Rescued from Death!

Wounded soldiers with little hope were crumbled in disarray on the battlefield. Too weak to move and covered with blood and flies, the merciless sun added to their thirst and fever. Many clutched the small Bible that was harbored in their breastpocket.

Suddenly they heard the rumbling of the Salvation Army truck and knew their prayers were answered. Out leaped the dedicated motherly women whose resourcefulness could ease any trauma. Their every action seemed to be imbued with divine purpose.

Within minutes the women stretched canvas pieces over the soldier's heads to protect them from the sun. Their gentle but strong hands then bathed away the blood and helped the fever-ridden men drink homemade lemonade.

War had swept away all differences. No Jew or Gentile, Protestant or Catholic, rich or poor, male or female existed now—only the brotherhood of Americans.

Tyndale House books by Grace Livingston Hill.
Check with your area bookstore for these best-sellers.

COLLECTOR'S CHOICE SERIES

Grace Livingston Hill

THE WAR ROMANCE
OF THE SALVATION ARMY

By Evangeline Booth
and
Grace Livingston Hill

LIVING BOOKS ®
Tyndale House Publishers, Inc.
Wheaton, Illinois

This Tyndale House book
by Grace Livingston Hill
contains the complete text
of the original hardcover edition
NOT ONE WORD
HAS BEEN OMITTED.

Printing History
J. B. Lippincott edition published 1919
Tyndale House edition/1991

Living Books is a registered trademark of Tyndale
House Publishers, Inc.

Library of Congress Catalog Card Number 91-65810
ISBN 0-8423-7911-8
Copyright © 1919 by Grace Livingston Hill.
Cover artwork copyright © 1991 by Steven H. Stroud

97   96   95   94   93   92
8   7   6   5   4   3   2

CONTENTS

Foreword

In presenting the narrative of some of the doings of the Salvation Army during the world's great conflict for liberty, I am but answering the insistent call of a most generous and appreciative public.

When moved to activity by the apparent need, there was never a thought that our humble services would awaken the widespread admiration that has developed. In fact, we did not expect anything further than appreciative recognition from those immediately benefited, and the knowledge that our people have proved so useful is an abundant compensation for all toil and sacrifice, for *service* is our watchword, and there is no reward equal to that of doing the most good to the most people in the most need. When our National Armies were being gathered for overseas work, the likelihood of a great need was self-evident, and the most logical and most natural thing for the Salvation Army to do was to hold itself in readiness for action. That we were straitened in our circumstances is well understood, more so by us than by anybody else. The story as told in these pages is necessarily incomplete, for the obvious reason that the work is yet in progress. We entered France ahead of our Expeditionary Forces, and it is my purpose to continue my people's ministries until the last of our troops return. At the present moment the number of our workers overseas equals that of any day yet experienced.

Because of the pressure that this service brings, together with the unmentioned executive cares incident to the vast work of the Salvation Army in these United States, I felt compelled to requisition some competent person to aid me in the literary work associated with the production of a concrete story. In this I was most fortunate, for a writer of established work and national fame in the person of Mrs. Grace Livingston Hill came to my assistance; and having for many days had the privilege of working with her in the sifting process, gathering from the mass of matter that had accumulated and which was being daily added to, with every confidence I am able to commend her patience and toil. How well she has done her work the book will bear its own testimony.

The foreword would be incomplete were I to fail in acknowledging in a very definite way the lavish expressions of gratitude that have abounded on the part of "The Boys" themselves. This is our reward, and is a very great encouragement to us to continue a growing and more permanent effort for their welfare, which is comprehended in our plans for the future.

The official support given has been of the highest and most generous character. Marshal Foch himself most kindly cabled me, and General Pershing has upon several occasions inspired us with commendatory words of the greatest worth.

Our beloved President has been pleased to reflect the people's pleasure and his own personal gratification upon what the Salvation Army has accomplished with the troops, which good-will we shall ever regard as one of our greatest honors.

The lavish eulogy and sincere affection bestowed by the nation upon the organization I can only account for by the simple fact that our ministering members have been in spirit and reality with the men.

True to our first light, first teaching, and first practices, we have always put ourselves close beside the man irrespective of whether his condition is fair or foul; whether his surroundings are peaceful or perilous; whether his prospects are promising or threatening. As a people we have felt that to be of true service to others we must be close enough to them to lift part of their load and thus carry out that grand injunction of the Apostle Paul, "Bear ye one another's burdens and so fulfill the law of Christ."

The Salvation Army upon the battlefields of France has but worked along the same lines as in the great cities of the nations. We are, with our every gift to serve, close up to those in need; and so, as Lieut.-Colonel Roosevelt put it, "Whatever the lot of the men, the Salvation Army is found with them."

We never permit any superiority of position, or breeding, or even grace to make a gap between us and any who may be less fortunate. To help another, you must be near enough to catch the heart-beat. And so a large measure of our success in the war is accounted for by the fact that we have been with them. With a hundred thousand Salvationists on all fronts, and tens and tens of thousands of Salvationists at their ministering posts in the homelands as well as overseas, from the time that each of the Allied countries entered the war the Salvation Army has been with the fighting-men.

With them in the thatched cottage on the hillside, and in the humble dwelling in the great towns of the home-lands, when they faced the great ordeal of wishing good-bye to mothers and fathers and wives and children.

With them in the blood-soaked furrows of old fields; with them in the desolation of No Man's Land; and with them amid the indescribable miseries and gory horrors of the battlefield. With them with the sweetest ministry, trained in the art of service, white-souled, brave, tender-hearted men and women could render.

Evangeline Booth
National Headquarters
Salvation Army
New York City.
April, 1919.

From the Commander's Own Pen

The war is over. The world's greatest tragedy is arrested. The awful pull at men's heart-strings relaxed. The inhuman monster that leapt out of the darkness and laid blood-hands upon every home of a peace-blest earth has been overthrown. Autocracy and diabolical tyranny lie defeated and crushed behind the long rows of white crosses that stand like sign-posts pointing heavenward, all the way from the English Channel to the Adriatic, linking the two by an inseverable chain.

While the nations were in the throes of the conflict, I was constrained to speak and write of the Salvation Army's activities in the frightful struggle. Now that all is over and I reflect upon the price the nations have paid I realize much hesitancy in so doing.

When I think of England—where almost every man you meet is but a piece of a man! France—one great graveyard! Its towns and cities a wilderness of waste! The allied countries—Italy, and deathless little Belgium, and Serbia—well-nigh exterminated in the desperate, gory struggle! When I think upon it—the price America has paid! The price her heroic sons have paid! They that come down the gangways of the returning boats on crutches! They that are carried down on stretchers! They that sail into New York Harbor, young and fair, but never again to see the Statue of Liberty! The price that dear mothers and fathers have paid! The price that the tens of thousands of little children have paid! The price they that sleep in the lands they made free have paid! When I think upon all this, it is with no little reluctance that I now write of the small part taken by the Salvation Army in the world's titanic sacrifice for liberty, but which part we shall ever regard as our life's crowning honor.

Expressions of surprise from officers of all ranks as well as the private soldier have vied with those of gratitude concerning the efficiency of this service, but no thought of having accomplished any achievement higher than their simplest duty is entertained by the Salvationists themselves; for uniformly they feel that they have but striven to measure up to the high standards of service maintained by the Salvation Army, which standards ask of its officers all over the world that no effort shall be left unprosecuted, no sacrifice unrendered, which will help to meet the *need at their door.*

And it is such high standards of devoted service to our fellow, linked with the practical nature of the movement's operations, the deeply religious character of its members, its intelligent system of government, uniting, and thus augmenting, all its activities; with the immense advantage of the military training provided by the organization, that give to its officers a potency and adaptability that have for the greater period of our brief lifetime made us an influential factor in seasons of civic and national disaster.

When that beautiful city of the Golden Gate, San Francisco, was laid low by earthquake and fire, the Salvationists were the first upon the ground with blankets, and clothes, and food, gathering frightened little children, looking after old age, and rescuing many from the burning and falling buildings.

At the time of the wild rush to the Klondike, the

Salvation Army was, with its sweet, pure women—the only women amidst tens of thousands of men—upon the mountain-side of the Chilcoot Pass saving the lives of the gold-seekers, and telling those shattered by disappointment of treasure that "doth not perish."

At the time of the Jamestown, the Galveston, and the Dayton floods the Salvation Army officer, with his boat laden with sandwiches and warm wraps, was the first upon the rising waters, ministering to marooned and starving families gathered upon the housetops.

In the direful disaster that swept over the beautiful city of Halifax, the Mayor of that city stated: "I do not know what I should have done the first two or three days following the explosion, when everyone was panic-stricken, without the ready, intelligent, and unbroken day-and-night efforts of the Salvation Army."

On numerous other similar occasions we have relieved distress and sorrow by our almost instantaneous service. Hence when our honored President decided that our National Emblem, heralder of the inalienable rights of man, should cross the seas and wave for the freedom of the peoples of the earth, automatically the Salvation Army moved with it, and our officers passed to the varying posts of helpfulness which the emergency demanded.

Now on all sides I am confronted with the question: *What is the secret of the Salvation Army's success in the war?*

Permit me to suggest three reasons which, in my judgment, account for it:

First, when the war-bolt fell, when the clarion call sounded, it found *the Salvation Army ready!*

Ready not only with our material machinery, but with that precious piece of human mechanism which is indispensable to all great and high achievement—the right calibre of man, and the right calibre of woman.

Men and women equipped by a careful training for the work they would have to do.

We were not many in number, I admit. In France our numbers have been regrettably few. But this is because I have felt it was better to fall short in quantity than to run the risk in falling short in quality. Quality is its own multiplication table. Quality without quantity will spread, whereas quantity without quality will shrink. Therefore, I would not send any officers to France except such as had been fully equipped in our training schools.

Few have even a remote idea of the extensive training given to all Salvation Army officers by our military system of education, covering all the tactics of that particular warfare to which they have consecrated their lives—*the service of humanity*.

We have in the Salvation Army thirty-nine Training Schools in which our own men and women, both for our missionary and home fields, receive an intelligent tuition and practical training in the minutest details of their service. They are trained in the finest and most intricate of all the arts, the art of dealing ably with human life.

It is a wonderful art which transfigures a sheet of cold grey canvas into a throbbing vitality, and on its inanimate spread visualizes a living picture from which one feels they can never turn their eyes away.

It is a wonderful art which takes a rugged, knotted block of marble, standing upon a coarse wooden bench, and cuts out of its uncomely crudeness—as I saw it done—the face of my father, with its every feature illumined with prophetic light, so true to life that I felt that to my touch it surely must respond.

But even such arts as these crumble; they are as dust under our feet compared with that much greater art, *the art of dealing ably with human life in all its varying conditions and phases*.

It is in this art that we seek by a most careful culture and training to perfect our officers.

They are trained in those expert measures which enable them to handle satisfactorily those that cannot handle themselves, those that have lost their grip on things, and that, if unaided go down under the high, rough tides.

Trained to meet emergencies of every character—to leap into the breach, to span the gulf, and to do it without waiting to be told *how*.

Trained to press at every cost for the desired and decided-upon end.

Trained to obey orders willingly, and gladly, and wholly—not in part.

Trained to give no quarter to the enemy, no matter what the character, nor in what form he may present himself, and to never consider what personal advantage may be derived.

Trained in the art of the winsome, attractive coquetries of the round, brown doughnut and all its kindred.

Trained, if needs be, to seal their services with their life's blood.

One of our women officers, on being told by the colonel of the regiment she would be killed if she persisted in serving her doughnuts and cocoa to the men while under heavy fire, and that she must get back to safety, replied: "Colonel, we can die with the men, but we cannot leave them."

When, therefore, I gathered the little companies together for their last charge before they sailed for France, I would tell them that while I was unable to arm them with many of the advantages of the more wealthy denominations; that while I could give them only a very few assistants owing to the great demand upon our forces; and that while I could promise them nothing beyond their bare expenses, yet I knew that without fear I could rely upon them for an unsurpassed devotion to the God-inspired standards of the emblem of this, the world's greatest Republic, the Stars and Stripes, now in the van for the freedom of the peoples of the earth. That I could rely upon them for unsurpassed devotion to the brave men who laid their lives upon the altar of their country's protection, and that I could rely upon them for an unsurpassed devotion to that other banner, the Banner of Calvary, the significance of which has not changed in nineteen centuries, and by the standards of which alone all the world's wrongs can be redressed, and by the standards of which alone men can be liberated from all their bondage. And they have not failed.

A further reason for the success of the Salvation Army in the war is, *it found us accustomed to hardship.*

We are a people who have thrived on adversity. Opposition, persecution, privation, abuse, hunger, cold and want were with us at the starting-post, and have journeyed with us all along the course.

We went to the battlefields *no strangers to suffering.* The biting cold winds that swept the fields of Flanders were not the first to lash our faces. The sunless cellars, with their mouldy walls and water-seeped floors, where our women sought refuge from shell-fire through the hours of the night, contributed no new or untried experience. In such cellars as these, in their home cities, under the flicker of a tallow candle, they have ministered to the sick and comforted the dying.

Wet feet, lack of sleep, being often without food, finding things different from what we had planned, hoped and expected, were frequent experiences with us. All such things we Salvationists encounter in our daily toils for others amid the indescribable miseries and inestimable sorrows, the sins and the tragedies of the underworlds of our great cities—the *underneath* of those great cities which upon the surface thunder with enterprise and glitter with brilliance.

We are not easily affrighted by frowns of fortune. We do not change our course because of contrary currents, nor put into harbor because of head-winds. Almost all our progress has been made in the teeth of the storm. We have always had to "tack," but as it is "the set of the sails, and not the gales" that decides the ports we reach, the competency of our seamanship is determined by the fact that we "get there."

Our service in France was not, therefore, an experiment, but an organized, tested, and proved system. We were enacting no new rôle. We were all through the Boer War. Our officers were with the besieged troops in Mafeking and Ladysmith. They were with Lord Kitchener in his victorious march through Africa. It was this grand soldier who afterwards wrote to my father, General William Booth, the Founder of our movement, saying: "Your men have given us an example both of how to live as good soldiers and how to die as heroes." And so it was quite natural that our men and women, with that fearlessness which characterizes our members, should take up positions under fire in France.

In fact, our officers would have considered themselves unfaithful to Salvation Army traditions and history, and untrue to those who had gone before, if they had deserted any post, or shirked any duty, because cloaked with the shadows of death.

This explains why their dear forms loomed up in the fog and the rain, in the hours of the night, on the roads, under shell fire, serving coffee and doughnuts.

This is how it was they were with them on the long dreary marches, with a smile and a song and a word of cheer.

This is how it is the Salvation Army has no "closing hours." "Taps" sounds for us *when the need is relieved*.

Three of our women officers in the Toul Sector had slept for three weeks in a hay-stack, in an open field, to be near the men of an ammunition train taking supplies to the front under cover of darkness. The boys had watched their continued, devoted service for them—the many nights without sleep—and noticing the shabby uniform of the little officer in charge, collected among themselves 1600 francs, and offered it to her for a new one, and some other comforts, the spokesman saying: "This is just to show you how grateful we are to you." The officer was deeply touched, but told them she could not think of accepting it for herself. "I am quite accustomed to hard toils," she said. "I have only done what all my comrades are doing—my duty," and offered to compromise by putting the money into a general fund for the benefit of all—to buy more doughnuts and more coffee for the boys.

Salvation Army teaching and practice is: Choose your purpose, then set your face as flint toward that purpose, permitting no enemy that can oppose, and no sacrifice that can be asked, to turn you from it.

Again, a reason for our success in the war is, *our practical religion*.

That is, our religion is *practicable*. Or, I would rather say, our Christianity is practicable. Few realize this as the secret of our success, and some who do realize it will not admit it, but this is what it really is.

We *do* worship; both in spirit and form, in public and in private. We rely upon prayer as the only line of communication between the creature and his Creator, the only wing upon which the soul's requirements and hungerings can be wafted to the Fount of all spiritual supply. Through our street, as well as our indoor meetings, perhaps oftener than any other people, we come to the masses with the divine benediction of prayer; and it would be difficult to find the Salvationist's home that does not regard the family altar as its most precious and priceless treasure.

We do preach. We preach God the Creator of earth and heaven, unerring in His wisdom, infinite in His love and omnipotent in His power. We preach Jesus Christ, God's only begotten Son, dying on Calvary for a world's transgressions, able to save to the uttermost "all those who come unto God by Him." We preach God the Holy Ghost, sanctifier and comforter of the souls of men, making white the life, and kindling lights in every dark landing-place. We preach the Bible, authentic in its statements, immaculate in its teaching, and glorious in its promises. We preach grace, limitless grace, grace enough for all men, and grace enough for each. We preach Hell, the irrevocable doom of the soul that rejects the Saviour. We preach Heaven, the home of the righteous, the reward of the good, the crowning of them that endure to the end.

Even as we preach, so we practice Christianity. We reduce theory to action. We apply faith to deeds. We confess and present Jesus Christ in things that can be done.

It is this that has carried our flag into sixty-three countries and colonies, and despite the bitterest opposition has given us the financial support of twenty-one national governments. It is this that has brought us up from a little handful of humble workers to an organization with 21,000 officers and workers, preaching the gospel in thirty-nine tongues. It is this that has multiplied the one bandsman and a despised big drum to an army of 27,000 musicians, and it is this—our practice of religion—that has placed *Christ in deeds*.

Arthur E. Copping gives as the reason for the movement's success—"the simple, thorough-going, uncompromising, seven-days-a-week character of its Christianity."

It is this every-day-use religion which has made us of infinite service in the places of toil, breakage, and suffering; this every-day-use religion which has made us the only resource for thousands in misery and vice; this every-day-use religion which has insured our success to an extent that has induced civic authorities, Judges, Mayors, Governors, and even National Governments—such as India with its Criminal Tribes—to turn to us with the problems of the poor and the wicked.

While the Salvationist is not of the generally understood ascetic or monastic type, yet his spirit and deeds are of the very essence of saintliness.

As man has arrested the lazy cloud sleeping on the brow of the hill, and has brought it down to enlighten our darkness, to carry our mail-bags, to haul our luggage, and to flash our messages, so, I would say with all reverence, that the Salvation Army in a very particular way has again brought down Jesus Christ from the high, high thrones, golden pathways, and wing-spread angels of Glory, to the common mud walks of earth, and has presented Him again in the flesh to a storm-torn world, touching and healing the wounds, the bruises, and the bleeding sores of humanity.

That was a wonderful sermon Christ preached on the Mount, but was it more wonderful than the ministry of the wounded man fallen by the roadside, or the drying of the tears from the pale, worn face of the widow of Nain? Or more wonderful than when He said, Let them come—let them come—mothers and the little children—and blessed them?

It has only been this same Christ, *this Christ in deeds,* when our women have washed the blood from the faces of the wounded, and taken the caked mud from their feet; when under fire, through the hours of the night, they have made the doughnuts; when instead of sleeping they have written the letters home to soldiers' loved ones, when they have lifted the heavy pails of water and struggled with them over the shell-wrecked roads that the dying soldiers might drink; when they have sewn the torn uniforms; when they have strewn with the first spring flowers the graves of those who died for liberty. Only *Christ in deeds* when our men went unarmed into the horrors of the Argonne Forest to gather the dying boys in their arms and to comfort them with love, human and divine.

That valiant champion of justice and truth; that faithful, able and brilliant defender of American standards, the late Honorable Theodore Roosevelt, told me personally a few days before he went into the hospital that his son wrote him of how our officer, fifty-three years of age, despite his orders, went unarmed over the top, in the whirlwind of the charge, amidst the shriek of shell and tear of shrapnel, and picked up the American boy left for dead in No Man's Land, carrying him on his back over the shell-torn fields to safety.

It is this *Christ in deeds* that has made the doughnut to take the place of the "cup of cold water" given in His name. It is this *Christ in deeds* that has brought from our humble ranks the modern Florence Nightingales and taken to the gory horrors of the battlefields the white, uplifting influences of pure womanhood. It is this *Christ in deeds* that made Sir Arthur Stanley say, when thanking our General for $10,000 donated for more ambulances: "I thank you for the money, but much more for the men; they are quite the best in our service."

It is this Christ who has given to our humblest service a sheen—something of a glory—which the troops have caught, and which will make these simple deeds to hold tenaciously to history, and to outlive the effacing fingers of time—even to defy the very dissolution of death.

As Premier Clemenceau said: "We must love. We must believe. This is the secret of life. If we fail to learn this lesson, we exist without living: we die in ignorance of the reality of life."

A senator, after several months spent in France, stated: "It is my opinion that the secret of the success of this organization is their complete abandonment to their cause, *the service of the man.*"

Of the many beautiful tributes paid to us by a most gracious public, and by the noblest-hearted and most kindly and gallant army that ever stood up in uniform, perhaps the most correct is this: *Complete abandonment to the service of the man.*

This, in large measure, is the cause of our success all over the world.

When you come to think of it, the Salvation Army is a remarkable arrangement. It is remarkable in its construction. It is a great empire. An empire geographically unlike any other. It is an empire without a frontier. It is an empire made up of geographical fragments, parted from each other by vast stretches of railroad and immense sweeps of sea. It is an empire composed of a tangle of races, tongues, and colors, of types of civilization and enlightened barbarism such as never before in all human history gathered together under one flag.

It is an army, with its titles rambling into all languages, a soldiery spreading over all lands, a banner upon which the sun never goes down—with its head in the heart of a cluster of islands set in the grey, wind-blown Northern seas, while its territories are scattered over every sea and under every sky.

The world has wondered what has been the controlling force holding this strange empire together. What is the electro-magnetism governing its furthest atom as though it were at your elbow? What is the magic sceptre that compels this diversity of peoples to act as one man? What is the master passion uniting these multifarious pulsations into one heart-beat?

Has it been a sworn-to signature attached to bond or paper? No; these can all too readily be designated "scraps" and be rent in twain. Has it been self-interest and worldly fame? No, for all selfish gain has had to be sacrificed upon the threshold of the contract. Has it been the bond of kinship, or blood, or speech? No, for under this banner the British master has become the servant of the Hindoo, and the American has gone to lay down his life upon the veldts of Africa. Has it been the bond of that almost supernatural force, glorious patriotism? No, not even this, for while we "know no man after the flesh," we recognize our brother in all the families of the earth, and our General infused into the breasts of his followers the sacred conviction that the Salvationist's country is the world.

What was it? What is it? Those ties created by a spiritual ideal. Our love for God demonstrated by our sacrifice for man.

My father, in a private audience with the late King Edward, said: "Your Majesty, some men's passion is gold; some men's passion is art; some men's passion is fame; my passion is man!"

This was in our Founder's breast the white flame which ignited like sparks in the hearts of all his followers.

Man is our life's passion.

It is for man we have laid our lives upon the altar. It is for man we have entered into a contract with our God which signs away our claim to any and all selfish ends. It is for man we have sworn to our own hurt, and —my God thou knowest—when the hurt came, hard and hot and fast, it was for man we held tenaciously to the bargain.

After the torpedoing of the *Aboukir* two sailors found themselves clinging to a spar which was not sufficiently buoyant to keep them both afloat. Harry, a Salvationist, grasped the situation and said to his mate: "Tom, for me to die will mean to go home to mother. I don't think it's quite the same for you, so you hold to the spar and I will go down; but promise me if you are picked up you will make my God your God and my people your people." Tom was rescued and told to a weeping audience in a Salvation Army hall the act of self-sacrifice which had saved his life, and testified to keeping his promise to the boy who had died for him.

When the *Empress of Ireland* went down with a hundred and thirty Salvation Army officers on board, one hundred and nine officers were drowned, and not one body that was picked up had on a life-belt. The few survivors told how the Salvationists, finding there were not enough life-preservers for all, took off their own belts and strapped them upon even strong men, saying, "I can die better than you can;" and from the deck of that sinking boat they flung their battle-cry around the world—*Others!*

Man! Sometimes I think God has given us special eyesight with which to look upon him. We look through the exterior, look through the shell, look through the coat, and find the man. We look through the ofttimes repulsive wrappings, through the dark, objectionable coating collected upon the downward travel of misspent years, through the artificial veneer of empty seeming—through to the *man*.

He that was made after God's image.

He that is greater than firmaments, greater than suns, greater than worlds.

Man, for whom worlds were created, for whom Heavens were canopied, for whom suns were set ablaze. He in whose being there gleams that immortal spark we call the soul.

And when this war came, it was natural for us to look to the man—the man under the shabby clothes, enlisting in the great armies of freedom; the man going down the street under the spick and span uniform; the man behind the gun, standing in the jaws of death hurling back world autocracy; the man, the son of liberty, discharging his obligations to them that are bound; the man, each one of them, although so young, who when the fates of the world swung in the balances proved to be *the man of the hour;* the man, each one of them, fighting not only for today but for to-morrow, and deciding the world's future; the man who gladly died that freedom might not be dead; the man dear to a hundred million throbbing hearts; the man God loved so much that to save him He gave His only Son to the unparalleled sacrifice of Calvary, with its measureless ocean of torment heaving up against His Heart in one foaming, wrathful, omnipotent surge.

Wherein is price? What constitutes cost, when the question is *THE MAN?*

Preface by the Writer

I wish I could give you a picture of Commander Evangeline Booth as I saw her first, who has been the Source, the Inspiration, the Guide of this story.

I went to the first conference about this book in curiosity and some doubt, not knowing whether it was my work; not altogether sure whether I cared to attempt it. She took my hand and spoke to me. I looked in her face and saw the shining glory of her great spirit through those wonderful, beautiful, wise, keen eyes, and all doubts vanished. I studied the sincerity and beauty of her vivid face as we talked together, and heard the thrilling tale she was giving me to tell because she could not take the time from living it to write it, and I trembled lest she would not find me worthy for so great a task. I knew that I was being honored beyond women to have been selected as an instrument through whom the great story of the Salvation Army in the War might go forth to the world. That I wanted to do it more than any work that had ever come to my hand, I was certain at once; and that my whole soul was enmeshed in the wonder of it. It gripped me from the start. I was overjoyed to find that we were in absolute sympathy from the first.

One sentence from that earliest talk we had together stands clear in my memory, and it has perhaps unconsciously shaped the theme which I hope will be found running through all the book:

"Our people," said she, flinging out her hands in a lovely embracing movement, as if she saw before her at that moment those devoted workers of hers who follow where she leads unquestioningly, and stay not for fire or foe, or weariness, or peril of any sort:

"Our people know that Christ is a living presence, that they can reach out and feel He is near: that is why they can live so splendidly and die so heroically!"

As she spoke a light shone in her face that reminded me of the light that we read was on Moses' face after he had spent those days in the mountain with God; and somewhere back in my soul something was repeating the words: "And they took knowledge of them that they had been with Jesus."

That seems to me to be the whole secret of the wonderful lives and wonderful work of the Salvation Army. They have become acquainted with Jesus Christ, whom to know is life eternal; they feel His presence constantly with them and they live their lives "as seeing Him who is invisible." They are a living miracle for the confounding of all who doubt that there is a God whom mortals may know face to face while they are yet upon the earth.

The one thing that these people seem to feel is really worth while is bringing other people to know their Christ. All other things in life are merely subservient to this, or tributary to it. All their education, culture and refinement, their amazing organization, their rare business ability, are just so many tools that they use for the uplift of others. In fact, the word "OTHERS" appears here and there, printed on small white cards and tacked up over a desk, or in a hallway near the elevator, anywhere, everywhere all over the great building of the New York Headquarters, a quiet, unobtrusive, yet startling reminder of a world of real things in the midst of the busy rush of life.

Yet they do not obtrude their religion. Rather it is a secret joy that shines unaware through their eyes, and seems to flood their whole being with happiness so that others can but see. It is there, ready, when the time comes to give comfort, or advice, or to tell the message of the gospel in clear ringing sentences in one of their meetings; but it speaks as well through a smile, or a ripple of song, or a bright funny story, or something good to eat when one is hungry, as it does through actual preaching. It is the living Christ, as if He were on earth again living in them. And when one comes to know them well one knows that He is!

"Go straight for the salvation of souls: never rest satisfied unless this end is achieved!" is part of the commission that the Commander gives to her envoys. It is worth while stopping to think what would be the effect on the world if every one who has named the name of Christ should accept that commission and go forth to fulfill it.

And you who have been accustomed to drop your pennies in the tambourine of the Salvation Army lassies at the street corners, and look upon her as a representative of a lower class who are doing good "in their way," prepare to realize that you have made a mistake. The Salvation Army is not an organization composed of a lot of ignorant, illiterate, reformed criminals picked out of the slums. There may be among them many of that class who by the army's efforts have been saved from a life of sin and shame, and lifted up to be useful citizens; but great numbers of them, the leaders and officers, are refined, educated men and women who have put Christ and His Kingdom first in their hearts and lives. Their young people will compare in every way with the best of the young people of any of our religious denominations.

After the privilege of close association with them for some time I have come to feel that the most noticeable and lovely thing about the girls is the way they wear their womanhood, as if it were a flower, or a rare jewel. One of these girls, who, by the way, had been nine months in France, all of it under shell fire, said to me:

"I used to wish I had been born a boy, they are not hampered so much as women are; but after I went to France and saw what a good woman meant to those boys in the trenches I changed my mind, and I'm glad I was born a woman. It means a great deal to be a woman."

And so there is no coquetry about these girls, no little personal vanity such as girls who are thinking of themselves often have. They take great care to be neat and sweet and serviceable, but as they are not thinking of themselves, but only how they may serve, they are blest with that loveliest of all adorning, a meek and quiet spirit and a joy of living and content that only forgetfulness of self and communion with Jesus Christ can bring.

I feel as if I would like to thank every one of them, men and women and young girls, who have so kindly and generously and wholeheartedly given me of their time and experiences and put at my disposal their correspondence to enrich this story, and have helped me to go over the ground of the great American drives in the war and see what they saw, hear what they heard, and feel as they felt. It has been one of the greatest experiences of my life.

And she, their God-given leader, that wonderful woman whose wise hand guides every detail of this marvellous organization in America, and whose well furnished mind is ever thinking out new ways to serve her Master, Christ; what shall I say of her whom I have come to know and love so well?

Her exceptional ability as a public speaker is of the widest fame, while comparatively few, beyond those of her most trusted Officers, are brought into admiring touch with her brilliant executive powers. All these, however, unite in most unstinted praise and declare that functioning in this sphere, the Commander even excels her platform triumphs. But one must know her well and watch her every day to understand her depth of insight into character, her wideness of vision, her skill of making adverse circumstances serve her ends. Born with an innate genius for leadership, swallowed up in her work, wholly consecrated to God and His service, she looks upon men, as it were, with the eyes of the God she loves, and sees the best in everybody. She sees their faults also, but she sees the good, and is able to take that good and put it to account, while helping them out of their faults. Those whom she has so helped would kiss the hem of her garment as she passes. It is easy to see why she is a leader of men. It is easy to see who has made the Army here in America. It is easy to see who has inspired the brave men and wonderful women who went to France and labored.

She would not have me say these things of her, for she is humble, as such a great leader should be, knowing all her gifts and attainments to be but the glory of her Lord; and this is her book. Only in this chapter can I speak and say what I will, for it is not my book. But here, too, I waive my privilege and bow to my Commander.

Grace Livingston Hill

The Story

INTO the heavy shadows that swathe the feet of the tall buildings in West Fourteenth Street, New York, late in the evening there slipped a dark form. It was so carefully wrapped in a black cloak that it was difficult to tell among the other shadows whether it was man or woman, and immediately it became a part of the darkness that hovered close to the entrances along the way. It slid almost imperceptibly from shadow to shadow until it crouched flatly against the wall by the steps of an open door out of which streamed a wide band of light that flung itself across the pavement.

Down the street came two girls in poke bonnets and hurried in at the open door. The figure drew back and was motionless as they passed, then with a swift furtive glance in either direction a head came cautiously out from the shadow and darted a look after the two lassies, watched till they were out of sight, and a form slid into the doorway, winding about the turning like a serpent, as if the way were well planned, and slipped out of sight in a dark corner under the stairway.

Half an hour or perhaps an hour passed, and one or

two hurrying forms came in at the door and sped up the stairs from some errand of mercy; then the night watchman came and fastened the door and went away again, out somewhere through a back room.

The interloper was instantly on the alert, darting out of its hiding place, and slipping noiselessly up the stairs as quietly as the shadow it imitated; pausing to listen with anxious mien, stepping as a cloud might have stepped with no creak of stairway or sound of going at all.

Up, up, up and up again, it darted, till it came to the very top, pausing to look sharply at a gleam of light under a door of some student not yet asleep.

From under the dark cloak slid a hand with something in it. Silently it worked, swiftly, pouring a few drops here, a few drops there, of some colorless, odorless matter, smearing a spot on the stair railing, another across from it on the wall, a little on the floor beyond, a touch on the window seat at the end of the hall, some more on down the stairs.

On rubbered feet the fiend crept down; halting, listening, ever working rapidly, from floor to floor and back to the entrance way again. At last with a cautious glance around, a pause to rub a match skilfully over the woolen cloak, and to light a fuse in a hidden corner, he vanished out upon the street like the passing of a wraith, and was gone in the darkness.

Down in the dark corner the little spark brooded and smouldered. The watchman passed that way but it gave no sign. All was still in the great building, as the smouldering spark crept on and on over its little thread of existence to the climax.

But suddenly, it sprang to life! A flame leaped up like a great tongue licking its lips before the feast it was about to devour; and then it sprang as if it were human, to another spot not far away; and then to another, and on, and on up the stair rail, across to the wall, leaping, roaring, almost shouting as if in fiendish glee. It flew to the top of the house and down again in a leap and the whole building was enveloped in a sheet of flame!

Some one gave the cry of FIRE! The night watchman darted to his box and sent in the alarm. Frightened girls in night attire crowded to their doors and gasping fell back for an instant in horror; then bravely obedient to their training dashed forth into the flame. Young men on other floors without a thought for themselves dropped into order automatically and worked like madmen to save everyone. The fire engines throbbed up almost immediately, but the building was doomed from the start and went like tinder. Only the fire drill in which they had constant almost daily practice saved those brave girls and boys from an awful death. Out upon the fire escapes in the bitter winter wind the girls crept down to safety, and one by one the young men followed. The young man who was fire sergeant counted his men and found them all present but one cadet. He darted back to find him, and that moment with a last roar of triumph the flames gave a final leap and the building collapsed, burying in a fiery grave two fine young heroes.

Afterward they said the building had been "smeared" or it never could have gone in a breath as it did. The miracle was that no more lives were lost.

So that was how the burning of the Salvation Army Training School occurred.

The significant fact in the affair was that there had been sleeping in that building directly over the place where the fire started several of the lassies who were to sail for France in a day or two with the largest party of war workers that had yet been sent out. Their trunks were packed, and they were all ready to go. The object was all too evident.

There was also proof that the intention had been to destroy as well the great fireproof Salvation Army National Headquarters building adjoining the Training School.

A few days later a detective taking lunch in a small German restaurant on a side street overheard a conversation:

"Well, if we can't burn them out we'll blow up the building, and get that damn Commander, anyhow!"

Yet when this was told her the Commander declined the bodyguard offered her by the Civic Authorities, to go with her even to her country home and protect her while the war lasted! She is naturally a soldier.

The Commander had stayed late at the Headquarters one evening to finish some important bit of work, and had given orders that she should not be interrupted. The great building was almost empty save for the night watchman, the elevator man, and one or two others.

She was hard at work when her secretary appeared with an air of reluctance to tell her that the elevator man said there were three ladies waiting downstairs to see her on some very important business. He had told them that she could not be disturbed but they insisted that they must see her, that she would wish it if she knew their business. He had come up to find out what he should answer them.

The Commander said she knew nothing about them and could not be interrupted now. They must be told to come again the next day.

The elevator man returned in a few minutes to say that the ladies insisted, and said they had a great gift for the Salvation Army, but must see the Commander at once and alone or the gift would be lost.

Quickly interested the Commander gave orders that they should be brought up to her office, but just as they were about to enter, the secretary came in again with great excitement, begging that she would not see the visitors, as one of the men from downstairs had 'phoned up to her that he did not like the appearance of the strangers; they seemed to be trying to talk in high strained voices, and they had very large feet. Maybe they were not women at all.

The Commander laughed at the idea, but finally yielded when another of her staff entered and begged her not to see strangers alone so late at night; and the callers were informed that they would have to return in the morning if they wished an interview.

Immediately they became anything but ladylike in their manner, declaring that the Salvation Army did not deserve a gift and should have nothing from them. The elevator man's suspicions were aroused. The ladies were attired in long automobile cloaks, and close caps with large veils, and he studied them carefully as he carried them down to the street floor once more, following them to the outer door. He was surprised to find that no automobile awaited them outside. As they turned to walk down the street, he was sure he caught a glimpse of a trouser leg from beneath one of the long cloaks, and with a stride he covered the space between the door and his elevator where was a telephone, and called up the police station. In a few moments more the three "ladies" found themselves in custody, and proved to be three men well armed.

But when the Commander was told the truth about them she surprisingly said: "I'm sorry I didn't see them. I'm sure they would have done me no harm and I might have done them some good."

But if she is courageous, she is also wise as a serpent, and knows when to keep her own counsel.

During the early days of the war when there were

many important matters to be decided and the Commander was needed everywhere, she came straight from a conference in Washington to a large hotel in one of the great western cities where she had an appointment to speak that night. At the revolving door of the hotel stood a portly servitor in house uniform who was most kind and noticeably attentive to her whenever she entered or went out, and was constantly giving her some pointed little attention to draw her notice. Finally, she stopped for a moment to thank him, and he immediately became most flattering, telling her he knew all about the Salvation Army, that he had a brother in its ranks, was deeply interested in their work in France, and most proud of what they were doing. He told her he had lived in Washington and said he supposed she often went there. She replied pleasantly that she had but just come from there, but some keen intuition began to warn this wise-hearted woman and when the next question, though spoken most casually, was: "Where are the Salvation Army workers now in France?" she replied evasively:

"Oh, wherever they are most needed," and passed on with a friend.

"I believe that man is a spy!" she said to her friend with conviction in her voice.

"Nonsense!" the friend replied; "you are growing nervous. That man has been in this hotel for several years."

But that very night the man, with five others, was arrested, and proved to be a spy hunting information about the location of the American troops in France.

Now these incidents do not belong in just this spot in the book, but they are placed here of intention that the reader may have a certain viewpoint from which to take the story. For well does the world of evil realize what a strong force of opponents to their dark deeds is found in this great Christian organization. Sometimes one is able the better to judge a man, his character and strength, when one knows who are his enemies.

It was the beginning of the dark days of 1917.

The Commander sat in her quiet office, that office through which, except on occasions like this when she locked the doors for a few minutes' special work, there marched an unbroken procession of men and affairs, affecting both souls and nations.

Before her on the broad desk lay the notes of a new address which she was preparing to deliver that evening, but her eyes were looking out of the wide window, across the clustering roofs of the great city to the white horizon line, and afar over the great water to the terrible scene of the Strife of Nations.

For a long time her thoughts had been turning that way, for she had many beloved comrades in that fight, both warring and ministering to the fighters, and she had often longed to go herself, had not her work held her here. But now at last the call had come! America had entered the great war, and in a few days her sons would be marching from all over the land and embarking for over the seas to fling their young lives into the inferno; and behind them would stalk, as always in the wake of War, Pain and Sorrow and Sin! Especially Sin. She shuddered as she thought of it all. The many subtle temptations to one who is lonely and in a foreign land.

Her eyes left the far horizon and hovered over the huddling roofs that represented so many hundreds of thousands of homes. So many mothers to give up their sons; so many wives to be bereft; so many men and boys to be sent forth to suffer and be tried; so many hearts already overburdened to be bowed beneath a heavier load! Oh, her people! Her beloved people, whose sorrows and burdens and sins she bore in her heart and carried to the feet of the Master every day! And now this war!

And those young men, hardly more than children, some of them! With her quick insight and deep knowledge of the world, she visualized the way of fire down which they must walk, and her soul was stricken with the thought of it! It was her work and the work of her chosen Army to help and save, but what could she do in such a momentous crisis as this? She had no money for new work. Opportunities had opened up so fast. The Treasury was already overtaxed with the needs on this side of the water. There were enterprises started that could not be given up without losing precious souls who were on the way toward becoming redeemed men and women, fit citizens of this world and the next. There was no surplus, ever! The multifarious efforts to meet the needs of the poorest of the cities' poor, alone, kept everyone on the strain. There seemed no possibility of doing more. Besides, how could they spare the workers to meet the new demand without taking them from places where they were greatly needed at home?

And other perplexities darkened the way. There were those sitting in high places of authority who had strongly advised the Salvation Army to remain at home and go on with their street meetings, telling them that the battlefield was no place for them, they would only be in the way. They were not adapted to a thing like war. But well she knew the capacity of the Salvation Army to adapt itself to whatever need or circumstance presented. The same standard they had borne into the most wretched places of earth in times of peace would do in times of war.

Out there across the waters the Salvation Brothers and Sisters were ministering to the British armies at the front, and now that the American army was going, too, duty seemed very clear; the call was most imperative!

The written pages on her desk loudly demanded attention and the Commander tried to bring her thoughts back to them once more, but again and again the call sounded in her heart.

She lifted her eyes to the wall across the room from her desk where hung the life-like portrait of her Christian-Warrior father, the grand old keen-eyed, wise-hearted General, founder of the movement. Like her father she knew they must go. There was no question about it. No hindrance should stop them. They MUST GO! The warrior blood ran in her veins. In this the world's greatest calamity they must fulfill the mission for which he lived and died.

"Go!" Those pictured eyes seemed to speak to her, just as they used to command her when he was here: "You must go and bear the standard of the Cross to the front. Those boys are going over there, many of them to die, and some are telling them that if they make the supreme sacrifice in this their country's hour of need it will be all right with them when they go into the world beyond. But when they get over there under shell fire they will know that it is not so, and they will need Christ, the only atonement for sin. You must go and take the Christ to them."

Then the Commander bowed her head, accepting the commission; and there in the quiet room perhaps the Master Himself stood beside her and gave her his charge—just as she would later charge those whom she would send across the water—telling her that He was depending upon the Salvation Army to bear His standard to the war.

Perhaps it was at this same high conference with her Lord that she settled it in her heart that Lieutenant-

Colonel William S. Barker was to be the pioneer to blaze the way for the work in France.

However that may be he was an out-and-out Salvationist, of long and varied experience. He was chosen equally for his proved consecration to service, for his unselfishness, for his exceptional and remarkable natural courage by which he was afraid of nothing, and for his unwavering persistence in plans once made in spite of all difficulties. The Commander once said of him: "If you want to see him at his best you must put him face to face with a stone wall and tell him he must get on the other side of it. No matter what the cost or toil, whether hated or loved, he would get there!"

Thus carefully, prayerfully, were each one of the other workers selected; each new selection born from the struggle of her soul in prayer to God that there might be no mistakes, no unwise choices, no messengers sent forth who went for their own ends and not for the glory of God. Here lies the secret which makes the world wonder to-day why the Salvation Army workers are called "the real thing" by the soldiers. They were hand-picked by their leader on the mount, face to face with God.

She took no casual comer, even with offers of money to back them, and there were some of immense wealth who pleaded to be of the little band. She sent only those whom she knew and had tried. Many of them had been born and reared in the Salvation Army, with Christlike fathers and mothers who had made their homes a little piece of heaven below. All of them were consecrated, and none went without the urgent answering call in their own hearts.

It was early in June, 1917, when Colonel Barker sailed to France with his commission to look the field over and report upon any and every opportunity for the Salvation Army to serve the American troops.

In order to pave his way before reaching France, Colonel Barker secured a letter of introduction from Secretary-to-the-President Tumulty, to the American Ambassador in France, Honorable William G. Sharp.

In connection with this letter a curious and interesting incident occurred. When Colonel Barker entered the Secretary's office, he noticed him sitting at the other end of the room talking with a gentleman. He was about to take a seat near the door when Mr. Tumulty beckoned to him to come to the desk. When he was seated, without looking directly at the other gentleman, the Colonel began to state his mission to Mr. Tumulty. Before he had finished the stranger spoke up to Mr. Tumulty: "Give the Colonel what he wants and make it a good one!" And lo! he was not a stranger, but a man whose reform had made no small sensation in New York circles several years before, a former attorney who through his wicked life had been despaired of and forsaken by his wealthy relatives, who had sunk to the lowest depths of sin and poverty and been rescued by the Salvation Army.

Continuing to Mr. Tumulty, he said, "You know what the Salvation Army has done for me; now do what you can for the Salvation Army."

Mr. Tumulty gave him a most kind letter of introduction to the American Ambassador.

On his arrival in Liverpool Colonel Barker availed himself of the opportunity to see the very splendid work being done by the Salvation Army with the British troops, both in France and in England, visiting many Salvation Army huts and hostels. He also put the Commander's plans for France before General Bramwell Booth in London.

As early as possible Colonel Barker presented his letter of introduction to the American Ambassador, who in turn provided him with a letter of introduction to General Pershing which insured a cordial reception by him. Mr. Sharp informed Colonel Barker that he understood the policy of the American army was to grant a monopoly of all welfare work to the Y.M.C.A. He feared the Salvation Army would not be welcome, but assured him that anything he could properly do to assist the Salvation Army would be most gladly done. In this connection he stated that he had known of and been interested in the work of the Salvation Army for many years, that several men of his acquaintance had been converted through their activities and been reformed from dissolute, worthless characters to kind husbands and fathers and good business men; and that he believed in the Salvation Army work as a consequence.

On many occasions during the subsequent months, Mr. Sharp was never too busy to see the Salvation Army representatives, and has rendered valuable assistance in facilitating the forwarding of additional workers by his influence with the State Department.

It appeared that among military officers a kind feeling existed toward the Salvation Army, though it was generally thought that there was no opening for their service. Their conception of the Salvation Army was that of street corner meetings and public charity. The officers at that time could not see that the soldiers needed charity or that they would be interested in religion. They could see how a reading-room, game-room and entertainments might be helpful, but anything further than that they did not consider necessary.

Colonel Barker presented his letter of introduction to General Pershing, and on behalf of Commander Booth offered the services of the Salvation Army in any form which might be desired.

General Pershing, who received the Colonel with

exceptional cordiality, suggested that he go out to the camps, look the field over, and report to him. Calling in his chief of staff he gave instructions that a side car should be placed at Colonel Barker's disposal to go out to the camps; and also that a letter of introduction to the General commanding the First Division should be given to him, asking that everything should be done to help him.

The first destination was Gondrecourt, where the First Division Headquarters was established.

2

The Gondrecourt Area

THE advance guard of the American Expeditionary Forces had landed in France, and other detachments were arriving almost daily. They were received by the French with open arms and a big parade as soon as they landed. Flowers were tossed in their path and garlands were flung about them. They were lauded and praised on every hand. On the crest of this wave of enthusiasm they could have swept joyously into battle and never lost their smiles.

But instead of going to the front at once they were billeted in little French villages and introduced to French rain and French mud.

When one discovers that the houses are built of stone, stuck together mainly by this mud of the country, and remembers how many years they have stood, one gets a passing idea of the nature of this mud about which the soldiers have written home so often. It is more like Portland cement than anything else, and it is most penetrative and hard to get rid of; it gets in the hair, down the neck, into the shoes and it sticks. If the soldier wears hip-boots in the trenches he must take them off every little while and empty the mud out of them which somehow manages to get into even hip-boots. It is said that one reason the soldiers were obliged to wear the wrapped leggings was, not that they would keep the water out, but that they would strain the mud and at least keep the feet comparatively clean.

There were sixteen of these camps at this time and probably twelve or thirteen thousand soldiers were already established in them.

There was no great cantonment as at the camps on this side of the water, nor yet a city of tents, as one might have expected. The forming of a camp meant the taking over of all available buildings in the little French peasant villages. The space was measured up by the town mayor and the battalion leader and the proper number of men assigned to each building. In this way a single division covered a territory of about thirty kilometers. This system made a camp of any size available in very short order and also fooled the Huns, who were on the lookout for American camps.

These villages were the usual farming villages, typical of eastern France. They are not like American villages, but a collection of farm yards, the houses huddled together years ago for protection against roving bands of marauders. The farmer, instead of living upon his land, lives in the village, and there he has his barn for his cattle, his manure pile is at his front door, the drainage from it seeps back under the house at will, his chickens and pigs running around the streets.

These houses were built some five or eight hundred years ago, some a thousand or twelve hundred years. One house in the town aroused much curiosity because it was called the "new" house. It looked just like all the others. One who was curious asked why it should have received this appellative and was told because it was the last one that was built—only two hundred and fifty years ago.

There is a narrow hall or court running through these houses which is all that separates the family from the horses and pigs and cows which abide under the same roof.

The whole place smells alike. There is no heat anywhere, save from a fireplace in the kitchen. There is a community bakehouse.

The soldiers were quartered in the barns and outhouses, the officers were quartered in the homes of these French peasants. There were no comforts for either soldier or officer. It rained almost continuously and at night it was cold. No dining-rooms could be provided where the men could eat and they lined up on the street, got their chow and ate it standing in the rain or under whatever cover they could find. Few of them could understand any French, and all the conditions surrounding their presence in France were most trying to them. They were drilled from morning to night. They were covered with mud. The great fight in which they had come to participate was still afar off. No wonder their hearts grew heavy with a great longing for home. Gloom sat upon their faces and depression grew with every passing hour.

Into these villages one after another came the little military side-car with its pioneer Salvationists, investigating conditions and inquiring the greatest immediate need of the men.

All the soldiers were homesick, and wherever the little car stopped the Salvation Army uniform attracted immediate and friendly attention. The boys expressed the liveliest interest in the possibility of the Salvation Army being with them in France. These troops composed the regular army and were old-timers. They showed at once their respect for and their belief in the Salvation Army. One poor fellow, when he saw the uniform, exclaimed: "The Salvation Army! I believe they'll be waiting for us when we get to hell to try and save us!"

It appeared that the pay of the American soldier was so much greater than that of the French soldier that he had too much money at his disposal; and this money was a menace both to him and to the French population. If some means could be provided for transferring the soldier's money home, it would help out in the one direction which was most important at that time.

It will be remembered that the French habit of drinking wine was ever before the American soldier, and with 165 francs a month in his pocket, he became an object of interest to the French tradespeople, who encouraged him to spend his money in drink, and who also raised the price on other commodities to a point where the French population found it made living for them most difficult.

The Salvation Army authorities in New York were all prepared to meet this need. The Organization has one thousand posts throughout the United States commanded by officers who would become responsible to get the soldier's money to his family or relatives in the United States. A simple money-order blank issued in France could be sent to the National Headquarters of the Salvation Army in New York and from there to the officer commanding the corps in any part of the United States, who would deliver the money in person.

In this way the friends and relatives of the soldier in France would be comforted in the knowledge that the Salvation Army was in touch with their boy; and if need existed in the family at home it would be discovered through the visit of the Salvation Army officer in the homeland and immediate steps taken to alleviate it.

Perhaps this has done more than anything else to bring the blessing of parents and relatives upon the organization, for tens of thousands of dollars that would have been spent in gambling and drink have been sent home to widowed mothers and young wives.

This suggestion appealed very strongly to the military general, who said that if the Salvation Army got into operation it could count upon any assistance which he could give it, and if they conducted meetings he would see that his regimental band was instructed to attend these meetings and furnish the music.

Several chaplains, both Protestant and Catholic, expressed themselves as being glad to welcome the Salvation Army among them.

Among the Regular Army officers there was rather a pessimistic attitude. It was in nowise hostile, but rather doubtful.

One general said that he did not see that the Salvation Army could do any good. His idea of the Salvation Army being associated altogether with the slums and men who were down and out. But on the other hand, he said that he did not see that the Salvation Army could do any harm, even if they did not do any good, and as far as he was concerned he was agreeable to their coming in to work in the First Division; and he would so report to General Pershing.

St. Nazaire, the base, was being used for the reception of the troops as they reached the shores of France. Here was a new situation. The men had been cooped up on transports for several days and on their landing at St. Nazaire they were placed in a rest camp with the opportunity to visit the city. Here they were a prey to immoral women and the officer commanding the base was greatly concerned about the matter and eagerly welcomed the idea of having the Salvation Army establish good women in St. Nazaire who would cope with the problem.

The report given to General Pershing resulted in an official authorization permitting the Salvation Army to open their work with the American Expeditionary Forces, and a suggestion that they go at once to the American Training Area and see what they could do to alleviate the terrible epidemic of homesickness that had broken out among the soldiers.

In the meantime, back in New York, the Commander had not been idle. Daily before the throne she had laid the great concerns of her Army, and daily she had been preparing her first little company of workers to go when the need should call.

There was no money as yet, but the Commander was not to be daunted, and so when the report came from over the water, she borrowed from the banks twenty-five thousand dollars.

She called the little company of pioneer workers together in a quiet place before they left and gave them such a charge as would make an angel search his heart. Before the Most High God she called upon them to tell her if any of them had in his or her heart any motive or ambition in going other than to serve the Lord Christ. She looked down into the eyes of the young maidens and bade them put utterly away from them the arts and coquetries of youth, and remember that they were sent forth to help and save and love the souls of men as God loved them; and that self must be forgotten, or their work would be in vain. She commanded them if even at this last hour any faltered or felt himself unfit for the God-given task, that he would tell her even then before it was too late. She begged them to remember that they held in their hands the honor of the Salvation Army, and the glory of Jesus Christ their Saviour as they went out to serve the troops. They were to be living examples of Christ's love, and they were to be willing to lay down their lives if need be for His sake.

There were tears in the eyes of some of those strong men that day as they listened, and the look of exaltation on the faces of the women was like a reflection from above. So must have looked the disciples of old when Jesus gave them the commission to go into all the world and preach the gospel. They were filled with His Spirit, and there was a look of utter joy and self-forgetfulness as they knelt with their leader to pray, in words which carried them all to the very feet of God and laid their lives a willing sacrifice to Him who had done so much for them. Still kneeling, with bowed heads, they sang, and their words were but a prayer. It is a way these wonderful people have of bursting into song upon their knees with their eyes closed and faces illumined by a light of another world, their whole souls in the words they are singing—"singing as unto the Lord!" It reminds one of the days of old when the children of Israel did everything with songs and prayers and rejoicing, and the whole of life was carried on as if in the visible presence of God, instead of utterly ignoring Him as most of us do now.

The song this time was just a few lines of consecration:

> *"Oh, for a heart whiter than snow!*
> *Saviour Divine, to whom else can I go?*
> *Thou who hast died, loving me so,*
> *Give me a heart that is whiter than snow!"*

The dramatic beauty of the scene, the sweet, holy abandonment of that prayer-song with its tender, appealing melody, would have held a throng of thousands in awed wonder. But there was no audience, unless, perchance, the angels gathered around the little company, rejoicing that in this world of sin and war there were these who had so given themselves to God; but from that glory-touched room there presently went forth men and women with the spirit in their hearts that was to thrill like an electric wire every life with which it came in contact, and show the whole world what God can do with lives that are wholly surrendered to Him.

It was a bright sunny afternoon, August 12th, when this first party of American Salvation Army workers set sail for France.

No doubt there was many a smile of contempt from the bystanders as they saw the little group of blue uniforms with the gold-lettered scarlet hatbands, and noticed the four poke bonnets among the number. What did the tambourine lassies know of REAL warfare? To those who reckoned the Salvation Army in terms of bands on the street corner, and shivering forms guarding Christmas kettles, it must have seemed the utmost audacity for this "play army" to go to the front.

When they arrived at Bordeaux on August 21st they went at once to Paris to be fitted out with French uniforms, as General Pershing had given them all the rank of military privates, and ordered that they should wear the regulation khaki uniforms with the addition of the red Salvation Army shield on the hats, red epaulets, and with skirts for the women.

A cabled message had reached France from the Commander saying that funds to the extent of twenty-five thousands dollars had been arranged for, and would be supplied as needed, and that a party of eleven officers were being dispatched at once. After that matters began to move rapidly.

A portable tent, 25 feet by 100 feet, was purchased and

shipped to Demange; and a touring car was bought with part of the money advanced.

Purchasing an automobile in France is not a matter merely of money. It is a matter for Governmental sanction, long delay, red tape—amazing good luck.

At the start the whole Salvation Army transportation system consisted of this one first huge limousine, heartlessly overdriven and overworked. For many weeks it was Colonel Barker's office and bedroom. It carried all of the Salvation Army workers to and from their stations, hauled all of the supplies on its roof, inside, on its fenders, and later also on a trailer. It ran day and night almost without end, two drivers alternating. It was a sort of supercar, still in the service, to which Salvationists still refer with an affectionate amazement when they consider its terrific accomplishments. It hauled all of the lumber for the first huts and a not uncommon sight was to see it tearing along the road at forty miles an hour, loaded inside and on top with supplies, several passengers clinging to its fenders, and a load of lumber or trunks trailing behind. For a long time Colonel Barker had no home aside from this car. He slept wherever it happened to be for the night—often in it, while still driven. One night he and a Salvation Army officer were lost in a strange woods in the car until four in the morning. They were without lights and there were no real roads.

Later, of course, after long waiting, other trucks were bought and to-day there are about fifty automobiles in this service. Chauffeurs had to be developed out of men who had never driven before. They were even taken from huts and detailed to this work.

In this first touring car Colonel Barker with one of the newly arrived adjutants for driver, started to Demange.

Twenty kilometers outside of Paris the car had a breakdown. The two clambered out and reconnoitered for help. There was nothing for it but to take the car back to Paris. A man was found on the road who was willing to take it in tow, but they had no rope for a tow line. Over in the field by the roadside the sharp eyes of the adjutant discovered some old rusty wire. He pulled it out from the tangle of long grass, and behold it was a part of old barbed-wire entanglements!

In great surprise they followed it up behind the camouflage and found themselves in the old trenches of 1914. They walked in the trenches and entered some of the dugouts where the soldiers had lived in the memorable days of the Marne fight. As they looked a little farther up the hillside they were startled to see great pieces of heavy field artillery, their long barrels sticking out from pits and pointing at them. They went closer to examine, and found the guns were made of wood painted black. The barrels were perfectly made, even to the breech blocks mounted on wheels, the tires of which were made of tin. They were a perfect imitation of a heavy ordnance piece in every detail. Curious, wondering what it could mean, the two explorers looked about them and saw an old Frenchman coming toward them. He proved to be the keeper of the place, and he told them the story. These were the guns that saved Paris in 1914.

The Boche had been coming on twenty kilometers one day, nineteen the next, fourteen the next, and were daily drawing nearer to the great city. They were so confident that they had even announced the day they would sweep through the gates of Paris. The French had no guns heavy enough to stop that mad rush, and so they mounted these guns of wood, cut away the woods all about them and for three hundred meters in front, and waited with their pitifully thin, ill-equipped line to defend the trenches.

Then the German airplanes came and took pictures of them, and returned to their lines to make plans for the next day; but when the pictures were developed and enlarged they saw to their horror that the French had brought heavy guns to their front and were preparing to blow them out of France. They decided to delay their advance and wait until they could bring up artillery heavier than the French had, and while they waited the Germans broke into the French wine cellars and stole the "vin blanche" and "vin rouge." The French call this "light" wine and say it takes the place of water, which is only fit for washing; but it proved to be too heavy for the Germans that day. They drank freely, not even waiting to unseal the bottles of rare old vintage, but knocked the necks off the bottles against the stone walls and drank. They were all drunk and in no condition to conquer France when their artillery came up, and so the wooden French guns and the French wine saved Paris.

When the two men finally arrived in Demange the Military General greeted them gladly and invited them to dine with him.

He had for a cook a famous French chef who provided delicious meals, but for dessert the chef had attempted to make an American apple pie, which was a dismal failure. The colonel said to the general: "Just wait till our Salvation Army women get here and I will see that they make you a pie that is a pie."

The General and the members of his staff said they would remember that promise and hold him to it.

The pleasure which the thought of that pie aroused furnished a suggestion for work later on.

Within two or three days the hut had arrived. The question of a lot upon which to place it was most important. The billeting officers stated that none could be had within the town and insisted that the hut would have to be placed in an inaccessible spot on the outskirts of the town, but Colonel Barker asked the General if he would mind his looking about himself and he readily assented. The indomitable Barker, true to the "never-say-die" slogan of the Salvation Army, went out and found a splendid lot on the main street in the heart of the town, which was being partly used by its owner as a vegetable garden. He quickly secured the services of a French interpreter and struck a bargain with the owner to rent the lot for the sum of sixteen dollars a year, and on his return with the information that this lot had been secured the General was greatly impressed.

A wire had been sent to Paris instructing the men of the party to come down immediately. A couple of tents were secured to provide temporary sleeping accommodation and the men lined up in the chow line with the doughboys at meal-time.

The six Salvationists pulled off their coats at once and went to work, much to the amusement of a few curious soldiers who stood idly watching them.

They discovered right at the start that the building materials which had been sent ahead of them had been dumped on the wrong lot, and the first thing they had to do was to move them all to the proper site. This was no easy task for men who had but recently left office chairs and clerical work. Unaccustomed muscles cried out in protest and weary backs ached and complained, but the men stubbornly marched back and forth carrying big timbers, and attracting not a little attention from soldiers who wondered what in the world the Salvation Army could be up to over in France. Some of them were suspicious. Had they come to try and stuff religion down their throats? If so, they would soon find out their mistake. So, half in belligerence, half in amusement, the soldiers watched their progress. It was a big joke to them, who had come here for *serious* business and longed to be at it.

Steadily, quietly, the work went on. They laid the timbers and erected the framework of their hut, keeping at it when the rain fell and soaked them to the skin. They were a bit awkward at it at first, perhaps, for it was new work to them, and they had but few tools. The hut was twenty-five feet wide and a hundred feet long. The walls went up presently, and the roof went on. One or two soldiers were getting interested and offered to help a bit; but for the most part they stood apart suspiciously, while the Salvation Army worked cheerily on and finished the building with their own hands.

Colonel Barker meanwhile had gone back to Paris for supplies and to bring the women overland in the automobile, because he was somewhat fearful lest they might be held up if they attempted to go out by train. The idea of women in the camps was so new to our American soldiers, and so distasteful to the French, that they presented quite a problem until their work fully justified their presence.

It got about that some real American girls were coming. The boys began to grow curious. When the big French limousine carrying them arrived in the camp it was greeted by some of the soldiers with the greatest enthusiasm while others looked on in critical silence. But very soon their influence was felt, for a commanding officer stated that his men were more contented and more easily handled since the unprecedented innovation of women in the camp than they had been within the experience of the old Regular Army officers. Profanity practically ceased in the vicinity of the hut and was never indulged in in the presence of the Salvationists.

While the hut was being erected meetings were conducted in the open air which were attended by great throngs, and after every meeting from one to four or five boys asked for the privilege of going into the tent at the back and being prayed with, and many conversions resulted from these first open-air meetings. Boys walked in from other camps from a distance as far away as five miles to attend these meetings and many were converted.

The hut was finally completed and equipped and was to be formally opened on Sunday evening.

In the meantime the Y.M.C.A. was getting busy also establishing its work in the camps; therefore, the Salvation Army tried to place their huts in towns where the Y. was not operating, so that they might be able to reach those who had the greatest need of them.

Officers had been appointed to take charge of the Demange hut and immediately further operations in other towns were being arranged.

A Y.M.C.A. hut, however, followed quickly on the heels of the Salvation Army at Demange and the night of the opening of the Salvation Army hut someone came to ask if they would come over to the Y. and help in a meeting. Sure, they would help! So the Staff-Captain took a cornetist and two of the lassies and went over to the Y.M.C.A. hut.

It was early dusk and a crowd was gathered about where a rope ring fenced off the place in which a boxing match had been held the day before, across the road from the hut. The band had been stationed there giving a concert which was just finished, and the men were sitting in a circle on the ground about the ring.

The Salvationists stood at the door of the hut and looked across to the crowd.

"How about holding our meeting over there?" asked the Staff-Captain of the man in charge.

"All right. Hold it wherever you like."

So a few willing hands brought out the piano, and the four Salvationists made their way across to the ring. The soldiers raised a loud cheer and hurrah to see the women stoop and slip under the rope, and a spirit of sympathy seemed to be established at once.

There were a thousand men gathered about and the cornet began where the band had left off, thrilling out between the roar of guns.

Up above were the airplanes throbbing back and forth, and signal lights were flashing. It was a strange place for a meeting. The men gathered closer to see what was going on.

The sound of an old familiar hymn floated out on the evening, bringing a sudden memory of home and days when one was a little boy and went to Sunday-school; when there was no war, and no one dreamed that the sons would have to go forth from their own land to fight. A sudden hush stole over the men and they sat enthralled watching the little band of singers in the changing flicker of light and darkness. Women's voices! Young and fresh, too, not old ones. How they thrilled with the sweetness of it:

> "Nearer, my God, to Thee,
> Nearer to Thee,
> E'en though it be a cross
> That raiseth me."

A cross! Was it possible that God was leading them to Him through all this awfulness? But the thought only hovered above them and hushed their hearts into attention as they gruffly joined their young voices in the melody. Another song followed, and a prayer that seemed to bring the great God right down in their midst and make Him a beloved comrade. They had not got

over the wonder of it when a new note sounded on
piano and cornet and every voice broke forth in the
words:

> *"When the trumpet of the Lord shall sound*
> *And time shall be no more—"*

How soon would that trumpet sound for many of
them! Time should be no more! What a startling
thought!

Following close upon the song came the sweet voice
of a young girl speaking. They looked up in wonder,
listening with all their souls. It was like having an angel
drop down among them to see her there, and hear her
clear, unafraid voice. The first thing that struck them was
her intense earnestness, as if she had a message of great
moment to bring to them.

Her words searched their hearts and found out the
weak places; those fears and misgivings that they had
known were there from the beginning, and had been
trying hard to hide from themselves because they saw no
cure for them. With one clear-cut sentence she tore
away all camouflage and set them face to face with the
facts. They were in a desperate strait and they knew it.
Back there in the States they had known it. Down in the
camps they had felt it, and had made various attempts to
find something strong and true to help them, but no one
had seemed to understand. Even when they went to
church there had been so much talk about the "supreme
sacrifice" and the glory of dying for one's country, that
they had a vague feeling that even the minister did not
believe in his religion any more. And so they had
whistled and tried to be jolly and forget. They were all
in the same boat, and this was a job that had to be done,
they couldn't get out of it; best not think about the

future! So they had lulled their consciences to sleep. But it was there, back in their minds all the time, a looming big awful question about the hereafter; and when the great guns boomed afar as a few were doing to-night and they thought how soon they might be called to go over the top, they would have been fools not to have recognized it.

But here at last was someone else who understood!

She was telling the old, old story of Jesus and His love, and every man of them as he listened felt it was true. It had been like a vague tale of childhood before; something that one outgrows and smiles at; but now it suddenly seemed so simple, so perfect, so fitted to their desperate need. Just the old story that everybody has sinned, and broken God's law: that God in His love provided a way of escape in the death of His Son Jesus on the Cross, from penalty for sin for all who would accept it; that He gave every one of us free wills; and it was up to us whether we would accept it or not.

There were men in that company who had come from college classes where they had been taught the foolishness of blood atonement, and who had often smiled disdainfully at the Bible; there were boys from cultured, refined homes where Jesus Christ had always been ignored; there were boys who had repudiated the God their mothers trusted in; and there were boys of lower degree whose lips were foul with blasphemy and whose hearts were scarred with sin; but all listened, now, in a new way. It was somehow different over here, with the thunder of artillery in the near distance, the hovering presence of death not far away, the flashing of signal lights, the hum of the airplanes, the whole background of war. The message of the gospel took on a reality it had never worn before. When this simple girl asked if they would not take Jesus to-night as their Saviour, there were many who raised their hands in the darkness and many more hearts were bowed whose owners could not quite bring themselves to raise their hands.

Then a lassie's voice began to sing, all alone:

> *"I grieved my Lord from day to day,*
> *I scorned His love, so full and free,*
> *And though I wandered far away,*
> *My Mother's prayers have followed me.*
> *I'm coming home, I'm coming home,*
> *To live my wasted life anew,*
> *For Mother's prayers have followed me,*
> *Have followed me, the whole world through.*
>
> *"O'er desert wild, o'er mountain high,*
> *A wanderer I chose to be—*
> *A wretched soul condemned to die;*
> *Still Mother's prayers have followed me.*
>
> *"He turned my darkness into light,*
> *This blessed Christ of Calvary;*
> *I'll praise His name both day and night,*
> *That Mother's prayers have followed me!*
> *I'm coming home, I'm coming home—"*

Only the last great day will reveal how many hearts echoed those words; but the voices were all husky with emotion as they tried to join in the closing hymn that followed.

There were those who lingered about the speakers and wanted to inquire the way of salvation, and some knelt in a quiet corner and gave themselves to Christ. Over all of them there was a hushed thoughtfulness. When the workers started back to their own hut the crowd went with them, talking eagerly as they went, hovering about wisfully as if here were the first real thing they had found since coming away from home.

Over at the Salvation Army hut another service had been going forward with equal interest, the dedication of the new building. The place was crowded to its utmost capacity, and crowds were standing outside and peering in at the windows. Some of the French people of the neighborhood, women and children and old men, had drifted over, and were listening to the singing in open-eyed wonderment. Among them one of the Salvation Army workers had distributed copies of the French "War Cry" with stories of Christ in their own language, and it began to dawn upon them that these people believed in the same Jesus that was worshipped in their French churches; yet they never had seen services like these. The joyous music thrilled them.

Before they slept that night the majority of the soldiers in that vicinity had lost most of their prejudice against the little band of unselfish workers that had dropped so quietly down into their midst. Word was beginning to filter out from camp to camp that they were a good sort, that they sold their goods at cost and a fellow could even "jawbone" when he was "broke."

Salvation Army huts gave the soldiers "jawbone," this being the soldier's name for credit. No accounts were kept of the amount allowed to each soldier. When a soldier came to the canteen and asked for "jawbone," he was asked how much he had already been allowed. If the amount owed by him already was large, he was cautioned not to go too deeply into his next pay check; but never was a man refused anything within reason. Frequently one hut would have many thousands of francs outstanding by the end of the month. But, although there was no check against them, soldiers always squared their accounts at pay-day and very little indeed was lost.

One man came in and threw 300 francs on the counter, saying: "I owe you 285 francs. Put the change in the coffee fund."

One Salvation Army Ensign frequently loaned sums of money out of his own pocket to soldiers, asking that, when they were in a position to return it, they hand it in to any Salvation Army hut, saying that it was for him. He says that he has never lost by doing this.

One day as he was driving from Havre to Paris he met six American soldiers whose big truck had broken down. They asked him where there was a Salvation Army hut; but there was none in that particular section. They had no food, no money, and no place to sleep. He handed them seventy francs and told them to leave it at any Salvation Army hut for him when they were able. Five months passed and then the money was turned in to a Salvation Army hut and forwarded to him. With it was a note stating that the men had been with the French troops and had not been able to reach a Salvation Army establishment. They were very grateful for the trust reposed in them by the Salvationist. Undoubtedly there are many such instances.

The Salvation Army officer who with his wife was put in charge of the hut at Demange, soon became one of the most popular men in camp. His generous spirit, no less than his rough–and–ready good nature, manful, soldier–like disposition, coupled with a sturdy self–respect and a ready humor, made him blood brother to those hard–bitten old regulars and National Guardsmen of the first American Expeditionary Force.

The Salvation Army quickly became popular. Meetings were held almost every night at that time with an average attendance of not less than five hundred. Meetings as a rule were confined to wonderful song services and brief, snappy talks. At first there were very few conversions, but there have been more since the great drives in which the Americans have taken so large a share. The Masons, the Moose and a Jewish fraternity used the hut for fraternal gatherings. Catholic priests held mass in it upon various occasions. The school for officers and the school for "noncoms" met in it. The band practiced in it every morning. Because of its popularity among the men it was known among the officers as "the soldiers' hut." General Duncan once addressed his staff officers in it upon some important matters.

It rained every day for three months. The hut was on rather low ground and in back of it ran the river, considerably swollen by the rains. One night the river rose suddenly, carried away one tent and flooded the other two and the hut. The Salvation Army men spent a wild, wet, sleepless night trying to salvage their scanty personal belongings and their stock of supplies. When the river retreated it left the hut floor covered with slimy black mud which the two men had to shovel out. This was a back-breaking task occupying the better part of two days.

The first snow fell on the bitterest night of the year. It was preceded by the rain and was damp and heavy. The soldiers suffered terribly, especially the men on guard duty who had perforce to endure the full blast of the storm. During the earlier hours of the night the girls served all comers with steaming coffee and filled the canteens of the men on guard (free). When they saw how severe the night would be they remained up to keep a supply of coffee ready for the Salvation Army men who went the rounds through the storm every half hour, serving the sentries with the warming fluid.

That first Expeditionary Force wanted for many things, and endured hardships unthought of by troops arriving later, after the war industries at home had swung into full production. It was almost impossible to secure stoves, and firewood was scarce. For every load that went to the Salvation Army Hut, men of the American Expeditionary Force had to do without, and yet wood was always supplied to the Salvationists (it could not be bought).

At St. Joire, the wood pile had entirely given out and it looked as if there was to be no heat at the Salvation Army hut that night. The sergeant promised them half a load, but the wood wagon lost a wheel about a hundred yards out of town.

"Never mind," said the sergeant to the girls, "the boys will see that you get some to-night."

So he requested every man going up to the Salvation Army hut that evening to carry a stick of wood with him ("a stick" may weigh anywhere from 10 to 100 pounds). By eight o'clock there was over a wagon load and a half stacked in back of the hut.

Two small stoves cast circles of heat in the big hut at Demange. Around them the men crowded with their wet garments steaming so profusely that the hut often took on the appearance of a steam-room in a Turkish bath. The rest of the hut was cold; but compared to the weather outside, it was heaven-like. For all of its size, the hut was frail, and the winter wind blew coldly through its many cracks; but compared with the soldier's billets, it was a cozy palace. The Salvationists spent hours each week sitting on the roof in the driving rain patching leaks with tar-paper and tacks.

The life was a hard one for the girls. They nearly froze during the days, and at nights they usually shivered themselves to sleep, only sleeping when sheer exhaustion overcame them. There were no baths at all. The experience was most trying for women and only the spirit of the great enterprise in which they were engaged carried them through the winter. Even soldiers were at times seen weeping with cold and misery.

One night the gasoline tank which supplied light to the hut exploded and set the place on fire. A whole regiment turned out of their blankets to put out the blaze. This meant more hours for those in charge repairing the roof in the snow. They also had to cut all of the wood for the hut. Later details were supplied to every hut by the military authorities to cut wood, sweep and clean up, carry water, etc. Soldiers used the hut for a mess hall. There was no other place where they could eat with any degree of comfort.

By this time the fact that the Salvation Army was established at Demange was becoming known throughout the division.

One of the towns where there had been no arrangements made for welfare workers at all was Montiers-sur-Saulx, where the First Ammunition Train was established, and here the officer temporarily commanding the ammunition train gave a most hearty welcome to the Salvation Army.

Two large circus tents had been sent on from New York and one of these was to be erected until a wooden building could be secured.

The touring car went back to Demange, picked up a Staff-Captain, a Captain, five white tents, the largest one thirty by sixty feet, the others smaller, carried them across the country and dropped them down at the roadside of the public square in Montiers.

There stood the Salvationists in the road wondering what to do next.

Then a hearty voice called out: "Are you locating with us?" and the military officer of the day advanced to meet them with a hand-shake and many expressions of his appreciation of the Salvation Army.

"We are going to stay here if you will have us," said the Staff-Captain.

"Have you! Well, I should say we would have you! Wait a minute and I'll have a detail put your baggage under cover for the night. Then we'll see about dinner and a billet."

Thus auspiciously did the work open in Montiers.

In a few minutes they were taken to a French café and a comfortable place found for them to spend the night.

Soon after the rising of the sun the next morning they were up and about hunting a place for the tents which were to serve for a recreation centre for the boys. The American Major in charge of the town personally assisted them to find a good location, and offered his aid in any way needed.

Before nightfall the five white tents were up, standing straight and true with military precision, and the two officers with just pride in their hard day's work, and a secret assurance that it would stand the hearty approval of the commanding officer whom they had not as yet met, went off to their suppers, for which they had a more than usually hearty appetite.

Suddenly the door of the dining-room swung open and a gruff voice demanded: "Who put up those tents?" The Salvation Army Staff-Captain stood forth saluting respectfully and responded: "I, sir." "Well," said the Colonel, "they look mighty fine up on that hill—mighty fine! Splendid location for them—splendid! But the enemy can spot them for a hundred miles, so I expect you had better get them down or camouflage them with green boughs and paint by to-morrow night at the latest. Good evening to you, sir!"

The Staff-Captain and his helper suddenly lost their fine appetites and felt very tired. Camouflage! How did they do that at a moment's notice? They left their unfinished dinner and hurried out in search of help.

The first soldier the Staff-Captain questioned reassured him.

"Aw, that's dead easy! Go over the hill into the woods and cut some branches, enough to cover your tents; or easier yet, get some green and yellow paint and splash over them. The worse they look the better they are!"

So the weary workers hunted the town over for paint, and found only enough for the big tent, upon which they worked hard all the next morning. Then they had to go to the woods for branches for the rest. Scratched and bleeding and streaked with perspiration and dirt, they finished their work at last, and the white tents had disappeared into the green and the yellow and the brown of the hillside. Their beautiful military whiteness was gone, but they were hidden safe from the enemy and the work might now go forward.

Then the girls arrived and things began to look a bit more cheerful.

"But where is the cook stove?" asked one of the lassies after they had set up their two folding cots in one of the smaller tents and made themselves at home.

Dismay descended upon the face of the weary Staff-Captain.

"Why," he answered apologetically, "we forgot all about that!" and he hurried out to find a stove.

A thorough search of the surrounding country, however, disclosed the fact that there was not a stove nor a field range to be had—no, not even from the commissary. There was nothing for it but to set to work and contrive a fireplace out of field stone and clay, with a bit of sheet iron for a roof, and two or three lengths of old sewer pipe carefully wired together for a stovepipe. It took days of hard work, and it smoked woefully except when the wind was exactly west, but the girls made fudge enough on it for the entire personnel of the ammunition train to celebrate when it was finished.

When the girls first arrived in Montiers the Salvation Army Staff-Captain was rather at a loss to know what to do with them until the hut was built. They were invited to chow with the soldiers, and to eat in an old French barn used as a kitchen, in front of which the men lined up at the open doorways for mess. It was a very dirty barn indeed, with heavy cobwebs hanging in weird festoons from the ceiling and straw and manure all over the floor; quite too barnlike for a dining-hall for delicately reared women. The Staff-Captain hesitated about bringing them there, but the Mess-Sergeant offered to clean up a corner for them and give them a comfortable table.

"I don't know about bringing my girls in here with the men," said the Staff-Captain still hesitating. "You know the men are pretty rough in their talk, and they're always cussing!"

"Leave that to me!" said the Mess-Sergeant. "It'll be all right!"

There was an old dirty French wagon in the barnyard where they kept the bread. It was not an inviting prospect and the Staff-Captain looked about him dubiously and went away with many misgivings, but there seemed to be nothing else to be done.

The boys did their best to fix things up nicely. When meal time arrived and the girls appeared they found their table neatly spread with a dish towel for a tablecloth. It purported to be clean, but there are degrees of cleanliness in the army and there might have been a difference of opinion. However, the girls realized that there had been a strenuous attempt to do honor to them and they sat down on the coffee kegs that had been provided *en lieu* of chairs with smiling appreciation.

The Staff-Captain's anxiety began to relax as he noticed the quiet respectful attitude of the men when they passed by the doorway and looked eagerly over at the corner where the girls were sitting. It was great to have American women sitting down to dinner with them, as it were. Not a "cuss word" broke the harmony of the occasion. The best cuts of meat, the largest pieces of pie, were given to the girls, and everybody united to make them feel how welcome they were.

Then into the midst of the pleasant scene there entered one who had been away for a few hours and had not yet been made acquainted with the new order of things at chow; and he entered with an oath upon his lips.

He was a great big fellow, but the strong arm of the Mess-Sergeant flashed out from the shoulder instantly, the sturdy fist of the Mess-Sergeant was planted most unexpectedly in the newcomer's face, and he found himself sprawling on the other side of the road with all his comrades glaring at him in silent wrath. That was the beginning of a new order of things at the mess.

The Colonel in charge of the regiment had gone away, and the commanding Major, wishing to make things pleasant for the Salvationists, sent for the Staff-Captain and invited them all to his mess at the chateau; telling him that if he needed anything at any time, horses or supplies, or anything in his power to give, to let him know at once and it should be supplied.

The Staff-Captain thanked him, but told him that he thought they would stay with the boys.

The boys, of course, heard of this and the Salvation Army people had another bond between them and the soldiers. The boys felt that the Salvationists were their very own. Nothing could have more endeared them to the boys than to share their life and hardships.

The Salvation Army had not been with the soldiers many hours before they discovered that the disease of homesickness which they had been sent to succor was growing more and more malignant and spreading fast.

The training under French officers was very severe. Trench feet with all its attendant suffering was added to the other discomforts. Was it any wonder that homesickness seized hold of every soldier there?

It had been raining steadily for thirty-six days, making swamps and pools everywhere. Depression like a great heavy blanket hung over the whole area.

The Salvation Army lassies at Montiers were in consultation. Their supplies were all gone, and the state of the roads on account of the rain was such that all transportation was held up. They had been waiting, hoping against hope, that a new load of supplies would arrive, but there seemed no immediate promise of that.

"We ought to have something more than just chocolate to sell to the soldiers, anyway," declared one lassie, who was a wonderful cook, looking across the big tent to the drooping shoulders and discouraged faces of the boys who were hovering about the Victrola, trying to extract a little comfort from the records. "We ought to be able to give them some real home cooking!"

They all agreed to this, but the difficulties in the way were great. Flour was obtainable only in small quantities. Now and then they could get a sack of flour or a bag of sugar, but not often. Lard also was a scarce article. Besides, there were no stoves, and no equipment had as yet been issued for ovens. All about them were apple orchards and they might have baked some pies if there had been ovens, but at present that was out of the question. After a long discussion one of the girls suggested doughnuts, and even that had its difficulties, although it really was the only thing possible at the time. For one thing they had no rolling-pin and no cake-cutter in the outfit. Nevertheless, they bravely went to work. The little tent intended for such things had blown down, so the lassie had to stand out in the rain to prepare the dough.

The first doughnuts were patted out, until someone found an empty grape-juice bottle and used that for a rolling-pin. As they had no cutter they used a knife, and twisted them, making them in shape like a cruller. They were cooked over a wood fire that had to be continually stuffed with fuel to keep the fat hot enough to fry. The pan they used was only large enough to cook seven at once, but that first day they made one hundred and fifty big fat sugary doughnuts, and when the luscious fragrance began to float out on the air and word went forth that they had real "hon-est-to-goodness" home doughnuts at the Salvation Army hut, the line formed away out into the road and stood patiently for hours in the rain waiting for a taste of the dainties. As there were eight hundred men in the outfit and only a hundred and fifty doughnuts that first day, naturally a good many were disappointed, but those who got them were appreciative. One boy as he took the first sugary bite exclaimed: "Gee! If this is war, let it continue!"

The next day the girls managed to make three hundred, but one of them was not satisfied with a doughnut that had no hole in it, and while she worked she thought, until a bright idea came to her. The top of the baking-powder can! Of course! Why hadn't they thought of that before? But how could they get the hole? There seemed nothing just right to cut it. Then, the very next morning the inside tube to the coffee percolator that somebody had brought along came loose, and the lassie stood in triumph with it in her hand, calling to them all to see what a wonderful hole it would make in the doughnut. And so the doughnut came into its own, hole and all.

That was at Montiers, the home of the doughnut.

One of the older Salvation Army workers remarked jocularly that the Salvation Army had to go to France and get linked up with the doughnut before America recognized it; but it was the same old Salvation Army and the same old doughnut that it had always been. He averred that it wasn't the doughnut at all that made the Salvation Army famous, but the wonderful girls that the Salvation Army brought over there; the girls that lay awake at night after a long hard day's work scheming to make the way of the doughboy easier; scheming how to take the cold out of the snow and the wet out of the rain and the stickiness out of the mud. The girls that prayed over the doughnuts, and then got the maximum of grace out of the minimum of grease.

The young Adjutant lassie who fried the first doughnut in France says that invariably the boys would begin to talk about home and mother while they were eating the doughnuts. Through the hole in the doughnut they seemed to see their mother's face, and as the doughnut disappeared it grew bigger and clearer.

The young Ensign lassie who had originated and *made* the first doughnut in France contrived to make many pies on a very tiny French stove with an oven only large enough to hold two pies at a time. Meanwhile, frying doughnuts on the top of the stove.

It wasn't long before the record for the doughnut makers had been brought up to five thousand a day, and some of the unresting workers developed "doughnut wrist" from sticking to the job too long at a time.

It was the original thought that pie would be the greatest attraction, but it was difficult to secure stoves with ovens adequate for baking pies, and after the ensign's experiment with doughnuts it was found that they could more easily be made and were quite as acceptable to the American boy.

Meantime, the pie was coming into its own, back in Demange also.

It was only a little stove, and only room to bake one pie at a time, but it was a savory smell that floated out on the air, and it was a long line of hungry soldiers that hurried for their mess kits and stood hours waiting for more pies to bake; and the fame of the Salvation Army began to spread far and wide. Then one day the "Stars and Stripes," the organ of the American Army, printed the following poem about the lassie who labored so far forward that she had to wear a tin hat:

> *"Home is where the heart is"—*
> *Thus the poet sang;*
> *But "home is where the pie is"*
> *For the doughboy gang!*
> *Crullers in the craters,*
> *Pastry in abris—*
> *This Salvation Army lass*
> *Sure knows how to please!*
>
> *Tin hat for a halo!*
> *Ah! She wears it well!*
> *Making pies for homesick lads*
> *Sure is "beating hell!"*
> *In a region blasted*
> *By fire and flame and sword,*
> *This Salvation Army lass*
> *Battles for the Lord!*

Call me sacrilegious
And irreverent, too;
Pies? They link us up with home
As naught else can do!
"Home is where the heart is"—
True, the poet sang;
But "home is where the pie is"—
To the Yankee gang!

It was no easy task to open up a chain of huts, for there was an amazing variety of details to be attended to, any one of which might delay the work. A hundred and one unexpected situations would develop during the course of a single day which must be dealt with quickly and intelligently. The fact that the Salvation Army section of the American Expeditionary Force is militarized and strictly accountable for all of its action to the United States military authorities is complicated in many places by the further fact that the French civil and military authorities must also be taken into consideration and consulted at every step. Nevertheless, in spite of all difficulties the work went steadily forward. The patient officers who were seeing to all these details worked almost night and day to place the huts and workers where they would do the most good to the greatest number; and steadily the Salvation Army grew in favor with the soldiers.

It was extremely difficult to obtain materials for the erection of huts—in many cases almost impossible. Once when Colonel Barker found troops moving, he discovered the village for which they were bound, rushed ahead in his automobile, and commandeered an old French barracks which would otherwise have been occupied by the American soldiers. When the soldiers arrived they were overjoyed to find the Salvation Army awaiting them with hot food. They were soaked through by the rain, and never was hot coffee more welcome. There was a little argument about the commandeered barracks. It was to have been used as headquarters, but when the commanding officer went out into the rain and saw for himself what service it was performing for his men, and how overjoyed they were by the entertainment he said: "We'll leave it to the men, whether they will be billeted here or let the Salvation Army have the place." The men with one accord voted to give it to the Salvation Army.

In one town, after an animated discussion with a crowd of enlisted men, a sergeant came to the Salvation Army Major as he worked away with his hammer putting up a hut and said: "Captain, would it make you mad if we offered our services to help?"

After that the work went on in record time. In less than a week the hut was finished and ready for business. Two self-appointed details of soldiers from the regulars employed all their spare time in a friendly rivalry to see which could accomplish the most work. When it was dedicated the popularity of the hut was well assured. Later, in another location, a hut 125 feet by 27 feet was put up with the assistance of soldiers in six hours and twenty minutes.

More men and women had arrived from America, and the work began to assume business-like proportions. There were huts scattered all through the American training area.

As other huts were established the making of pies and doughnuts became a regular part of the daily routine of the hut. It was found that a canteen where candy and articles needed by the soldiers could be obtained at moderate prices would fill a very pressing need and this was made a part of their regular operation.

The purchase of an adequate quantity of supplies was a great problem. It was necessary to make frequent trips to Paris, to establish connections with supply houses there, and to attend to the shipping of the supplies out to the camps. At first it was impossible to purchase any quantity of supplies from any house. The demand for everything was so great that wholesale dealers were most independent. Three hundred dollars' worth of supplies was the most that could be purchased from any one house, but in course of time, confidence and friendly relations being established, it became possible to purchase as much as ten thousand dollars' worth at one time from one dealer.

The first twenty-five thousand dollars, of course, was soon gone, but another fifty thousand dollars arrived from Headquarters in New York, and after a little while another fifty thousand; which hundred thousand dollars was loaned by General Bramwell Booth from the International Treasury. The money was not only borrowed, but the Commander had promised to pay it back in twelve months (which guarantee it is pleasant to state was made good long before the promised time), for the Commander had said: "It is only a question of our getting to work in France, and the American public will see that we have all the money we want."

So it has proved.

In the meantime another hut was established at Houdelainecourt.

The American boys were drilling from early morning until dark; the weather was wet and cold; the roads were seas of mud and the German planes came over the valleys almost nightly to seek out the position of the American troops and occasionally to drop bombs. It was necessary that all tents should be camouflaged, windows darkened so that lights would not show at night, and every means used to keep the fact of the Americans' presence from the German observers and spies.

Another party of Salvation Army officers, men and women, arrived from New York on September 23rd, and these were quickly sent out to Demange which for the time being was used as the general base of supplies, but later a house was secured at Ligny-en-Barrios, and this was for many months the Headquarters.

One interesting incident occurred here in connection with this house. One of its greatest attractions had been that it was one of the few houses containing a bathroom, but when the new tenants arrived they found that the anticipated bathtub had been taken out with all its fittings and carefully stowed away in the cellar. It was too precious for the common use of tenants.

All Salvation Army graduates from the training school have a Red Cross diploma, and many are experienced nurses.

A Salvation Army woman Envoy sailed for France with a party of Salvationists about the time that the epidemic of influenza broke out all over the world. Even before the steamer reached the quarantine station in New York harbor a number of cases of Spanish influenza had developed among the several companies of soldiers who were aboard, a number of whom were removed from the ship. So anxious were others of these American fighting men to reach France that they hid away until the steamer had left port.

Land was hardly out of sight before more cases of the disease were reported—so many, in fact, that special hospital accommodations had to be immediately arranged. The ship's captain after consulting with the American military officers, requested the Salvation Army Envoy to take entire responsibility for the hospital, which responsibility, after some hesitation, she accepted.

Under her were two nurses, three dieticians (Y.M.C.A. and Red Cross), a medical corps sergeant (U.S.A.), and twenty-four orderlies. She took charge on the fourth day of a thirteen day voyage, working in the sick bay from 12 noon to 8 P.M., and from 12 midnight to 8 A.M. every day. She had with her a mandolin and a guitar with which, in addition to her sixteen hours of duty in the sick bay, she every day spent some time (usually an hour or two) on deck singing and playing for the soldiers who were much depressed by the epidemic. To them she was a very angel of good cheer and comfort.

Many amusing incidents occurred on the voyage.

Stormy weather had added to the discomforts of the trip and most of the passengers suffered from seasickness during the greater part of the voyage.

On board there was also a woman of middle age who could not be persuaded to keep her cabin porthole closed at night. Again and again a ray of light was projected through it upon the surface of the water and the quartermaster, whose duty it was to see that no lights were shown, was at his wit's end. His difficulty was the greater because he could speak no English, and she no French. Finally, a passenger took pity on the man, and, as the light was really a grave danger to the ship's safety, promised to speak to the woman, who insisted that she was not afraid of submarines and that it was foolish to think they could see her light.

"Madam," he said, "the quartermaster here tells me that the sea in this locality is infested with flying fish, who, like moths, fly straight for any light, and he is afraid that if you leave your porthole open they will dive in upon you during the night."

If he had said that the sea was infested with flying mice, his statement could not have been more effective. Thereafter the porthole stayed closed.

When the first man died on board, the Captain commanding the soldiers and the ship's Captain requested a Salvation Army Adjutant to conduct the funeral service.

At 4:30 P.M. the ship's propeller ceased to turn and the steamer came up into the wind. The United States destroyer acting as convoy also came to a halt. The French flag on the steamer and the American flag on the destroyer were at half-mast. Thirty-two men from the dead man's company lined up on the after-deck. The coffin (a rough pine box), heavily weighted at one end, lay across the rail over the stern. Here a chute had been rigged so that the coffin might not foul the ship's screws. The flags remained at half-mast for half an hour. The Salvation Army Adjutant read the burial service and prayed. Passengers on the promenade deck looked on. Then a bugler played taps. Every soldier stood facing the stern with hat off and held across the breast. As the coffin slipped down the chute and splashed into the sea a firing squad fired a single rattling volley. The ship came about and, with a shudder of starting engines, continued her voyage, the destroyer doing likewise.

During the passage the Adjutant conducted six such funerals, two more being conducted by a Catholic priest. Four more bodies of men who died as they neared port were landed and buried ashore.

In the hospital the Envoy was undoubtedly the means of saving several lives by her endless toil and by the encouragement of her cheerful face in that depressing place. The sick men called her "Mother" and no mother could have been more tender than she.

"You look so much like mother," said one boy just before he died. "Won't you please kiss me?"

Another lad, with a great convulsive effort, drew her hand to his lips and kissed her just as he passed away.

All of the American officers and two French officers

attended the funerals in full dress uniform and ten sailors of the French navy were also present.

The night before the ship docked at Bordeaux a letter signed by the Captain of the ship and the American officers was handed to the Envoy lady. It contained a warm statement of their appreciation of her service. Officers of the Aviation Corps who were aboard the ship arranged a banquet to be held in her honor when they should reach port; but she told them that she was under orders even as they were and that she must report to Paris Headquarters at once. And so the banquet did not take place.

As she left the ship, the soldiers were lined up on the wharf ready to march. When she came down the gang-plank and walked past them to the street, they cheered her and shouted: "Good-bye, mother! Good luck!"

As the fame of the doughnuts and pies spread through the camps a new distress loomed ahead for the Salvation Army. Where were the flour and the sugar and the lard and the other ingredients to come from wherewith to concoct these delicacies for the homesick soldiers?

It was of no use to go to the French for white flour, for they did not have it. They had been using war bread, dark mixtures with barley flour and other things, for a long time. Besides, the French had a fixed idea that everyone who came from America was made of money. Wood was thirty-five dollars a load (about a cord) and had to be cut and hauled by the purchaser at that. There was a story current throughout the camps that some Frenchmen were talking together among themselves, and one asked the rest where in the world they were going to get the money to rebuild their towns. "Oh," replied another; "haven't we the only battlefields in the world? All the Americans will want to come over after the war to see them and we will charge them enough for the sight to rebuild our villages!"

But even at any price the French did not have the materials to sell. There was only one place where things of that sort could be had and that was from the Americans, and the question was, would the commissary allow them to buy in large enough quantities to be of any use? The Salvation Army officers as they went about their work, were puzzling their brains how to get around the American commissary and get what they wanted.

Meantime, the American Army had slipped quietly into Montiers in the night and been billeted around in barns and houses and outhouses, and anywhere they could be stowed, and were keeping out of sight. For the German High Council had declared: "As soon as the American Army goes into camp we will blow them off the map."

Day after day the Germans lay low and watched. Their airplanes flew over and kept close guard, but they could find no sign of a camp anywhere. No tents were in sight, though they searched the landscape carefully; and day after day, for want of something better to do they bombarded Bar-le-Duc. Every day some new ravishment of the beautiful city was wrought, new victims buried under ruins, new terror and destruction, until the whole region was in panic and dismay.

Now Bar-le-Duc, as everyone knows, is the home of the famous Bar-le-Duc jam that brings such high prices the world over, and there were great quantities stored up and waiting to be sold at a high price to Americans after the war. But when the bombardment continued, and it became evident that the whole would either be destroyed or fall into the hands of the Germans, the owners were frightened. Houses were blown up, burying whole families. Victims were being taken hourly from the ruins, injured or dying.

A Salvation Army Adjutant ran up there one day with his truck and found an awful state of things. The whole place was full of refugees, families bereft of their homes, everybody that could trying to get out of the city. Just by accident he found out that the merchants were willing to sell their jam at a very reasonable price, and so he bought tons and tons of Bar-le-Duc jam. That would help out a lot and go well on bread, for of course there was no butter. Also it would make wonderful pies and tarts if one only had the flour and other ingredients.

As he drove into Montiers he was still thinking about it, and there on the table in the Salvation Army hut stood as pretty a chocolate cake as one would care to see. A bright idea came to the Adjutant:

"Let me have that cake," said he to the lassie who had baked it, "and I'll take it to the General and see what I can do."

It turned out that the cake was promised, but the lassie said she would bake another and have it ready for him on his return trip; so in a few days when he came back there was the cake.

Ah! That was a wonderful cake!

The lassie had baked it in the covers of lard tins, fourteen inches across and five layers high! There was a layer of cake, thickly spread with rich chocolate frosting, another layer of cake, overlaid with the translucent Bar-le-Duc jam, a third layer of cake with chocolate, another layer spread with Bar-le-Duc jam, then cake again, the whole covered smoothly over with thick dark chocolate, top and sides, down to the very base, without a ripple in it. It was a wonder of a cake!

With shining eyes and eager look the Adjutant took that beautiful cake, took also twelve hundred great brown sugary doughnuts, and a dozen fragrant apple pies just out of the oven, stowed them carefully away in his truck, and rustled off to the Officers' Headquarters. Arrived there he took his cake in hand and asked to see the General. An officer with his eye on the cake said the General was busy just now but he would carry the cake to him. But the Adjutant declined this offer firmly, saying: "The ladies of Montiers-sur-Saulx sent this cake to the General, and I must put it into his hands."

He was finally led to the General's room and, uncovering the great cake, he said:

"The Salvation Army ladies of Montiers-sur-Saulx have sent this cake to you as a sample of what they will do for the soldiers if we can get flour and sugar and lard."

The General, greatly pleased, took the cake and sent for a knife, while his officers stood about looking on with much interest. It appeared as if every one were to have a taste of the cake. But when the General had cut a generous slice, held it up, observing its cunning workmanship, its translucent, delectable interior, he turned with a gleam in his eye, looked about the room and said: "Gentlemen, this cake will not be served till the evening's mess, and I pity the gentlemen who do not eat with the officer's mess, but they will have to go elsewhere for their cake."

The Adjutant went out with his pies and doughnuts and distributed them here and there where they would do the most good, getting on the right side of the Top Sergeant, for he had discovered some time ago that even with the General as an ally one must be on the right side of the "old Sarge" if one wanted anything. While he was still talking with the officers he was handed an order from the General that he should be supplied with all that he needed, and when he finally came out of Headquarters he found that seven tons of material were being loaded on his car. After that the Salvation Army never had any trouble in getting all the material they needed.

After the tents in Montiers were all settled and the work fully started, the Staff-Captain and his helpers settled down to a pleasant little schedule of sixteen hours a day work and called it ease; but that was not to be enjoyed for long. At the end of a week the Salvation Army Colonel swooped down upon them again with orders to erect a hut at once as the tents were only a makeshift and winter was coming on. He brought materials and selected a site on a desirable corner.

Now the corner was literally covered with fallen walls of a former building and wreckage from the last year's raid, and the patient workers looked aghast at the task before them. But the Colonel would listen to no arguments.

"Don't talk about difficulties," he said, brushing aside a plea for another lot, not quite so desirable perhaps, but much easier to clear. "Don't talk about difficulties; get busy and have the job over with!"

One big reason why the Salvation Army is able to carry on the great machinery of its vast organization is that its people are trained to obey without murmuring.

Cheerfully and laboriously the men set to work. Winter rains were setting in, with a chill and intensity never to be forgotten by an American soldier. But wet to the skin day after day all day long the Salvationists worked against time, trying to finish the hut before the snow should arrive. And at last the hut was finished and ready for occupancy.

Such tireless devotion, such patient, cheerful toil for their sake was not to be passed by nor forgotten by the soldiers who watched and helped when they could. Day after day the bonds between them and the Salvation Army grew stronger. Here were men who did not have to, and yet who for the sake of helping them, came and lived under the same conditions that they did, working even longer hours than they, eating the same food, enduring the same privations, and whose only pay was their expenses.

At the first the Salvationists took their places in the chow line with the rest, then little by little men near the head of the line would give up their places to them, quietly stepping to the rear of the line themselves. Finally, no matter how long the line was the men with one consent insisted that their unselfish friends should take the very head of the line whenever they came and always be served first.

One day one of the Salvation Army men swathed in a big raincoat was sitting in a Ford by the roadside in front of a Salvation Army hut, waiting for his Colonel, when two soldiers stopped behind him to light their cigarettes. It was just after sundown, and the man in the car must have seemed like any soldier to the two as they chatted.

"Bunch of grafters, these Y.M.C.A. and Salvation Army outfits!" grumbled one as he struck a match. "What good are the 'Sallies' in a soldier camp?"

"Well, Buddy," said the other somewhat excitedly, "there's a whole lot of us think the Salvation Army is about *it* in this man's outfit. For a rookie you sure are picking one good way to make yourself unpopular *tout de suite!* Better lay off that kind of talk until you kind of find out what's what. I didn't have much use for them myself back in the States, but here in France they're real folks, believe me!"

So the feeling had grown everywhere as the huts multiplied. And the huts proved altogether too small for the religious meetings, so that as long as the weather permitted the services had to be held in the open air. It was no unusual thing to see a thousand men gathered in the twilight around two or three Salvation Army lassies, singing in sweet wonderful volume the old, old hymns. The soldiers were no longer amused spectators, bent on mischief; they were enthusiastic allies of the organization that was theirs. The meeting was theirs.

"We never forced a meeting on them," said one of the girls. "We just let it grow. Sometimes it would begin with popular songs, but before long the boys would ask for hymns, the old favorites, first one, then another, always remembering to call for "Tell Mother I'll Be There."

Almost without exception the boys entered heartily into everything that went on in the organization. The songs were perhaps at first only a reminder of home, but soon they came to have a personal significance to many. The Salvation Army did not have movies and theatrical singers as did the other organizations, but they did not seem to need them. The men liked the Gospel meetings and came to them better than to anything else. Often they would come to the hut and start the singing themselves, which would presently grow into a meeting of evident intention.

The Staff-Captain did not long have opportunity to enjoy the new hut which he had labored so hard to finish at Montiers, for soon orders arrived for him to move on to Houdelainecourt to help put up the hut there, and leave Montiers in charge of a Salvation Army Major.

The Salvation Army was with the Eighteenth Infantry at Houdelainecourt.

It was an old tent that sheltered the canteen, and it had the reputation of having gone up and down five times. When first they put it up it blew down. It was located where two roads met and the winds swept down in every direction. Then they put it up and took it down to camouflage it. They got it up again and had to take it down to camouflage it some more. The regular division helped with this, and it was some camouflage when it was done, for the boys had put their initials all over it, and then, had painted Christmas trees everywhere, and on the trees they had put the presents they knew they never would get, and so in all the richness of its record of homesickness the old tent went up again. They kept warm here by means of a candle under an upturned tin pail. The tent blew down again in a big storm soon after that and had to be put up once more, and then there came a big rain and flooded everything in the neighborhood. It blew down and drowned out the Y.M.C.A. and everything else, and only the old tent stood for awhile. But at last the storm was too much for it, too, and it succumbed again.

After that the Salvation Army put up a hut for their work. A number of soldiers assisted. They put up a stove, brought their piano and phonograph, and made the place look cheerful. Then they got the regimental band and had an opening, the first big thing that was recognized by the military authorities. The Salvation Army Staff-Captain in charge of that zone took a long board and set candles on it and put it above the platform like a big chandelier. The Brigade Commander was there, and a Captain came to represent the Colonel. A chaplain spoke. The lassies who took part in the entertainment were the first girls the soldiers had seen for many months.

Long before the hour announced for the service the soldier boys had crowded the hutment to its greatest capacity. Game and reading tables had been moved to the rear and extra benches brought in. The men stood three deep upon the tables and filled every seat and every inch of standing room. When there was no more room on the floor, they climbed to the roof and lined the rafters. There was no air and the Adjutant came to say there was too much light, but none of these things damped the enthusiasm.

With the aid of the regimental chaplain, the Staff-Captain had arranged a suitable program for the occasion, the regimental band furnishing the music.

When the General entered the hutment all of the men stood and uncovered and the band stopped abruptly in the middle of a strain. "That's the worst thing I ever did—stopping the music," he exclaimed ruefully. He refused to occupy the chair which had been prepared for him, saying: "No, I want to stand so that I can look at these men."

The records of the work in that hut would be precious reading for the fathers and mothers of those boys, for the Fighting Eighteenth Infantry are mostly gone, having laid their young lives on the altar with so many others.

Here is a bit from one lassie's letter, giving a picture of one of her days in the hut:

> "Well, I must tell you how the days are spent. We open the hut at 7; it is cleaned by some of the boys; then at 8 we commence to serve cocoa and coffee and make pies and doughnuts, cup cakes and fry eggs and make all kinds of eats until it is all you see. Well, can you think of two women cooking in one day 2500 doughnuts, 8 dozen cup cakes, 50 pies, 800 pancakes and 225 gallons of cocoa, and one other girl serving it? That is a day's work in my last hut. Then meeting at night, and it lasts two hours."

A lieutenant came into the canteen to buy something and said to one of the girls: "Will you please tell me something? Don't you ever rest?" That is how both the men and officers appreciated the work of these tireless girls.

Men often walked miles to look at an American woman. Once acquainted with the Salvation Army lassies they came to them with many and strange requests. Having picked a quart or so of wild berries and purchased from a farmer a pint of cream they would come to ask a girl to make a strawberry shortcake for them. They would buy a whole dozen of eggs apiece, and having begged a Salvation Army girl to fry them would eat the whole dozen at a sitting. They would ask the girls to write their love letters, or to write assuring some mother or sweetheart that they were behaving themselves.

Soldiers going into action have left thousands of dollars in cash and in valuables in the care of Salvation Army officers to be forwarded to persons designated in case they are killed in action or taken prisoner. In such cases it is very seldom that a receipt is given for either money or valuables, so deeply do the soldiers trust the Salvation Army.

One of the girl Captains wears a plain silver ring, whose intrinsic value is about thirty cents, but whose moral value is beyond estimate. The ring is not the Captain's. It belongs to a soldier, who, before the war, had been a hard drinker and had continued his habits after enlisting. He came under the influence of the Salvation Army and swore that he would drink no more. But time after time he fell, each time becoming more desperate and more discouraged. Each time the young lassie-Captain dealt with him. After the last of his failures, while she was encouraging him to make another try, he detached the ring from the cord from which it had dangled around his neck and thrust it at her.

"It was my mother's," he explained. "If you will wear

it for me, I shall always think of it when the temptation comes to drink, and the fact that someone really cares enough about my worthless hide to take all the trouble you have taken on my behalf, will help me to resist it."

"No one will misunderstand," he cried, seeing that the lassie was about to decline, "not even me. I shall tell no one. And it would help."

"Very well," agreed the girl, looking steadily at him for a moment, "but the first time that you take a drink, off will come the ring! And you must promise that you will tell me if you do take that drink."

The soldier promised. The lassie still wears the ring. The soldier is still sober. Also he has written to his wife for the first time in five years and she has expressed her delight at the good news.

On more than one occasion American aviators have flown from their camps many miles to villages where there were Salvation lassies and have returned with a load of doughnuts. On one occasion a bird-man dropped a note down in front of the hut where two sisters were stationed, circling around at a low elevation until certain that the girls had picked up the note, which stated that he would return the following afternoon for a mess of doughnuts for his comrades. When he returned, the doughnuts were ready for him.

The Adjutant of the aerial forces attached to the American Fifth Army around Montfaucon on the edge of the Argonne Forest, before that forest was finally captured at the point of American bayonets, drove almost seventy miles to the Salvation Army Headquarters at Ligny for supplies for his men. He was given an automobile load of chocolate, candies, cakes, cookies, soap, toilet articles, and other comforts, without charge. He said that he *knew* that the Salvation Army would have what he wanted.

The two lassies who were in Bure had a desperate time of it. Things were most primitive. They had no stove, just an old travelling field range, and for a canteen one end of Battery F's kitchen. They were then attached to the Sixth Field Artillery. This was the regiment that fired the first shot into Germany.

The smoke in that kitchen was awful and continuous from the old field range. The girls often made doughnuts out-of-doors, and they got chilblains from standing in the snow. All the company had chilblains, too, and it was a sorry crowd. Then the girls got the mumps. It was so cold here, especially at night, they often had to sleep with their clothes on. There was only one way they could have meetings in that place and that was while the men were lined up for chow near to the canteen. They would start to sing in the gloomy, cold room, the men and girls all with their overcoats on, and fingers so cold that they could hardly play the concertina, for there was no fire in the big room save from the range at one end where they cooked. Then the girls would talk to them while they were eating. Perhaps they did not call these meetings, but they were a mighty happy time to the men, and they liked it.

A minister who had taken six months' leave of absence from his church to do Y.M.C.A. work in France asked one of the boys why he liked the Salvation Army girls and he said: "Because they always take time to cheer us up. It's true they do knock us mighty hard about our sins, but while it hurts they always show us a way out." The minister told some one that if he had his work to do over again he would plan it along the lines of the Salvation Army work.

You may hear it urged that one reason the boys liked the Salvation Army people so much was because they did not preach, but it is not so. They preached early and often, but the boys liked it because it was done so simply, so consistently and so unselfishly, that they did not recognize it as preaching.

In Menaucourt as Christmas was coming on some United States officers raised money to give the little refugee children a Christmas treat. There was to be a tree with presents, and good things to eat, and an entertainment with recitations from the children. The schoolteacher was teaching the children their pieces, and there was a general air of delightful excitement everywhere. It was expected that the affair was to be held in the Catholic church at first, but the priest protested that this was unseemly, so they were at a loss what to do. The school-house was not large enough.

The Salvation Army Staff-Captain found this out and suggested to the officers that the Salvation Army hut was the very place for such a gathering. So the tree was set up, and the officers went to town and bought presents and decorations. They covered the old hut with boughs and flags and transformed it into a wonderland for the children. The officers were struggling helplessly with the decorations of the tree when the Salvation Army man happened in and they asked him to help.

"Why, sure!" he said heartily. "That's my regular work!" So they eagerly put it into his hands and departed. The Staff-Captain worked so hard at it and grew so interested in it that he forgot to go for his chow at lunch-time, and when supper-time came the hall was so crowded and there was so much still to be done that he could not get away to get his supper. But it was a grand and glorious time. The place was packed. There were two American Colonels, a French Colonel, and several French officers.

The soldiers crowded in and they had to send them out again, poor fellows, to make room for the children, but they hung around the doors and windows eager to see it all.

The regimental band played, there were recitations in French and a good time generally.

The seats were facing the canteen where the supplies were all stocked neatly, boxes of candy and cakes and good things. The Colonel in charge of the regiment looked over to them wistfully and said to the Staff-Captain: "Are you going to sell all those things?" The Staff-Captain, with quick appreciation, said: "No, Colonel, Christmas comes but once a year and there's a present up there for you." And the Colonel seemed as pleased as the children when the Staff-Captain handed him a big box of candy all tied up in Christmas ribbons.

In the huts, phonographs are never silent as long as there is a single soldier in the place. One night two of the Salvation Army girls, who slept in the back room of a certain hut, had closed up for the night and retired. They were awakened by the sound of the phonograph, and wondered how anyone got into the hut and who it might happen to be. They were a little bit nervous, but went to investigate. They found that a soldier on guard had raised a window, and although this did not allow him room to enter the hut, he was able to reach the table where the phonograph stood. He had turned the talking machine around so that it faced the window, and, placing a record in position, had started it going. He was leaning up against the outer wall of the hut, smoking a cigarette in the moonlight, and enjoying his concert. The girls returned to bed without disturbing the audience.

One of the most popular French confections sold in the huts was a variety of biscuits known under the trade name of "Boudoir Biscuits." One day a soldier entered a hut and said, "Say, miss, I want some of them there—

them there—Dang me if I can remember them French names!—them there (suddenly a great light dawned)—some of them there bedroom cookies." And the lassie got what he wanted.

The Salvation Army men who worked among the soldiers in advanced positions from which all women are barred are among the heroes of the war. Here during the day they labored in dugouts far below the shell-tortured earth, often going out at night to help bring in the wounded; always in danger from shells and gas; some with the ammunition trains; others driving supply trucks; still others attached to units and accompanying the fighting men wherever they went, even to the active combat of the firing trench and the attack. These are unofficial chaplains. Such a one was "La Petit Major," as the soldiers called him, because of his smallness of stature.

The Little Major commenced his service in the field with the Twenty-sixth Infantry, First Division, at Menaucourt. Soon he was transferred to command the hut at Boviolles. At this place was the battalion of the Twenty-sixth Infantry, commanded by Major Theodore Roosevelt. His brother, Captain Archie Roosevelt, commanded a company in this battalion. He was for the greater part of the time alone in the work at Boviolles.

By his consistent life and character and his willingness to serve both men and officers, he won their esteem.

When they left the training area for the trenches the Major was requested to go with them. He turned the key in the canteen door and went off with them across France and never came back, establishing himself in the front-line trenches with the men and acting as unofficial chaplain to the battalion.

There is an interesting incident in connection with his introduction to Major Roosevelt's notice.

For some reason the Salvation Army had been made to feel that they were not welcome with that division. But the Little Major did not give up like that, and he lingered about feeling that somehow there was yet to be a work for him there.

A young private from a far Western state, a fellow who, according to all reports, had never been of any account at home, was convicted of a most horrible murder and condemned to die by hanging because the commanding officer said that shooting was too good for him.

He accepted his fate with sullen ugliness. He would not speak to anyone and he was so violent that they had to put him in chains. No one could do anything with him. He had to be watched day and night; and it was awful to see him die this way with his sin unconfessed. Many attempts were made to break through his silence, but all to no effect. Several chaplains visited him, but he would have nothing to do with them.

On the morning of his execution, to the surprise of everybody he said that he had heard that there was a Salvation Army man around and he would like to see him. The authorities sent and searched everywhere for the Little Major, and some thought he must have left, but they found him at last and he came at once to the desperate man.

The criminal sat crouched on his hard bench, chained hand and foot. He did not look up. He was a dreadful sight, his brutal face haggard, unshaven, his eyes bloodshot, his whole appearance almost like some low animal. Through the shadowy prison darkness the Little Major crept to those chains, those symbols of the man's degradation; and still the man did not look up.

"You must be in great trouble, brother. Can I help

you any?" asked the Little Major with a wonderful Christlike compassion in his voice.

The man lifted his bleared eyes under the shock of unkempt hair, and spoke, startled:

"You call me brother! You know what I'm here for and you call me brother! Why?"

The Little Major's voice was steady and sweet as he replied without hesitation:

"Because I know a great deal about the suffering of Christ on the Cross, all because He loved you so! Because I know He said He was wounded for your transgressions, He was bruised for your iniquities! Because I know He said, 'Though your sins be as scarlet they shall be as white as snow, though they be red like crimson they shall be as wool!' So why shouldn't I call you brother?"

"Oh," said the man with a groan of agony and big tears rolling down his face. "Could I be made a better man?"

Then they went down on their knees together beside the hard bench, the man in chains and the man of God, and the Little Major prayed such a wonderful prayer, taking the poor soul right to the foot of the Throne; and in a few minutes the man was confessing his sin to God. Then he suddenly looked up and exclaimed:

"It's true, what you said! Christ has pardoned me! Now I can die like a man!"

With that great pardon written across his heart he actually went to his death with a smile upon his face. When the Chaplain asked him if he had anything to say he publicly thanked the military authorities and the Salvation Army for what they had done for him.

The Colonel, greatly surprised at the change in the man, sent to find out how it came about and later sent to thank the Little Major. Two days later Major Roosevelt came in person to thank him:

"I knew that someone who knew how to deal with men had got hold of him," he said, "but I almost doubted the evidence of my own eyes when I saw how cheerfully he went to his death, it all seemed too wonderful!"

The Little Major was with this battalion in all of its engagements, and on several occasions went over the top with the men and devoted himself to first aid to the wounded and to bringing the men back to the dressing station on stretchers. Between the times of active engagements, the Major gave himself to supplying the needs of the men and made daily trips out of the trenches to obtain newspapers, writing material, and to perform errands which they could not do for themselves.

One of the lieutenants said of him: "He is worth more than all the chaplains that were ever made in the United States Army. He will walk miles to get the most trivial article for either man or officer. The men know that he loves them or he would not go into the trenches with them, for he does not have to go. You can tell the world for me that he is a real man!"

One of the fellows said of him he had seen him take off his shoes and bring away pieces of flesh from the awful blisters got from much tramping.

The men soon learned to love their gray haired Salvation Army comrade. When an enemy attack was to be met with cold steel he was the first to follow the company officers "over the top," to cheer and encourage the onrushing Americans in the anxious semi-calm which follows the lifting of a barrage. A non-combatant, unarmed and fifty-three years of age, he was always in the van of the fierce onslaught with which our men repulsed the enemy, ready to pray with the dying or help bring in the wounded, and always fearless no matter what the conditions. By his unfearing heroism as well as his willingness to share the hardships and dangers of the men, he so won their confidence that it was frequently said that they would not go into battle except the Major was with them. The men would crouch around him with an almost fantastic confidence that where he was no harm could come. Knowing that many earnest Christian people were praying for his safety and having seen how safely he and those with him had come through dangers, they thought his very presence was a protection. Who shall say that God did not stay on the battlefield living and speaking through the Little Major?

When the first division was moved from the Montdidier Sector he travelled with the men as far as they went by train. When they detrained and marched he marched with them, carrying his seventy pound pack as any soldier did. He was by the side of Captain Archie Roosevelt when he received a very dangerous wound from an exploding shell, and was in the battle of Cantigny in the Montdidier Sector, where his company lost only two men killed and four wounded, while other companies' losses were much more severe.

Protestant, Catholic and Jew were all his friends. One Catholic boy came crawling along in the waist-deep trench one day to tell the Major about his spiritual worries. After a brief talk the Major asked him if he had his prayer book. The boy said yes. "Then take it out and read it," said the Major. "God is here!" And there in the narrow trench with lowered heads so that the snipers could not see them, they knelt together and read from the Catholic prayer book.

In one American attack the Little Major followed the Lieutenant over the top just as the barrage was lifted. The Lieutenant looking back saw him struggling over the crest of the parapet, laughed and shouted: "Go back, Major, you haven't even a pistol!" But the Major did not go back. He went with the boys. "I have no hesitancy in laying down my life," he once said, "if it will help or encourage anyone else to live in a better or cleaner way."

He was always striving for the salvation of his boys, and in his meetings men would push their way to the front and openly kneel before their comrades registering their determination to live in accordance with the teachings of Jesus. One tells of seeing him kneel beside an empty crate with three soldiers praying for their souls.

It was because of all these things that the men believed in him and in his God. He used to say to the men in the meetings, "We are not afraid because we have a sense of the presence of God right here with us!"

One night the battalion was "in" after a heavy day's work strengthening the defenses and trying to drain the trenches, and the men were asleep in the dugouts. The Major lay in his little chicken-wire bunk, just drowsing off, while the water seeped and dripped from the earthen roof, and the rats splashed about on the water covered floor.

Across from him in a bunk on the other side of the dugout tossed a boy in his damp blankets who had just come to the front. He was only eighteen and it was his first night in the line. It had been a hard day for him. The shells screamed overhead and finally one landed close somewhere and rocked the dugout with its explosion.

The old-timers slept undisturbed, but the boy started up with a scream and a groan, his nerves a-quiver, and cried out: "Oh, Daddy! Daddy! Daddy!"

The Little Major was out and over to him in a flash, and gathered the boy into his arms, soothing him as a mother might have done, until he was calmed and strengthened; and there amid the roaring of guns, the screaming of shells, the dripping of water and splashing of rats, the youngest of the battalion found Christ.

An old soldier came down from the front and a Salvationist asked him if he knew the Little Major.

"Well, you just bet I know the Major—sure thing!" And the Major is always on hand with a laugh and his fun-making. In the trenches or in the towns, where the shells are flying, the Little Major is with his boys. No words of mine could express the admiration the boys have for him. The boys love him. He calls them "Buddie." They salute and are ready to do or die. The last time I saw him he had hiked in from the trenches with the boys. He carried a heavy "war baby" on his back and a tin hat on his head. He was tired and footsore, but there was that laugh, and before he got his pack off he jabbed me in the ribs. "No, sir, we can't get along without our Major!" So says "Buddie."

A request came from a chaplain to open Salvation Army work near his division. The Brigade Commander was most favorable to the suggestion until he learned that the Salvation Army would have women there and that religious meetings would be conducted. As this was explained the General's manner changed and he declared he did not know that the work was to be carried on in this way; that he did not favor the women in camps, or any religion, but thought it would make the soldier soft, and the business of the soldier was to kill, to kill in as brutal a manner as possible; and to kill as many of the enemy as possible; and he did not propose to have any work conducted in the camps or any influence on the soldiers that would tend to soften them.

He ordered them, therefore, not to extend the work of the Salvation Army within his brigade. It was explained to him that Demange was now within the territory named. He appeared to be put out that the Salvation Army was already established in his district, but said that if they behaved themselves they could go on, but that they must not extend.

He reported the matter to the Divisional Headquarters and an investigation of the Salvation Army activities was ordered. A major who was a Jew was appointed to look into the matter. During the next two weeks he talked with the men and officers and attended Salvation Army meetings. The leaders, of course, knew nothing about this, but they could not have planned their meetings better if they had known. It seemed as though God was in it all. At the end of two weeks there came a written communication from the General stating that after a thorough examination of the Salvation Army work he withdrew his objections and the Salvation Army was free to extend operations anywhere within his brigade.

The Salvation Army hut was a scene of constant activity.

At one place in a single day there was early mass, said by the Catholic chaplain, later preaching by a Protestant chaplain, then a Jewish service, followed by a company meeting where the use of gas masks was explained. All this, besides the regular uses of the hut, which included a library, piano, phonograph, games, magazines, pies, doughnuts and coffee; the pie line being followed by a regular Salvation Army meeting where men raised their hands to be prayed for, and many found Christ as their Saviour.

It was in an old French barracks that they located the Salvation Army canteen in Treveray. One corner was boarded off for a bedroom for the girls. There were windows but not of glass, for they would have soon been shattered, and, too, they would have let too much light through. They were canvas well camouflaged with paint so that the enemy shells would not be attracted at night, and, of course, one could not see through them.

Inside the improvised bedroom were three little folding army cots, a board table, a barrack bag and some boxes. This was the only place where the girls could be by themselves. On rainy days the furniture was supplemented by a dishpan on one cot, a frying-pan on another, and a lard tin on the third, to catch the drops from the holes in the roof. The opposite corner of the barracks was boarded off for a living-room. In this was a field range and one or two tables and benches.

The rest of the hut was laid out with square bare board tables. The canteen was at one end. The piano was at one side and the graphophone at the other. Sometimes in places like this, the hut would be too near the front for it to be thought advisable to have a piano. It was too liable to be shattered by a chance shell and the management thought it unwise to put so much money into what might in a moment be reduced to worthless splinters. Then the boys would come into the hut, look around disappointedly and say: "No piano?"

The cheerful woman behind the counter would say sympathetically: "No, boys, no piano. Too many shells around here for a piano."

The boys would droop around silently for a minute or two and then go off. In a little while back they would come with grim satisfaction on their faces bearing a piano.

"Don't ask us where we got it," they would answer with a twinkle in reply to the pleased inquiry. "This is war! We salvaged it!"

Around the room on the tables were plenty of magazines, books and games. Checkers was a favorite game. No card playing, no shooting crap. The canteen contained chocolate, candy, writing materials, postage stamps, towels, shaving materials, talcum powder, soap, shoestrings, handkerchiefs in little sealed packets, buttons, cootie medicine and other like articles. The Salvation Army did not sell nor give away either tobacco or cigarettes. In a few cases where such were sent to them for distribution they were handed over to the doctors for the badly wounded in the hospitals or the very sick men accustomed to their use, who were almost insane with their nerves. They also procured them from the Red Cross for wounded men, sometimes, who were fretting for them, but they never were a part of their supplies and far from the policy of the Salvation Army. Furthermore, the Salvation Army sent no men to France to work for them who smoked or used tobacco in any form, or drank intoxicating liquors. No man can hold a commission in the Salvation Army and use tobacco! It is a remarkable fact that the boys themselves did not want the Salvation Army lassies to deal in cigarettes because they knew it would be going against their principles to do so.

Occasionally a stranger would come into the canteen and ask for a package of cigarettes. Then some soldier would remark witheringly: "Say, where do you come from? Don't you know the Salvation Army don't handle tobacco?"

The men were always deeply grateful to get talcum powder for use after shaving. It seemed somehow to help to keep up the morale of the army, that talcum powder, a little bit of the soothing refinement of the home that seemed so far away.

To this hut whenever they were at liberty came Jew and Gentile, Protestant and Catholic, rich and poor. War is a great leveler and had swept away all differences. They were a great brotherhood of Americans now, ready, if necessary, to die for the right.

To one of the huts came a request from the chaplain of a regiment which was about to move from its temporary billet in the next village. The men had not been so fortunate as to be stationed at a town where there was a Salvation Army hut and it had been over four months since they had tasted anything like cake or pie. Would the Salvation Army lassies be so good as to let them have a few doughnuts before they moved that night? If so the chaplain would call for them at five o'clock.

The lassies worked with all their might and fried thirty-five hundred doughnuts. But something happened to the ambulance that was to take them to the boys, and over an hour was lost in repairs. Back at the camp the boys had given up all hope. They were to march at eight o'clock and nothing had been heard of the doughnuts. Suddenly the truck dashed into view, but the boys eyed it glumly, thinking it was likely empty after all this time. However, the chaplain held up both hands full of golden brown beauties, and with a wild shout of joy the men sprang to "attention" as the ambulance drew up, and more soldiers crowded around. The villagers rushed to their doors to see what could be happening now to those crazy American soldiers.

When the chaplain stood up in the car flinging doughnuts to them and shouting that there were thousands, enough for everybody, the enthusiasm of the soldiers knew no bounds. The girls had come along and now they began to hand out the doughnuts, and the crowd cheered and shouted as they filed up to receive them. And when it came time for the girls to return to their own village the soldiers crowded up once more to say good-bye, and give them three cheers and a "tiger."

These same girls a few days before had fed seven hundred weary doughboys on their march to the front with coffee, hot biscuits and jam.

In one of the Salvation Army huts one night the usual noisy cheerfulness was in the air, but apart from the rest sat a boy with a letter open on the table before him and a dreamy smile of tender memories upon his face. Nobody noticed that far-away look in his eyes until the lassie in charge of the hut, standing in the doorway surveying her noisy family, searched him out with her discerning eyes, and presently happened down his way and inquired if he had a letter. The boy looked up with a wonderful smile such as she had never seen on his face before, and answered:

"Yes, it's from mother!" Then impulsively, "She's the nearest thing to God I know!"

Mother seemed to be the nearest thought to the heart of the boys over there. They loved the songs best that spoke about mother. One boy bought a can of beans at the canteen, and when remonstrated with by the lassie who sold them, on the ground that he was always complaining of having to eat so many beans, he replied, "Aw, well, this is different. These beans are the kind that mother used to buy."

In the dark hours of the early morning a boy who belonged to the ammunition train sat by one of the little wooden tables in the hut, just after he had returned from his first barrage, and pencilled on its top the following words:

> Mother o' mine, what the words mean to me
> Is more than tongue can say;
> For one view to-night of your loving face,
> What a price I would gladly pay!
> The wonderful face . . .
> . . . smiling still despite loads of care,
> 'Tis crowned by a silvering sheen.
> Your picture I carry next to my heart;

With it no harm can befall.
It has helped me to smile through many a care,
Since I heeded my country's call.
O mother who nursed me as a babe

And prayed for me as a boy,
Can I not show, now at man's estate,
That you are my pride and joy?
Good night! God guard you, way over the ocean blue,
Your boy loves you and his dreams are bright,
For he's dreaming of home and you.

One of the letters that was written home for "Mother's Day" in response to a suggestion on the walls of the Salvation Army hut was as follows:

Dearest Little Mother of Mine:

They started a campaign to write to mother on this day, and, believe me, I didn't have to be urged very hard. If I wrote you every time I think of you this war would go hang as far as I am concerned, for I think of you always and there are hundreds of things that serve as an eternal reminder.

Near our billet is one lone, scrubby little lilac bush that has a dozen blossoms, and it doesn't take much mental work to connect lilacs with mother. Then, too, the distant whistle of a train 'way down the valley reminds me of how you would listen for the whistle of the Montreal train on Saturday morning and then fix up a big feed for your boy to offset a week of boarding-house grub. Those and many other things remind me many times a day of the one who bid me good-by with a smile and saved her tears 'till she was home alone; who knit helmets, wristlets and sweaters to keep out the cold when she should have been sleeping; who (I'll bet a hat) didn't sleep one of the thirteen nights I was on the ocean, and who writes me cheerful, newsy letters when all others fail.

And I appreciate all those things too, although I'm not much on showing affection. I haven't always been as good to you as I ought, but I'm going to make up by being the soldier and the man "me mudder" thinks I am.

And when I come back home, all full of prunes and glory, we're going to have the grandest time you ever dreamed of. We'll go joy riding, eat strawberry shortcake and pumpkin pie, and have all the lilacs in the U.S.A. Wait till I walk down Main Street with you on my arm all fixed up in a swell dress and a new bonnet and me with a span new uniform, with sergeant-major's chevrons, about steen service stripes, a Mex. campaign badge and a Croix de Guerre (maybe), then you'll be glad your boy went to be a soldier.

I was on the road all of night before last and on guard last night and I'm a wee bit tired so I'm making this kinder short; but it's a little reminder that the boy who is 5,000 miles away is thinking, "I love you my ma," same as I always did.

And, by gosh, don't forget about that pumpkin pie!

Good-night, mother of mine; your soldier boy loves you a whole dollar's worth.

The Salvation Army hut was home to the boys over there. They came to it in sorrow or joy. They came to ask to scrape out the bowl where the cake batter had been stirred because mother used to let them do it; they came to get their coats mended and have their buttons sewed on. Sometimes it seemed to the long-suffering, smiling woman who sewed them on, as if they just ripped them off so she could sew them on again; if so, she did not mind. They came to mourn when they received no word from home; and when the mail came in and they were fortunate they came first to the hut waving their letter to tell of their good luck before they even opened it to read it. It is remarkable how they pinned their whole life on what these consecrated American women said to them over there. It is wonderful how they opened their hearts to them on religious subjects, and how they flocked to the religious meetings, seeming to really be hungry for them.

Word about these wonderful meetings that the soldiers were attending in such numbers got to the ears of another commanding officer, and one day there came a summons for the Salvation Army Major in charge at Gondrecourt to appear before him. An officer on a motor cycle with a side car brought the summons, and the Major felt that it practically amounted to an arrest. There was nothing to do but obey, so he climbed into the side car and was whirled away to Headquarters.

The Major-General received him at once and in brusque tones informed him most emphatically:

"We want you to get out! We don't want you nor your meetings! We are here to teach men to fight and your religion says you must not kill. Look out there!" pointing through the doorway, "we have set up dummies and teach our men to run their bayonets through them. You teach them the opposite of that. You will unfit my men for warfare!"

The Salvationist looked through the door at the line of straw dummies hanging in a row, and then he looked back and faced the Major-General for a full minute before he said anything.

Tall and strong, with soldierly bearing, with ruddy health in the glow of his cheeks, and fire in his keen blue eyes, the Salvationist looked steadily at the Major-General and his indignation grew. Then the good old Scotch burr on his tongue rolled broadly out in protest:

"On my way up here in your automobile"—every word was slow and calm and deliberate, tinged with a fine righteous sarcasm—"I saw three men entering your Guard House who were not capable of directing their own steps. They had been off on leave down to the town and had come home drunk. They were going into the Guard House to sleep it off. When they come out to-morrow or the next day with their limbs trembling, and their eyes bloodshot and their heads aching, do you think they will be fit for warfare?

"You have men down there in your Guard House who are loathsome with vile diseases, who are shaken with self-indulgence, and weakened with all kinds of excesses. Are they fit for warfare?

"Now, look at me!"

He drew himself up in all the strength of his six feet, broad shoulders, expanded chest, complexion like a baby, muscles like iron, and compelled the gaze of the officer.

"Can you find any man—" The Salvationist said "mon" and the soft Scotch sound of it sent a thrill down the Major-General's back in spite of his opposition. "Can you find any mon at fifty-five years who can follow these in your regiment, who can beat me at any game whatever?"

The officer looked, and listened, and was ashamed.

The Major rose in his righteous wrath and spoke mighty truths clothed in simple words, and as he talked the tears unbidden rolled down the Major-General's face and dropped upon his table.

"And do you know," said the Salvationist, afterward telling a friend in earnest confidence, "do you *know,* before I left we *had prayer together!* And he became one of the best friends we have!"

Before he left, also, the Major-General signed the authority which gave him charge of the Guard Houses, so that he might talk to the men or hold meetings with them whenever he liked. This was the means of opening up a new avenue of work among the men.

The Scotch Major had a string of hospitals that he visited in addition to his other regular duties. He knew that the men who are gassed lose all their possessions when their clothes are ripped off from them. So this Salvationist made a delightful all-the-year-round Santa Claus out of himself: dressing up in old clothes, because of the mud and dirt through which he must pass, he would sling a pack on his back that would put to shame the one Old Santa used to carry. Shaving things and soap and toothbrushes, handkerchiefs and chocolate and writing materials. How they welcomed him wherever he came! Sick men, Protestants, Jews, Catholics. He talked and prayed with them all, and no one turned away from his kindly messages.

Six miles from Neufchauteul is Bazoilles, a mighty city of hospital tents and buildings, acres and acres of them, lying in the valley. Whenever this man heard the rumbling of guns and knew that something was doing, he took his pack and started down to go the rounds, for there were always men there needing him.

Then he would hold meetings in the wards, blessed meetings that the wounded men enjoyed and begged for.

They all joined in the singing, even those who could not sing very well. And once it was a blind boy who asked them to sing "Lead Kindly Light Amid the Encircling Gloom, Lead Thou Me On."

One Sunday afternoon two Salvation Army lassies had come with their Major to hold their usual service in the hospital, but there were so many wounded coming in and the place was so busy that it seemed as if perhaps they ought to give up the service. The nurses were heavy-eyed with fatigue and the doctors were almost worked to death. But when this was suggested with one accord both doctors and nurses were against it. "The boys would miss it so," they said, "and we would miss it, too. It rests us to hear you sing."

After the Bible reading and prayer a lassie sang: "There Is Sunshine in My Heart To-day," and then came a talk that spoke of a spiritual sunshine that would last all the year.

The song and talk drifted out to another little ward where a doctor sat beside a boy, and both listened. As the physician rose to go the wounded boy asked if he might write a letter.

The next day the doctor happened to meet the lassie who sang and told her he had a letter that had been handed to him for censorship that he thought she would like to see. He said the writer had asked him to show it to her. This was the letter:

> Dear Mother: You will be surprised to hear that I am in the hospital, but I am getting well quickly and am having a good time. But best of all, some Salvation Army people came and sang and talked about sunshine, and while they were talking the sunshine came in through my window—not into my room alone, but into my heart and life as well, where it is going to stay. I know how happy this will make you.

The hospital work was a large feature of the service performed by the Salvation Army. In every area this testimony comes from both doctors, nurses and wounded men. Yet it was nothing less than a pleasure for the workers to serve those patient, cheerful sufferers.

A lassie entered a ward one day and found the men with combs and tissue paper performing an orchestra selection. They apologized for the noise, declaring that they were all crazy about music and that was the only way they could get it.

"How would you like a phonograph?" she asked.

"Oh, Boy! If we only had one! I'll tell the world we'd like it," one declared wistfully.

The phonograph was soon forthcoming and brought much pleasure.

A lassie offered to write a letter for a boy whose foot had just been amputated and whose right arm was bound in splints. He accepted her offer eagerly, but said:

"But when you write promise me you won't tell mother about my foot. She worries! She wouldn't understand how well off I really am. Maybe you had better let me try to write a bit myself for you to enclose. I guess I could manage that. So, with his left hand, he wrote the following:

> Dearest Mother:—I am laid up in the hospital here with a very badly sprained ankle and some bruises, and will be here two or three weeks. Do not worry, I am getting along fine. Your loving Son.

Two automobiles, an open car and a limousine, were maintained in Paris for the sole purpose of providing outings for wounded men who were able to take a little drive. It was said by the doctors and nurses that nothing helped a rapid recovery like these little excursions out into an every-day beautiful world.

A boy on one of the hospital cots called to a passing lassie:

"I am going to die, I know I am, and I'm a Catholic. Can you pray for me, Salvation Army girl, like you prayed for that fellow over there?"

The young lassie assured him that he was not going to die yet, but she knelt by his cot and prayed for him, and soothed him into a sleep from which he awoke refreshed to find that she was right, he was not going to die yet, but live, perhaps, to be a different lad.

A sixteen-year-old boy who at the first declaration of war had run away from home and enlisted was wounded so badly that he was ordered to go back to the evacuation hospital. He was determined that he could yet fight, and was almost crying because he had to leave his comrades, but on the way back he discovered the entrance to a German dugout and thought he heard someone down in there moving.

"Come out," he shouted, "or I'll throw in a hand grenade!"

A few minutes later he reached the evacuation hospital with thirty prisoners of war, his useless arm hanging by his side. That is the kind of stuff our American boys are made of, and those are the boys who are praising the Salvation Army!

It was sunset at the Gondrecourt Officers' Training Camp. On the big parade ground in back of the Salvation Army huts three companies were lined up for "Colors." The sun was sinking into a black mass of storm clouds, painting the Western sky a dull blood red with here and there a thread of gleaming gold etched on the rim of a cloud. Three French children trudged sturdily, wearily, back from the distant fields where they had toiled all day. The elder girl pushed a wheelbarrow heavily laden with plunder from the fields. All bore farming implements, the size of which dwarfed them by comparison. They had almost reached the end of the drill ground when the military band blared out the opening notes of the "Star Spangled Banner," and the flag slipped slowly from its high staff. Instantly the farming tools were dropped and the three childish figures swung swiftly to "attention," hands raised rigidly to the stiff French salute. So they stood until the last note had died. Then on they tramped, their backs all bent and weary, over the hill and down into the grey, evening-shadowed village of the valley.

In a shell-marred little village at the American front, the Salvation Army once brought the United States Army to a standstill. Several hundred artillerymen had gathered for the regular Wednesday night religious service, held in the hutment, conducted by that organization at this point, and, in closing, sang vigorously three verses of "The Star Spangled Banner." A Major who was passing came immediately to attention, his example being followed by all of the men and officers within hearing, and also by a scattering of French soldiers who were just emerging from the Catholic church. By the time the second verse was well under way three companies of infantry, marching from a rest camp toward the front, had also come to a rigid salute, blocking the road to a quartermaster's supply train, who had, perforce, to follow suit. The "Star Spangled Banner" has a deeper meaning to the man who has done a few turns in the trenches.

They had a pie-baking contest in Gondrecourt one day, where the renowned "Aunt Mary" was located, with her sweet face and sweeter heart.

One of the other huts had baked two hundred and

thirty-five pies in a day. The people in Gondrecourt believed they could do better than that, so they made their preparations and set to work.

The soldiers were all interested, of course. Who was to eat those pies? The more pies the merrier! The engineers had constructed a rack to hold them, so that they might be easily counted without confusion. The soldiers had appointed a committee to do the counting with a representative from the cooks to be sure that everything went right. Even the officers and chaplain took an interest in it.

This hut was in one of the largest American sectors. It was so well patronized that they used on an average fifty gallons of coffee every evening and seventy-five or more gallons of lemonade every afternoon. You can imagine the pies and doughnuts that would find a welcome here. One day they made twenty-seven hundred sugar cookies, and another day they fried eighteen hundred and thirty-six doughnuts, at the same time baking cake and pies; but this time they were going to try to bake three hundred pies between the rising and setting of the sun.

An army field oven only holds nine pies at a time, so every minute of the day had to be utilized. The fires were started very early in the morning and everything was ready for the girls to begin when the sun peeped over the edge of the great battlefield. They sprang at their task as though it were a delightful game of tennis, and not as though they had worked hard and late on the day before, and the many days before that.

It was very hot in the little kitchen as the sun waxed high. An army range never tries to conserve its heat for the benefit of the cooks. In fact that kitchen was often used for a Turkish bath by some poor wet soldiers who were chilled to the bone.

But the heat did not delay the workers. They flew at

their task with fingers that seemed to have somehow borrowed an extra nimbleness. All day long they worked, and the pies were marshalled out of the oven by nines, flaky and fragrant and baked just right. The rack grew fuller and fuller, and the soldiers watched with eager eyes and watering mouths. Now and then one of the soldiers' cooks would put his head in at the door, ask how the score stood, and shake his head in wonder. On and on they worked, mixing, rolling, filling, putting the little twists and cuts on the upper crust, and slipping in the oven and out again! Mixing, rolling, filling and baking without any let-up, until the sun with a twinkle of glowing appreciation slipped regretfully down behind the hills of France again as if he were sorry to leave the fun, and the time was up. The committee gave a last careful glance over the filled racks and announced the final score, three hundred and sixteen pies, in shining, delectable rows!

By seven o'clock that evening the pie line was several hundred yards long. It was eleven o'clock when the last quarter of a pie went over the counter, with its accompanying mug of coffee. Think what it was just to have to cut and serve that pie, and make that coffee, after a long day's work of baking!

One of the officers receiving his change after having paid for his pie looked at it surprisedly:

"And you mean to tell me that you girls work so hard for such a small return? I don't see where you make any profit at all."

"We don't work for profit, Captain," answered the lassie. "I don't think any amount of money would persuade us to keep going as we have to here at times."

"You mean you sort of work for the joy of working?" he asked, puzzled.

"I don't know what you mean," responded the lassie

pleasantly, "but when we are tired we look at the boys drilling in the sun and working early and late. They are splendid and we feel we must do our part as unreservedly as they do theirs."

"No wonder my men have so many good things to say about the Salvation Army!" said the Captain, turning to his companions. But as he went out into the night his voice floated back in a puzzled sort of half-conviction, as if he were thinking out something more than had been spoken:

"It takes more than patriotism to keep refined women working like that!"

These same girls were commissioned also to make frequent visits to the hospitals and talk with the sick soldiers. Often they read the Bible to them, and many a man through these little talks has found the way to eternal life. This in addition to their other work.

One night after a meeting in the hut a lad wanted to come into the room at the back and speak to one of the women about his soul. They knelt and prayed together, and the boy when he rose had a light of real happiness on his face. But suddenly the happiness faded and he exclaimed:

"But I can't read!"

"Read? What do you mean?" asked the lassie.

"My Bible. Nobody never learned me to read, and I can't read my Bible like you said in the meeting I should."

The lassie thought for a minute, and then suggested that he come to the hut every morning just before first call and she would teach him a verse of scripture and read him a chapter. This meant that the lassie must rise that much earlier, but what of that for a servant of the King?

Just a month this program was carried out, and then came marching orders for the boy, but by this time he had a rich store of God's word safe in his heart from the verses he had memorized. The last night when he came to say good-bye he said to his teacher:

"Your kindness has meant a lot of trouble for you, miss, but for me it has meant life! Before, I was afraid to fight; but now I don't even fear death. I know now that it can only mean a new life. Thank God for your goodness to me!"

There was one soldier who went by the name of Scoop. He had been a reporter back in the States and learned to love drink. When he joined the army he did not give up his old habits. Whenever anybody remonstrated with him he invariably replied gaily, "I'm out to enjoy life." On pay-days Scoop celebrated by drinking more than ever.

One day he happened into the Salvation Army hut. Whether the pie or the doughnuts or the homeyness of the place first attracted him no one knows. He said it was the pie. Something held him there. He came every night. The spirit of the Lord that lived and breathed in those consecrated men and girls began to work in his heart and conscience, and speak to him of better things that might even be for him.

When he felt the desire for drink or gambling coming on he gave his money to the girls to keep for him.

On the last pay-day before he was sent to another location he took a paint-brush and some paint and made a little sign which he set up in a prominent place in the hut, his silent testimony to what they had done for him: "FOR THE FIRST TIME ON PAY-DAY SCOOP IS SOBER!"

One morning a lassie was frying some doughnuts in the Gondrecourt hut, another was rolling and cutting, and both were very busy when a soldier came in with the mail. The girls went on with their work, though one could easily see that they were eager for letters. One was handed to the lassie who was frying the doughnuts. When she opened it she found it was an official dispatch. The others saw the change of her expression and asked what was the matter, but she made no reply while tears started down her cheeks. She, however, went on frying doughnuts. The others asked again what was the trouble and for answer the girl handed them the open dispatch, which stated briefly that one of her three brothers, who were all in the service, had been killed in action on the previous day. The others sympathetically tried to draw her away from her work, but she said: "No, nothing will help me to bear my sorrow like doing something for others." This is the spirit of the Salvation Army workers. Personal sorrows, personal feelings, personal difficulties, hardships, dangers, are not allowed to interrupt their labors of love. Fortunately, it was later discovered that this message about her brother was unfounded.

A boy told this lassie one day that the next day was his birthday, and she saw the homesickness and yearning in his eyes as he spoke. Immediately she told him she would have a birthday party for him and bake a cake for it.

She found some tiny candles in the village and placed nineteen upon the pretty frosted cake. They had to use a white bed-quilt for a tablecloth, and none of the cups and saucers matched, but the table looked very pretty when it was set, with little white paper baskets of almonds which the girls had made at each place, and all the candles lit on the white cake in the middle. The boy brought three of his comrades, and there were the Salvation Army Major in charge and the lassies. They had a beautiful time. Of course it was quite a little extra work for the lassie, but when someone asked her why she took so much trouble she had a faraway look in her eyes, and said she guessed it was for the sake of the boy's mother, and those who heard remembered that her own three brothers were in United States uniform somewhere facing the enemy.

There were several instances in which American soldiers coming from British and French Sectors, where they had been brigaded with armies of those nations, have upon entering a Salvation Army hut for the first time without noticing the sign over the door started to talk to the girls in French—very fragmentary French at that. When they found the girls to be Americans they were almost beside themselves with mingled feelings of bashfulness and delight. Most of the soldiers exhibit the former trait.

One boy approached one of our men officers.

"Can them girls speak American?" he asked, pointing at the girls.

On being assured that they could, he said: "Will they mind if I go up and speak to them? I ain't talked to an American woman in seven months."

Two soldiers were walking along the dusty roadway.

First soldier: "Let's go to the Salvation Army hut."

Second soldier: "No, I don't want to."

First soldier: "They've got a piano and a phonograph and lots of records."

Second soldier: "No, I don't want to."

First soldier: "They've got books and *beaucoup* games."

Second soldier: "No, I don't want to."

First soldier: "Two American ladies there!"

Second soldier: "No, I don't want to."

First soldier: "They've got swell coffee and doughnuts!"

Second soldier (angrily): "No! I said NO!"

First soldier: "Aw, come on. They got real homemade pie!"

Second soldier: "I don't care!"

First soldier: "They cut their own wood and do their own work!"

Second soldier: "Well, that's different! Why didn't you say that right off, you bonehead? Come on. Where is it?"

And they entered the Salvation Army hut smiling.

One dear Salvation Army lady had a little hand sewing machine which she took about with her and wherever she landed she would sit down on an orange crate, put her machine on another and set up a tailor shop: sewing up rips; refitting coats that were too large; letting out a seam that was too tight; and helping the boys to be tidy and comfortable again. A good many of our boys lost their coats in the Soissons fight, and when they got new ones they didn't always fit, so this little sewing machine that went to war came in very handy. Sometimes the owner would rip off the collar or rip out the sleeves, or almost rip up the whole coat and with her mouthful of pins skillfully put it together again until it looked as if it belonged to the laddie who owned it. Then with some clever chalk marks replacing the pins she would run it through her little machine, and off went another boy well-clothed. One week she altered more than thirty-three coats in this way. The soldiers called her "mother" and loved to sit about and talk with her while she worked.

The men went in battalions to the Luneville Sector for Trench Training facing the enemy. Of course, the Salvation Army sent a detachment also.

Over here they had to give up huts. No huts at all were allowed so near the front. No light of fire or even stove, no lights of any kind or everything would be destroyed by shell fire at once. An order went out that all huts near the front must be under ground. Yet neither did this daunt the faithful men and women whom God Himself had sent to help those boys at the front.

The work was extended to other camps in the Gondrecourt area and finally the time came for the troops to move up to the front to occupy part of a sector.

3

The Toul Sector

HEADQUARTERS of the First Division were established at Menil-la-Tour and that of the First Brigade at Ansauville. Information came on leaving the Gondrecourt Area, that the district would be abandoned to the French, so the wooden hut at Montiers was moved and set up again at Sanzey, which then became the Headquarters of the First Ammunition Train. Huts were established at Menil-la-Tour and other points in the Toul Sector.

It took three days to erect the hut at Sanzey, but within an hour the field range was set up, and a piece of tarpaulin stretched over it to keep the rain off the girls and the doughnuts.

Hour after hour the girls stood there making doughnuts, and hour after hour the line moved slowly along waiting patiently for doughnuts. The Adjutant went away a little while and returned to find some of the same boys standing in line as when he left. Some had been standing five hours! It was the only pastime they had, just as soon as they were off duty, to line up again for doughnuts.

The hut at Sanzey was used mostly by men of an Ammunition Train. As in other places where the Salvation Army huts catered to the American troops, an all-night service of hot coffee or chocolate and doughnuts or cookies was provided for the men as they returned from their dangerous nightly trips to the front. When men were killed their comrades usually brought them back and laid them in this hut until they could be buried. One night a man was killed and brought back in this fashion. The chaplain was holding a service over his body in the hut. The Salvation Army man was talking to the man who had been the dead lad's "buddie." "I wish it was me instead of him, Cap," said this soldier, "he was his mother's oldest son and she will take it hard."

The Salvation Army was told that Ansauville was too far front for any women to be allowed to go. They felt, however, that it was advisable for women to be there and determined to bring it about if possible. On scouting the town there was found no suitable place in any of the buildings except one that was occupied as the General's garage. The Salvation Army was not permitted to erect any additional buildings as it was feared they would attract the fire of the Germans, for Ansauville was well within the range of the German guns.

After deciding that the General's garage was the only logical place for them the Salvation Army representative called upon the General, who asked him where he would propose establishing a hut. The Salvationist told him the only suitable place in the town was that used by him as a garage. He immediately gave most gracious and courteous consent and ordered his aide to find another garage.

The place in question was an old frame barn with a lofty roof which had already been partly shot away and was open to the sky. They were not permitted to repair the roof because the German airplane observers would notice it and know that some activity was going on there which would call for renewed shell fire. However, the top of one of the circus tents was easily run up in the barn so as to form a ceiling.

Ansauville was between Mandres and Menil-la-Tour, not far from advanced positions in the Toul Sector. Five hundred French soldiers had been severely gassed there the night before the Staff-Captain and his helper arrived, and every day people were killed on the streets by falling shells. There was not a house in the village that had not suffered in some way from shell fire; very few had a door or a window left, and many were utterly demolished.

Approaching the town the roads were camouflaged with burlap curtains hanging on wires every little way, so that it was impossible to see down the streets very far in either direction. There were signs here and there: "ATTENTION! THE ENEMY SEES YOU!"

About midnight the Staff-Captain and his officer arrived and after some difficulty found the old barn that the Colonel had told them was to be their hut, but to their dismay there were half a dozen cars parked inside, including the Commanding General's, and it looked as if it were being used for the Staff Garage. Looking up they could see the stars peeping through the shell holes in the tiled roof. It was the first time either of them had been in a shelled town and the experience was somewhat awe-inspiring. Moreover they were both hungry and sleepy and the situation was by no means a cheerful one. They had a large tent and a load of supplies with them and were at a loss where to bestow them.

In the midst of their perturbation a courier arrived with a side car and dismounted. He stumbled in on them and peered at them through the darkness.

"As I live, it's the Salvation Army!" he cried joyfully,

shaking hands with both of them at once. "All of the boys have been asking when you were coming. Are you looking for a place to chow and sleep? There's no place in town for a billet, but we have a kitchen down the street. We can give you some chow, and it's warm there. You can roll up in your blankets and sleep by the stove till morning. Come with me."

The cook awakened them in the morning with his clatter of pots and pans in preparation for breakfast. They arose and began to roll up their blanket packs.

"Don't worry about getting up yet," said the chief cook kindly. "Sleep a little longer. You are not in my way." But the two men thanked him and declined to rest longer.

"Where are you going to chow?" asked the chief cook.

The Salvationists allowed that they didn't know.

"Well, you boys line up with this outfit, see?" insisted the chief cook. "We eat three times a day and you're welcome to everything we have!"

This settled the question of board, and after a good breakfast the two started out to report to the General in command.

He greeted them most kindly and made them feel welcome at once.

When they asked about the barn he smiled pleasantly:

"That Colonel of yours is a fine fellow," he said. "He told me that there was only one place in this town that would do for your hut and that was my garage. He said he was afraid he would have to ask me to move my car. Just as though my car were of more importance than the souls of my men! Gentlemen, you can have anything you want that is mine to give. The barn is yours! And if there's anything I can do, command me!"

It was a very dirty stable and needed a deal of cleaning,

but the strong workers bent to their task with willing hands, and soon had it in fine order. There was no possibility of mending the roof, but they camouflaged the old tent top and ran it up inside, and it kept the rain and snow off beautifully. Of course, it was no protection against shells, but when they commenced to arrive everybody departed in a hurry to the nearby dugouts, returning quietly when the firing had ceased. The nights were so cold that they had to sleep with all their clothes on, even their overcoats. Often in the mornings their shoes were frozen too stiff to put on until they were thawed over a candle. One soldier broke his shoe in two trying to bend it one morning. Sometimes the men would sleep with their shoes inside their shirts to keep the damp leather from freezing. Two yards from the stove the milk froze!

A field range had been secured and the chimney extended up from the roof for a distance of forty or fifty feet. It smoked terribly, but on this range was cooked many a savory meal and tens of thousands of doughnuts.

Among the doughboys who loved to help around the Salvation Army hut was a quiet fellow who never talked much about himself, yet everybody liked him and trusted him. No one knew much about him, or where he came from, and he never told about his folks at home as some did. But he used to come in from the trenches during the day and do anything he could to be useful around the hut, which was run by two sisters. Even when he had to stand watch at night he would come back in the daytime and help. They could not persuade him to sleep when he ought. Other fellows came and went, talked about their troubles and their joys, got their bit of sympathy or cheer and went their way, but this fellow came every day and worked silently, always on the job. They made him their chief doughnut dipper and he seemed to love the work and did it well.

Then one day his company moved, and he came no more. The girls often asked if anyone knew anything about him, but no one did. Once in a while a brief note would come from him up at the front in the trenches a few miles to the north, but never more than a word of greeting.

One morning the girls were making doughnuts, hard at work, and suddenly the former chief doughnut dipper stumbled into the hut. He looked tired and dusty and it was evident by the way he walked that he was footsore.

"Gee! It's good to see you," he said, sinking down in his old place by the stove.

They gave him a cup of steaming coffee and all the doughnuts he could eat and waited for his story, but he did not begin.

"Well, how are you?" asked one of the girls, hoping to start him.

"Oh, all right, thanks," he said meekly.

"Where is your company?"

"Up the line in some woods."

"How far is it?"

"About ten miles."

The girls felt they were not getting on very fast in acquiring information.

"Did you walk all that way in the dust and sun?"

"Most of it. Sometimes I was in the fields."

"Were you on watch last night?"

"Ye-ah."

"Then you didn't have any sleep?"

"No."

"Why did you come over here then?"

"I wanted to see you." There was a sound of a deep hunger in his voice.

"Well, we're awfully glad to see you, surely. Is there anything we can do for you?"

"No. Just let me look at you"—there was frank honesty in his eyes, a deep undertone of reverence in his voice, not even a hint of gallantry or flattery, only a loyal homage.

"Just let me look at you—and—" he hesitated.

"And what?"

"And cook some doughnuts."

"Why, of course!" said the girls cheerily, "but you must lie down and sleep awhile first. We'll fix a place for you."

"I don't want to lie down," said the soldier determinedly, "I don't want to waste the time."

"But it wouldn't be wasted. You need the sleep."

"No, that isn't what I need. I want to look at you," he reiterated. "I've got a wife and a little baby at home, and I love them. I like to be here because seeing you takes me back to them. This morning I knew I ought to sleep, but I just couldn't go over the top to-night without seeing you again. That's why I want to see you and fry a few doughnuts for you. It takes me back to them."

He finished with a far-away look in his eyes. He was not thinking what impression his words would make, his thoughts were with his wife and little baby.

He worked around for a couple of hours, saying very little, but seeming quite content. Then he looked at his watch and said it was time to go, as it was quite a walk back to his company. Just so quietly he took his leave and went out to take his chance with Death.

The two girls thought much about him that night as they went about their work, and later lay down and tried to sleep, and their prayers went up for the faithful soul who was doing his duty out there under fire, and for the anxious wife and little one who waited to know the outcome. Sleep did not come soon to their eyes, as they lay in the darkness and prayed.

The next day about noon as the girls were dipping doughnuts the chief doughnut dipper stumbled once more into the hut, tired, dirty, dusty and worn, but with his eyes sparkling:

"Just thought I ought to come back and tell you I'm all right," he said. "I was afraid you'd be worried. My wife and baby would, anyway."

The girls received him with exultant smiles.

"You go out there under the trees and go to sleep!" they ordered him.

"All right, I will," he said. "I feel like sleeping now. Say, you don't think I'm crazy, do you? I just had to see you! It took me back to them!"

It was one of those chill rainy nights which have caused the winter of 1917–1918 to be remembered with shudders by the men of the earlier American Expeditionary Forces. A large part of the American forces were billeted in the weathered, age-old little villages of the Gondrecourt area. They slept in barns, haylofts, cowsheds and even in pig sties. The roads were mere ditches running knee deep in sticky, clogging mud. Shoes, soaked through from the muddy road, froze as the men slept and in the morning had to be thawed out over a candle before they could be drawn on. Frequently men were late at roll-call simply because their shoes were frozen so stiff that they were unable to don them, and their leggings so icy that they could not be wound. After sundown there were no lights, because lights invited air-raids and might well expose the position of troops to the enemy observers. Only in towns where there were Salvation Army or Y.M.C.A. huts could men find any artificial warmth during the day or night, and only in these places were there any lights after nightfall. Such huts afforded absolutely the only available recreation facilities. But in countless villages where Americans were billeted there was not even this small comfort to be had.

On this particular night, in such a village, an eighteen-year-old boy sat in the orderly room of a regimental headquarters, which was housed in a once pretentious but now sadly decrepit house. Rain leaked through the tiled roof and dribbled down into the room. Windows were long ago shattered and through cracks in the rude board barricades which had replaced the glass a rising wind was driving the rain. The boy sat at a rough wooden table waiting orders. Two weeks previously a letter had come, saying that his mother was seriously ill. Since that he had had no further word. He was desperately homesick. There had been as yet none of the danger and none of the thrill which seems to settle a man down to the serious business of war.

A passing soldier had just told him that in a village some twelve kilometers distant two Salvation Army women were operating a hut. He longed desperately for the comfort of a woman of his own people and, sitting in the drafty, damp room, he wished that these two Salvationists were not so far away—that he could talk with them and confide in them. At last the wish grew so strong that he could no longer resist it.

He got up quietly, and silently slipped out into the rainy night. The darkness was so thick that he could not see objects six feet away. Walking through the mud was out of the question. He stumbled down the street, once falling headlong into a muddy puddle, finally reaching the horse-lines, where, saying that he had an errand for the Colonel, he saddled a horse and slopped off into the night.

For a while he kept to the road, his horse occasionally taking fright, as a truck passed clanking slowly in the opposite direction, or a staff car turned out to pass him like a fleeting, ghostly shadow. By following the trees which lined the road at regular intervals he was fairly sure to keep the road. He was very tired and soon began to feel sleepy, but the driving storm, which by this time had assumed the proportions of a tempest, stung him to wakefulness. Once, at a cross-roads a Military Police stopped and questioned him and gave him directions upon his saying that he was carrying dispatches.

He went on. He dozed, only to be sharply awakened by a truck which almost ran him down. He must be more careful, he thought to himself, feeling utterly alone and miserable. But in spite of his resolution his eyes soon closed again. He was awakened, this time by his horse stumbling over some unseen obstacle. He could see nothing in any direction. The blackness and rain shut him in like a fog. He turned at right angles to find the trees which lined the road, but there were no trees. He swung his horse around and went in the other direction, but he found no trees—only an impenetrable darkness which pressed in upon him with a heaviness which might almost have been weighed. He was lost—utterly lost.

He guided his steed in futile circles, hoping to regain the road, but all to no avail. Fear of the night fell upon him. He was wet to the skin and chilled to the bone. He shivered with cold and with fright. Dropping from his horse he pulled from his pocket an electric flashlight and began throwing its slender beam in widening arcs over the ground. The light revealed a stubble field. Surely there must be a path which would lead to the road, thought the boy. Backward and forward over the field he waved the light. His hands trembled so that he could not hold the switch steady, and the lamp blinked on and off.

On the storm-swept, night-hidden hillside which overhung the field was established an anti-aircraft battery. The sound detectors had just registered the intermittent hum of an enemy plane. It was unusual that an enemy aviator should fight his way over the lines in the face of such a storm, but such things had occurred before and the Captain in charge of the battery searched the tempestuous skies for the intruder, waiting for the sound to grow until he should know that the searchlights had at least a chance of locating the venturesome plane instead of merely giving away their position.

Suddenly, cutting the night in the field below, a tiny ray of light cut the darkness, sweeping back and forward, flashing on and off. For a moment the officer watched it, then, with a muttered curse, he raced down the hillside followed by one of his men. The noise of the storm hid their approach. The boy collapsed into a trembling heap, as the officer grasped him and wrested the flash-light from his chilled fingers. He made no protest as they led him down into a dark, deserted village. He followed his captors into a candle-lighted room where sat a staff officer.

Briefly the Captain explained the situation.

"Caught him in the act of signaling to an enemy plane, sir," he said.

The boy was too cold to venture a protest.

"Bring him to me again in the morning," said the Colonel, shrugging his shoulders. "Hold on, though! What are you going to do with him? He will die unless you get him warmed up."

"Don't know what to do with him, sir, unless I take him down to the Salvation Army . . . they have a fire there."

"Very good, Captain, see that he is properly guarded and if they will have him, leave him there for the night."

And so it came to pass that the boy reached his destination. It was past closing time—long past; but the motherly Salvationist in charge knew just what to do. Within ten minutes, wrapped in a warm blanket, the boy sat with his feet in a pan of hot water, with the Salvation Army woman feeding him steaming lemonade. Between gulps, he told his story and was comforted. Soon he was snugly tucked into an army cot, and still grasping the Salvationist's hand, was sleeping peacefully.

The next day a little investigation assured the Colonel that the boy's story was a true one, and with a reprimand for leaving his post without orders he was allowed to return. The delay, however, had absented him, of course, from morning roll-call, and he was sentenced to thirty days repairing wire on the front-line trenches, which was often equivalent to a death sentence, for as many men were shot during the performance of this duty as came in safely.

He had done fifteen days of his time at this sentence when the Salvation Army woman from the Ansauville hut which the boy had visited that rainy night happened over to his Officers' Headquarters, and by chance learned of his unhappy fate. It took but a few words from her to his commanding officer to set matters right; his sentence was revoked, and he was pardoned.

Ansauville was a point of peculiar importance in that all the troops passing into or out from the sector stopped there. It was here that cocoa and coffee were first provided for the troops. Afterwards it came to be the habit to serve them with the doughnuts and pie. It was when the Twenty-sixth Division came into the line. They had marched for hours and had been without any warm meal for a long time. Detachments of them reached Ansauville at night, wet and cold, too late to secure supper that night, and hearing they were coming, the lassies put on great boilers of coffee and cocoa, and as the men arrived they were given to them freely.

A hut was established at Mandres. This was some distance in advance of Ansauville and lay in the valley. At first a wooden building was secured. It had nothing but a dirt floor but lumber was hauled from Newchateau by truck—a distance of sixty miles, and the place was made comfortable.

For some little time the boys enjoyed this hut, but on one occasion the Germans sent over a heavy barrage; they hit the hut, destroying one end of it, scattering the supplies, ruining the victrola, and after that the military authorities ordered that the men should not assemble in such numbers.

When this order was given, the Salvation Army had no intention of discontinuing work at Mandres and so found a cellar under a partially destroyed building. This cellar was vaulted and had been used for storing wine. It was wet and in bad condition, but with some labor it was made fit to receive the men; and tables and benches were placed there, the canteen established and a range set up. It was at this place that a very wonderful work was carried on. The Salvation Army Ensign who had charge, for a time, scoured the country for miles around to purchase eggs, which he transferred to his hut in an old baby carriage. The eggs were supplied to the men at cost and they fried them themselves on the range, which was close at hand. This was considered by the military authorities too far front for women to come and only men were allowed here.

The Ensign also mixed batter for pan cakes and established quite a reputation as a pan-cake maker. Here was a place where the soldiers felt at home. They could come in at any time and on the fire cook what they pleased. They could purchase at the canteen such articles as were for sale and it was home to them. Very wonderful meetings were held in this spot and many men found Christ at the penitent-form, which was an old bench placed in front of the canteen.

On the wharf in New York when the soldiers were returning home some soldiers were talking about the Salvation Army. "Did you ever go to one of their meetings?" asked one. "I sure did!" answered a big fine fellow—a college man, by the way, from one of the well known New England universities. "I sure did!—and it was the most impressive service I ever attended. It was down in an old wine cellar, and the house over it *wasn't* because it had been blown away. The meeting was led by a little Swede, and he gave a very impressive address, and followed it by a wonderful prayer. And it wasn't because it was so learned either, for the man was no college chap, but it stirred me deeply. I used to be a good deal of a barbarian before I went to France, but that meeting made a big change in me. Things are going to be different now.

"The place was lit by a candle or two and the guns were roaring overhead, but the room was packed and a great many men stood up for prayers. Oh, I'll never forget that meeting!"

That meeting was in the old wine cellar in Mandres.

The town of Mandres was shelled daily and it was an exceptional day that passed without from one to ten men being killed as a result of this shelling.

Here are some extracts from letters written by the Ensign from the old wine cellar in Mandres:

"Somewhere in France,"
May 15, 1918.

I am still busy in my old wine-cellar in France. I must give you an idea of my daily routine: Get up early and go to my cellar. Get wood and make fire; go for some water to put on stove. Take my mess kit, helmet, gas mask and cane, walk about one block to the part of the church standing by the artillery kitchen and get my hand-out mess, go back to my cellar and have my breakfast, see to the fire, fuel, clean and light the lamps, dip and carry out some water and mud (but have now found a place to drain off the water by cutting through the heavy stone wall and digging a ditch underneath). I dig whenever I have time. Then the boys begin to come in—some right from the trenches, others who are resting up after a siege in the trenches. They are all covered with mud when they come in and have to talk, stand and even sleep in mud. Then I must have the cocoa and coffee ready and serve also the candy, figs, nuts, gum, chocolate, shaving-sticks, razors, watches, knives, gun oil, paper, envelopes, etc. I mostly wear my rubber boots and stand in a little boot "slouched" down so I can stand straight. Almost every evening we have a little "sing-song," or regular service, and on Sunday two or three services.

Our wine-cellar is supposed to be bomb-proof. First the roof, the ceiling, the floor, then the three-feet stone and concrete under the floor and along the wine-cellar. I am all alone for all this business. Sometimes the boys help me to cut wood and keep the fire and carry water, but the companies are changed so often that they go and come every five days, and when they come from the trenches they are so tired and sleepy they need all the rest they can get. Yesterday I had to change the stove and stovepipes because it smoked so bad that it almost smoked us out. So I had to run through the ruins and find old stovepipes. I could not find enough elbows, so I had to make some with the help of an old knife. We ran the pipes through the low window bars and up the side of the house to the top, and plastered up poor joints with mud, but it burns better and does not smoke. The boys claim I make the best coffee they have had in France, and also cocoa. I am glad I know something of cooking. You see, they don't permit girls so near the trenches and in the shell fire.

My dear Major:

Grace, love and peace unto you! Many thanks for the beautiful letter I received from you full of love, Christian admonition and encouragement. Such letters are much appreciated over here.

I have been very busy. The last week, in addition to running the ordinary business, I have used the pick and shovel and wheel-barrow in lowering our wine-cellar floor (now used as a Salvation Army rest room), so we can walk straight in. I have also done some white-washing to brighten things up and have some flowers in bowls, large French wine bottles and big brass shells, which makes a great improvement. I now expect to pick up pieces and erect a range, so we can cook and make things faster. I secured two hams and am having them cooked, and expect to serve ham sandwiches by Decoration Day, two days hence, when there is to be a great time in decorating the graves of our heroes. I am also trying to get some lemons so that

I can make lemonade for the boys besides the coffee and cocoa. You can get an idea of the immensity of our business when I tell you I got 999.25 francs worth of butter-scotch candy alone with the last lot of goods, besides a dozen other kinds of candy, nuts, toilet articles, etc., and this will be sold and given out in a very few days.

We had very good meetings last Sunday. I spoke at night. A glorious time we had, indeed. Praise God for the opportunity of working among the New England braves!

At Menil-la-Tour the French forbade any huts at all to be put up at first, but finally they gave permission for one hut. The Staff-Captain wanted to put up two, but as that wasn't allowed he got around the order by building five rooms on each side of the one big hut and so had plenty of room. It is pretty hard to get ahead of a Salvation Army worker when he has a purpose in view. Not that they are stubborn, simply that they know how to accomplish their purpose in the nicest way possible and please everybody.

There were some American railroad engineers here, working all night taking stuff to the front. They came over and asked if they could help out, and so instead of taking their day for sleep they spent most of it putting tar paper on the roof of the Salvation Army hut.

It was in this place that there seemed to be a strong prejudice among some of the soldiers against the Salvation Army for some reason. The soldiers stood about swearing at the Staff-Captain and his helper as they worked, and saying the most abusive and contemptible things to them. At last the Staff-Captain turned about and, looking at them, in the kindliest way said:

"See here, boys, did you ever know anything about the Salvation Army before?"

They admitted that they had not.

"Well, now, just wait a little while. Give us fair play and see if we are like what you say we are. Wait until we get our hut done and get started, and then if you don't like us you can say so."

"Well, that's fair, Dad," spoke up one soldier, and after that there was no more trouble, and it wasn't long before the soldiers were giving the most generous praise to the Salvation Army on every side.

L'Hermitage, nestled in the heart of a deep woods, was no quiet refuge from the noise of battle and the troubles of a war-weary world, as one might suppose. It was surrounded by swamps everywhere. And it had been raining, of course. It always seems to have been raining in France during this war. There were duck boards over the swampy ground, and a single mis-step might send one prone in the ooze up to the elbows.

It was a very dangerous place, also.

There was a large ammunition dump in the town, and besides that there was a great balloon located there which the Boche planes were always trying to get. It was the nearest to the front of any of our balloons and, of course, was a great target for the enemy. There was a lot of heavy coast artillery there, also, and there were monster shell holes big enough to hold a good audience.

At last one day the enemy did get the ammunition dump, and report after report rent the air as first one shell and then another would burst and go up in flame. It was fourteen hours going off and the military officer ordered the girls to their billets until it should be over. It was like this: First a couple of shells would explode, then there would be a second's quiet and a keg of powder would flare; then some boxes of ammunition would go off;

then some more shells. It was a terrible pandemonium of sound. Thirty miles away in Gondrecourt they saw the fire and heard the terrific explosions.

The Zone Major and one of his helpers had been to Nancy for a truck load of eggs and were just unloading when the explosions began. Together they were carefully lifting out a crate containing a hundred dozen eggs when the mammoth detonations began that rocked the earth beneath them and threatened to shake them from their feet. They staggered and tottered but they held onto the eggs. One of the sayings of Commander Eva Booth is, "Choose your purpose and let no whirlwind that sweeps, no enemy that confronts you, no wave that engulfs you, no peril that affrights you, turn you from it." The Zone Major and his helper had chosen the purpose of landing those eggs safely, and eggs at five francs a dozen are not to be lightly dropped, so they staggered but they held onto the eggs.

The girls in the canteen went quietly about their work until ordered to safety; but over in Sanzey and Menil-la-Tour their friends watched and waited anxiously to hear what had been their fate.

The General who was in charge of the Twenty-sixth Division was exceedingly kind to the Salvation Army girls. He acted like a father toward them: giving up his own billet for their use; sending an escort to take them to it through the woods and swamps and dangers when their work at the canteen was over for a brief respite; setting a sentry to guard them and to give a gas alarm when it became necessary; and doing everything in his power for their comfort and safety.

4

The Montdidier Sector

SPRING came on even in shell-torn France, lovely like the miracle it always is. Bare trees in a day were arrayed in wondrous green. A camouflage of beauty spread itself upon the valleys and over the hillsides like a garment sewn with colored broidery of blossoms. Great scarlet poppies flamed from ruined homes as if the blood that had been spilt were resurrected in a glorious color that would seek to hide the misery and sorrow and touch with new loveliness the war-scarred place. Little birds sent forth their flutey voices where mortals must be hushed for fear of enemies.

The British had been driven back by the Huns until they admitted that their backs were against the wall, and it was an anxious time. Daily the enemy drew nearer to Paris.

When the great offensive was started by the Germans in March, 1918, and American troops were sent up to help the British and French, the Division was located at Montdidier. Under the rules for the conduct of war, they were not permitted to know where they were destined to go, and so the Salvation Army could not secure that information. They knew it was to be north of Paris, but where, was the problem.

The French were opposed to any relief organizations going into the Sector, and rules and regulations were made which were calculated to discourage or to keep them out altogether.

It was urgent that the Salvation Army should be there at the earliest possible moment and as they could not secure permits, especially for the women, they decided to get there without permits.

The first contingent was put into a big Army truck, the cover was put down and they were started on the road, to a point from which they hoped to secure information of the movements of their outfit. From place to place this truck proceeded until, finally, detachments of the troops were located in the vicinity of Gisors. Contact was immediately established. The girls were received with the greatest joy and portable tents were set up. It seemed as if every man in the Division must come to say how glad he was to see them back. The men decided that if it was in their power they would never again allow the Salvation Army to be separated from them. A few days later when the Division was ordered to move they took these same lassies with them riding in army trucks. The troops were on their way to the front and seldom remained more than three days in one place, and frequently only one day. On arrival at the stopping-place, fifteen or twenty of the boys would immediately proceed to erect the tent and within an hour or two a comfortable place would be in operation, a field range set up, the phonograph going, and the boys had a home.

At Courcelles the Salvation Army set up a tent, started a canteen, and had it going four days in charge of two sisters just come from the States. Then one morning they woke up and found their outfit gone, they knew not where, and they had to pick up and go after them. An all-day journey took them to Froissy, where they found their special outfit.

There was no place for a tent at Froissy, but there was an old dance hall, where they had their canteen. The Division stayed there five weeks—under a roar of guns. But in spite of this there were wonderful meetings every night in Froissy.

This work was exceedingly trying on the girls. Permits were never secured for any of the Salvation Army workers in this Sector. They were applied for regularly through the French Army. About three months after application was made, they were all received back with the statement from the French that, seeing the workers were already there, it was not now necessary that permits should be issued. It must be reported that the French Army was opposed to the presence of women in any of the camps of the soldiers. This prejudice existed for a long time, but it was finally broken down because of the good work done by Salvation Army women, which came to be fully recognized by the French Army.

The work in the Montdidier Sector was particularly hard. Permanent buildings could not be established. The best that could be done was to erect portable tents, which were about twenty feet wide and fifty-seven feet long. Huts were established in partially destroyed buildings or houses or stores that had been vacated by their owners, and on the extreme front canteens were established in dugouts and cellars and the entire district was under bombardment from the German guns as well as from the airplane bombs. The Salvation Army had no place there that was not under bombardment continually. The huts were frequently shelled and there was imminent danger for a long time that the German Army would break through, which, of course, added to the strain.

The Zone Major went back and forth bringing more men and more lassies and more supplies from the Base at Paris to the front, and many a new worker almost lost his life in a baptism of fire on his way to his post of duty for the first time. But all these men and women, as a soldier said, were made of some fine high stuff that never faltered at danger or fatigue or hardship.

They rode over shell-gashed roads in the blackest midnight in a little dilapidated Ford; made wild dashes when they came to a road upon which the enemy's fire was concentrated, looking back sometimes to see a geyser of flame leap up from a bend around which they had just whirled. Shells would rain in the fields on either side of them; cars would leap by them in the dark, coming perilously close and swerving away just in time; and still they went bravely on to their posts.

Everything would be blackest darkness and they would think they were stealing along finely, when all of a sudden an incendiary bomb would burst and flare up like a house-on-fire lighting up the whole country for miles about, and there you were in plain sight of the enemy! And you couldn't turn back nor hesitate a second or you would be caught by the ever watchful foe! You had to go straight ahead in all that blare of light!

The S.A. Adjutant's headquarters were fifty feet below the ground; sometimes the earth would rock with the explosives. Two of the dugouts were burrowed almost beneath the trenches and S.A. Officers here looked after the needs of the men who were actually engaged in fighting. Every night the shattered villages were raked and torn above them. Such dugouts could only be left at night or when the firing ceased. The two men who operated these lived a nerve-racking existence. Of course, all pies and doughnuts for these places had to be prepared far to the rear, and no fire could be built as near to the front as this. It was no easy task to bring the supplies back and forth. It was almost always done at the risk of life.

The Staff-Captain and the Adjutant were speeding over a shell-swept road one cold, black, wet night at reckless speed without a light, their hearts filled with anxiety, for a rumor had reached them that two Salvation Army lassies had been killed by shell fire. The night was full of the sound of war, the distant rumble of the heavy guns, the nervous stutter of machine guns, the tearing screech of a barrage high above the road.

Suddenly in front of them yawned a black gulf. The Adjutant jammed on his brakes, but it was too late. The game little Ford sailed right into a big shell hole, and settled down three feet below the road right side up but tightly wedged in. The two travelers climbed out and reconnoitered but found the situation hopeless. There had been many sleepless nights before this one, and the men, weary beyond endurance, rolled up in their blankets, climbed into the car, and went to sleep, regardless of the guns that thundered all about them.

They were just lost to the land of reality when a soldier roused them summarily, saying:

"This is a heck of a place for the Salvation Army to go to sleep! If you don't mind I'll just pick your old bus out of here and send you on your way before it's light enough for Fritzy to spot you and send a calling card."

He was grinning at them cheerfully and they roused to the occasion.

"How are you going to do it?" asked the Adjutant,

who, by the way, was Smiling Billy, the same one the soldiers called "one game little guy." "It will take a three-ton truck to get us out of this hole!"

"I haven't got a truck but I guess we can turn the trick all right!" said the soldier.

He disappeared into the darkness above the crater and in a moment reappeared with ten more dark forms following him, and another soldier who patrolled the rim of the crater on horseback.

"How do you like 'em?" he chuckled to the Salvation Army men, as he turned his flashlight on the ten and showed them to be big German prisoners of war. Under his direction they soon had the little Ford pushed and shouldered into the road once more. In a little while the Salvationists reached their destination and found to their relief that the rumor about the lassies was untrue.

At Mesnil-St.-Firmin one of the lassies, a young woman well known in New York society circles, but a loyal Salvationist and in France from the start, drove a little flivver carrying supplies for several nights, accompanied only by a young boy detailed from the Army. Every mile of the way was dark and perilous, but there was no one else to do the work, so she did it.

Here they were under shell fire every night. The girls slept in an old wine cellar, the only comparatively safe place to be found. It was damp, with a fearful odor they will never forget—moreover, it was already inhabited by rats. They frequently had to retire to the cellar during gas attacks, and stay for hours, sometimes having only time to seize an overcoat and throw it over their night-clothes. They were here through ten counter-attacks and when Cantigny was taken.

There seemed to be big movements among the Germans one day. They were bringing up reinforcements, and a large attack was expected. The airplanes were dropping bombs freely everywhere and it looked as if there would not be one brick left on the top of another in a few hours. Then the military authorities ordered the two girls to leave town.

When the boys heard that the hut was being shelled and the girls were ordered to leave they poured in to tell them how much they would miss them. They well knew from experience that their staunch hardworking little friends would not have left them if they could have helped it. Also, they dreaded to lose these consecrated young women from their midst. They had a feeling that their presence brought the presence of the great God, with His protection, and in this they had come to trust in their hour of danger. Often the boys would openly speak of this, owning that they attributed their safety to the presence of their Christian friends.

One young officer from the officers' mess where the girls had dined once at their invitation, brought them boxes of candy, and in presenting them said:

"Gee! We shall miss you like the devil!"

The lassie twinkled up in a merry smile and answered: "That sure is some comparison!"

The officer blushed as red as a peony and tried to apologize:

"Well, now, you know what I mean. I don't know just how to say how much we shall miss you!"

They left at midnight on foot accompanied by one of the Salvation Army men workers who had been badly gassed and needed to get back of the lines and have some treatment. It was brilliant moonlight as they hiked it down the road, the airplanes were whizzing over their heads and the anti-aircraft guns piling into them.

They started for La Folie, the Headquarters of the Staff-Captain of that zone, but they lost their way and got far out of the track, arriving at last at Breteuil. Coming to the woods a Military Police stationed at the crossroads told them:

"You can't go into Breteuil because they have been shelling it for twenty minutes. Right over there beyond where you are standing a bomb dropped a few minutes ago and killed or wounded seven fellows. The ambulance just took them away."

However, as they did not know where else to go they went into Breteuil, and found the village deserted of all but French and American Military Police. They tried to get directions, and at last found a French mule team to take them to La Folie, where they finally arrived at four o'clock in the morning.

The next day they went on to Tartigny, where they were to be located for a time.

One of the lassies left her sister with the canteen one day and started out with another Officer to the Divisional Gas Officer to get a new gas mask, for something had happened to hers. As they reached a crossroads a boy on a wheel called out: "Oh, they're shelling the road! Pull into the village quick!"

When they arrived in the village there was a great shell just fallen in the very centre of the town. The girl thought of her sister all alone in the canteen, for the shells were falling everywhere now, and they started to take a short cut back to Tartigny, but the Military Police stopped them, saying they couldn't go on that road in the daytime as it was under observation, so they had to go back by the road they had come. The canteen was at the gateway of a chateau, and when they reached there they saw the shells falling in the chateau yard and through the glass roof of the canteen. It was a trying time for the two brave girls.

They had been invited out to dinner that evening at

the Officers' Mess. As a rule, they did not go much among the officers, but this was a special invitation. The shells had been falling all the afternoon, but they were quite accustomed to shells and that did not stop the festivities. During the dinner the soldier boys sang and played on guitars and banjos. But when the dinner was over they asked the girls to sing.

It was very still in the mess hall as the two lovely lassies took their guitars and began to sing. There was something so strong and sweet and pure in the glance of their blue eyes, the set of their firm little chins, so pleasant and wholesome and merry in the very curve of their lips, that the men were hushed with respect and admiration before this highest of all types of womanhood.

It was a song written by their Commander that the girls had chosen, with a sweet, touching melody, and the singers made every word clear and distinct:

> *Bowed beneath the garden shades,*
> *Where the Eastern sunlight fades,*
> *Through a sea of griefs He wades,*
>   *And prays in agony.*
> *His sweat is of blood,*
> *His tears like a flood*
>   *For a lost world flow down.*
> *I never knew such tears could be—*
>   *Those tears He wept for me!*
>
> *Hung upon a rugged tree*
> *On the hill of Calvary,*
> *Jesus suffered death, to be*
>   *The Saviour of mankind.*
> *His brow pierced by thorn,*
> *His hands and feet torn,*
>   *With broken heart He died.*

> *I never knew such pain could be,*
>   *This pain He bore for me!*

Suddenly crashing into the midst of the melody came a great shell, exploding just outside the door and causing everyone at the table to spring to his feet. The singers stopped for a second, wavered, as the reverberation of the shock died away, and then went on with their song; and the officers, abashed, wondering, dropped back into their seats marvelling at the calmness of these frail women in the face of death. Surely they had something that other women did not have to enable them to sing so unconcernedly in such a time as this!

> *Love which conquered o'er death's sting,*
> *Love which has immortal wing,*
> *Love which is the only thing*
>   *My broken heart to heal.*
> *It burst through the grave,*
> *It brought grace to save,*
>   *It opened Heaven's gate.*
> *I never knew such love could be—*
>   *This love He gave to me!*

It needs some special experience to appreciate what Salvation Army lassies really are, and what they have done. They are not just any good sort of girl picked up here and there who are willing to go and like the excitement of the experience; neither are they common illiterate girls who merely have ordinary good sense and a will to work. The majority of them in France are fine, well-bred, carefully reared daughters of Christian fathers and mothers who have taught them that the home is a little bit of heaven on earth, and a woman God's means of drawing man nearer to Him. They have been especially trained from childhood to forget self and to live for others. The great slogan of the Salvation Army is "Others." Did you ever stop to think how that would take the coquetry out of a girl's eyes, and leave the sweet simplicity of the natural unspoiled soul? We have come to associate such a look with a plain, homely face, a dull complexion, careless, severe hair-dressing and unbeautiful clothes. Why?

Righteousness from babyhood has given to these girls delicate beautiful features, clear complexions that neither faded nor had to be renewed in the thick of battle, eyes that seemed flecked with divine lights and could dance with mirth on occasion or soften exquisitely in sympathy, furtive dimples that twinkled out now and then; hands that were shapely and did not seem made for toil. Yet for all that they toiled night and day for the soldiers. They were educated, refined, cultured, could talk easily and well on almost any subject you would mention. They never appeared to force their religious views to the front, yet all the while it was perfectly evident that their religion was the main object of their lives; that this was the secret source of strength, the great reason for their deep joy, and abiding calm in the face of calamities; that this was the one great purpose in life which overtopped and conquered all other desires. And if you would break through their sweet reserve and ask them they would tell you that Jesus and the winning of souls to Him was their one and only ambition.

And yet they have not let these great things keep them from the pleasant little details of life. Even in the olive drab flannel shirt and serge skirt of their uniform, or in their trim serge coats, the exact counterpart of the soldier boy's, except for its scarlet epaulets, and the little close trench hat with its scarlet shield and silver lettering, they are beautiful and womanly. Catch them with the coat off and a great khaki apron enveloping the rest of their uniform, and you never saw lovelier women. No wonder the boys loved to see them working about the hut, loved to carry water and pick up the dishes for washing, and peel apples, and scrape out the bowl after the cake batter had been turned into the pans. No wonder they came to these girls with their troubles, or a button that needed sewing on, and rushed to them first with the glad news that a letter had come from home even before they had opened it. These girls were real women, the kind of woman God meant us all to be when He made the first one; the kind of woman who is a real helpmeet for all the men with whom she comes in contact, whether father, brother, friend or lover, or merely an acquaintance. There is a fragrance of spirit that breathes in the very being, the curve of the cheek, the glance of the eye, the grace of a movement, the floating of a sunny strand of hair in the light, the curve of the firm red lips that one knows at a glance will have no compromise with evil. This is what these girls have.

You may call it what you will, but as I think of them I am again reminded of that verse in the Bible about those brave and wonderful disciples: "And they took knowledge of them that they had been with Jesus."

Two of the Salvation Army men went back to Mesnil-St.-Firmin the day after the lassies had been obliged to leave, to get some of their belongings which they had not been able to take with them, and one of them, a Salvation Army Major, stayed to keep the place open for the boys. He was the only Salvation Army man who is entitled to wear a wound stripe. By his devotion to duty, self-sacrifice, and contempt of danger, he won the confidence of the men wherever he was. He chiefly worked alone and operated a canteen usually in a dugout at the front.

On one occasion a soldier was badly wounded at the door of a hut, by an exploding gas-shell. He fell into the dugout and while the Major worked over him, the Major himself was gassed and had to be removed to the rear and undergo hospital treatment. For this service he was awarded a wound stripe. During the St. Mihiel offensive he was appointed in the Toul Sector and followed up the advancing soldiers, and later was active in the Argonne. He is essentially a front-line man and always takes the greatest satisfaction in being in the place of most danger.

The following is a brief excerpt from his diary when he manned the dugout hut in Coullemelle:

May 12.

"Arrived in Coullemelle Sunday night, May 12. Was busy with my work by mid-day, Monday, 13. After cleaning our dugout, gave medicine to sick man, who refused to sleep in my bed because he was not fit. However, I made him feel fine, helped. I had a long talk with the boys.

Tuesday, 14: Shell struck opposite to dugout and sent tiles down steps. The Captain of E Battery visited me to-day, and then I visited the Battery and had chow with them. Airplane fight: while batteries were roaring, the Germans came down in flames.

Wednesday, 15: No coming to dugout in the day-time on account of shelling. I did good business in the evening and also had long services by request of the boys. Received a letter from B—— here to-day, I slept good.

Thursday, 16: I visited army, the officers and men of F Battery. Their chow kitchen is in a bad place, all men coming down sick. I had an arrangement with the doughboys that they might come in my dugout any hour in the night, whenever they wanted. I visited infantry officers to-day, Capt. Cribbs and Capt. Crisp, I had a lovely talk with them. I offered to go to the trenches with my goods, but Capt. Cribbs said I would just be killed without doing what he knew I wanted to do, namely, serve the boys with food and encourage them.

Friday, 17: I was startled by a fearful barrage at four o'clock when I got up, washed my clothes: was visited by the Y.M.C.A. Secretary: was shelled from five o'clock till ten o'clock. I went for chow and found shell ball gone through kitchen. High explosive, black smoke shells bursting intermittently, tiles fell into my dugout. I took pick shovel in with me; my kitten ran away but came back. A three-legged cat came to the ruined home where I am; its leg evidently had been cut off by shrapnel. Great air fight all day. Incendiary shells were fired into the town and burnt for a long time. I visited Battery F, and gave the fellows medicine. To-day both officers and men were in the gun pits and I with them, while they were deviling with Fritzy. Big business in evening with long service, gave out Testaments and held service in dugout; got a Frenchman to interpret the scripture to his comrades. Requests for prayer. Doughboys came in 12:30, through a barrage, and got sixty-five bars of chocolate, others got biscuits. I am very, very tired; artillery is roaring as I go to sleep.

Saturday, 18: Capt. Cribbs came down to dugout and said he was worried to death over me (thought I was killed). I assured him I was all O.K., and that it was their end of the town that needed looking after. He laughed and enjoyed it. My supplies are kept up by the courage and devotion of the Staff-Captain and Billy, who, taking their lives in their hands, bring the Ford with supplies along the shell-torn road at great peril. Capt. Corliss also came.

During the day, the officer of Battery F wanted the Victrola and got the use of it in their dugout for three days. In the meantime I had furnished Battery D the use of the Victrola and the day I made the promise, I found the boys without chow for twelve hours. When about to serve it, the town was gassed and their food with it and no one was permitted to touch a thing, they were blessing the Kaiser as only soldiers can under such circumstances. When I arrived among them, after finding out the way of things, I suggested to the officers that I should be permitted to supply them with such food as I had. They assured me it would be a mighty good thing for them if I would, and I took four boxes of biscuits and six pots of jam and other things to their trench in the rear of their batteries—they surely thought I was an angel and I left them pretty happy. This was all done under fire and at great risk. I chowed with Battery E and saw shell hole through building which was new since my last visit—boys offer to teach me how to work gun, their spirit is wonderful under the terrific strain which they labor. I visited ruined church and went inside; here were some graves of the French soldiers, some of the bodies being exposed. Could not stay very long. Overtook soldier-boy limping, got him to stay awhile and gave him hot chocolate; persuaded him to let his limb be seen to, which he did, and was sent to hospital. I visited hospital corps-fellows and arranged that in case of gas, they would visit and rouse me at night. They are fine fellows. Doughboys bought lots of goods and blessed the Salvation Army a thousand times. These lads come in from the trenches and have some hair-raising stories to tell.

Sunday, 19: Quiet till the afternoon when a gas barrage started. I was driven out of my dugout. I had a narrow escape, while reaching the hospital corps dugout. Lieut. Roolan (since promoted), of the Fifth Field Artillery, was there for two hours and half. 480 shells, I was informed, came down, averaging up three and four per minute. All night, from 6 o'clock to 3 A.M., 3000 shells are sent into the town. I slept in the Headquarters Signal Corps dugout with my gas mask on all night.

Monday, 20: Visited Y.M.C.A. and found their dugout had been struck and the Secretary's eyes were gassed after a man took his place. I saw Colonel Crane to try and get out of my dugout and get the one he had left. He gave me permission, assuring me that it was not a very good one at that. I took my Victrola with two of the battery boys from F Battery. I carried the records and they the Victrola. We dodged the shelling all the way and I had the pleasure of hearing the "Swanee River" song at the same time as the firing of the big guns much to the enjoyment of the boys. I understand that General Summerall visited and heard the Victrola soon after I had taken it to the boys. I placed about fifty books among officers of the Hospital Corps, Infantry officers, Battery officers. They were highly appreciated. I slept with Signal Corps boys again as Fritzy decided to continue the bombardment of the town which he did from 5.30 P.M. to 5.30 A.M. I slept with mask on and had no ill effects of the gas at all so far; but about five o'clock a terrific crash just outside of my dugout followed by a man shouting as he rushed down the dugout steps, "Oh, God, get me to the doctor right away." That shell nearly got me. I was only eight feet from it. I sprung up and rushed him from the dugout over to the hospital. I had to chase around from one dugout to another and finally landed my man (his name was Harry), who was taken to the hospital.

Tuesday, 21: After taking the man to the doctor, I went to my own place and found a nine-inch gas shrapnel shell had burst 15 or 20 feet from my dugout, about fifteen holes were torn through the door, the top of the shell lay six feet from the top of the steps, pieces of the shell were scattered down the steps and my dugout to the gas curtain, was full of gas. If Staff-Captain and Billy had been visiting me that night, the shell would have hit the Ford right in the center. Fierce bombardment all the day. Houses were struck on the entire street from end to end. Shells fell in the yard, one struck the corner of the house. The soldiers next door have gone, and my place can only be opened in the evenings. Things are pretty hot, I started out visiting the batteries to-day, but was driven back and could get out only by the back entrance to the yard. I am told by a soldier of the Intelligence Dept., that their bombardment is what is known as a "Million-Dollar Barrage," and that all were fortunate to have passed through it, he also told me the number and nature of the shells. I served hot chocolate this Tuesday night and noticed that my hands were very red.

Wednesday, 22: I visited the Battery in their trenches again and took them food. My eyes are affected by the gas, and I got treatment at the Evacuating Hospital. Some shells come very close to my dugout—to-day thirty feet, fifty feet and twenty feet. I gather up a box full of remnants. I find I am gassed by a contact with the poor fellow coming in whom I took to the doctor. I get treatment two or three times for my eyes and throat. My hands begin to crack and smart. The flesh comes off from my neck and other parts of my body. I had a fine meeting with boys in dugout and am again visited by the doughboys and officers. I visit the ruined church area again and get a few relics.

Thursday, 23: My eyes are very red and becoming painful and also my throat and nose, etc. I plan to move my dugout and pack up accordingly. Things are quieter to-day; had services again in the evening. French schoolmaster among the number, six requests for prayer.

Friday, 24: Am all ready to move to a new dugout when Staff-Captain arrives and tells me I am ordered out by the military."

Here is the Military Order received by the Staff-Captain:

"To Major Coe,
    "Salvation Army:
    "(1) Major Wilson, Chief G1, directs that the Salvation Army evacuate 'Coullemelle' as soon as possible:

"(2) He desires that they leave to-night if possible.

"(3) This message was received by me from the office of G1.

"L. Johnson,

"1st Lieut., F.A."

Orders also arrived soon for the removal of the Salvation Army workers in Broyes:

"Headquarters, 1st Division, G-1.

"American Expeditionary Forces,

"June 3, 1919.

"Memorandum: To Mr. L. A. Coe, Salvation Army, La Folie.

"The hut, which it is understood the Salvation Army is operating in Broyes, will, for military reasons, be removed from there as soon as practicable.

"It is contrary to the desire of the Commanding General that women workers be employed in huts or canteens east of the line Mory-Chepoix-Tartigny, and if any are now so located they are to be removed.

"The operations of technical services, Red Cross, Y.M.C.A., and other similar agencies is a function of this section of the General Staff and all questions pertaining to your movements and location of huts should in the future be referred by G.-1.

"By command of Major General Bullard.

"G. K. Wilson,

"Major, General Staff,

"A. C. of S., G.-1."

In Tartigny they found a house with five rooms, one of them very large. The billeting officer turned this over to the Salvation Army.

There was plenty of space and the girls might have a room to themselves here, instead of just curtaining off a corner of a tent or making a partition of supply boxes in one end of the hut as they often had to do. There was also plenty of furniture in the house, and they were allowed to go around the village and get chairs and tables or anything they wanted to fix up their canteen. The girls had great fun selecting easy-chairs and desks and anything they desired from the deserted houses, and before long the result was a wonderfully comfortable, cozy, home-like room.

"Gee! This is just like heaven, coming in here!" one of the boys said when he first saw it.

Just outside Tartigny there was a large ammunition dump, piles of shells and boxes of other ammunition. It was under the trees and well camouflaged, but night after night the enemy airplanes kept trying to get it. The girls used to sit in the windows and watch the airplane battles. They would stay until an airplane got over the house and then they would run to the cellar. They came so close one night that pieces of shell from the anti-aircraft guns fell over the house.

Sometimes the airplanes would come in the daytime, and the girls got into the habit of running out into the street to watch them. But at this the boys protested:

"Don't do that, you will get hit!" they begged. And one day the nose of an unexploded shell fell in the street just outside the door. After that they were more careful.

In this town one afternoon a whole truck-load of oranges arrived, being three hundred crates, four hundred oranges to a crate, for the canteen, and they were all gone by four o'clock!

The Headquarters of the Division Commander were in a beautiful old stone chateau of a peculiar color that seemed to be invisible to the airplanes. There were woods all around it and the house was never shelled. It was filled with rare old tapestries and beautiful furniture.

The Count who owned the chateau asked the Major General to get some furniture that belonged to him out of the village that was being shelled. Later the Count asked the General if he ever got that furniture. The General asked his Colonel, "What did you do with that furniture?" "Oh," the Colonel said, "it's down there all right!" "And where is the piano?" "Oh, I gave that to the Salvation Army."

In this area it was one lassie's first bombardment; it came suddenly and without warning. The soldiers in the hut decamped without ceremony for the safety of their dugouts. One soldier who had been detailed to help the lassie, shouted: "Come on! Follow me to your dugout!" Without further talk he turned and started for cover. The girl had been baking. A tray full of luscious lemon cream pies stood on the table. She did not want to leave those pies to the tender mercies of a shell. Also she had some new boots standing beneath the table, and she was not going to lose those. Without stopping to think, she seized the shoes in one hand and the tray in the other and rushed after the soldier. A little gully had to be crossed on the way to the dugout and the only bridge was a twelve-inch plank. The soldier crossed in safety and turned to look after the girl. Just as she reached the middle of the plank a shell burst not far away. The lassie was so startled that she nearly lost her balance, swaying first one way and then the other. In an attempt to stop the tray of pies from slipping, she almost lost the shoes, and in recovering the shoes, the pies just escaped sliding overboard into the thick mud below.

The soldier registered deep agitation.

"Drop the shoes!" he shouted. "I can clean the shoes,

but for heaven's sake don't drop them pies!" And the lassie obeyed meekly.

In the little town of Bonnet where the rest room was located in an old barn connected with a Catholic convent, one Salvation Army Envoy and his wife from Texas began their work. They soon became known to the soldiers familiarly as "Pa" and "Ma."

It was in this old barn that the tent top, later made famous at Ansauville, was first used. Stoves were almost impossible to obtain at that time, but "Ma" was determined that she would bake pies for the men, so the Envoy constructed an oven out of two tin cake boxes and using a small two-burner gasoline stove, "Ma" baked biscuits and pies that made her name famous. Through her great motherly heart and her willingness to serve the boys at all times, under all circumstances, she won their confidence and love. One soldier said he would walk five miles any day to look into "Ma's" gray eyes.

From Bonnet they were transferred to command a hut at Ansauville, but "Ma" could never rest so long as there was a soldier to be served in any way. She worked early and late, and she made each individual soldier who came to the hut her special charge as if he were her own son. She could not sleep when they were going over the top unless she prayed with each one before he went.

The meetings which she and her husband held were full of life and power and were never neglected, no matter how hard the strain might be from other lines of service.

It was not long before "Ma's" strength gave out and it was necessary to move her to a quieter place. She was transferred to Houdelainecourt. She would not go until they carried her away.

Houdelainecourt at this time was on the main road

travelled by trucks, taking supplies by train from the railroad at Gondrecourt to the front. Truck drivers invariably made it a point to stop at "Ma's" hut and here they were always sure to receive a welcome and the most delicious doughnuts and pies and hot biscuit which loving hands could make.

Not satisfied with this service alone, she undertook to fry pancakes for the officers' breakfast. It was through these kindly services, ungrudgingly done, at any time of the day or night, that her name was established as one of the most potent factors in contributing to the comfort and welfare of the men, and there was no hole or tear of the men's clothes that "Ma" could not mend.

A short time after the pie contest over at Gondrecourt, "Ma" and one of her lassie helpers set out to break the record of 316 pies as a day's work. Their oven would hold but six pies at a time; their hut had but just been opened and all their equipment had not yet arrived, so they were short a rolling pin, which had to be carved from a broken wagon-shaft with a jack-knife before they could begin; but they achieved the baking of 324 pies between 6 A.M. and 6 P.M. that day. It is fair to state for the sake of the doubter, however, that the pie fillers, both pumpkin and apple, were all prepared and piping hot on the stove ready to be poured into the pastry as it was put into the oven, which, of course, helped a good deal.

A sign was put out announcing that pie would be served at seven o'clock, but the lines formed long before that. The pies were unusually large and cut into fifths, but even at that they were much larger pieces than are usually served at the ordinary restaurant.

By half-past eight some men were falling in for a second helping, but "Ma" had been watching long a little company of men off to one side who hovered about yet never dropped into line themselves, and made up her mind that these were some of those who perhaps sent much of their money home and found it a long time between pay-days. Casting her kindly eye comprehendingly toward these men she mounted a chair and requested:

"All of the men who have already had pie, please step out of the line; and all of those boys who want coffee and pie but have no money, step into line and get some, *anyhow!*"

She gave the boys one of her beautiful motherly smiles and that made them feel they had all got home, and they hesitated no longer. "Ma," however, was more deeply interested in her meetings than in mere pie. The Sunday before this contest over five hundred soldiers had attended the evening meeting, and almost as many had been present at the morning service. Also, there had been twenty-eight members added to her Bible class. Though the hut was a large one it had been crowded to its utmost capacity in the evening, with men packed into the open doorways and windows on either side, and forty of the men who announced their determination to follow Christ that night could not get inside to come forward. More than a dozen gave personal testimony of what Christ had done for them. One notable testimony was as follows:

"I used to be a hard guy fellers," he said, "and maybe I had some good reasons when I used to say that nothing was ever going to scare me, but when we lay out there with a six-hour barrage busting right in front of us and 'arrivals' busting all around us, I did a whole lot of thinking. It seemed as though every shell had my number on it! And when we went over and ran square into their barrage, I'll admit I was scared yellow and was darned afraid I was going to show it! We were under a barrage for ten hours. A shell buried me under about a foot of earth, and for the first time I can remember, while my bunkie was digging me out, I prayed to God. And I want to say that I believe He answered my prayer, and that is the only reason I came out uninjured. I promised if I got out I'd call for a new deal, and I want to say that I'm going to keep that promise!"

A boy who had been converted in one of the meetings a few nights before came into the hut and sought her out. He told her he was going over the top that night, and he had something he wanted to confess before he went. He had told a lie and he had felt terrible remorse about it ever since he was converted. He had treated his mother badly, and gone and enlisted, saying he was eighteen when he was only sixteen. "Now," said he with relief after he had told the story, "that's all clear. And say, if I'm killed, will you go through my pockets and find my Testament and send it to mother? And will you tell my mother all about it and tell her it is all right with me now? Tell mother I went over the top a Christian. You'll know what to say to her to help her bear up."

She promised and the boy went away content. That night he was killed, and, true to her promise, she went through his pockets when he was brought back, and found the little Testament close over his heart; and in it a verse was marked for his mother:

"The blood of Jesus Christ His Son cleanseth us from all sin."

During the early days of the Salvation Army work in France, while the work was still under inspection as to its influence on the men, and one Colonel had sent a Captain around to the meetings to report upon them to him, "Ma's" was one of the meetings to which the Captain came.

She did not know that she was under suspicion, but

that night she spoke on obedience and discipline, taking as her text: "Take heed to the law," and urging the men to obey both moral and military laws so that they might be better men and better soldiers. The Captain reported on her sermon and said that he wished the regiment had a Salvation Army chaplain for every company.

The hospital visitation work was started by "Ma" in the Paris hospitals while she was in that city for several months regaining her strength after a physical breakdown at the front. She was idolized by the wounded. If she walked along any hospital passageway or through any ward, a crowd of men were sure to call her by name. They knew her as "Ma," and frequently, overworked nurses have called up the Paris Salvation Army Headquarters asking if Ma could not find time to come down and sit with a dying boy who was calling for her. She observed their birthdays with books and other small presents, wrote to their mothers, wives and sweethearts, and performed a multitude of invaluable, precious little services of love. For weeks after she left Paris, returning to the front, the wounded called for her. She is one of the outstanding figures of the Salvation Army's work with the American Expeditionary Forces in France. She is indelibly enshrined in the hearts of hundreds of American soldiers.

A Salvation Army lassie bent over the bed of a wounded boy recently arrived in the Paris hospital from the front, and gave him an orange and a little sack of candy.

"I know the Salvation Army," he said with a faint smile, "I knew I should find you here."

She asked him his division and he told her he belonged to one that had been cooperating with the French.

"But how can that be?" she asked in surprise, "we

have never worked with your division. How do you know about us?"

"I only saw the Salvation Army once," he replied, "but I'll never forget it. It was when I came back to consciousness in the Dressing Station at Cheppy, and the first thing I saw was a Salvation Army girl bending over me washing the blood and dirt off my face with cold water. She looked like an angel and she was that to me. She gave me a drink of cold lemonade when I was burning up with fever, and she lifted my head to pour it between my lips when I had not strength to move myself. No, I shall not forget!"

One bright young fellow with a bandaged eye turned a cheerful grin toward the Salvation Army visitor as she said with compassion: "Son, I'm sorry you've lost your eye."

"Oh, that's nothing," was the gay reply, "I can see everything out of the other eye. I've got seven holes in me, too, but believe me I'm not going home for the loss of an eye and seven holes! I'll get out yet and get into the fight!"

The Salvation Army officer and his wife who were stationed at Bonvillers visited every man in the local hospital every day, sleeping every night in the open fields. As they are quite elderly, this was no little hardship, especially in rainy weather.

Five lassies stationed at Noyers St. Martin were for several weeks forced by the nightly shelling and air-raids to take their blankets out into the fields at night and sleep under the stars. One of these girls was called "Sunshine" because of her smile.

On the eve of Decoration Day a military Colonel visited her in the hut. He seemed rather depressed, perhaps by the ceremonies of the day, and said that he had come to be cheered up. In parting he said, "Little girl, you had better get out of town early to-night; I feel as though something is going to happen." Less than an hour later, while the girls were just preparing for the night in a field half a mile distant, an aerial bomb dropped by an aviator on the house in which he was billeted killed him and two other Captains who were sitting with him at the time. He had been a great friend of the Salvation Army.

Out in a little village in Indiana there grew a fair young flower of a girl. Her mother was a dear Christian woman and she was brought up in her mother's church, which she loved. When she was only twelve years old she had a remarkable and thorough old-fashioned conversion, giving herself with all her childish heart to the Saviour. She feels that she had a kind of vision at that time of what the Lord wanted her to be, a call to do some special work for Christ out in the world, helping people who did not know Him, people who were sick and poor and sorrowful. She did not tell her vision to anyone. She did not even know that anywhere in the world were any people doing the kind of work she felt she would like to do, and God had called her to do. She was shy about it and kept her thoughts much to herself. She loved her own church, and its services, but somehow that did not quite satisfy her.

One day when she was about fourteen years old the Salvation Army came to the town where she lived and opened work, holding its meetings in a large hall or armory. With her young companions she attended these meetings and was filled with a longing to be one of these earnest Christian workers.

Her mother, accustomed to a quiet conventional church and its way of doing Christian work, was horrified; and in alarm sent her away to visit her uncle, who was a Baptist minister. The daughter, dutiful and sweet, went willingly away, although she had many a longing for these new friends of hers who seemed to her to have found the way of working for God that had been her own heart's desire for so long.

Meantime her gay young brother, curious to know what had so stirred his bright sister, went to the Salvation Army meetings to find out, and was attracted himself. He went again and found Jesus Christ, and himself joined the Salvation Army. The mother in this case did not object, perhaps because she felt that a boy needed more safeguards than a girl, perhaps because the life of publicity would not trouble her so much in connection with her son as with her daughter.

The daughter after several months away from home returned, only to find her longing to join the Salvation Army stronger. But quietly and sweetly she submitted to her mother's wish and remained at home for some years, like her Master before her, who went down to His home in Nazareth and was subject to His father and mother; showing by her gentle submission and her lovely life that she really had the spirit of God in her heart and was not merely led away by her enthusiasm for something new and strange.

When she was twenty her mother withdrew her objections, and the daughter became a Salvationist, her mother coming to feel thoroughly in sympathy with her during the remaining years she lived.

This is the story of one of the Salvation Army lassies who has been giving herself to the work in the huts over in France. She is still young and lovely, and there is something about her delicate features and slender grace that makes one think of a young saint. No wonder the soldiers almost worshipped her! No wonder these lassies were as safe over there ten miles from any other woman or any other civilian alone among ten thousand soldiers, as if they had been in their own homes. They breathed the spirit of God as they worked, as well as when they sang and prayed. To such a girl a man may open his heart and find true help and strength.

It was no uncommon thing for our boys who were so afraid of anything like religion or anything personal over here, to talk to these lassies about their souls, to ask them what certain verses in the Bible meant, and to kneel with them in some quiet corner behind the chocolate boxes and be prayed with, yes, and *pray!* It is because these girls have let the Christ into their lives so completely that He lives and speaks through them, and the boys cannot help but recognize it.

Not every boy who was in a Salvation hut meeting has given himself to Christ, of course, but every one of them recognizes this wonderful something in these girls. Ask them. They will tell you "She is the real thing!" They won't tell you more than that, perhaps, unless they have really grown in the Christian life, but they mean that they have recognized in her spirit a likeness to the spirit of Christ.

Now and then, of course, there was a thick-headed one who took some minutes to recognize holiness. Such would enter a hut with an oath upon his lips, or an unclean story, and straightway all the men who were sitting at the tables writing or standing about the room would come to attention with one of those little noisy silences that mean so much; pencils would click down on the table like a challenge, and the newcomer would look up to find the cold glances of his fellows upon him.

The boys who frequented the huts broke the habit of swearing and telling unclean stories, and officers began to realize that their men were better in their work because of this holy influence that was being thrown about them. One officer said his men worked better, and kept their engines oiled up so they wouldn't be delayed on the road, that they might get back to the hut early in the evening. The picture of a girl stirring chocolate kept the light of hope going in the heart of many a homesick lad.

One ignorant and exceedingly "fresh" youth, once walked boldly into a hut, it is said, and jauntily addressed the lassie behind the counter as "Dearie." The sweet blue eyes of the lassie grew suddenly cold with aloofness, and she looked up at the newcomer without her usual smile, saying distinctly: *"What did you say?"*

The soldier stared, and grew red and unhappy:

"Oh! I beg your pardon!" he said, and got himself out of the way as soon as possible. These lassies needed no chaperon. They were young saints to the boys they served, and they had a cordon of ten thousand faithful soldiers drawn about them night and day. As a military Colonel said, the Salvation Army lassie was the only woman in France who was safe unchaperoned.

When this lassie from Indiana came back on a short furlough after fifteen months in France with the troops, and went to her home for a brief visit, the Mayor gave the home town a holiday, had out the band and waited at the depot in his own limousine for four hours that he might not miss greeting her and doing her honor.

Here is the poem which Pte. Joseph T. Lopes wrote about "Those Salvation Army Folks" after the Montdidier attack:

> *Somewhere in France, not far from the foe,*
> *There's a body of workers whose name we all know;*
> *Who not only at home give their lives to make right,*
> *But are now here beside us, fighting our fight.*
> *What care they for rest when our boys at the front,*
> *Who, fighting for freedom, are bearing the brunt,*

And so, just at dawn, when the caissons come home,
With the boys tired out and chilled to the bone,
The Salvation army with its brave little crew,
Are waiting with doughnuts and hot coffee, too.
When dangers and toiling are o'er for awhile,
In their dugouts we find comfort and welcome their smile.
There's a spirit of home, so we go there each night,
And the thinking of home makes us sit down and write,
So we tell of these folks to our loved ones with pride,
And are thanking the Lord to have them on our side.

The Toul Sector Again

WHEN the German offensive was definitely checked in the Montdidier Sector, the First Division was transferred back to the Toul Sector and the Salvation Army moved with it. They had in the meantime maintained all the huts which had been established originally, and with the return of the First Division, they established additional huts between Font and Nancy. When the St. Mihiel drive came off, they followed the advancing troops, establishing huts in the devastated villages, keeping in as close contact with the extreme front as was possible, serving the troops day and night, always aiming to be at the point where the need was the greatest, and where they could be of the greatest service.

The first Americans to pay the supreme sacrifice in the cause of liberty were buried in the Toul Sector.

As it drew near to Decoration Day there came a message from over the sea from the Commander to her faithful band of workers, saying that she was sending American flags, one for every American soldier's grave, and that she wanted the graves cared for and decorated;

and at all the various locations of Salvation Army workers they prepared to do her bidding.

The day before the thirtieth of May they took time from their other duties to clear away the mud, dead grass and fallen leaves from the graves, and heap up the mounds where they had been washed flat by the rains, making each one smooth, regular and tidy. At the head of each grave was a simple wooden cross bearing the name of the soldier who lay there, his rank, his regiment and the date of his death. Into the back of each cross they drove a staple for a flag, and they swept and garnished the place as best they could.

One Salvation Army woman writing home told of the plans they had made in Treveray for Decoration Day; how Commander Booth was sending enough American flags to decorate every American grave in France, and how they meant to gather flowers and put with the flags, and have a little service of prayer over the graves.

In the gray old French cemetery of Treveray five American boys lay buried. The flowers upon their graves were dry and dead, for their regiments had moved on and left them. The graves had been neglected and only the guarding wooden crosses remained above the rough earth to show that someone had cared and had stopped to put a mark above the places where they lay. It was these graves the Salvation Army woman now proposed to decorate on Memorial Day.

The letter went to the Captain for censorship, and soon the Salvation Army woman had a call from him.

"I understand by one of your letters that you are thinking of decorating the American graves," he said. "We would like to help in that, if you don't mind. I would like the company all to be present."

The day before Memorial Day this woman with two

of the lassies from the hut went to the cemetery and prepared for the morrow.

In the morning they gathered great armfuls of crimson poppies from the fields, creamy snowballs from neglected gardens, and blue bachelor buttons from the hillsides, which they arranged in bouquets of red, white and blue for the graves. They had no vases in which to place the flowers but they used the apple tins in which the apples for their pies had been canned.

The centuries-old gray cemetery nestled in a curve of the road between wheat fields on every side. A gray, moss-covered, lichen-hung wall surrounded it. The five American graves were under the shadow of the Western wall, and the sun was slowly sinking in his glory as the company of soldiers escorted the women into the cemetery. They passed between the ponderous old gray stones, and beaded wreaths of the French graves; and the officers and men lined up facing the five graves. The women placed the tricolored flowers in the cans prepared for them, and planted the flags beside them. Then the elder woman, who had sons of her own, stepped out and saluted the military commanding officer: "Colonel," said she, "with your permission we would like to follow our custom and offer a prayer for the bereaved." Instantly permission was given and every head was uncovered as the Salvationist poured out her heart in prayer to the Everlasting Father, commending the dead into His tender keeping, and pleading for the sorrow-stricken friends across the sea, until the soldiers' tears fell unchecked as they stood with rifles stiffly in front of them listening to the quiet voice of the woman as she prayed. God seemed Himself to come down, and the living boys standing over their five dead comrades could not help but be enfolded in His love, and feel the sense of His presence. They knew that they, too, might soon be sleeping even as these at their feet. It seemed but a step to the other life.

When the prayer was finished a firing squad fired five volleys over the graves, and then the bugler played the taps and the little service was over. The lassies lingered to take pictures of the graves and that night they wrote letters describing the ceremony, to be sent with the photographs to the War Department at Washington with the request that they be forwarded to the nearest relatives of the five men buried at Treveray.

There were exercises at Menil-la-Tour and here they had built a simple platform in the centre of the ground and erected a flagpole at one corner.

When the morning came two regimental bands took up their positions in opposite corners of the cemetery and began to play. The French populace had turned out en masse. They took up their stand just outside the little cemetery, next to them the soldiers were lined up, then the Red Cross, then the Y.M.C.A. Beyond, a little hill rose sloping gently to the sky line, and over it a mile away was the German front, with the shells coming over all the time.

It was an impressive scene as all stood with bared heads just outside the little enclosure where eighty-one wooden crosses marked the going of as many brave spirits who had walked so blithely into the crisis and given their young lives.

Some French officers had brought a large, beautiful wreath to do honor to the American heroes, and this was placed at the foot of the great central flagpole.

The bands played, and they all sang. It was announced that but for the thoughtfulness and kindness of Commander Evangeline Booth in sending over flags those graves would have gone undecorated that day.

The Commanding General then came to the front

and behind him walked the Salvation Army lassies bearing the flags in their arms.

Down the long row of graves he passed. He would take a flag from one of the girls, slip it in the staple back of the cross, stand a moment at salute, then pass on to the next. It was very still that May morning, broken only by the awesome boom of battle just over the hill, but to that sound all had grown accustomed. The people stood with that hush of sorrow over them which only the majesty of death can bring to the hearts of a crowd, and there were tears in many eyes and on the faces of rough soldiers standing there to honor their comrades who had been called upon to give their lives to the great cause of freedom.

A little breeze was blowing and into the solemn stillness there stole a new sound, the silken ripple of the flags as one by one they were set fluttering from the crosses, like a soft, growing, triumphant chorus of those to come whose lives were to be made safe because these had died. As if the flag would waft back to the Homeland, and the stricken mothers and fathers, sisters and sweethearts, some idea of the greatness of the cause in which they died to comfort them in their sorrow.

Out through each line the General passed, placing the flags and solemnly saluting, till eighty graves had been decorated and there was only one left; but there was no flag for the eighty-first grave! Somehow, although they thought they had brought several more than were needed, they were one short. But the General stood and saluted the grave as he had the others, and later the flag was brought and put in place, so that every American grave in the Toul Sector that day had its flag fluttering from its cross.

Then the General and the soldiers saluted the large flag. It was an impressive moment with the deep thunder of the guns just over the hill reminding of more battle and more lives to be laid down.

The General then addressed the soldiers, and facing toward the West and pointing he said:

"Out there in that direction is Washington and the President, and all the people of the United States, who are looking to you to set the world free from tyranny. Over there are the mothers who have bade you good-bye with tears and sent you forth, and are waiting at home and praying for you, trusting in you. Out there are the fathers and the sisters and the sweethearts you have left behind, all depending on you to do your best for the Right. Now," said he in a clear ringing voice, "turn and salute America!" And they all turned and saluted toward the West, while the band played softly "My Country 'Tis of Thee!"

It was a wonderful, beautiful, solemn sight, every man standing and saluting while the flags fluttered softly on the breeze.

Behind the little French Catholic church in the village of Bonvilliers there was quite a large field which had been turned over to the Americans for a cemetery. The Military Major had caused an arch to be made over the gateway inscribed with the words: "NATIONAL CEMETERY OF THE AMERICAN EXPEDITIONARY FORCES." There were over two hundred graves inside the cemetery.

On Decoration Day the Regimental Band led a parade through the village streets to the graveyard, the French women in black and little French children, with wreaths made of wonderful beaded flowers cunningly constructed from beads strung on fine wires, marching in the parade. Arrived at the cemetery they all stood drawn up in line while the Military Major gave a beautiful address, first in French and then in English. He then told the French children and women to take their places one at each grave, and lay down their tributes of flowers for the Americans. Following this the Salvation Army placed flags on each on behalf of the mothers of the boys who were lying there.

It was noon-day. The sun was very bright and every white cross bearing the name of the fallen glittered in the sun. Even the worst little hovel over in France is smothered in a garden and bright with myriads of flowers, so everything was gay with blossoms and everybody had brought as many as could be carried.

Over in one corner of the cemetery were two German graves, and one of the lassies of that organization which proclaims salvation for all men went and laid some blossoms there also.

At La Folie one of the Salvation Army lassies going across the fields on some errand of mercy found three American graves undecorated and bare on Memorial Day, and turning aside from the road she gathered great armfuls of scarlet poppies from the fields and came and laid them on the three mounds, then knelt and prayed for the friends of the boys whose bodies were lying there.

The whole world was startled and saddened when the news came that Lieutenant Quentin Roosevelt had been shot down in his airplane in action and fallen within the enemy's lines.

He was crudely buried by the Germans where he fell, near Chambray, and a rude cross set up to mark the place. All around were pieces of his airplane shattered on the ground and left as they had fallen.

When the spot fell into the hands of the Allies, the grave was cared for by the Salvation Army; a new white cross set up beside the old one, and gentle hands smoothed the mound and made it shapely. On Decoration Day Colonel Barker placed upon this grave the beautiful flowers arranged for by cable by Commander Booth.

The girls went down to decorate the two hundred American graves at Mandres, and even while they bent over the flaming blossoms and laid them on the mounds an air battle was going on over their heads. Close at hand was the American artillery being moved to the front on a little narrow-gauge railroad that ran near to the graveyard, and the Germans were firing and trying to get them.

But the girls went steadily on with their work, scattering flowers and setting flags until their service of love was over. Then they stood aside for the prayer and a song. One of the Salvation Army Captains with a fine voice began to sing:

> *"My loved ones in the Homeland*
> *Are waiting me to come,*
> *Where neither death nor sorrow*
> *Invades their holy home;*
> *O dear, dear native country!*
> *O rest and peace above!*
> *Christ, bring us all to the Homeland*
> *Of Thy redeeming love."*

Into the midst of the song came the engine on the little narrow track straight toward where he stood, and he had to step aside onto a pile of dirt to finish his song.

That same Captain went on ahead to the Home Land not long after when the epidemic of influenza swept over the world; and he was given the honor of a military funeral.

6

The Baccarat Sector

BACCARAT was the Zone Headquarters for that Sector.

Down the Main street there hung a sign on an old house labeled "MODERN BAR."

Inside everything was all torn up. It had never been opened since the battles of 1914. The Germans had lived there and everything was in an awful condition. One wonders how they endured themselves. The Military detailed two men for two days to spade up and carry away the filth from the bedrooms, and it took two women an entire week all but one day, scrubbing all day long until their shoulders ached, to scrub the place clean. But they got it clean. They were the kind of women that did not give up even when a thing seemed an impossibility. This was the sort of thing they were up against continually. They could have no meetings that week, because they had to scrub and make the place fit for a Salvation Army hut.

Two of the lassies were awakened early one bright morning by the sound of an axe ringing rhythmically on wood, just back of their canteen. It was a cheerful sound to wake to, for the girls had been through a long wearing day and night, and they knew when they went to sleep that the wood was almost gone. It was always so pleasant to have someone offer to cut it for them, for they never liked to have to ask help of the soldiers if they could possibly avoid it. But there was so much else to be done besides cutting wood. Not that they could not do that, too, when the need offered. The sisters looked sleepily at one another, thinking simultaneously of the poor homesick doughboy who had told them the day before that chopping wood for them made him think of home and mother and that was why he liked to do it. Of course, it was he hard at work for them before they were up, and they smiled contentedly, with a lifted prayer for the poor fellow. They knew he had received no mail for four months and that only a few days before he had read in a paper sent to one of his pals of the death of his sister. Of course, his heart was breaking, for he knew what his widowed mother was suffering. They knew that his salvation from homesickness just now lay in giving him something to do, so they lingered a little just to give him the chance, and planned how they would let him help with the doughnuts, and fix the benches, later, when the wood was cut.

In a few minutes the girls were ready for the day's work and went around to the kitchen, where the sound of the ringing axe was still heard in steady strokes. But when they rounded the corner of the kitchen and greeted the wood-chopper cheerily, he looked up, and lo! it was not the homesick doughboy as they had supposed, but the Colonel of the regiment himself who smiled half apologetically at them, saying he liked his new job; and when they invited him to breakfast he accepted the invitation with alacrity.

After breakfast the girls went to work making pies. There had been no oven in the little French town in which they were stationed, and so baking had been impossible, but the boys kept talking and talking about pies until one day a Lieutenant found an old French stove in some ruins. They had to half bury it in the earth to make it strong enough for use, but managed to make it work at last, and though much hampered by the limitations of the small oven, they baked enough to give all the boys a taste of pie once a week or so. Pie day was so welcomed that it almost made a riot, so many boys wanted a slice.

They were having a meeting one night at Baccarat. There was a great deal of noise going on outside the dugout. The shells were falling around rather indiscriminately, but it takes more than shell fire to stop a Salvation Army meeting at the front. There is only one thing that will stop it, and that is a sudden troop movement. It is the same way with baseball, for the week before this meeting two regimental baseball teams played seven innings of air-tight ball while the shells were falling not three hundred yards away at the roadside edge of their ball-ground. During the seven innings only eight hits were allowed by the two pitchers. The score was close and when at the end of the seventh a shell exploded within fifty yards of the diamond and an officer shouted: "Game called on account of shell fire!" there was considerable dissatisfaction expressed because the game was not allowed to continue. It is with the same spirit that the men attend their religious meetings. They come because they want to and they won't let anything interfere with it.

But on this particular night the meeting was in full force, and so were the shells. It had been a meeting in which the men had taken part, led by one of the women whose leadership was unquestioned among them, a personal testimony meeting in which several soldiers and an officer had spoken of what Christ had done for them. Then there was a solo by one of the lassies, and the Adjutant opened his Bible and began to read. He took as his text Isaiah 55:1. "Ho, every one that thirsteth, come ye to the waters, and he that hath no money; come ye, buy, and eat."

Those boys knew what it was to be thirsty, terrible thirst! They had come back from the lines sometimes their tongues parched and their whole bodies feverish with thirst and there was nothing to be had to drink until the Salvation Army people had appeared with good cold lemonade; and when they had no money they had given it to them just the same. Oh, they knew what that verse meant and their attention was held at once as the speaker went on to show plainly how Jesus Christ would give the water of life just as freely to those who were thirsty for it. And they were thirsty! They did not wish to conceal how thirsty they were for the living water.

Just in the midst of the talk the lights went out. Many a church under like conditions would have had a panic in no time, but this crowded audience sat perfectly quiet, listening as the speaker went on, quoting his Bible from memory where he could not read.

Over there in the corner on a bench sat the lassies, the women who had been serving them all through the hard days, as quiet and calm in the darkness as though they sat in a cushioned pew in some well-lit church in New York. It was as if the guns were like annoying little insects that were outside a screen, and now and then slipped in, so little attention did the audience pay to them. When all those who wished to accept this wonderful invitation were asked to come forward, seven men arose and stumbled through the darkness. The light from a bursting shell revealed for an instant the forms of these men as they knelt at the rough bench in front, one of them with his steel helmet hanging from his arm as he prayed aloud for his own salvation. No one who was in that meeting that night could doubt but that Jesus Christ Himself was there, and that those men all felt His presence.

In Bertrichamps the Salvation Army was given a large glass factory for a canteen. It made a beautiful place, and there was room to take care of eight hundred men at a time. This building was also used by the Y.M.C.A. as well as the Jews and the Catholics for their services, there being no other suitable place in town. But everybody worked together, and got along harmoniously.

Here there were some wonderful meetings, and it was great to hear the boys singing "When The Roll Is Called Up Yonder, I'll Be There." Perhaps if some of the half-hearted Christians at home could have caught the echo of that song sung with such earnestness by those boyish voices they would have had a revelation. It seemed as if the earth-film were more than half torn away from their young, wise eyes over there; and they found that earthly standards and earthly false-whisperings did not fit. They felt the spirit of the hour, they felt the spirit of the place, and of the people who were serving them patiently day by day; who didn't have to stay there and work; who might have kept in back of the lines and worked and sent things up now and then; but who chose to stay close with them and share their hardships. They felt that something more than just love to their fellow-men had instigated such unselfishness. They knew it was something they needed to help them through what was before them. They reached hungrily after the Christ and they found Him.

Then they testified in the meetings. Often as many as

twelve or more before an audience of five hundred would get up and tell what Jesus had become to them. In one meeting in this glass factory two hundred soldiers pledged to serve the Lord, to read their Bibles, and to pray.

There were in this place some Christian boys who came from families where they had been accustomed to family worship, and who now that they were far away from it, looked back with longing to the days when it had been a part of every day. Things look different over there with the sound of battle close at hand, and customs that had been a part of every-day life at home became very dear, perhaps dearer than they had ever seemed before. They found out that the Salvation Army people had prayers every night after they closed the canteen at half-past nine and went to their rooms in a house not far away, and so they begged that they might share the worship with them. So every night they took home fifteen or twenty men to the living-room of the house where they stayed just as many as they could crowd in, and there they would have a little Bible reading and prayer together. The Father only knows how many souls were strengthened and how many feet kept from falling because of those brief moments of worship with these faithful men and women of God.

"Oh, if you only knew what it means to us!" one of the men tried to tell them one day.

Sometimes men who said they hadn't prayed nor read their Bibles for years would be found in little groups openly reading a testament to each other.

When the girls opened their shutters in the morning they could look out over the spot in No Man's Land which was the scene of such frightful German atrocities in 1914.

Our field artillery, stationed in the woods, sent over to the Salvation Army to know if they wouldn't come over and cook something for them, they were starving for some home cooking. So two of the women put on their steel helmets and their gas masks, for the Boche planes were flying everywhere, and went over across No Man's Land to see if there was a place where they could open up a hut. They were walking along quietly, talking, and had not noticed the German plane that approached. They were so accustomed to seeing them by twos and threes that a single one did not attract their attention. Suddenly almost over their heads the Boche dropped a shell, trying to get them. But it was a dud and did not explode. Two American soldiers came tearing over, crying: "Girls! Are you hurt?"

"Oh, no," said one of them brightly. "The Lord wouldn't let that fellow get us."

The soldiers used strong language as they looked after the fast-vanishing plane, but then they glanced back at the women again with something unspoken in their eyes. They believed, those boys, they really did, that God protected those women; and they used to beg them to remain with their regiment when they were going near the front, because they wanted their prayers as a protection. Some of the regiments openly said they thought those girls' prayers had saved their lives.

That Boche plane, however, had not far to go. Before it reached Baccarat the Americans trained their guns on it and brought it down in flames.

The house occupied by the Salvation Army girls as a billet had a sad story connected with it. When the Germans had come the father was soon killed and four German officers had taken possession of the place for their Headquarters. They also took possession of the two little girls of the family, nine and fourteen years of age, to wait upon them. And the first command that was given these children was that they should wait upon the men nude! The youngest child was not old enough to understand what this meant, but the older one was in terror, and they begged and cried and pleaded but all to no purpose. The officer was inexorable. He told them that if they did not obey they would be shot.

The poor old grandfather and grandmother, too feeble to do anything, and powerless, of course, to aid, could only endure in agony. The grandmother, telling the Salvation Army women the story afterward, pointed with trembling fingers and streaming eyes to the two little graves in the yard and said: "Oh, it would have been so much better if he had shot them! They lie out there as the result of their infamous and inhuman treatment."

Some most amusing incidents came to the knowledge of the Salvation Army workers.

An old French woman, over eighty years of age, lived in one of the stricken villages on the Vosges front. Her home had been several times struck by shells and was frequently the target for enemy bombing squadrons. All through the war she refused to leave the home in which she had lived from earliest childhood.

"It is not the guns, nor the bombs which can frighten me," she told a Salvation Army lassie who was billeted with her for a time, "but I am very much afraid of the submarines."

The village was several hundred miles inland.

The activity was all at night, for no one dared be seen about in the daytime. It must be a very urgent duty that would call men forth into full view of the enemy. But as soon as the dark came on the men would crawl into the trenches, stick their rifles between the sandbags and get ready for work.

It seemed to be always raining. They said that when it wasn't actually raining it was either clearing off or just getting ready to rain again. Twenty minutes in the trenches and a man was all over mud, wet, cold, slippery mud. In his hair, down his neck, in his boots, everywhere.

Through the trenches just behind the standing place ran a deeper trench or drain to carry the water away, and this was covered over with a rough board called a duck-board. Underneath this duck-board ran a continual stream of water. A man would go along the trench in a hurry, make a misstep on one end of the duck-board and down he would go in mud and freezing water to the waist. In these cold, wet garments he must stay all night. The tension was very great.

As the soldiers had to work in the night, so the Salvation Army men and women worked in the night to serve them.

The Salvation Army men would visit the sentries and bring them coffee and doughnuts prepared in the dug-outs by the girls. It was exceedingly dangerous work. They would crawl through the connecting trenches, which were not more than three feet deep, and one must stoop to be safe, and get to the front-line trenches with their cans of coffee. They would touch a fellow on the shoulder, fill his mug with coffee, and slip him some doughnuts. At such times the things were always given, not sold. They did not dare even to whisper, for the enemy listening posts were close at hand and the slightest breath might give away their position. The sermon would be a pat of encouragement on a man's shoulder, then pass on to the next.

One morning at three o'clock a Salvationist carried a

second supply of hot coffee to the battery positions. One gunner with tense, strained face eyed his full coffee mug with satisfaction and said with a sigh: "Good! That is all I wanted. I can keep going until morning now!"

When the men were lined up for a raid there would be a prayer-meeting in the dugout, thirty inside and as many as could crowded around the door. Just a prayer and singing. Then the boys would go to the girls and leave their little trinkets or letters, and say: "I'm going over the top, Sister. If I don't come back—if I'm kicked off—you tell mother. You will know what to say to her to help her bear up."

Three-quarters of an hour later what was left of them would return and the girls would be ready with hot coffee and doughnuts. It was heart-breaking, back-aching, wonderful work, work fit for angels to do, and these girls did it with all their souls.

"Aren't you tired? Aren't you afraid?" asked someone of a lassie who had been working hard for forty consecutive hours, aiding the doctors in caring for the wounded, and in a lull had found time to mix up and fry a batch of doughnuts in a corner from which the roof had been completely blown by shells.

"Oh, no! It's great!" she replied eagerly. "I'm the luckiest girl in the world."

By this time the Salvation Army had acquired many great three-ton trucks, and the drivers of these risked their lives daily to carry supplies to the dugouts and huts that were taking care of the men at the front.

There were signs all over everywhere: "ATTENTION! THE ENEMY SEES YOU!" Trucks were not allowed to go in daytime except in case of great emergency. Sometimes in urgent cases day-passes would be given with the order: "If you have to go, go like the devil!"

The enemy always had the range on the road where the trucks had to pass, and especially in exposed places and on cross-roads a man had no chance if he paused. Once he had been sighted by the enemy he was done for. A man driving on a hasty errand once dropped his crank, and stopped his truck to pick it up. Even as he stooped to take it a shell struck his truck and smashed it to bits.

Most of the travelling had to be done at night. Silently, without a light over roads as dark as pitch, where the only possible guide was the faint line above where the trees parted and showed the sky; over rough, muddy roads, filled with shell-holes, the trucks went nightly. Just fall in line, keep to the right, and whistle softly when something got in the way. No claxon horns could be used, for that was the gas alarm. A man could not even wear a radiolight watch on his wrist or a driver smoke a cigarette.

One very dark night a truck came through with a man sitting away out on the radiator watching the road and telling the driver where to go. The only light would be from shells exploding or occasional signal lights for a moment.

To get supplies from where they were to where they were needed was an urgent necessity which often arose with but momentary warning—frequently with no warning at all. The American front was a matter not of miles, but of hundreds of miles, and the call for supplies might come from any point along that front. Sometimes the call meant the immediate shipment of tons of blankets, oranges, lemons, sugar, flour for doughnuts, lard, chocolate and other materials, to a point 200 miles distant. At times a railroad may supply a part of the route, but always there is a long, dangerous truck haul, and usually the entire route must be covered by truck.

During the winter there were many thrills added to the already strenuous task of the Salvation Army truck drivers. One of them driving late at night in a snow-storm, mistook a river for the road for which he was searching, and turned from the real road to the snow-covered surface of the river, which he followed for some little distance before discovering his mistake. Fortu-nately, the ice was solid and the truck unloaded—an unusual combination.

Another missed the road and drove into a field, where his wheels bogged down. His fellow-traveller, driving a Ford, went for help, leaving him with his truck, for if it had been left unguarded it would have soon been stripped of every movable part by passing truck drivers. Here he remained for almost forty-eight hours, during which time there was considerable shelling.

A Catholic Chaplain told the Salvation Army Staff-Captain that he thought the reason the Salvation Army was so popular with his men was because the Salvation Army kept its promises to the men.

When the Salvation Army officer went to open work in the town of Baccarat it was so crowded that he was unable to secure accommodations. He was having din-ner in the café, but could get no bread because he had no bread tickets. The local K. of C. man, observing his difficulty, supplied tickets, and, finding that he had no place to sleep, offered to share his own meagre accom-modations. For several nights he shared his bed with him and the Salvation Army officer was greatly assisted by him in many ways. The Salvation Army is popular not alone among the soldiers.

While the offensive was on in Argonne and north of Verdun, those who were in the huts in the old training area, which were then used as rest buildings, decided to do something for the boys, and on one occasion they fried fourteen thousand doughnuts and took them to the boys at the front. They traveled in the trucks, and distributed the doughnuts to the boys as they came from the trenches and sent others into the trenches.

By the time they were through, the day was far spent and it was necessary for them to find some place to stay over night. Verdun was the only large city anywhere near but it had either been largely destroyed or the civil population had long since abandoned it and there was no place available.

Underneath the trenches, however, there had been constructed in ancient times, underground passages. There are fifty miles of these underground galleries honeycombed beneath the city, sufficiently large to shelter the entire population. There are cross sections of galleries, between the longer passage ways, and winding stairways here and there. Air is supplied by a system of pumps. There are theatres and a church, also. The Army protecting Verdum had occupied these underground passages.

When the officer commanding the French troops learned that the Salvation Army girls were obliged to stay over night, he arranged for their accommodation in the underground passage and here they rested in perfect security with such comforts as cots and blankets could insure.

It was said that they were the only women ever permitted to remain in these underground passages.

7

The Chateau-Thierry-Soissons Drive

WHEN the trouble at Seicheprey broke out the Germans began shelling Beaumont and Mandres, and things took on a very serious look for the Salvation Army. Then the Military Colonel gave an order for the girls to leave Ansauville, and loading them up on a truck he sent them to Menil-la-Tour. They never allowed girls again in that town until after the St. Mihiel drive.

That was a wild ride in the night for those girls sitting in an army truck, jolted over shell holes with the roar of battle all about them; the blackness of night on every side, shells bursting often near them, yet they were as calm as if nothing were the matter; finally the car got stuck under range of the enemy's fire, but they never flinched and they sat quietly in the car in a most dangerous position for twenty minutes while the Colonel and the Captain were out locating a dugout. Plucky little girls!

The Salvation Army Staff-Captain of that zone went back in the morning to Ansauville to get the girls' personal belongings, and when he entered the canteen he stood still and looked about him with horror and thankfulness as he realized the narrow escape those girls had had. The windows and roof were full of shell holes. Shrapnel had penetrated everywhere. He went about to examine and took pieces of shrapnel out of the flour and sugar and coffee which had gone straight through the tin containers. The vanilla bottles were broken and there was shrapnel in the vanilla, shrapnel was embedded in the wooden tops of the tables, and in the walls.

He went to the billet where two of the girls had slept. Opposite their bed on the other side of the room was a window and over the bed was a large picture. A shell had passed through the window and smashed the picture, shattering the glass in fragments all over the bed. Another shell had entered the window, passed over the pillows of the bed and gone out through the wall by the bed. It would have gone through the temples of any sleeper in that bed. After this they kept men in Ansauville instead of girls.

The next day the girls opened up the canteen at Menil-la-Tour as calmly as if nothing had happened the day before.

The boys were going down to Nevillers to rest, and while they rested the girls cooked good things for them and used that sweet God-given influence that makes a little piece of home and heaven wherever it is found.

The girls did not get much rest, but then they had not come to France to rest, as they often told people who were always urging them to save themselves. They did get one bit of luxury in the shape of passes down to Beauvais. There it was possible to get a bath and the girls had not been able to have that from the first of April to the first of July. They had to stand in line with the officers, it is true, to take their turn at the public bath houses, but it was a real delight to have plenty of water for once, for their appointments at the front had been most restricted and water a scarce commodity. Sometimes it had been difficult to get enough water for the cooking and the girls had been obliged to use cold cream to wash their faces for several days at a time. Of course, it was an impossibility for them to do any laundry work for themselves, as there was neither time nor place nor facilities. Their laundry was always carried by courier to some near-by city and brought back to them in a few days.

The Zone Major had supper with the Colonel, who told him that none of the organizations would be allowed on the drive. The Zone Major asked if they might be allowed to go as far as Crepy. The Colonel much excited said: "Man, don't you know that town is being shelled every night?" The next morning a party of sixteen Salvation Army men and women started out in the truck for Crepy. It was a beautiful day and they rode all day long. At nightfall they reached the village of Crepy where they were welcomed eagerly. The Zone Major had to leave and go back and wanted them all to stay there, but they were unwilling to do so because their own outfit was going over the top that night and they wanted to be with them before they left. They started from Crepy about five o'clock and got lost in the woods, but finally, after wandering about for some hours, landed in Roy St. Nicholas where was the outfit to which one of the girls belonged.

The Salvation Army boys had just pulled in with another truck and were getting ready for the night, for they always slept in their trucks. The girls decided to sit down in the road until the billeting officer arrived, but time passed and no billeting officer came. They were growing very weary, so they got into the Colonel's car, which stood at the roadside, and went to sleep. A little later the billeting officer appeared with many apologies and offered to take them to the billet that had been set aside for them. They took their rolls of blankets, and climbed sleepily out of the car, following him two blocks down the street to an old building. But when they reached there they found that some French officers had taken possession and were fast asleep, so they went back to the car and slept till morning. At daylight they went down to a brook to wash but found that the soldiers were there ahead of them, and they had to go back and be content with freshening up with cold cream. Thus did these lassies, accustomed to daintiness in their daily lives, accommodate themselves to the necessities of war, as easily and cheerfully as the soldier boys themselves.

That day the rest of the outfits arrived, and they all pulled into Morte Fontaine.

Morte Fontaine was well named because there was no water in the town fit to use.

The girls felt they were needed nearer the front, so they went to Major Peabody and asked permission.

"I should say not!" he replied vigorously with yet a twinkle of admiration for the brave lassies. "But you can take anything you want in this town."

So the girls went out and found an old building. It was very dirty but they went cheerfully to work, cleaned it up, and started their canteen.

There was a hospital in the town; they knew that by the many ambulances that were continually going back and forth; so they offered their services to the doctors, which were eagerly accepted. After that they took turns staying in the canteen and going to the hospital.

The hospital was fearfully crowded, though it was in no measure the fault of the hospital authorities, for they were doing their best, working with all their might; but it had not been expected that there would be so many wounded at this point and they had not adequate accommodations. Many of the wounded boys were lying on the ground in the sun, covered with blood and flies, and parched with thirst and fever. There were not enough ambulances to carry them further back to the base hospitals.

The girls stretched pieces of canvas over the heads of the poor boys to keep off the sun; they got water and washed away the blood; and they sent one of their indefatigable truck drivers after some water to make lemonade. The little Adjutant twinkled his nice brown eyes and set his firm merry lips when they told him to get the water, in that place of no water, but he took his little Ford car and whirled away without a word, and presently he returned with a barrel of ice-cold water from a spring he had found two miles away. How the girls rejoiced that it was ice cold! And then they started making lemonade. They had known that the Adjutant would find water somewhere. He was the man the doughboys called "one game little guy," because he was so fearless in going into No Man's Land after the wounded, so indefatigable in accomplishing his purpose against all odds, so forgetful of self.

They had but one crate of lemons, one crate of oranges and one bag of sugar when they began making lemonade, but before they needed more it arrived just on the minute. It was almost like a miracle. For a whole car load of oranges and lemons had been shipped to Beauvais and arrived a day too late—after the troops had gone. They were of no use there, so the Zone Major had them shipped at once to the railhead at Crepy, and got a special permit to go over with trucks and take them up to Morte Fontaine.

The Salvation Army never does things by halves. Colonel Barker sent to Paris to get some mosquito netting to keep the flies off those soldiers, and failing to find any in the whole city he bought $10,000 worth of white net, such as is used for ladies' collars and dresses—ten thousand yards at a dollar a yard—and sent it down to the hospital where it was used over the wounded men, sometimes over a wounded arm or leg or head, sometimes over a whole man, sometimes stretched as netting in the windows. And no ten thousand dollars was ever better spent, for the flies occasioned indescribable suffering as well as the peril of infection.

Wonderful relief and comfort all these things brought to those poor boys lying there in agony and fever. How delicious were the cooling drinks to their parched lips! The doctors afterward said that it was the cool drinks those girls gave to the men that saved many a life that day.

There were some poor fellows hurt in the abdomen who were not allowed to drink even a drop and who begged for it so piteously. For these the girls did all in their power. They bathed their faces and hands and dipping gauze in lemonade they moistened their lips with it.

The other day, after the war was over and a ship came sailing into New York harbor, one of these same fellows standing on the deck looked down at the wharf and saw one of these same girls standing there to welcome him. As soon as he was free to leave the ship he rushed down to find her, and gripping her hand eagerly he cried out so all around could hear: "You saved my life that day. Oh, but I'm glad to see you! The doctor said it was that cold lemonade you gave me that kept me from dying of fever!"

In one base hospital lay a boy wounded at Chateau-Thierry. Of course, when wounded, he lost all his possessions, including a Testament which he very much treasured. The Salvation Army supplied him with another, but it did not comfort him as the old one had done. He said that it could never be the same as the one he had carried for so long. He worried so much about his Testament, that one of the lassies finally attempted to recover it, and, after much trouble, succeeded through the Bureau of Effects. The little book, which the soldier had always carried with him, was blood-soaked and mud-stained; but it was an unmistakable aid in the lad's recovery.

But the honor of those days in Morte Fontaine was not all due to the Salvation Army lassies. The Salvation army truck drivers were real heroes. They came with their ambulances and their trucks and they carried the poor wounded fellows back to the base hospitals. The hospitals were full everywhere near there, and sometimes they would go from one to another and have to drive miles, and even go from one town to another to find a place where there was room to receive the men they carried. Then back they would come for another load. They worked thus for three days and five nights steadily, before they slept, and some of them stripped to the waist and bared their breasts to the sharp night wind so that the cold air would keep them awake to the task of driving their cars through the black night with its precious load of human lives. They had no opportunity for rest of any kind, no chance to shave or wash or sleep, and they were a haggard and worn looking set of men when it was over.

While all this was going on the Zone Major kept out of sight of the Colonel who had told him he couldn't go out on that drive; but two days later he saw his familiar car coming down the road and the Colonel seemed greatly agitated. He was shaking his fist in front of him.

The Zone Major pondered whether he would not better drive right on without stopping to talk, but he reflected that he would have to take his punishment some time and he might as well get it over with, so when the Colonel's car drew near he stopped. The Colonel got out and the Zone Major got out, and it was apparent that the Colonel was very angry. He forgot entirely that the Zone Major was a Salvationist and he swore roundly: "I'm out with you for life," declared the Colonel angrily. "The General's upset and I'm upset."

"Why, what's the matter, Colonel?" asked the Zone Major innocently.

"Matter enough! You had no business to bring those girls up here!"

The Colonel said more to the same effect, and then got into his car and drove off. The Zone Major wisely kept out of his way; but a few days later met him again and this time the Colonel was smiling:

"Dog-gone you, Major, where've you been keeping yourself? Why haven't you been around?" and he put out his hand affably.

"Why, I didn't want to see a man who bawled me out in the public highway that way," said the Zone Major.

"Well, Major, you had no business to bring those girls up here and you know it!" said the Colonel rousing to the old subject again.

"Why not, Colonel, didn't they do fine?"

"Yes, they did," said the Colonel with tears springing suddenly into his eyes and a huskiness into his voice, "but, Major, think what if we'd lost one of them!"

"Colonel," said the Zone Major gently, "my girls are soldiers. They come up here to share the dangers with the soldiers, and as long as they can be of service they feel this is the place for them."

The Colonel struggled with his emotion for a moment and then said gruffly: "Had anything to eat? Stop and take a bite with me." And they sat down under the trees and had supper together.

It was at this town that the girls slept in a German-dug cave, in which our boys had captured seven hundred Germans, the commanding officer of whom said that according to his rank in Germany he ought to have a car to take him to the rear. However, he was compelled to leg it at the point of an American bayonet in the hands of an American doughboy. The cave was of chalk rock made to store casks of wine.

The airplanes were bad in this place. One speaks of airplanes in such a connection in the same way one used to mention mosquitoes at certain Jersey seashore resorts. But they were particularly bad at Morte Fontaine, and Major Peabody ordered the canteen to be moved out of the village to the cave. More Salvation Army girls came to look after the canteen leaving the first girls free for longer hours at the hospital.

One beautiful moonlight night the girls had just started out from the hospital to go to their cave when they heard a German airplane, the irregular chug, chug of its engine distinguishing it unmistakably from the smooth whirr of the Allies' planes. The girls looked up and almost over their heads was an enemy plane, so low that they could see the insignia on his machine, and see the man in the car. He seemed to be looking down at them. In sudden panic they fled to a nearby tree and hid close under its branches. Standing there they saw the enemy make a low dip over the hospital tents, drop a bomb in the kitchen end just where they had been working five minutes before, and slide up again through the silvery air, curve away and dive down once more.

The scene was bright as day for the moon was full and very clear that night, and the roads stretched out in every direction like white ribbons. One block away the girls could see a regiment of Scotch soldiers, the famous Highland Regiment called "The Ladies From Hell," marching up to the front that night, and singing bravely as they marched, their skirling Scotch songs accompanied by a bagpipe. And even as they listened with bated breath and straining eyes the airplane dipped and dropped another bomb right into the midst of the brave men, killing thirty of them, and slid up and away before it could be stopped. These were the scenes to which they grew daily accustomed as they plied their angel mission, and daily saw themselves preserved as by a miracle from constant peril.

We had about eight or ten German prisoners here, who were employed as litter bearers, and very good workers they were, tickled to death to be there instead of over on their own side fighting. Most of the prisoners, except some of the German officers, seemed glad to be taken.

These German prisoners were sitting in a row on the ground outside the hospital one day when the Salvation Army girls and men were picking over a crate of oranges. The Germans sat watching them with longing eyes.

"Let's give them each one," proposed one of the girls.

"No! Give them a punch in the nose!" said the boys.

The girls said nothing more and went on working. Presently they stepped away for a few minutes and when they came back the Germans sat there contentedly eating oranges. Questioningly the girls looked at their male co-workers and with lifted brows asked: "What does this mean?"

"Aw, well! The poor sneaks looked so longingly!" said one of the boys, grinning sheepishly.

There in the hospital the girls came into contact with the splendid spirit of the American soldier boys. "Don't help me, help that fellow over there who is suffering!" was heard over and over again when they went to bring comfort to some wounded boy.

When the supplies in the canteen would run out, and

the last doughnut would be handed with the words: "That's the last," the boy to whom it was given would say: "Don't give it to me, give it to Harry. I don't want it."

It was during that drive and there was a farewell meeting at one of the Salvation Army huts that night for the boys who were going up to the trenches. It was a beautiful and touching meeting as always on such occasions. Starting with singing whatever the boys picked out, it dropped quickly into the old hymns that the boys loved and then to a simple earnest prayer, setting forth the desperate case of those who were going out to fight, and appealing to the everlasting Saviour for forgiveness and refuge. They lingered long about the fair young girl who was leading them, listening to her earnest, plain words of instruction how to turn to the Saviour of the world in their need, how to repent of their sins and take Christ for their Saviour and Sanctifier. No man who was in that meeting would dare plead ignorance of the way to be saved. Many signified their desire to give their lives into the keeping of Christ before they went to the front. The meeting broke up reluctantly and the men drifted out and away, expecting soon to be called to go. But something happened that they did not go that night. Meantime, a company had just returned from the front, weary, hungry, worn and bleeding, with their nerves unstrung, and their spirits desperate from the tumult and horror of the hours they had just passed in battle. They needed cheering and soothing back to normal. The girls were preparing to do this with a bright, cheery entertainment, when a deputation of boys from the night before returned. There was a wistful gleam in the eyes of the young Jew who was spokesman for the group as he approached the lassie who had led the meeting.

"Say, Cap, you see we didn't go up."

"I see," she smiled happily.

"Say, Cap, won't you have another farewell meeting to-night?" he asked with an appealing glance in his dark eyes.

"Son, we've arranged something else just now for the fellows who are coming back," she said gently, for she hated to refuse such a request.

"Oh, say, Cap, you can have that later, can't you? We want another meeting now."

There was something so pleading in his voice and eyes, so hungry in the look of the waiting group, that the young Captain could not deny him. She looked at him hesitatingly, and then said:

"All right. Go out and tell the boys."

He hurried out and soon the company came crowding in. That hour the very Lord came down and communed with them as they sang and knelt to pray, and not a heart but was melted and tender as they went out when it was over in the solemn darkness of the early morning. A little later the order came and they "went over."

It was a sharp, fierce fight, and the young Jew was mortally wounded. Some comrades found him as he lay white and helpless on the ground, and bending over saw that he had not long to stay. They tried to lift him and bear him back, but he would not let them. He knew it was useless.

They asked him if he had any message. He nodded. Yes, he wanted to send a message to the Salvation Army girls. It was this:

"Tell the girls I've gone West; for I will be by the time you tell them; and tell them it's all right for at that second meeting I accepted Christ and I die resting on the same Saviour that is theirs."

One of our wonderful boys out on the drive had his hand blown off and didn't realize it. His chum tried to drag him back and told him his hand was gone.

"That's nothing!" he cried. "Tie it up!"

But they forced him back lest he would bleed to death. In the hospital they told him that now he might go home.

"Go home!" he cried. "Go home for the loss of a left hand! I'm not left-handed. Maybe I can't carry a gun, but I can throw hand grenades!"

He went to the Major and the Major said also that he must go home.

The boy looked him straight in the eye:

"Excuse me, Major, saying I won't. But *I won't let go your coat* till you say I can stay," and finally the Major had to give in and let him stay. He could not resist such pleading.

One poor fellow, wounded in his abdomen, was lying on a litter in a most uncomfortable position suffering awful pain. The lassie came near and asked if she could do anything for him. He told her he wanted to lie on his stomach, but the doctor, when she asked him, said "No" very shortly and told her he must lie on his back. She stooped and turned him so that his position was more comfortable, put his gas mask under his head, rolled his blanket so as to support his shoulders better, and turned to go to another, and the poor suffering lad opened his eyes, held out his hand and smiled as she went away.

The doctors said to the girls: "It is wonderful to have you around."

The Red Cross men and their rolling kitchens came to the front, but no women. Somehow in pain and sickness no hand can soothe like a woman's. Perhaps God meant it to be so. Here at Morte Fontaine was the first time a woman had ever worked in a field hospital.

The Salvation Army women worked all that drive.

It was a sad time, though, for the division went in to stay until they lost forty-five hundred men, but it stayed two days after reaching that figure and lost about seventy-five thousand.

The doctor in charge of the evacuation hospital at Crepy spoke of the effect of the Salvation Army girls, not alone upon the wounded, but also upon the medical-surgical staff and the men of the hospital corps who acted as nurses in that advanced position. "Before they came," he said, "we were overwrought, everyone seemed at the breaking point, what with the nervous tension and danger. But the very sight of women working calmly had a soothing effect on everyone."

When the drive was over orders came to leave. The following is the official notice to the Salvation Army officers:

G-1   Headquarters, 1st Division,
                    American Expeditionary Forces,
                                July 26, 1918.

Memorandum.

To Directors, Y.M.C.A., Red Cross, Salvation Army Services, 1st Division.

1. This division moves by rail to destination unknown beginning at 6.00 A.M., July 28th. Motor organizations of the Division move overland. Your motorized units will accompany the advanced section of the Division Supply Train, and will form a part of that train.

2. Time of departure and routes to be taken will be announced later.

3. Secretaries attached to units may accompany units, if it is so desired.

By command of Major-General Summerall.

P.E. Peabody,

Captain, Infantry,
G–1

Copies:
YMCA
Red Cross
Salvation Army
G–3
C. of S.
File

The girls stowed themselves and their belongings into the big truck. Just as they were about to start they saw some infantry coming, seven men whom they knew, but in such a plight! They were unshaven, with white, sunken faces, and great dark hollows under their eyes. They were simply "all in," and could hardly walk.

Without an instant's hesitation the girls made a place for those poor, tired, dirty men in the truck, and the invitation was gratefully accepted.

There were more poor forlorn fellows coming along the road. They kept meeting them every little way, but they had no room to take in any more so they piled oranges in the back end of the truck and gave them to all the boys they passed who were walking.

Now the girls were on their way to Senlis, where they had planned to take dinner at a hotel in which they had dined before. It was one of the few buildings remaining in the town for the Germans, when they left Senlis, had set it on fire and destroyed nearly everything. But as the girls neared the town they began to think about the boys asleep in the back of the truck, who probably hadn't had a square meal for a week, and they decided to take them with them. So they woke them up when they arrived at the hotel. Oh, but those seven dirty, unshaven soldiers were embarrassed with the invitation to dinner! At first they declined, but the girls insisted, and they found a place to wash and tidy up themselves a bit. In a few minutes into the big dining-room filled with French soldiers and a goodly sprinkling of French officers, marched those two girls, followed by their seven big unshaven soldiers with their white faces and hollow eyes, sat proudly down at a table in the very centre and ordered a big dinner. That is the kind of girls Salvation Army lassies are. Never ashamed to do a big right thing.

After the dinner they took the boys to their divisional headquarters, where they found their outfit.

They went on their way from Senlis to Dam-Martin to stay for a week back of the lines for rest.

There was a big French cantonment building here built for moving pictures, which was given to them for a canteen, and they set up their stove and went to work making doughnuts, and doing all the helpful things they could find to do for the boys who were soon to go to the front again.

Then orders came to move back to the Toul Sector.

Those were wonderful moonlight nights at Saizerais, but the Boche airplanes nearly pestered the life out of everybody.

"Gee!" said one of the boys, "if anybody ever says 'beautiful moonlight nights' to me when I get home I don't know what I'll do to 'em!"

The boys were at the front, but not fighting as yet. Occasional shells would burst about their hut here and there, but the girls were not much bothered by them. The thing that bothered them most was an old "Vin" shop across the street that served its wine on little tables set out in front on the sidewalk. They could not help seeing that many of the boys were beginning to drink. Poor souls! The water was bad and scarce, sometimes poisoned, and their hearts were sick for something, and this was all that presented itself. It was not much wonder. But when the girls discovered the state of things they sent off three or four boys with a twenty-gallon tank to scout for some water. They found it after much search and filled the big tank full of delicious lemonade, telling the boys to help themselves.

All the time they were in that town, which was something like a week, the girls kept that tank full of lemonade close by the door. They must have made seventy-five or a hundred gallons of lemonade every day, and they had to squeeze all the lemons by hand, too! They told the boys: "When you feel thirsty just come here and get lemonade as often as you want it!" No wonder they almost worship those girls. And they had the pleasure of seeing the trade of the little wine shop decidedly decrease.

However near the front you may go you will always find what is known over there in common parlance as a "hole in the wall" where "vin blanche" and "vin rouge" and all kinds of light wines can be had. And, of course, many soldiers would drink it. The Salvation Army tried to supply a great need by having carloads of lemons sent to the front and making and distributing lemonade freely.

One cannot realize the extent of this proposition without counting up all the lemons and sugar that would be required, and remembering that supplies were obtained only by keeping in constant touch with the Headquarters of that zone and always sending word immediately when any need was discovered. There is nothing slow about the Salvation Army and they are not troubled with too much red tape. If necessity presents itself they will even on occasion cut what they have to help someone.

The airplanes visited them every night that week, and sometimes they did not think it worth while to go to bed at all; they had to run to the safety trenches so often. It was just a little bit of a village with dugouts out on the edge.

One night they had gone to bed and a terrific explosion occurred which rocked the little house where they were. They thought of course the bomb had fallen in the village, but they found it was quite outside. It had made such a big hole in the ground that you could put a whole truck into it.

The trenches in which they hid were covered over with boards and sand, and were not bomb proof, but they were proof against pieces of shell and shrapnel.

It was a very busy time for the girls because so many different outfits were passing and repassing that they had to work from early morning till late at night.

At Bullionville the hut was in a building that bore the marks of much shelling. The American boys promptly dubbed the place "Souptown."

The Division moved to Vaucouleurs for rest and replacements. At Vaucouleurs there was a great big hut with a piano, a victrola, and a cookstove.

They started the canteen, made doughnuts and pies, and gave entertainments.

But best of all, there were wonderful meetings and numbers of conversions, often twenty and twenty-five at a time giving themselves to Christ. The boys would get up and testify of their changed feelings and of what Christ now meant to them, and the others respected them the more for it.

They stayed here two weeks and everybody knew they were getting ready for a big drive. It was a solemn time for the boys and they seemed to draw nearer to the Salvation Army people and long to get the secret of their brave, unselfish lives, and that light in their eyes that defied danger and death. In the distance you could hear the artillery, and the night before they left, all night long, there was the tramp, tramp, tramp of feet, the boys "going up."

The next day the girls followed in a truck, stopping a few days at Pagny-sur-Meuse for rest.

The Saint Mihiel Drive

THE HUT in Raulecourt was an old French barracks. Outside in the yard was an old French anti-aircraft gun and a mesh of barbed wire entanglement. The woods all around was filled with our guns. To the left was the enemy's third line trench. Three-quarters of the time the Boche were trying to clean us up. Less than two miles ahead were our own front line trenches.

The field range was outside in the back yard.

One hot day in July a Salvation Army woman stood at the range frying doughnuts from eleven in the morning until six at night without resting, and scarcely stopping for a bite to eat. She fried seventeen hundred doughnuts, and was away from the stove only twice for a few minutes. She claims, however, that she is not the champion doughnut fryer. The champion fried twenty-three hundred in a day.

One day a soldier watching her tired face as she stood at the range lifting out doughnuts and plopping more uncooked ones into the fat, protested.

"Say, you're awfully tired turning over doughnuts.

Let me help you. You go inside and rest a while. I'm sure I can do that."

She was tired and the boy looked eager, so she decided to accept his offer. He was very insistent that she *go away* to rest, so she slipped in behind a screen to lie down, but peeped out to watch how he was getting on. She saw him turn over the first doughnuts all right and drain them, but he almost burned his fingers trying to eat one before it was fairly out of the fat; and then she understood why he had been so anxious for her to *"go away"* and rest.

Often the boys would come to the lassies and say: "Say, Cap, I can help you. Loan me an apron." And soon they would be all flour from their chin to their toes.

They would come about four o'clock to find out what time the doughnuts would be ready for serving, and the girls usually said six o'clock so that they would be able to fry enough to supply all the regiment. But the men would start to line up at half-past four, knowing that they could not be served until six, so eager were they for these delicacies. When six o'clock came each man would get three doughnuts and a cup of delicious coffee or chocolate. A great many doughnut cutters were worn out as the days went by and the boys frequently had to get a new cutter made. Sometimes they would take the top of quite a large-sized can or anything tin that they could lay hands on from which to make it. One boy found the top of an extra large sized baking powder tin and took it to have a smaller cutter soldered in the center. Sometimes they used the top of the shaving soap box for this. When he got back to the hut the cook exclaimed in dismay: "Why, but it's too big!"

"Oh, that's all right," said the doughboy nonchalantly. "That'll be all the better for us. We'll get more doughnut. You always give us three anyway, you know. The size don't count."

They were always scheming to get more pie and more doughnuts and would stand in line for hours for a second helping. One day the Salvation Army woman grew indignant over a noticeably red-headed boy who had had three helpings and was lining up for a fourth. She stood majestically at the head of the line and pointed straight at him: "You! With the red head down there! Get out of the line!"

"She's got my number all right!" said the red-headed one, grinning sheepishly as he dropped back.

The town of Raulecourt was often shelled, but one morning just before daybreak the enemy started in to shell it in earnest. Word came that the girls had better leave as it was very dangerous to remain, but the girls thought otherwise and refused to leave. One might have thought they considered that they were real soldiers, and the fate of the day depended upon them. And perhaps more depended upon them than they knew. However that was they stayed, having been through such experiences before. For the older woman, however, it was a first experience. She took it calmly enough, going about her business as if she, too, were an older soldier.

On the evening of June 14th they made fudge for the boys who were going to leave that night for the front lines.

For several hours the tables in the hut were filled with men writing letters to loved ones at home, and the women and girls had sheets of paper filled with addresses to which they had promised to write if the boys did not come back.

At last one of the men got up with his finished letter and quietly removed the phonograph and a few of its devotees who were not going up to the front yet, placing them outside at a safe distance from the hut. A soldier followed, carrying an armful of records, and the hut was cleared for the men who were "going in" that night.

For a little while they ate fudge and then they sang hymns for another half hour, and had a prayer. It was a very quiet little meeting. Not much said. Everyone knew how solemn the occasion was. Everyone felt it might be his last among them. It was as if the brooding Christ had made Himself felt in every heart. Each boy felt like crying out for some strong arm to lean upon in this his sore need. Each gave himself with all his heart to the quiet reaching up to God. It was as if the eating of that fudge had been a solemn sacrament in which their souls were brought near to God and to the dear ones they might never see on this earth again. If any one had come to them then and suggested the Philosophy of Nietzsche it would have found little favor. They knew, here, in the face of death, that the Death of Jesus on the Cross was a soul satisfying creed. Those who had accepted Him were suddenly taken within the veil where they saw no longer through a glass darkly, but with a face-to-face sense of His presence. They had dropped away their self assurance with which they had either conquered or ignored everything so far in life, and had become as little children, ready to trust in the Everlasting Father, without whom they had suddenly discovered they could not tread the ways of Death.

Then came the call to march, and with a last prayer the boys filed silently out into the night and fell into line. A few minutes later the steady tramp of their feet could be heard as they went down the street that led to the front.

Later in the night, quite near to morning, there came a terrific shock of artillery fire that heralded a German raid. The fragile army cots rocked like cradles in the hut, dishes rolled and danced on the shelves and tables, and were dashed to fragments on the floor. Shells wailed and screamed overhead; and our guns began, until it seemed that all the sounds of the universe had broken forth. In the midst of it all the gas alarm sounded, the great electric horns screeching wildly above the babel of sound. The women hurried into their gas masks, a bit flustered perhaps, but bearing their excitement quietly and helping each other until all were safely breathing behind their masks.

The next day several times officers came to the hut and begged the women to leave and go to a place of greater safety, but they decided not to go unless they were ordered away. On June 19th one of them wrote in her diary: "Shells are still flying all about us, but our work is here and we must stay. God will protect us." Once when things grew quiet for a little while she went to the edge of the village and watched the shells falling on Boucq, where one of her friends was stationed, and declared: "It looks awfully bad, almost as bad as it sounds."

The next morning as the firing gradually died away, Salvation Army people hurried up to Raulecourt from near-by huts to find out how these brave women were, and rejoiced unspeakably that every one was safe and well.

That night there was another wonderful meeting with the boys who were going to the front, and after it the weary workers slept soundly the whole night through, quietly and undisturbed, the first time for a week.

It was a bright, beautiful Sunday morning, June 23, 1918, when a little party of Salvationists from Raulecourt started down into the trenches. The muddy, dirty, unpleasant trenches! Sometimes with their two feet firmly planted on the duck-board, sometimes in the mud! Such mud! If you got both feet on it at once you were sure you were planted and would soon begin to grow!

As soon as they reached the trenches they were told: "Keep your heads down, ladies, the snipers are all around!" It was an intense moment as they crept into the narrow housings where the men had to spend so much time. But it was wonderful to watch the glad light that came into the men's eyes as they saw the women.

"Here's a real, honest-to-goodness American woman in the trenches!" exclaimed a homesick lad as they came around a turn.

"Yes, your mother couldn't come to-day," said the motherly Salvationist, smiling a greeting, "so I've come in her place."

"All right!" said he, entering into the game. "This is Broadway and that's Forty-second Street. Sit down."

Of course there was nothing to sit down on in the trenches. But he hunted about till he found a chow can and turned it up for a seat, and they had a pleasant talk.

"Just wait," he said. "I'll show you a picture of the dearest little girl a fellow ever married and the darlingest little kid ever a man was father to!" He fumbled in his breast pocket right over his heart and brought out two photographs.

"I'd give my right arm to see them this minute, but for all that," he went on, "I wouldn't leave till we've fought this thing through to Berlin and given them a dose of what they gave little Belgium!"

They went up and down the trenches, pausing at the entrances to dugouts to smile and talk with the men. Once, where a grassy ridge hid the trench from the enemy snipers, they were permitted to peep over, but there was no look of war in the grassy, placid meadow full of flowers that men called "No Man's Land." It seemed hard to believe, that sunny, flower-starred morning, that Sin and Hate had the upper hand and Death was abroad stalking near in the sunlight.

It was a twelve-mile walk through the trenches and back to the hut, and when they returned they found the men were already gathering for the evening meeting.

That night, at the close of a heart-searching talk, eighty-five men arose to their feet in token that they would turn from the ways of sin and accept Christ as their Saviour, and many more raised their hands for prayers. One of the women of this party in her three months in France saw more than five hundred men give themselves to Christ and promise to serve Him the rest of their lives.

A little Adjutant lassie who was stationed at Boucq went away from the town for a few hours on Saturday, and when she returned the next day she found the whole place deserted. A big barrage had been put over in the little, quiet village while she was away and the entire inhabitants had taken refuge in the General's dugout. Her husband, who had brought her back, insisted that she should return to the Zone headquarters at Ligny-en-Barrios, where he was in charge, and persuaded her to start with him, but when they reached Menil-la-Tour and found that the division Chaplain was returning to Boucq she persuaded her husband that she must return with the Chaplain to her post of duty.

That night she and the other girls slept outside the dugout in little tents to leave more room in the dugout for the French women with their little babies. At half-past three in the morning the Germans started their shelling once more. After two hours, things quieted down somewhat and the girls went to the hut and prepared a large urn of coffee and two big batches of hot biscuits. While they were in the midst of breakfast there was another barrage. All day they were thus moving backward and forward between the hut and the dugout, not knowing when another barrage would arrive. The Germans were continually trying to get the chateau where the General had his headquarters. One shell struck a house where seven boys were quartered, wounding them all and killing one of them. Things got so bad that the Divisional Headquarters had to leave; the General sent his car and transferred the girls with all their things to Trondes. This was back of a hill near Boucq. They arrived at three in the afternoon, put up their stove and began to bake. By five they were serving cake they had baked. The boys said: "What! Cake already?" The soldiers put up the hut and had it finished in six hours.

While all this was going on the Salvation Army friends over at Raulecourt had been watching the shells falling on Boucq, and been much troubled about them.

These were stirring times. No one had leisure to wonder what had become of his brother, for all were working with all their might to the one great end.

Up north of Beaumont two aviators were caught by the enemy's fire and forced to land close to the enemy nests. Instead of surrendering the Americans used the guns on their planes and held off the Germans until darkness fell, when they managed to escape and reach the American lines. This was only one of many individual feats of heroism that helped to turn the tide of battle. The courage and determination, one might say the enthusiasm, of the Americans knew no bounds. It awed and overpowered the enemy by its very eagerness. The Americans were having all they could do to keep up with the enemy. The artillerymen captured great numbers of enemy cannon, ammunition, food and other supplies, which the trucks gathered up and carried far to the front, where they were ready for the doughboy-when they arrived. One of the greatest feats of engineering ever accomplished by the American Army was the bridging of the Meuse, in the region of Stenay, under terrible shell fire, using in the work of building the pontoons the Boche boats and materials captured during the fighting at Chateau-Thierry and which had been brought from Germany for the Kaiser's Paris offensive in July. The Meuse had been flooded until it was a mile wide, yet there was more than enough material to bridge it.

As the Americans advanced, village after village was set free which had been robbed and pillaged by the Germans while under their domination. The Yankee trucks as they returned brought the women and children back from out of the range of shell fire, and they were filled with wonder as they heard the strange language on the tongues of their rescuers. They knew it was not the German, but they had many of them never seen an American before. The Germans had told them that Americans were wild and barbarous people. Yet these men gathered the little hungry children into their arms and shared their rations with them. There were three dirty, hungry little children, all under ten years of age, Yvonne, Louisette and Jeane, whose father was a sailor stationed at Marseilles. Yvonne was only four years of age, and she told the soldiers she had never seen her father. They climbed into the big truck and sat looking with wonder at the kindly men who filled their hands with food and asked them many questions. By and by, they comprehended that these big, smiling, cheerful men were going to take the whole family to their father. What wonder, what joy shone in their eager young eyes!

Strange and sad and wonderful sights there were to see as the soldiers went forward.

A pioneer unit was rushed ahead with orders to conduct its own campaign and choose its own front, only so that contact was established with the enemy, and to this unit was attached a certain little group of Salvation Army people. Three lassies, doing their best to keep pace with their own people, reached a battered little town about four o'clock in the morning, after a hard, exciting ride.

The supply train had already put up the tent for them, and they were ordered to unfold their cots and get to sleep as soon as possible. But instead of obeying orders these indomitable girls set to work making doughnuts and before nine o'clock in the morning they had made and were serving two thousand doughnuts, with the accompanying hot chocolate.

The shells were whistling overhead, and the dough-boys dropped into nearby shell holes when they heard them coming, but the lassies paid no heed and made doughnuts all the morning, under constant bombardment.

Bouconville was a little village between Raulecourt and the trenches. In it there was left no civilian nor any whole house. Nothing but shot-down houses, dugouts and camouflages, Y.M.C.A., Salvation Army and enlisted men.

Dead Man's Curve was between Mandres and Beaumont. The enemy's eye was always upon it and had its range.

Before the St. Mihiel drive one could go to Bouconville or Raulecourt only at night. As soon as it was dark the supply outfits on the trucks would be lined up awaiting the word from the Military Police to go.

Everyone had to travel a hundred yards apart. Only three men would be allowed to go at once, so dangerous was the trip.

Out of the night would come a voice:

"Halt! Who goes there? Advance and give the counter-sign."

Every man was regarded as an enemy and spy until he was proven otherwise. And the countersign had to be given mighty quick, too. So the men were warned when they were sent out to be ready with the countersign and not to hesitate, for some had been slow to respond and had been promptly shot. The ride through the night in the dark without lights, without sound, over rough, shell-plowed roads had plenty of excitement.

Bouconville for seven months could never be entered by day. The dugout wall of the hut was filled with sandbags to keep it up. It was at Bouconville, in the Salvation Army hut, that the raids on the enemy were organized, the men were gathered together and instructed, and trench knives given out; and here was where they weeded out any who were afraid they might sneeze or cough and so give warning to the enemy.

Not until after the St. Mihiel drive when Montsec was behind the line instead of in front did they dare enter Bouconville by day.

Passing through Mandres, it was necessary to go to Beaumont, around Dead Man's Curve and then to Rambucourt, and proceed to Bouconville. Here the Salvation Army had an outpost in a partially destroyed residence. The hut consisted of the three ground floor rooms, the canteen being placed in the middle. The sleeping quarters were in a dugout just at the rear of these buildings. It was in the building adjoining this hut that three men were killed one day by an exploding shell, and gas alarms were so frequent in the night that it was very difficult for the Salvation Army people to secure sufficient rest as on the sounding of every gas alarm it was necessary to rise and put on the gas mask and keep it on until the "alerte" was removed. This always occurred several times during the night.

It was just outside of Bouconville that the famous doughnut truck experience occurred. The supply truck, driven by two young Salvation Army men, one a mere boy, was making its rounds of the huts with supplies and in order to reach Raulecourt, the boy who was driving decided to take the shortest road, which, by the way, was under complete observation of the Germans located at Montsec. The truck had already been shelled on its way to Bouconville, several shells landing at the edge of the road within a few feet of it. They had not noticed the first shell, for shells were a somewhat common thing, and the old truck made so much noise that they had not heard it coming, but when the second one fell so close one of the boys said: "Say, they must be shooting at *us!*" as though that were something unexpected.

They stepped on the accelerator and the truck shot forward madly and tore into the town with shells breaking about it. Having escaped thus far they were ready to take another chance on the short cut to Raulecourt.

They proceeded without mishaps for some distance. Just outside of Bouconville was a large shell hole in the road and in trying to avoid this the wheels of the truck slipped into the ditch, and the driver found he was stuck. It was impossible to get out under his own power. While working with the truck, the Germans began to shell him again. At first the two boys paid little heed to it, but when more began to come they knew it was time to leave. They threw themselves into a communicating trench, which was really no more than a ditch, and wiggled their way up the bank until they were able to drop into the main trenches, where they found safety in a dugout.

The Germans meantime were shelling the truck furiously, the shells dropping all around on either side, but not actually hitting it. This was about two o'clock in the afternoon.

At Headquarters they were becoming anxious about the non-appearance of the truck and started out in the touring car to locate it. Commencing at Jouey-les-Cotes they went from there to Boucq and Raulecourt, which were the last places the truck was to visit. Not hearing of it at Raulecourt, the search was continued out to Bouconville, again by a short road. Montsec was in full view. There were fresh shell holes all along the road since the night before. Things began to look serious.

A short distance ahead was an army truck, and even as they got abreast of it a shell went over it exploding about twenty-five feet away, and one hit the side of the road just behind them. It seemed wise to put on all speed.

But when they reached Bouconville and found that the truck they had passed was the Salvation Army truck, they were unwilling to leave it to the tender mercies of the enemy as everybody advised. That truck cost fifty-five hundred dollars, and they did not want to lose it.

As soon as it was dark a detail of soldiers volunteered to go with the Salvation Army officers to attempt to get it out, but the Germans heard them and started their shelling furiously once more, so that they had to retreat for a time; but later, they returned and worked all night trying to jack it up and get a foundation that would permit of hauling it out. Every little while all night the Germans shelled them. About half-past four in the morning it grew light enough for the enemy to see, and the top was taken off the truck so that it would not be so good a mark.

That day they went back to Headquarters and secured permission for an ammunition truck to come down and give them a tow, as no driver was permitted out on that road without a special permit from Headquarters. The journey back was filled with perils from gas shells, especially around Dead Man's Curve, but they escaped unhurt. That night they attached a tow line to the front of the truck, started the engine quietly, and waited until the assisting truck came along out of the darkness. They then attached their line without stopping the other truck and with the aid of its own power the old doughnut truck was jerked out of the ditch at last and sent on its way. In spite of the many shells for which it had been a target it was uninjured save that it needed a new top. The knowledge that the truck was stuck in the ditch and was being shelled aroused great excitement among all the troops in the Toul Sector and it was thereafter an object of considerable interest. Newspaper correspondents telegraphed reports of it around the world.

In most of the huts and dugouts Salvation Army workers subsist entirely upon Army chow. At Bouconville the chow was frequently supplemented by fresh fish. The dugout here was very close to the trenches, less than five minutes' walk. Just behind the trenches to the left was a small lake. When there was sufficient artillery fire to mask their attack, soldiers would toss a hand grenade into this lake, thus stunning hundreds of fish which would float to the surface, where they were gathered in by the sackful. The Salvation Army dugout was never without its share of the spoils.

Before the soldiers began to think, as they do now, that being detailed to the Salvation Army hut was a privilege, an Army officer sent one of his soldiers, who seemed to be in danger of developing a yellow streak, to sweep the hut and light the fires for the lassies. "You are only fit to wash dishes, and hang on to a woman's skirts," he told the soldier in informing him that he was detailed. That night the village was bombed. The boy, who wa really frightened, watched the two girls, being too proud to run for shelter while they were so calm. He trembled and shook while they sat quietly listening to the swish of falling bombs and the crash of anti-aircraft guns. In spite of his fright, he was so ashamed of his fears that he forced himself to stand in the street and watch the progress of the raid. The next day he reported to his Captain that he had vanquished his yellow streak and wanted a chance to demonstrate what he said. The demonstration was ample. The example of these brave lassies had somehow strengthened his spirit.

Back of Raulecourt the woods were full of heavy artillery. Raulecourt was the first town back of the front lines. The men were relieved every eight days and passed through here to other places to rest.

The military authorities sent word to the Salvation Army hut one day that fifty Frenchmen would be going through from the trenches at five o'clock in the morning who would have had no opportunity to get anything to eat.

The Salvation Army people went to work and baked up a lot of biscuits and doughnuts and cakes, and got hot coffee ready. The Red Cross canteen was better situated to serve the men and had more conveniences, so they took the things over there, and the Red Cross supplied hot chocolate, and when the men came they were well served. This is a sample of the spirit of cooperation which prevailed. One Sunday night they were just starting the evening service when word came from the military authorities that there were a hundred men coming through the town who were hungry and ought to be fed. They must be out of the town by nine-thirty as they were going over the top that night. Could the Salvation Army do anything?

The woman officer who was in charge was perplexed.

She had nothing cooked ready to eat, the fire was out, her detailed helpers all gone, and she was just beginning a meeting and hated to disappoint the men already gathered, but she told the messenger that if she might have a couple of soldiers to help her she would do what she could. The soldiers were supplied and the fire was started. At ten minutes to nine the meeting was closed and the earnest young preacher went to work making biscuits and chocolate with the help of her two soldier boys. By ten o'clock all the men were fed and gone. That is the way the Salvation Army does things. They never say "I can't." They always CAN.

In Raulecourt there were several pro-Germans. The authorities allowed them to stay there to save the town. The Salvation Army people were warned that there were spies in the town and that they must on no account give out information. Just before the St. Mihiel drive a special warning was given, all civilians were ordered to leave town, and a Military Police knocked at the door and informed the woman in the hut that she must be careful what she said to anybody with the rank of a second lieutenant, as word had gone out there was a spy dressed in the uniform of an American second lieutenant.

That night at eleven o'clock the young woman was just about to retire when there came a knock at the canteen door. She happened to be alone in the building at the time and when she opened the door and found several strange officers standing outside she was a little frightened. Nor did it dispel her fears to have them begin to ask questions:

"Madam, how many troops are in this town? Where are they? Where can we get any billets?"

To all these questions she replied that she could not tell or did not know and advised them to get in tou with the town Major. The visitors grew impatient. Then three more men knocked at the door, also in uniform, and began to ask questions. When they could get no information one of them exclaimed indignantly:

"Well, I should like to know what kind of a town this is, anyway? I tried to find out something from a Military Police outside and he took me for a SPY! Madam, we are from Field Hospital Number 12, and we want to find a place to rest."

Then the frightened young woman became convinced that her visitors were not spies; all the same, they were not going to leave her any the wiser for any information she would give.

Several times men would come to the town and find no place to sleep. On such occasions the Salvation Army hut was turned over to them and they would sleep on the floor.

The St. Mihiel drive came on and the hut was turned over to the hospital. The supplies were taken to a dugout and the canteen kept up there. Then the military authorities insisted that the girls should leave town, but the girls refused to go, begging, "Don't drive us away. We know we shall be needed!" The Staff-Captain came down and took some of the girls away, but left two in the canteen, and others in the hospital.

It rained for two weeks in Raulecourt. The soldiers slept in little dog tents in the woods.

The meetings held the boys at the throne of God each night, they were the power behind the doughnut, and the boys recognized it.

"One hesitated to ask them if they wanted prayers because we knew they did," said one sweet woman back from the front, speaking about the time of the St. Mihiel drive. "We couldn't say how many knelt at the altar because they all knelt. Some of them would walk five miles to attend a meeting."

It poured torrents the night of the drive and nearly drowned out the soldiers in their little tents.

They came into the hut to shake hands and say good-bye to the girls; to leave their little trinklets and ask for prayers; and they had their meeting as always before a drive.

But this was an even more solemn time than usual, for the boys were going up to a point where the French had suffered the fearful loss of thirty thousand men trying to hold Mt. Sec for fifteen minutes. They did not expect to come back. They left sealed packages to be forwarded if they did not return.

One boy came to one of the Salvation Army men Officers and said: "Pray for me. I have given my heart to Jesus."

Another, a Sergeant, who had lived a hard life, came to the Salvation Army Adjutant and said: "When I go back, if I ever go, I'm going to serve the Lord."

After the meeting the girls closed the canteen and on the way to their room they passed a little sort of shed or barn. The door was standing open and a light streaming out, and there on a little straw pallet lay a soldier boy rolled up in his blanket reading his Testament. The girls breathed a prayer for the lad as they passed by and their hearts were lifted up with gladness to think how many of the American boys, fully two-thirds of them, carried their Testaments in the pockets over their hearts; yes, and read them, too, quite openly.

Two young Captains came one night to say good-bye to the girls before going up the line. The girls told them they would be praying for them and the elder of the two, a doctor, said how much he appreciated that, and then told them how he had promised his wife he would read a chapter in his Testament every day, and how he had never failed to keep his promise since he left home.

Then up spoke the other man:

' Well, I got converted one night on the road. The shells were falling pretty thick and I thought I would never reach my destination and I just promised the Lord if He would let me get safely there I would never fail to read a chapter, and I never have failed yet!" This young man seemed to think that the whole plan of redemption was comprised in reading his Bible, but if he kept his promise the Spirit would guide him.

On the way back to the hut one morning the girls picked marguerites and forget-me-nots and put them in a vase on the table in the hut, making it look like a little oasis in a desert, and no doubt, many a soldier looked long at those blossoms who never thought he cared about flowers before.

Within thirty-six hours after the first gun was fired in the St. Mihiel drive seven Salvation Army huts were established on the territory.

Three days before the drive opened twenty Salvation Army girls reached Raulecourt, which was a little village half a mile from Montsec. They had been travelling for hours and hours and were very weary.

The Salvation Army hut had been turned over to the hospital, so they found another old building.

That night there was a gas alarm sounded and everybody came running out with their gas masks on. The officer who had them in charge was much worried about his lassies because some of them had a great deal of hair, and he was afraid that the heavy coils at the back of their heads would prevent the masks from fitting tightly and let in the deadly gas, but the lassies were level-headed girls, and they came calmly out with their masks on tight and their hair in long braids down their backs, much to the relief of their officer.

It had been raining for days and the men were wet to the skin, and many of them had no way to get dry except to roll up in their blankets and let the heat of their body dry their clothes while they slept. It was a great comfort to have the Salvation Army hut where they could go and get warm and dry once in awhile.

The night of the St Mihiel drive was the blackest night ever seen. It was so dark that one could positively see nothing a foot ahead of him. The Salvation Army lassies stood in the door of the canteen and listened. All day long the heavy artillery had been going by, and now that night had come there was a sound of feet, tramping, tramping, thousands of feet, through the mud and slush as the soldiers went to the front. In groups they were singing softly as they went by. The first bunch was singing "Mother Machree."

> *"There's a spot in me heart that no colleen may own,*
> *There's a depth in me soul never sounded or known;*
> *There's a place in me memory, me life, that you fill,*
> *No other can take it, no one ever will;*
> *Sure, I love the dear silver that shines in your hair,*
> *And the brow that's all furrowed and wrinkled with care.*
> *I kiss the dear fingers, so toil-worn for me;*
>   *O, God bless you and keep you!*
>   *Mother Machree!"*

The simple pathos of the voices, many of them tramping forward to their death, and thinking of mother, brought the tears to the eyes of the girls who had been mothers and sisters, as well as they could, to these boys during the days of their waiting.

Then the song would die slowly away and another

group would come by singing: "Tell mother I'll be there!" Always the thought of mother. A little interval and the jolly swing of "Pack up your troubles in your old kit bag and smile, smile, smile!" came floating by, and then sweetly, solemnly, through the chill of the darkness, with a thrill in the words, came another group of voices:

> *"Abide with me; fast falls the eventide,*
> *The darkness deepens; Lord, with me abide!"*

There had been rumors that Montsec was mined and that as soon as a foot was set upon it it would blow up.

The girls went and lay down on their cots and tried to sleep, praying in their hearts for the boys who had gone forth to fight. But they could not sleep. It was as though they had all the burden of all the mothers and wives and sisters of those boys upon them, as they lay there, the only women within miles, the only women so close to the lines.

About half-past one a big naval gun went off. It was as though all the noises of the earth were let loose about them. They could lie still no longer. They got up, put on their rain-coats, rubber boots, steel helmets, took their gas masks and went out in the fields where they could see. Soon the barrage was started. Darkness took on a rosy hue from shells bursting. First a shell fell on Montsec. Then one landed in the ammunition dump just back of it and blew it up, making it look like a huge crater of a volcano. It seemed as if the universe were on fire. The noise was terrific. The whole heavens were lit up from end to end. The beauty and the horror of it were indescribable.

At five o'clock they went sadly back to the hut.

The hospital tents had been put up in the dark and now stood ready for the wounded who were expected momentarily. The girls took off their rain-coats and reported for duty. It was expected there would be many wounded. The minutes passed and still no wounded arrived. Day broke and only a few wounded men had been brought in. It was reported that the roads were so bad that the ambulances were slow in getting there. With sad hearts the workers waited, but the hours passed and still only a straggling few arrived, and most of those were merely sick from explosives. There were almost no wounded! Only ninety in all.

Then at last there came one bearing a message. There *were* no wounded! The Germans had been taken so by surprise, the victory had been so complete at that point that the boys had simply leaped over all barriers and gone on to pursue the enemy. Quickly packing up seven outfits a little company of workers started after their divisions on trucks over ground that twenty-four hours before had been occupied by the Germans, on roads that were checkered with many shell holes which American road makers were busily filling up and bridging as they passed.

One of the Salvation Army truck drivers asked a negro road mender what he thought of his job. He looked up with a pearly smile and a gleam of his eye and replied: "Boss, I'se doin' mah best to make de world safe foh Democrats!"

They had to stop frequently to remove the bodies of dead horses from the way so recently had that place been shelled. They passed through grim skeletons of villages shattered and torn by shell fire; between tangles of rusty barbed wire that marked the front line trenches. Then on into territory that had long been held by the Huns. More than half of the villages they passed were partially burned by the retreating enemy. All along the way the pitiful villagers, free at last, came out to greet them with shouts of welcome, calling "Bonnes Americaines! Bonnes Americaines!" Some flung their arms about the Salvation Army lassies in their joy. Some of the villagers had not even known that the Americans were in the war until they saw them.

In the village of Nonsard a little way beyond Mt. Sec they found a building that twenty-four hours before had been a German canteen. Above the entrance was the sign "KAMERAD, tritt' sin."

The Salvation Army people stepped in and took possession, finding everything ready for their use. They even found a lard can full of lard and after a chemist had analyzed it to make sure it was not poisoned they fried doughnuts with it. In one wall was a great shell hole, and the village was still under shell fire as they unloaded their truck and got to work. One lassie set the water to heat for hot chocolate, while another requisitioned a soldier to knock the head off a barrel of flour and was soon up to her elbows mixing the dough for doughnuts. Before the first doughnut was out of the hot fat several hundred soldiers were waiting in long, patient, ever-growing lines for free doughnuts and chocolate. These thing were always served free after the men had been over the top.

The lassies had had no sleep for thirty-six hours, but they never thought of stopping until everybody was served. In that one day their three tons of supplies entirely gave out.

The Red Cross was there with their rolling kitchen. They had plenty of bread but nothing to put on it. The Salvation Army had no stove on which to cook anything, but they had quantities of jam and potted meats. They turned over ten cases of jam, some of the cases containing as many as four hundred small jars, to the Red Cross, who served it on hot biscuits. Some one put up a sign: "THIS JAM FURNISHED BY THE SALVA-

TION ARMY!" and the soldiers passed the word along the line: "The finest sandwich in the world, Red Cross and Salvation Army!"

The first day two Salvation Army girls served more than ten thousand soldiers in their canteen. They did not even stop to eat. The Red Cross brought them over hot chocolate as they worked.

Evening brought enemy airplanes, but the lassies did not stop for that and soon their own aerial forces drove the enemy back.

That night the girls slept in a dirty German dugout, and they did not dare to clean up the place, or even so much as to move any of the *débris* of papers and old tin and pasteboard cracker boxes, or cans that were strewn around the place until the engineer experts came to examine things, lest it might be mined and everything be blown up. The girls set up their cots in the clearest place they could find, and went to sleep. One of the women, however, who had just arrived, had lost her cot, and being very weary crawled into a sort of berth dug by the Germans in the wall, where some German had slept. She found out from bitter experience what cooties are like.

The next morning they were hard at work again as early as seven o'clock. Two long lines of soldiers were already patiently waiting to be served. The girls wondered whether they might not have been there all night. This continued all day long.

"We had to keep on a perpetual grin," said one of the lassies, "so that each soldier would think he had a smile all his own. We always gave everything with a smile."

Yet they were not smiles of coquetry. One had but to see the beautiful earnest faces of those girls to know that nothing unholy or selfish entered into their service. It was more like the smile that an angel might give.

Here is one of the many popular songs that have been written on the subject which shows how the soldiers felt:

Salvation Lassie of Mine

They say it's in Heaven that all angels dwell,
    But I've come to learn they're on earth just as well;
And how would I know that the like could be so,
    If I hadn't found one down here below?

Chorus.
A sweet little Angel that went o'er the sea,
    With the emblem of God in her hand;
A wonderful Angel who brought there to me
    The sweet of a war-furrowed land.
The crown on her head was a ribbon of red,
    A symbol of all that's divine;
Though she called each a brother she's more like a mother,
    Salvation Lassie of Mine.

Perhaps in the future I'll meet her again,
    In that world where no one knows sorrow or pain;
And when that time comes and the last word is said,
    Then place on my bosom her band of red.
                    By "Jack" Caddingan and "Chick" Stoy.

That day a shell fell on the dugout where they had slept the night before, and a little later one dropped next door to the canteen; another took seven men from the signal corps right in the street near by, and the girls were ordered out of the village because it was no longer safe for them.

One of the boys had been up on a pole putting up wires for the signal corps. These boys often had to work as now under shell fire in daytime because it was necessary to have telephone connections complete at once. A shell struck him as he worked and he fell in front of the canteen. They had just carried him away to the ambulance when his chum and comrade came running up. A pool of blood lay on the floor in front of the canteen, and he stood and gazed with anguish in his face. Suddenly he stooped and patted the blood tenderly murmuring, "My Buddy! My Buddy!" Then like a flash he was off, up the pole where his comrade had been killed to finish his work. That is the kind of brave boys those girls were serving.

The Argonne Drive

THAT night they slept in the woods on litters, and the next day they went on farther into the woods, twelve kilometres beyond what had been German front.

Here they found a whole little village of German dugouts in the form of log cabin bungalows in the woods. It was a beautifully laid out little village, each bungalow complete with running water and electric lights and all conveniences. There were a dance hall, a billiard room, and several pianos in the woods. There were also fine vegetable gardens and rabbit hutches full of rabbits, for the Germans had been obliged to leave too hastily to take anything with them.

The boys were hungry, some of them half starved for something different from the hard fare they could take with them over the top, and they made rabbit stews and cooked the vegetables and had a fine time.

The girls up at the front had no time for making doughnuts, so the girls back of the lines made 8000 doughnuts and sent them up by trucks for distribution. They also distributed oranges to the soldiers.

News came to the girls after they had been for a week in Nonsard that they were to make a long move.

Back to Verdun they went and stopped just long enough to look at the city. They were much impressed with St. Margaret's school for young ladies, and a wonderful old cathedral standing on the hill with a wall surrounding it. Just the face of the building was left, all the rest shot away, and through the concrete walls were holes, with guns bristling from every one.

They did not linger long for duty called them forward on their journey. At dusk they stopped in a little village, bought some stuff, and asked a French woman to cook it for them. They inquired for a place in which to wash and were given a bar of soap and directed to the village pump up the street. After supper they went on their way to Benoitvaux. Here they found difficulty in getting quarters, but at last an old French woman agreed to let them sleep in her kitchen and for a couple of days they were quartered with her. The word went forth that there were two American girls there and people were most curious to see them. One afternoon two French soldiers came to the kitchen to visit them. It was raining, as usual, and the girls had stayed in because there was really nothing to call them out. The soldiers sat for some time talking. They had heard that America was a wild place with *beaucoup* Indians who wore scalps in their belts, and they wanted to know if the girls were not afraid. It was a bit difficult conversing, but the girls got out their French dictionary and managed to convey a little idea of the true America to the strangers. At last one of the soldiers in quite a matter of fact tone informed one of the girls that he was pleased with her and loved her very much. This put a hasty close to the conversation, the lassie informing him with much dignity that men did not talk in that way to girls they had just met in America and that she did not like it. Whereupon the girls withdrew to the other end of the kitchen and turned their backs on their callers, busying themselves with some reading, and the crest-fallen gallants presently left.

They only had a canteen here one day when they were called to go on to Neuvilly.

When the offensive was extended to the Argonne the Salvation Army followed along, keeping in touch with the troops so that they felt that the Salvation Army was ever with them, sharing their hardships and dangers, and always ready to serve them.

Just before a drive, close to the front, there are always blockades of trucks going either way.

The Salvation Army truck filled with the workers on their way to Neuvilly one dark night was caught in such a blockade. They crawled along making only about a mile an hour and stopping every few minutes until there was a chance to go on again. At last the wait grew longer and longer, the mud grew deeper, and the truck was having such a hard time that the little company of travellers decided to abandon it to the side of the road till morning and get out and walk to Neuvilly. There was a field hospital there and they felt sure they could be of use; and anyway, it was better than sitting in the truck all night. They were then about eight kilometers from the front. So they all got off and walked. But when they reached the place, found the hospital, and essayed to go in, the mud was so deep that they were stuck and unable to move forward. Some soldiers had to rescue them and carry them to the hospital on litters.

Their help was accepted gladly, and they went to work at once. There were many shell-shocked boys coming in who needed soothing and comforting, and a woman's hand so near the front was gratefully appreciated.

When at last there was a lull in the stream of wounded men the girls went to find a place to sleep for a little while. It was early morning, and sad sights met their eyes as they hurried down what had once been a pleasant village street. Destruction and desolation everywhere. The house that had been selected for a Salvation Army canteen was nearly all gone. One end was comparatively intact, with the floor still remaining, and this was to be for the canteen. The rest of the building was a series of shell holes surrounding a cellar from which the floor had been shot away.

The women reconnoitred and finally decided to unfold their cots and try to get a wink of sleep down in that cellar. It did not take them long to get settled. The cots were brought down and placed quickly among the fallen rafters, stone and tiling. Part of the walls that were standing leaned in at a perilous slant, threatening to fall at the slightest wind, but the lassies took off their shoes, rolled up in their blankets, and were at once oblivious to all about them, for they had been travelling all the day before and had worked hard all night.

One hour later, still early in the morning, they were awakened by the arrival of the truck and the thumping of boxes, tables and supplies as the Salvation Army truck drivers unloaded and set up the paraphernalia of the canteen. The girls opened their eyes and looked about them, and there all around the building were American soldiers, a head in every shell hole, watching them sleep. There was something thrilling in the silent audience looking down with holy eyes—yes, I said holy eyes!— for whatever the American soldier may be in his daily life he had nothing in his eyes but holy reverence for these women of God who were working night and day for him. There was something touching, too, in their attitude, for perhaps each one was thinking of his mother or sister at home as he looked down on these weary girls, rolled up in the brown blankets, with their neat little brown shoes in couples under their cots, nothing visible above the blankets but their pretty rumpled brown hair.

The women did not waste much more time in sleeping. They arose at once and got busy. There were five tables in the canteen above and already from each one there stretched a long line of men waiting silently, patiently for the time to arrive when there would be something good to eat. The girls had no more sleep that day, and there simply was no seclusion to be had anywhere. Everything was shell-riddled.

When night came on the question of beds arose again. The cellar seemed hardly possible, and the military officers considered the question.

Across the road from the most ruined end of the canteen building stood an old church. All of its north wall was gone save a supporting column in the middle, all the north roof gone. There were holes in all the other walls, and all the windows were gone. The floor was covered with *débris* and wreckage. It had been used all day for an evacuation hospital.

Just over the altar was a wonderful picture of the Christ ascending to heaven. It was still uninjured save for a shot through the heart.

The military officer stood on the steps of this ruined church, and, looking around in perplexity, remarked:

"Well, I guess this is the wholest place in town." Then stepping inside he glanced about and pointed:

"And this is the most secluded spot here!"

The seclusion was a pillar! But the girls were glad to get even that for there was no other place, and they were very weary. So they set up their little cots, and prepared to roll themselves in their blankets for a well-earned rest.

The boys had built a small bonfire on the stone floor

against a piece of one wall that was still standing, and now they sent a deputation to know if the girls would bring their guitars over and have a little music. The boys, of course, had no idea that the girls had not slept for more than twenty-four hours, and the girls never told them. They never even cast one wistful glance toward their waiting cots, but smilingly assented, and went and got their instruments.

Beneath the picture of the Christ, in front of the altar a few men were at work in an improvised office with four candles burning around them. In the rear of the church Lt.-Col. Frederick R. Fitzpatrick of the One Hundred and Tenth Ammunition Train had his office, and there another candle was burning. Some wounded men lay on stretchers in the shadowed northwest corner, and around the little fire the five Salvation Army lassies sat among two hundred soldiers. They sang at first the popular songs that everybody knew: "The Long, Long Trail," "Keep the Home Fires Burning," "Pack Up Your Troubles in Your Old Kit Bag and Smile! Smile! Smile!" and "Keep Your Head Down, Fritzie Boy!"

By and by some one called for a hymn, and then other hymns followed: "Jesus Lover of My Soul," "When the Roll Is Called Up Yonder," and, as always, the old favorite, "Tell Mother I'll Be There!"

They sang for at least an hour and a half, and then they did not want to stop. Oh, but it was a great sound that rolled through the old broken walls of the church and floated out into the night! One of the lassies said she would not change crowds with the biggest choir in New York.

Then they asked the girls to sing and the room was very still as two sweet voices thrilled out in a tender melody, speaking every word distinctly:

Beautiful Jesus, Bright Star of earth!
Loving and tender from moment of birth,
Beautiful Jesus, though lowly Thy lot,
Born in a manger, so rude was Thy cot!

Beautiful Jesus, gentle and mild,
Light for the sinner in ways dark and wild,
Beautiful Jesus, O save such just now,
As at Thy feet they in penitence bow!

Beautiful Christ! Beautiful Christ!
Fairest of thousands and Pearl of great price!
Beautiful Christ! Beautiful Christ!
Gladly we welcome Thee, Beautiful Christ!

Before they had finished many eyes had turned instinctively toward the picture in the weirdly flickering light.

Then the young Captain-lassie asked her sister to read the Ninety-first Psalm, "He that dwelleth in the secret place of the Most High shall abide under the shadow of the Almighty," and she told them that was a promise for those who trusted in God, and she wished they would think about it while they were going to sleep.

"This evening has made me think so much of home," she said thoughtfully, drooping her lashes and then raising them with a sweeping glance that included the whole group, while the firelight flickered up and lit her lovely serious face, and touched her hair with lights of gold, "I suppose it has made every one else feel that way," she went on; "I mean especially the evenings at home when the family gathered in the parlor, with one at the piano and brothers with their horns, and the rest with some kind of instrument, and we had a good 'sing;' and afterward father took the Bible and read the evening chapter, and then we had family prayers and kissed Mamma and Papa good night and went to bed. I shouldn't wonder if many of you used to have homes like that?"

The lassie raised her eyes again and looked on them. Many of the men nodded. It was beautiful to see the look that came into their faces at these recollections.

"And you used to have family prayers, too, didn't you?" she asked eagerly.

They nodded once more but some of them turned their faces away from the light quickly and brushed the back of their hands across their eyes.

"To-night has been a family gathering," she went on. "We girls are little sisters to all you big brothers, and we have had a delightful time with just the family, and the evening chapter has been read, and now I think it would not be complete if we did not have the family prayers before we separate and go to sleep."

Down went the heads in response, with reverent mien, and the place was very still while the lassie prayed. Afterward the boys joined their gruff voices, husky now with emotion, into the universal prayer with which she closed: "Our Father which are in heaven——"

They were all sorts and conditions of men gathered around the little fire in that old shell-torn church in Neuvilly that night. To quote from a letter written by a military officer, Lt.-Col. Frederick R. Fitzpatrick, to his wife:

There was the lad who was willing but not strong enough for field work, who was in the rear with the office; the walking wounded who had stopped for something to eat; the big, strong mule skinner who could throw a mule down or lift a case of ammunition, who was rough in appearance and speech and who would deny that the moisture in his eye was anything but the effects of the cold. There were the men who had been facing death a thousand times an hour for the last three days, who had not had a wash or a chance to take off their shoes and had been lying in mud in shell holes—men who looked as though they were chilled through and through; men on their way to the front, well knowing all the hardships and dangers which were ahead of them, but who were worried only about the delay in the traffic; doctors who had been working for three days without rest; men off ammunition and ration trucks, who had been at the wheel so long that they had forgotten whether it was three or four days and nights; wounded on their stretchers enjoying a smoke. And as I stepped in the door there were the feminine voices singing the good old tunes we all know so well, and not a sound in the church but as an accompaniment the distant booming of big guns, the rattle of small arms, the whirl of air craft, the passing of the ever-present column of trucks with rations and ammunition going up, and the wounded coming back; the shouted directions of the traffic police, the sound of the ammunition dump just outside the door and the rattle of the kitchens which surround the church, and which are working twenty-four hours a day.

There was the crowd of men, each uncovered, giving absolute undivided attention to the good, brave girls who were not making a meeting of it; it was just a meeting which grew—men who in their minds were back with mother and sister. The girls sang the good old songs, and then one of them offered a short prayer, in which all the men joined in spirit, and as I tip-toed out of the church it seemed to me that the four candles at the altar did not give all the light that was shown on the picture of Christ our Saviour. Every man in the building that night was in the very presence of God. It was not a religious meeting; it was a meeting full of religion. And it was a picture that will ever stand fresh in my memory and which will be an inspiration in time of doubt. There was nothing there but the real things, absolutely no sham of any kind. Oh, it was wonderful! I hope you can get just a little idea of what it was. I wish you would keep this letter. I want to be able to read it in future years.

In what remained of another village not far distant from Neuvilly, the lassies had a tent erected. The rain was endless—a driving drizzle which quickly soaked through everything but the staunchest raincoats in a very few moments. The ground was so thickly covered by shell craters that they could find no clear space wide enough for the tent. It so happened that almost in the centre of the tent there was a big shell crater. In this the girls lighted a fire. All through the night, and through nights to follow, wounded men limping back through the rain and mud to the dressing stations came in to warm themselves around the fire in the shell hole, and to drink of the coffee prepared by the girls. As they sat around the blazing wood, the fire cast strange shadows on the bleached brown canvas of the tent. In spite of their wounds, they were very cheerful, singing as lightly as though they were safe at home.

Everybody had worked hard at Neuvilly, but they felt they must get to their own outfit as soon as possible at the Field Hospital up in Cheppy where the wounded were coming in droves and the boys were pouring in from the front half-starved, having been fighting all night with nothing to eat except reserve rations. Some had been longer with only such rations as they took from their dead comrades. The need was most urgent, but the puzzle was how to get there. The roads had been shelled and ploughed by explosives until there was no possible semblance of a way, and there were no conveyances to be had. The Zone Major had gone back for supplies, telling the girls to get the first conveyance possible going up the road. That was enough for the girls. "We've *got* to get there" they said, and when they said that one knew they would. They searched diligently and at last found a way. One girl rode on a reel cart, one on a mule team and one went with an old wagon. They went over roads that had to be made ahead of them by the engineers, and late in the night, bruised and sore from head to foot, they arrived at their destination.

The next morning they reported at the hospital for work and the Major in charge said: "I never was so glad to see anybody in my life!"

They went straight to work and served coffee and sandwiches to the poor half-starved men. The Red Cross men were there, also, with sandwiches, hot chocolate and candy.

The wounded men continued to pour in, later to be evacuated to the base hospital; they kept coming and coming, a thousand men where two hundred had been expected. There was plenty to be done. The girls were put in charge of different wards. They were under shell fire continually, but they were too busy to think of that as they hurried about ministering to the brave soldiers, who gave never a groan from their white lips no matter what they suffered.

The girls worked about eighteen hours a day, and slept from about one or two at night to five or six in the morning. The hospital was in front of the artillery and every shell that went over to Germany passed over their heads. When they had been there five days under continual shell fire from the enemy the General gave orders that they *must* leave, that it was no fit place for women so near to the front.

When the Salvation Army Zone Major brought this order to the girls rebellion shone in their eyes and they declared they would not leave! They knew they were needed there, and there they would stay! The Zone Major surveyed them with intense satisfaction. He turned on his heel and went back to the General:

"General," he said, with a twinkle, "my girls say they won't go."

The General's face softened, and the twinkle flashed across to his eyes, with something like a tear behind its fire. Somehow he didn't look like a Commanding Officer who had just been defied. A wonderful light broke over his face and he said:

"Well, if the Salvation Army wants to stay let them stay!" And so they stayed.

It was in a German-dug cave that they had their headquarters, cut out of the side of a hill and opening into the hospital yard. It was a work of art, that cave. There was a passage-way a hundred feet long with avenues each side and places for cots, room enough to accommodate a hundred men.

The German airplanes came in droves. When the bugle sounded every one must get under cover. There must be nobody in sight for the Germans were out to get individuals, and even one person was not too insignificant for them to waste their ammunition upon. They had a mistaken idea, perhaps, that this sort of thing destroyed our morale. The tents, of course, were no protection against shells and bombs, and presently the

Boche began to shell the town in good earnest, especially at night. Gas alarms, also, would sound out in the middle of the night and everybody would have to rush out and put on their gas masks. They would not last long at a time, of course, but it broke up any rest that might have been had, and it was only too evident that the enemy was trying to get the range on the hospital.

One morning, standing by the window making cocoa for the boys, one of the lassies saw an eight-inch shell land between the hospital tents, ten feet in front of the window, and only five feet from the door of the place where the severely wounded were lying. These shells always kill at two hundred feet. All that saved them was that the shell buried itself deep in the soft earth and was a dud.

The shells were coming every twenty minutes and there was no time to lose for now the enemy had their range. At once all hands got busy and began to evacuate the wounded men into the Salvation Army cave. The cave would accommodate seventy men, but they managed to get a hundred men inside, most of them on litters. They were all safe and the girls heard the whistle of the next shell and made haste toward safety themselves. But someone had carelessly dropped a whole outfit of blankets and things across the passageway of the dugout and the first woman to enter fell across it, shutting out the other two. Before anything could be done the next shell struck the doorway, partly burying the fallen young woman. Inside the dugout rocks came down on some of the men on litters, and anxious hands extricated the lassie from the *débris* that had fallen upon her, and lifted her tenderly. She was pretty badly bruised and lamed, besides being wounded on her leg, but the brave young woman would not claim her wound, nor let it become known to the military authorities lest they would forbid the girls to stay at the front any longer. So for three weeks she patiently limped about and worked with the rest, quietly bearing her pain, and would not go to the hospital. One lassie outside was struck on the helmet by a piece of falling rock. If she had not had on her helmet she would have been killed.

The shelling continued for six hours.

The hospital was all the time filled with wounded men and there was plenty to be done twenty-four hours out of every day. The women moved about among the men as if they were their own brothers.

A poor shell-shocked boy lay on his cot talking wildly in delirium, living over the battle again, charging his men, ordering them to advance.

"Company H. Advance! See that hill over there? It's full of Germans, but *we've got to take it!*"

Then he turned over and began to sob and cry, "Oh God! Oh God!"

A lassie went to him and soothed him, talking to him gently about home, asking him questions about his mother, until he grew calm and began to answer her, and rested back quite rationally. The stretcher-bearers came to take him to another hospital, and he started up, put out his hand and cried: "Oh nurse! I've got to get back to my men! *I'm the only one left!*"

Thus the heart-breaking scenes were multiplied.

One boy came back to the hospital in the Argonne badly wounded. He called the lassie to him one day as she passed through the ward, and motioned her to lean down so he could talk to her. He said he knew he was hard hit and he wanted to tell her something.

"I was wounded, lying on the ground over there in No Man's Land," he went on. "It was all dark and I was waiting for someone to come along and help me. I thought it was all up with me and while I was lying there

I felt something. I can't explain it, but I knew it was there and I saw my mother and I prayed. Then my Buddy came along and I asked him if he could baptize me. He said he wasn't very good himself but he guessed the heavenly Father would understand. So he stooped down and got some muddy water out of a shell hole close by and put it on my forehead, and prayed; and now I know it's all right. I wanted you to know."

Often the boys, just before they went over the top, would come to these girls and say:

"We're going up there, now. You pray for us, won't you?"

One day some boys came to the hut when there were not many about and asked the girls if they might talk with them. These boys were going over the top that night.

"We fellows want to ask you something," they said. "Some of the chaplains have been telling us that if we go over there and die for liberty that it'll be all right with us afterward. But we don't believe that dope and we want to know the truth. Do you mean to tell me that if a man has lived like the devil he's going to be saved just because he got killed fighting? Why, some of us fellows didn't even go of our own accord. We were drafted. And do you mean to tell me that counts just the same? We want to know the truth!"

And then the girls had their opportunity to point the way to Jesus and speak of repentance, salvation from sin, and faith in the Saviour of the world.

A lassie was stooping over one young boy lying on a cot, washing his face and trying to make him more comfortable, and she noticed a hole in his breast pocket. Stooping closer she examined it and found it was a piece of high explosive shell that had gone through the cloth of his pocket and was embedded in his Testament, which he, like many of the boys, always kept in his breast pocket.

Another boy lay on a cot biting his lips to bear the agony of pain, and she asked him what was the matter, was the wound in his leg so bad? He nodded without opening his eyes. She went to ask the doctor if the boy couldn't have some morphine to dull the pain. The Sergeant in charge came over and looked at him, examined the bandage on the boy's leg and then exclaimed: "Who bandaged this leg?"

"I did," said the boy weakly, "I did the best I could."

The poor fellow had bandaged his own leg and then walked to the hospital. The bandage had looked all right and no one had examined it until then, but the Sergeant found that it was so tight that it had stopped the circulation. He took off the bandage and made him comfortable, and the agony left him. In a little while the Salvation Army lassie passed that way again and found the boy with a little book open, reading.

"What is it?" she asked, looking at the book.

"My Testament," he answered with a smile.

"Are you a Christian?"

"Oh, yes," he said with another smile that meant volumes.

It grew dark in the tent for they dared not have lights on account of the enemy always watching, but stooping near a little later she could see that his lips were murmuring in prayer. There was an angelic smile on his white, dead face in the morning when they came to take him away.

There was a funeral every day in that place. A hundred boys were buried that week. Always the girls sang at the graves, and prayed. There would be just the grave digger, a few people, and some of the boys. Off to one side the Germans were buried. When the simple services over our own dead were complete one of the girls would say: "Now, friends, let us go and say a prayer beside our enemy's graves. They are some mother's boys, and some woman is waiting for them to come home!"

And then the prayers would be said once more, and another song sung.

Those were solemn, sorrowful times, death and destruction on every side. The fighting was everywhere. United States anti-aircraft guns firing at German planes; Germans firing at us; air fights in the sky above.

And in the midst of it all the boys had meetings every night on log piles out in the open. These meetings would begin with popular songs, but the boys would soon ask for the hymns and the meetings would work themselves out without any apparent leading up to it. The boys wanted it. They wanted to hear about religious things. They hungered for it. So they were held at the throne of God each night by the wonderful men and girls who had learned to know human hearts, and had attained such skill in leading them to the Christ for whom they lived.

It was not alone the doughnut that bound the hearts of the boys to the Salvation Army in France, it was what was behind the doughnut; and here, in these wonderful God-led meetings they found the secret of it all. Many of them came and told the girls they did not believe in the so-called "trench religion" and wanted to know the truth from them. And those girls told them the way of eternal life in a simple, beautiful way, not mincing matters, nor ignoring their sins and unworthiness, but pointing the way to the Christ who died to save them from sin, and who even now was waiting in silent Presence to offer them Himself. Great numbers of the men accepted Christ, and pledged themselves to live or die for Him whatever came to them.

How close the Salvation Army people had grown to the hearts and lives of the men was shown by the fact that when they came back from the fight they would always come to them as if they had come to report at home:

"We've escaped!" they would say. "We don't know how it is, but we think it's because you girls were praying for us, and the folks at home were praying, too!"

There were three cardinal principles which were deemed necessary to success in this work. The first and most important depended upon winning the confidence of the boys. This was a prime requisite in any work with the boys, especially by a religious organization.

The first quality looked for in a person professing religion is always consistency. It was felt that if the boys saw that the Salvation Army was consistent, that it stood only for those things in France which it was known to stand for in the United States, that the first step would be established in winning the confidence of the boy. It was therefore determined that the Salvation Army would not, under any circumstances, compromise, and that it should stand out in its religious work and adhere to its teachings as firmly and as vigorously as it was known to do at home.

A stand upon the tobacco question was, therefore, highly important. Other organizations were encouraging the use of tobacco but those who had come in contact with the Salvation Army at home knew that it had always discouraged its use, and although the officers had to go against the judgment of many high military authorities who thought they should handle it, they decided that the Salvation Army would not handle tobacco and that no one wearing its uniform should use it. The consistency of the Salvation Army and the careful conduct of its workers won the esteem of the boys.

The second requisite was that the Salvation Army should be willing to share their hardships. To accomplish this, it was made a rule that Salvation Army workers should not mess with the officers but should draw their rations at the soldiers' mess, also that they should not associate with the officers more than was absolutely necessary and that in the huts. It was neither possible nor desirable that officers should be kept out of the huts, but as far as possible soldiers were made to feel that the Salvation Army was in France to serve them and not for its own pleasure or convenience.

The third requisite was that the Salvation Army should be willing to share their dangers and this was proved to them when they went to the trenches—the Salvation Army moved to the trenches with them and established huts and outposts as close to the front line as was permitted.

The Armistice

AFTER the Armistice was signed, on November 11th, it was a great question what disposition would be made of the troops. It was concluded that they would be sent home as rapidly as possible and that the three ports—Brest, St. Nazaire and Bordeaux—would be used for that purpose. Immediately arrangements were made for the opening of Salvation Army work at the base ports with a view to letting the boys have a last sight of the Salvation Army as they left the shores of France. The Salvation Army had served them in the training area and at the front and were still serving them as they left the shores of the old world and it would meet them again when they arrived on the shores of the home-land. In this way the contact of the Salvation Army would be continuous, so that when they returned, it would be able to reach their hearts and affect their lives with the Gospel of Christ.

The problem of buildings was, of course, the first one and a very difficult one. To secure buildings of adequate size, which could be constructed in a short space of time, was almost out of the question, but it occurred to the officers that the aviation section would be demobilizing and that they had brought over portable steel buildings, for use as hangars. The matter was taken up at once with the military authorities and twenty of these steel buildings were secured—each of them sixty-six feet wide by one hundred feet long. It was planned to place eight of them at Bordeaux, six at St. Nazaire and six at Brest. By placing two of them end to end it was possible to secure one auditorium sixty-six feet wide by two hundred feet long—capable of seating three thousand men. Adjoining that could be another building sixty-six feet by one hundred feet, to be used for canteen and rest room.

It was planned to proceed with a religious campaign at these Base Ports, holding Salvation meetings in these extensive departments.

When the Army of Occupation was started for Germany, two Salvation Army trucks were assigned to go along with the Army. Whenever the Army of Occupation stopped for a space of two or three days, places were secured where doughnuts could be fried, pies made, and at all times hot coffee and chocolate were available for the men.

When the American soldiers marched through the villages of Alsace-Lorraine the Salvationists marched with them. At Esch and Luxemburg they were in all the rejoicing and triumph of the parade, bringing succor and comfort wherever they could find an opportunity.

When the men arrived at Coblenz the Salvation Army was there before them, and on their crossing the Rhine, arrangements had been made for the location of the Salvation Army work at the principal points in the

Rhinehead. They are now conducting Salvation Army operations with the Army of Occupation.

One of the occasions when President Wilson clapped for the Salvation Army was at the inauguration of the Soldiers' Association in Paris. The Y had invited all the other organizations to be present. The meeting was held in the Palais de Glace, which seats about ten thousand people.

President and Mrs. Wilson were present, accompanied by many prominent American officials. Representatives of the various War Work Organizations spoke.

The Salvationist who had been selected to represent the Army at this meeting had been in the United States Navy for twelve years and was a chaplain.

When he was called upon to speak the boys with one accord as if by preconcerted action arose to their feet and gave him an ovation. Of course, it was not given to the man but to the uniform.

A soldier of the Rainbow Division sitting next to one of the Salvation Army workers over there, kept telling him what the boys thought of the Salvation Army, and when the cheering began he poked the Salvationist in the ribs and whispered joyously:

"I told you! I told you! We've just been waiting for eight months to pull this off! Now, you see!"

The speaker when given opportunity did not attempt to make a great speech. He told in simple, vivid sentences of the services of the Salvation Army just back of the trenches under fire; and President Wilson sat listening and applauding with the rest.

The chaplain paid a tribute to President Wilson, finishing with these words:

"President Wilson was not man-elected, but God-selected!"

CHAPLAINS

For some little time after the War started it was a question as to whether the Salvation Army was entitled to any representation in the realm of Chaplaincies of the United States forces. During the progress of the consideration Adjutant Harry Kline secured an appointment with the Nebraska National Guard, and his regiment being made a part of the National Army, he was received as an officer of the same and thus became our first Army Chaplain.

The War Office decided favorably with regard to the question of our general representation, and shortly thereafter Adjutant John Allan, of Bowery fame, was given a first lieutenancy and then followed, in the order given, Captain Ernest Holz, Adjutant Ryan and Captain Norman Marshall.

The exceptional service that these men have rendered is of sufficient importance to have a much wider notice than where only the barest of reference is possible. Shortly after arrival in France Chaplain Allan was being very favorably noticed because of the character of the work which he was doing, and it was gratifying to learn that this confidence was reflected in his appointment as Senior Chaplain of his regiment and his assignment to special service where probity and wisdom were essential. Shortly thereafter he was taken to the Army Headquarters, where up to the present time he is most highly esteemed as a co-laborer with Bishop Brent, the Chaplain-General of the overseas forces.

Typical of the enthusiasm of each of the five men appointed as Chaplains, the following story is told of First Lieutenant Ernest Holz, who was inducted into his office as Senior Chaplain of his regiment right at the commencement of his career.

At the beginning of the year, when Chaplain Holz knew his Salvation Army comrades would, as usual, be engaged in special revival work, he thought it would be a worthy thing to time a similar effort among the men of his regiment. Approaching the Colonel, he found him in hearty agreement concerning the effort, and so securing the assistance of his fellow chaplains they arranged for a series of meetings nightly for one week, with the result that two hundred of the men of the regiment confessed Christ and practically all of them were deeply interested.

The effort was wholly directed to the uplift of the men and God commanded His blessing in a most gratifying manner.

Homecoming

THE BOAT docked that morning, and one soldier at least, as he stood on the deck and watched the shores of his native land draw nearer, felt mingling with the thrill of joy at his return a vague uneasiness. He was coming back, it is true, but it had been a long time and a lot of things had happened. For one thing he had lost his foot. That in itself was a pretty stiff proposition. For another thing he was not wearing any decorations save the wound stripes on his sleeve. Those would have been enough, and more than enough, for his mother if she were alive, but she had gone away from earth during his absence, and the girl he had kissed good-bye and promised great things was peculiar. The question was, would she stand for that amputated foot? He didn't like to think it of her, but he found he wasn't sure. Perhaps, if there had been a croix de guerre! He had promised her to win that and no end of other honors, when he went away so buoyant and hopeful; but almost on his first day of real battle he had been hurt and tossed aside like a derelict, to languish in a hospital, with no more hope of wining anything. And now he had come home with one foot gone, and no distinction!

He hadn't told the girl yet about the foot. He didn't know as he should. He felt lonely and desolate in spite of his joy at getting back to "God's Country." He frowned at the hazy outline of the great city from which tall buildings were beginning to differentiate themselves as they drew nearer. There was New York. He meant to see New York, of course. He was a Westerner and had never had an opportunity to go about the metropolis of his own country. Of course, he would see it all. Perhaps, after he was demobilized he would stay there. Maybe he wouldn't send word he had come back. Let them think he was killed or taken prisoner, or missing, or anything they liked. There were things to do in New York. There were places where he would be welcome even with one foot gone and no cross of war. Thus he mused as the boat drew nearer the shore and the great city loomed close at hand. Then, suddenly, just as the boat was touching the pier and a long murmur of joy went up from the wanderers on board, his eyes dropped idly to the dock and there in her trim little overseas uniform, with the sunlight glancing from the silver letters on the scarlet shield of her trench cap and the smile radiating from her sweet face, stood the very same Salvation Army lassie who had bent over him as he lay on the ground just back of the trenches waiting to be put in the ambulance and taken to the hospital after he had been wounded. He could feel again the throbbing pain in his leg, the sickening pain of his head as he lay in the hot sun, with the flies swarming everywhere, the horrible din of battle all about, and his tongue parched and swollen with fever from lying all night in pain on the wet ground of No Man's Land. She had laid a soft little hand on his hot forehead, bathed his face, and brought him a cold drink of lemonade. If he lived to be a hundred years old he would never taste anything so good as that lemonade had been. Afterward the doctor said it was the good cold drink that day that saved the lives of those fever patients who had lain so long without attention. Oh, he would never forget the Salvation lassie! And there she was alive and at home! She hadn't been killed as the fellows had been afraid she would. She had come through it all and here she was always ahead and waiting to welcome a fellow home. It brought the tears smarting to his eyes to think about it, and he leaned over the rail of the ship and yelled himself hoarse with the rest over her, forgetting all about his lost foot.

It was hours before they were off the ship. All the red tape necessary for the movement of such a company of men had to be unwound and wound up again smoothly, and the time stretched out interminably; but somehow it did not seem so hard to wait now, for there was someone down there on the dock that he could speak to, and perhaps—just *perhaps*—he would tell her of his dilemma about his girl. Somehow he felt that she would understand.

He watched eagerly when he was finally lined up on the wharf waiting for roll-call, for he was sure she would come; and she did, swinging down the line with her arms full of chocolate, handing out telegraph blanks and postal cards, real postal cards with a stamp on them that could be mailed anywhere. He gripped one in his big, rough hand as if it were a life preserver. A real, honest-to-goodness postal card! My it was good to see the old red and white stamp again! And he spoke impulsively:

"You're the girl that saved my life out there in the field, don't you remember? With the lemonade!"

Her face lit up. She had recognized him and somehow cleared one hand of chocolate and telegrams to grasp his with a hearty welcome: "I'm so glad you came through all right!" her cheery voice said.

All right! *All right!* Did she call it all right? He looked down at his one foot with a dubious frown. She was quick to see. She understood.

"Oh, but that's nothing!" she said, and somehow her voice put new heart into him. "Your folks will be so glad to have you home you'll forget all about it. Come, aren't you going to send them a telegram?" And she held out the yellow blank.

But still he hesitated.

"I don't know," he said, looking down at his foot again. "Mother's gone, and——"

Instantly her quick sympathy enveloped his sore soul, and he felt that just the inflection of her voice was like balm when she said: "I'm so sorry!" Then she added:

"But isn't there somebody else? I'm sure there was. I'm sure you told me about a girl I was to write to if you didn't come through. Aren't you going to let her know? Of course you are."

"I don't know," said the boy. "I don't think I am. Maybe I'll never go back now. You see, I'm not what I was when I went away."

"Nonsense!" said the lassie with that cheerful assurance that had carried her through shell fire and made her merit the pet name of "Sunshine" that the boys had given her in the trenches. "Why, that wouldn't be fair to her. Of course, you're going to let her know right away. Leave it to me. Here, give me her address!"

Quick as a flash she had the address and was off to a telephone booth. This was no message that could wait to go back to headquarters. It must go at once.

He saw her again before he left the wharf. She gave him a card with two addresses written on it:

"This first is where you can drop in and rest when you

are tired," she explained. "It's just one of our huts; the other is where you can find a good bed when you are in the city."

Then she was off with a smile down the line, giving out more telegraph blanks and scattering sunshine wherever she went. He glanced back as he left the pier and saw her still floating eagerly here and there like a little sister looking after more real brothers.

The next day, when he was free and on a few days leave from camp, he started out with his crutch to see the city, but the thought of her kept him from some of the places where his feet might have strayed. Yet she had not said a word of warning. Her smile and the look in her eyes had placed perfect confidence in him, and he could remember the prayer she had uttered in a low tone back there at the dressing station behind the trenches in the ear of a companion who was not going to live to get to the Base Hospital, and who had begged her to pray with him before he went. Somehow it lingered with him all day and changed his ideas of what he wanted to see in New York.

But it was a long hard tramp he had set for himself to see the town with that one foot. He hadn't much money for cars, even if he had known which cars to take, so he hobbled along and saw what he could. He was all alone, for the fellows he started with went so fast and wanted to do so many things that he could not do, that he had made an excuse to shake them off. They were kind. They would not have left him if they had known; but he wasn't going to begin his new life having everybody put out on his account, so he was alone. And it was toward evening. He was very tired. It seemed to him that he couldn't go another block. If only there were a place somewhere where he could sit down a little while and rest; even a doorstep would do if there were only one near at hand. Of course, there were saloons, and there would always be soldiers in them. He would likely be treated, and there would be good cheer, and a chance to forget for a little while; but somehow the thought of that Salvation lassie and the cheery way she had made him send that telegram kept him back. When a girl with painted cheeks stopped and smiled in his face he passed her by, and half wondered why he did it. He must go somewhere presently and get a bite to eat, but it couldn't be much for he wanted to save money enough and hunt up that lodging house where there were nice beds. How much he wanted that bed!

It was quite dark now. The lights were lit everywhere. He was coming to a great thoroughfare. He judged by his slight knowledge of the city that it might be Broadway. There would likely be a restaurant somewhere near. He hurried on and turned into the crowded street. How cold it was! The wind cut him like a knife. He had been a fool to come off alone like this! Just out of the hospital, too. Perhaps he would get sick and have to go to another hospital. He shivered and stopped to pull his collar up closer around his neck. Then suddenly he stood still and stared with a dazed, bewildered expression, straight ahead of him. Was he getting a bit leary? He passed his hand over his eyes and looked again. Yes, there it was! Right in the midst of the busy, hurrying throng of Union Square! He made sure it was Union Square, for he looked up at the street sign to be certain it wasn't Willow Vale—or Heaven—right there where streets met and crossed, and cars and trolleys and trucks whirled, and people passed in throngs all day, just across the narrow road, stood the loveliest, most perfect little white clapboard cottage that ever was built on this earth, with porches all around and a big tree growing up through the roof of one porch. It stood out against the night like a wonderful mirage, like a heavenly dove descended into the turmoil of the pit, like home and mother in the midst of a rushing pitiless world. He could have cried real tears of wonder and joy as he stood there, gazing. He felt as though he were one of those motion pictures in which a lone Klondiker sits by his campfire cooking a can of salmon or baked beans, and up above him on the screen in one corner appears the Christmas tree where his wife and baby at home are celebrating and missing him. It seemed just as unreal as that to see that little beautiful home cottage set down in the midst of the city.

The windows were all lit up with a warm, rosy light and there were curtains at the windows, rosy pink curtains like the ones they used to have at the house where his girl lived, long ago before the War spoiled him. He stood and continued to gaze until a lot of cash-boys, let loose from the toil of the day, rushed by and almost knocked his crutch from under him. Then he determined to get nearer this wonder. Carefully watching his opportunity he hobbled across the street and went slowly around the building. Yes, it was real. Some public building, of course, but how wonderful to have it look so like a home! Why had they done it?

Then he came around toward the side, and there in plain letters was a sign: "SOLDIERS AND SAILORS IN UNIFORM WELCOME." What? Was it possible? Then he might go in? What kind of a place could it be?

He raised his eyes a little and there, slung out above the neatly shingled porch, like any sign, swung an immense fat brown doughnut a foot and a half in diameter, with the sugar apparently still sticking to it, and inside the rough hole sat a big white coffee cup. His heart leaped up and something suddenly gave him an idea. He fumbled in his pocket, brought out a card, saw that this was the Salvation Army hut, and almost shouted with joy. He lost no time in hurrying around to the door and stepping inside.

There revealed before him was a great cozy room, with many easy-chairs and tables, a piano at which a young soldier sat playing ragtime, and at the farther end a long white counter on which shone two bright steaming urns that sent forth a delicious odor of coffee. Through an open door behind the counter he caught a glimpse of two Salvation Army lassies busy with some cups and plates, and a third enveloped in a white apron was up to her elbows in flour, mixing something in a yellow bowl. By one of the little tables two soldier boys were eating doughnuts and coffee, and at another table a sailor sat writing a letter. It was all so cozy and homelike that it took his breath away and he stood there blinking at the lights that flooded the rooms from graceful white bowl-like globes that hung suspended from the ceiling by brass chains. He saw that the rosy light outside had come from soft pink silk sash curtains that covered the lower part of the windows, and there were inner draperies of some heavier flowered material that made the whole thing look real and substantial. The willow chairs had cushions of the same flowered stuff. The walls were a soft pearly gray below and creamy white above, set off by bands of dark wood, and a dark floor with rush mats strewn about. He looked around slowly, taking in every detail almost painfully. It was such a contrast to the noisy, rushing street, a contrast to the hospital, and the trenches and all the life with which he had been familiar during the past few dreadful months. It made him think of home and mother. He began to be afraid he was going to cry like a great big baby, and he looked around nervously for a place to get out of sight. He saw a fellow going upstairs and at a distance he followed him. Up there was another bright, quiet room, curtained and cushioned like the other, with more easy willow chairs, round willow tables, and desks over by the wall where one might write. The soldier who had come up ahead of him was already settled writing now at a desk in the far corner. There were bookcases between the windows with new beautifully bound books in them, and there were magazines scattered around, and no rules that one must not spit on the floor, or put their feet in the chairs, or anything of the sort. Only, of course, no one would ever dream of doing anything like that in such a place. How beautiful it was, and how quiet and peaceful! He sank into a chair and looked about him. What rest!

And now there were real tears in his eyes which he hastened to brush roughly away, for someone was coming toward him and a hand was on his shoulder. A man's voice, kindly, pleasant, brotherly, spoke:

"All in, are you, my boy? Well, you just sit and rest yourself awhile. What do you think of our hut? Good place to rest? Well, that's what we want it to be to you, Home. Just drop in here whenever you're in town and want a place to rest or write, or a bite of something homelike to eat."

He looked up to the broad shoulders in their well-fitting dark blue uniform, and into the kindly face of the gray-haired Colonel of the Salvation Army who happened to step in for a minute on business and had read the look on the lonesome boy's face just in time to give a word of cheer. He could have thrown his arms around the man's neck and kissed him if he only hadn't been too shy. But in spite of the shyness he found himself talking with this fine strong man and telling him some of his disappointments and perplexities, and when the older man left him he was strengthened in spirit from the brief conversation. Somehow it didn't look quite so black a prospect to have but one foot.

He read a magazine for a little while and then, drawn by the delicious odors, he went downstairs and had some coffee and doughnuts. He saw while he was eating that the front porch opened out of the big lower room and was all enclosed in glass and heated with radiators. A lot of fellows were sitting around there in easy-chairs, smoking, talking, one or two sleeping in their chairs or reading papers. It had a dim, quiet light, a good place to rest and think. He was more and more filled with wonder. Why did they do it? Not for money, for they charged hardly enough to pay for the materials in the food they sold, and he knew by experience that when one had no money one could buy of them just the same if one were in need.

Later in the evening he took out the little card again and looked up the other address. He wanted one of those clean, sweet beds that he had been hearing about, that one could get for only a quarter a night, with all the shower-bath you wanted thrown in. So he went out again and found his way down to Forty-first Street.

There was something homelike about the very atmosphere as he entered the little office room and looked about him. Beyond, through an open door he could see a great red brick fireplace with a fire blazing cheerfully and a few fellows sitting about reading and playing checkers. Everybody looked as if they felt at home.

When he signed his name in the big register book the young woman behind the desk who wore an overseas uniform glanced at his signature and then looked up as if she were welcoming an old friend:

"There's a telegram here for you," she said pleasantly. "It came last night and we tried to locate you at the camp but did not succeed. One of our girls went over to camp

this afternoon, but they said you were gone on a furlough, so we hoped you would turn up."

She handed over the telegram and he took it in
wonder. Who would send him a telegram? And here of
all places! Why, how would anybody know he would be
here? He was so excited his crutch trembled under his
arm as he tore open the envelope and read:

"Dear Billy (It was a regular letter!):
"I am leaving to-night for New York. Will meet
you at Salvation Hostel day after to-morrow
morning. What is a foot more or less? Can't I be
hands and feet for you the rest of your life? I'm
proud, proud, proud of you!
Signed "Jean."

He found great tears coming into his eyes and his
throat was full of them, too. It didn't matter if that
Salvation Army lassie behind the counter did see them
roll down his cheeks. He didn't care. She would understand anyway, and he laughed out loud in his joy and
relief, the first joy, the first relief since he was hurt!

Some one else was coming in the door, another fellow
maybe, but the lassie opened a door in the desk and drew
him behind the counter in a shaded corner where no one
would notice and brought him a cup of tea, which she
said was all they had around to eat just then. She didn't
pay any attention to him till he got his equilibrium again.

She was the kind of woman one feels is a natural-born
mother. In fact, the fellows were always asking her
wistfully: "May we call you Mother?" Young enough to
understand and enter into their joys and sorrows, yet old
enough to be wise and sweet and true. She mothered
every boy that came.

A sailor boy once asked if he might bring his girl to

see her. He said he wanted her to see her so she could tell his mother about her.

"But can't you tell her about your girl?" she asked.

"Oh, yes, but I want you to tell her," he said. "You see, whatever you say mother'll know is true."

So presently she turned to this lonely boy and took him upstairs through the pleasant upper room with its piano and games, its sun parlor over the street, lined with trailing ferns, with cheery canaries in swinging tasseled cages, who looked fully as happy and at home as did the soldier boys who were sitting about comfortably reading.

She found him a room with only one other bunk in it. Nice white beds with springs like air and mattresses like down. She showed him where the shower-baths were, and with a kindly good-night left him. He almost wanted to ask her to kiss him good-night, so much like his own mother she seemed.

Before he got into that white bed he knelt beside it, all clean and comfortable and happy like a little child that had wandered a long way from home and got back again, and he told God he was sorry and ashamed for all the way he had doubted, and sinned, and he wanted to live a new life and be good. Then he lay down to sleep. Tomorrow morning Jean would be there. And she didn't mind about the foot! She didn't mind! How wonderful!

And then he had a belated memory of the little Salvation Army lassie on the wharf who had brought all this about, and he closed his eyes and murmured out loud to the clean, white walls: "God bless her! Oh, God bless her!"

This is only one of the many stories that might be told about the boys who have been helped by the various activities of the Salvation Army, both at home and abroad.

It would be well worth one's while to visit their Brooklyn Hospital and their New York Hospital and all their other wonderful institutions. In several of them are many little children, some mere infants, belonging to soldiers and sailors away in the war. In some instances the mother is dead, or has to work. If she so desires she is given work in the institution, which is like a real home, and allowed to be with her child and care for it. Where both mother and father are dead the child remains for six years or until a home elsewhere is provided for it. Here the little ones are well cared for, not in the ordinary sense of an institution, but as a child would be cared for in a home, with beauty and love, and pleasure mingling with the food and shelter and raiment that is usually supplied in an institution. These children are prettily, though simply, dressed and not in uniform; with dainty bits of color in hair ribbon, collar, necktie or frock; the babies have wee pink and blue wool caps and sacks like any beloved little mites, they ride around on Kiddie Cars, play with doll houses and have a fine Kindergarten teacher to guide their young minds, and the best of hospital service when they are ailing. But that is another story, and there are yet many of them. If everybody could see the beautiful life-size painting of Christ blessing the little children which is painted right on the very wall and blended into the tinting, they could better comprehend the spirit which pervades this lovely home.

The New York Hospital, which has just been rebuilt and refurnished with all the latest appliances, is in charge of a devoted woman physician, who has given her life to healing, and has at the head of its Board one of the most noted surgeons in the city, who gives his services free, and boasts that he enjoys it best of all his work. Here those of small means or of no means at all, especially those belonging to soldiers and sailors, may find healing of the wisest and most expert kind, in cheery, airy, sanitary and beautiful rooms. But here, too, to understand, one must see. Just a peep into one of those dainty white rooms would rest a poor sick soul; just a glance at the room full of tiny white basket cribs with dainty blue satin-bound blankets—real wool blankets—and white spreads, would convince one.

And what one sees in New York in the line of such activities is duplicated in most of the other large cities of the United States.

Not the least of the Salvation Army service for the returning soldiers is the work that is done on the docks by the lassies meeting returning troop ships. They send telegrams free, not C.O.D., for them, give the men stamped postal cards, hunt up relatives, answer questions, and give them chocolate while they wait for the inevitable roll call before they can entrain. Often these girls will sit up half the night after having met boats nearly all day, to get the telegrams all off that night. It is interesting to note that on one single day, April 20th, 1919, the Salvation Army Headquarters in New York sent 2900 such free telegrams for returning soldiers.

The other day the father of a soldier came to Headquarters with an anxious face, after a certain unit from overseas had returned. It was the unit in which his boy had gone to France, but he had written saying he was in the hospital without stating what was the matter or how serious his wound. No further word had been received and the father and mother were frenzied with grief. They had tried in every way to get information but could find out nothing. The Salvation Army went to work on the telephone and in a short time were able to locate the missing boy in a Casual Company soon to return, and to report to his anxious father that he was recovering rapidly.

Another soldier arrived in New York and sent a Salvation Army telegram to his father and mother in California who had previously received notification that he was dead. A telegram came back to the Salvation Army almost at once from the West stating this fact and begging someone to go to the camp where the boy's Casual Company was located and find out if he were really living. One of the girls from the office went over to the Debarkation Hospital immediately and saw the boy, and was able to telegraph to his parents that he was perfectly recovered and only awaiting transportation to California. He was overjoyed to see someone who had heard from his parents.

A portion of one troop ship had been reserved for soldiers having influenza. These men were kept on board long after all the others had left the ship. A Salvation Army worker seeing them with the white masks over their faces went on board and served them with chocolate, distributing post cards and telegraph blanks. When she was leaving the ship a Captain said to her rather brusquely: "Don't you realize that you have done a foolish thing? Those men have influenza and your serving them might mean your death!"

Looking up into the man's eyes the Salvationist said: "I am ready to die if God sees fit to call me."

The officer laughed and told her that was the first time in his life he had known anyone to say they were ready to die and would willingly expose themselves to such a contagious disease.

"Aren't you ready to die?" asked the girl. "Certainly not," replied the Captain. "Sometimes I think I am hardly fit to live, much less die."

"Don't you realize that there is a Power which can enable you to live in such a way as to make you ready to die?"

"Oh, well, I don't bother about going to church, in fact, I don't bother about religion at all, although I must say once or twice when I was up the line over there I wished I did know something about religion, that is, the kind that makes a fellow feel good about dying; but I don't want to go to church and go through all that business."

"It is possible to accept Christ here and now on this very spot—on this ship—if you'll only believe," said the girl wistfully.

The Captain could not help being interested and thoughtful. When she left after a little more talk he put out his hand and said:

"Thank you. You've done me more good than any sermon could have done me, and believe me, I am going to pray and trust God to help me live a different life."

Sad things are seen on the docks at times when the ships come into port, and the boys are coming home.

A soldier in a basket, with both arms and both legs gone and only one eye, was being carried tenderly along.

"Why do you let him live?" asked one pityingly of the Commanding Officer.

The gruff, kindly voice replied:

"You don't know what life is. We don't live through our arms and legs. We live through our hearts."

Some of our boys have learned out there amid shell fire to live through their hearts.

One of these lying on a litter greeted the lassie from Indiana, just come back to New York from France to meet the boys when they landed:

"Hello, Sister! *You here?*"

Her eyes filled with tears as she recognized one of her

old friends of the trenches, and noticed how helpless he was now, he who had been the strongest of the strong. She murmured sympathetically some words of attempted cheer:

"Oh, that's all right, Sister," he said, "I know they got me pretty hard, but I don't mind that. I'm not going to feel bad about it. I got something better than arms and legs over in one of your little huts in France. I found Jesus, and I'm going to live for Him. I wanted you to know."

A few days later she was talking with another boy just landed. She asked him how it seemed to be home again, and to her surprise he turned a sorrowful face to her:

"It's the greatest disappointment of my life," he said sadly, "the folks here don't understand. They all want to make me forget, and I don't want to forget what I learned out there. I saw life in a different way and I knew I had wasted all the years. I want to live differently now, and mother and her friends are just getting up dances and theatre parties for me to help me to forget. They don't understand."

Forty miles west of Chicago is Camp Grant and there the Salvation Army has put up a hut just outside of the camp.

During the days when the boys were being sent to France, and were under quarantine, unable to go out, no one was allowed to come in and there was great distress. Mothers and sisters and friends could get no opportunity to see them for farewells.

The Salvation officer in charge suggested to the military authorities that the Salvation Army hut be the clearing place for relatives, and that he would come in his machine and bring the boys to the hut, taking them back again afterwards, that they might have a few hours with their friends before leaving for France.

This offer was readily accepted by the authorities, and so it was made possible for hundreds and hundreds of mothers to get a last talk with their boys before they left, some of them forever.

One day a young man came to the Salvation Army officer and told him that his regiment was to depart that night and that he was in great distress about his wife who on her way to see him had been caught in a railroad wreck, and later taken on her way by a rescue train. "I think she is in Rockford somewhere," he said anxiously, "but I don't know where, and I have to leave in three hours!"

The Ensign was ready with his help at once. He took the young soldier in his car to Rockford, seven miles away, and they went from hotel to hotel seeking in vain for any trace of the wife. Then suddenly as they were driving along the street wondering what to try next the young soldier exclaimed: "There she is!" And there she was, walking along the street!

The two had a blessed two hours together before the soldier had to leave. But it was all in the day's work for the Salvation Army man, for his main object in life is to help someone, and he never minds how much he puts himself out. It is always reward enough for him to have succeeded in bringing comfort to another.

One of the Salvation Army Ensigns who was assigned to work at Camp Grant hut had been an all-around athlete before he joined the Salvation Army, a boxer and wrestler of no mean order.

The fame of the Ensign went abroad and the doctor at the Base Hospital asked him to take charge of athletics in the hospital. He was also appointed regularly as chaplain in the hospital. Every day he drilled the five hundred women nurses in gymnastics, and put the men attendants and as many of the patients as were able through a set of exercises. Thus mingling his religion with his athletics he became a great power among the men in the hospital.

The Salvation Army asked the hospital if there was anything they could do for the wounded men. The reply was, that there were eighty wards and not a graphophone in one of them, nothing to amuse the boys. The need was promptly filled by the Salvation Army which supplied a number of graphophones and a piano. Then, discovering that the nurses who were getting only a very small cash allowance out of which they had to furnish their uniforms, were short of shoes, the indefatigable good Samaritan produced a thousand dollars to buy new shoes for them. The Salvation Army has always been doing things like that.

The Salvation Army built many huts, locating them wherever there was need among the camps. They have a hut at Camp Grant, one at Camp Funston, one at Camp Travis, San Antonio, one at Camp Logan, Houston, Texas, one at Camp Bowie, Fort Worth, one at Camp Cody, Deming, New Mexico, one at Camp Lewis, Tacoma, a Soldiers' Club at Des Moines, a Soldiers' Club with Sitting Room, Dining Room, and rooms for a hundred soldiers just opened at Chicago. There is a charge of twenty-five cents a night and twenty-five cents a meal for such as have money. No charge for those who have no money. There is such a Soldiers' Club at St. Louis, Kansas City, St. Paul and Minneapolis. All of these places at the camps have accommodations for women relatives to visit the soldiers, and all of the rooms are always full to the limit.

In Des Moines the Army has an interesting institution which grew out of a great need.

The Federal authorities have placed a Woman's Protective Agency in all Camp towns. At Des Moines the woman representative of the Federal Government sent word to the Salvation Army that she wished they would help her. She said she had found so many young girls between the ages of fourteen and sixteen who were being led into an immoral life through the soldiers, and she wished the Salvation Army would open a home to take care of such girls.

With their usual swiftness to come to the rescue the Salvation Army opened such a home. The Brigadier up in Chicago gave up his valued private secretary, a lovely young girl only twenty-four years old, to be at the head of this home. It may seem a pretty big undertaking for so young a girl, but these Salvation Army girls are brought up to be wonderfully wise and sweet beyond others, and if you could look into her beautiful eyes you would have an understanding of the consecration and strength of character that has made it possible for her to do this work with marvellous success, and reach the hearts and turn the lives of these many young girls who have come under her influence in this way. In her work she deals with the individual, always giving immediate relief for any need, always pointing the way straight and direct to a better life. The young girls are kept in the home for a week or more until some near relative can be sent for, or longer, until a home and work can be found for them. Every case is dealt with on its own merits; and many young girls have had their feet set upon the right road, and a new purpose in life given to them, with new ideals, from the young Christian girl whom they easily love and trust.

So great has been the success of the Salvation Army hut and women's hostel at Camp Lewis that the United States Government has asked the Salvation Army to put up a hundred thousand dollar hotel at that camp which is located twenty miles out of Tacoma. The Salvation Army hut at this place was recently inspected by Secretary of War Baker and Chief of Staff who highly complimented the Salvationists on the good work being done.

A Christmas box was sent by the Salvation Army to each soldier in every camp and hospital throughout the West. Each box contained an orange, an apple, two pounds of nuts, one pound of raisins, one pound of salted peanuts, one package of figs, two handkerchiefs in sealed packets, one book of stamps, a package of writing paper, a New Testament, and a Christmas letter from the Commissioner at Headquarters in Chicago.

No Officer in the Salvation Army has been more successful in ingenious efforts to further all activities connected with the work than Commissioner Estill in command of the Western forces. He is an indefatigable and tireless worker, is greatly beloved, and his efforts have met with exceptional success.

It was a new manager who had taken hold of the affairs of the Salvation Army Hostel in a certain city that morning and was establishing family prayers. A visitor, waiting to see someone, sat in an alcove listening.

There in the long beautiful living-room of the Hostel sat a little audience, two black women—the cooks— several women in neat aprons and caps as if they had come in from their work, a soldier who had been reading the morning paper and who quietly laid it aside when the Bible reading began, a sailor who tiptoed up the two low steps from the café beyond the living-room where he had been having his morning coffee and doughnuts—the young clerk from behind the office desk. They all sat quiet, respectful, as if accorded a sudden, unexpected privilege.

The reading was a few well-chosen verses about Moses in the mount of vision and somehow seemed to

have a strange quieting influence and carried a weight of
reality read thus in the beginning of a busy day's work.

The reader closed the book and quite familiarly, not
at all pompously, he said with a pleasant smile that this
was a lesson for all of them. Each one should have his
vision for the day. The cook should have a vision as she
made the doughnuts—and he called her by her name—
to make them just as well as they could be made; and the
women who made the beds should have a vision of how
they could make the beds smooth and soft and fine to
rest weary comers; and those who cleaned must have a
vision to make the house quite pure and sweet so that it
would be a home for the boys who came there; the clerk
at the desk should have a vision to make the boys
comfortable and give them a welcome; and everyone
should have a vision of how to do his work in the best
way, so that all who came there for a day or a night or
longer should have a vision when they left that God was
ruling in that place and that everything was being done
for His praise.

Just a few simple words bringing the little family of
workers into touch with the Divine and giving them a
glimpse of the great plan of laboring with God where no
work is menial, and nothing too small to be worth doing
for the love of Christ. Then the little company dropped
upon their knees, and the earnest voice took up a prayer
which was more an intimate word with a trusted beloved Companion; and they all arose to go about that
work of theirs with new zest and—a vision!

In her alcove out of sight the visitor found refresh-
ment for her own soul, and a vision also.

This is the secret of this wonderful work that these
people do in France, in the cities, everywhere; they have
a vision! They have been upon the Mountain with God
and they have not forgotten the injunction:

"See that thou do all things according to the pattern given thee in the Mount."

But the stories multiply and my space is drawing to a close. I am minded to say reverently in words of old:

"And there are also many other things which these disciples of Jesus did, the which if they should be written every one, I suppose that even the world itself could not contain the books that should be written;" but are they not graven in the hearts of men who found the Christ on the battlefield or the hospital cot, or in the dim candle-lit hut, through these dear followers of His?

12

Letters of Appreciation

My Dear Miss Booth:

You may be sure that your telegram of November fifteenth warmed my heart and brought me very real cheer and encouragement. It is a message of just the sort that one needs in these trying times, and I hope that you will express to your associates my profound appreciation and my entire confidence in their loyalty, their patriotism, and their enthusiasm for the great work they are doing.

Cordially and sincerely yours,
Woodrow Wilson.
Nov. 30, 1917.

My Dear Miss Booth:

I am very much interested to hear of the campaign the Salvation Army has undertaken for money to sustain its war activities, and want to take the opportunity to express my admiration for the work that it has done and my sincere hope that it may be fully sustained.

(Signed) Woodrow Wilson.

The President of the United States of America.
Commander Evangeline Booth,
Paris, 7 April, 1919.
122 W. 14th Street, New York, U.S.A.

I am very much interested to know that the Salvation Army is about to enter into a campaign for a sustaining fund.

I feel that the Salvation Army needs no commendation from me. The love and gratitude it has elicited from the troops is a sufficient evidence of the work it has done and I feel that I should not so much commend as congratulate it.

Cordially and sincerely yours,
Woodrow Wilson.

British Delegation, Paris, 8th April, 1919.
Dear Madam:

I have very great pleasure in sending you this letter to say how highly I think of the great work which has been done by the Salvation Army amongst the Allied Armies in France and the other theatres of war. From all sides I hear the most glowing accounts of the way in which your people have added to the comfort and welfare of our soldiers. To me it has always been a great joy to think how much the sufferings and hardships endured by our troops in all parts of the world have been lessened by the self-sacrifice and devotion shown to them by that excellent organization, the Salvation Army.

Yours faithfully,
W. Lloyd George.

General J. J. Pershing, France.

The Salvation Army of America will never cease to hail you with devoted affection and admiration for your valiant leadership of your valiant army. You have rushed the advent of the world's greatest peace, and all men honor you. To God be all the glory!

Commander Evangeline Booth.

Commander Evangeline Booth, New York City.

Many thanks for your cordial cable. The American Expeditionary Forces thank you for all your noble work that the Salvation Army has done for them from the beginning.

General Pershing.

With deep feeling of gratitude for the enormous contribution which the Salvation Army has made to the moral and physical welfare of this expedition all ranks join me in sending heartiest Christmas greetings and cordial best wishes for the New Year.

(Signed) Pershing.

Salvation, New York.
Paris, April 22, 1919.

The following cable received, Colonel William S. Barker, Director of the Salvation Army, Paris: My dear Colonel Barker—I wish to express to you my sincere appreciation, and that of all members of the American Expeditionary Forces, for the splendid services rendered by the Salvation Army to the American Army in France. You first submitted your plans to me in the summer of 1917, and before the end of that year you had a number of Huts in operation in the Training Area of the First Division, and a group of devoted men and women who laid the foundation for the affectionate regard in which the workers of your organization have always been held by the American soldiers. The outstanding features of the work of the Salvation Army have been its disposition to push its activities as far as possible to the Front, and the trained and experienced character of its workers whose one thought was the well-being of its soldiers they came to serve. While the maintenance of these standards has necessarily kept your work within narrow bounds as compared to some of the other welfare agencies, it has resulted in a degree of excellence and self-sacrifice in the work performed which has been second to none. It has endeared your organization and its individual men and women workers to all those Divisions and other units to which they have been attached and has published their good name to every part of the American Expeditionary forces. Please accept this letter as a personal message to each one of your workers.

> Very sincerely,
> John J. Pershing.

Marshal Foch, Paris, France:

Your brilliant armies, under blessing of God, have triumphed. The Salvation Army of America exults with war-worn but invincible France. We must consolidate for God of Peace all the good your valor has secured.

> Commander Evangeline Booth.

Just before leaving London on Thursday for his provincial campaigns, General Booth received the following letter from Field Marshal Sir Douglas Haig. The generous tribute will be read with intense satisfaction by Salvationists the world over:

General Headquarters, British Armies in France.
March 27, 1918.

I am glad to have the opportunity of congratulating the Salvation Army on the service which its representatives have rendered during the past year to the British Armies in France.

The Salvation Army workers have shown themselves to be of the right sort and I value their presence here as being one of the best influences on the moral and spiritual welfare of the troops at the bases. The inestimable value of these influences is realized when the morale of the troops is afterwards put to the test at the front.

The huts which the Salvation Army has staffed have besides been an addition to the comfort of the soldiers which has been greatly appreciated.

I shall be glad if you will convey the thanks of all ranks of the British Expeditionary Forces in France to the Salvation Army for its continued good work.

> D. Haig, Field Marshal,
> Commanding British Armies in France.

The following message from Marshal Joffre:

Miss Evangeline Booth, Apr. 9, 1919.
New York City.

President Wilson has said that the work of the Salvation Army on the Franco-American front needs no praise in view of the magnificent results obtained and remains only to be admired and congratulated. I cannot do better than to use the same words which I am sure express the sentiments of all French soldiers.

> J. Joffre.

From Field Marshal Viscount French.

Of all the organizations that have come into existence during the past fifty years none has done finer work or achieved better results in all parts of the Empire than the

Salvation Army. In particular, its activities have been of the very greatest benefit to the soldiers in this war.

June 16, 1918.

Colonel Theodore Roosevelt, writing from Oyster Bay, Long Island, under date of April 11, 1918, has the following to say to the War Work Executive of the Salvation Army:

I was greatly interested in your letter quoting the letter from my son now with Pershing in France. His testimony as to the admirable work done by the Salvation Army agrees with all my own observations as to what the Salvation Army has done in war and in peace. You have had to enlarge enormously your program and readjust your work in order to meet the need of the vast number of soldiers and sailors serving our country overseas; and you must have funds to help you. I am informed that over 40,000 Salvationists are in the ranks of the Allied armies. I can myself bear testimony to the fact that you have a practical social service, combined with practical religion, that appeals to multitudes of men who are not reached by the regular churches; and I know that you were able to put your organization to work in France before the end of the first month of the World War. I am glad to learn that you do not duplicate or parallel the work done by any other organization, and that you are in constant touch with the War Work Councils of such organizations as the Y.M.C.A. and the Red Cross. I happen to know that you are now maintaining and operating 168 huts behind the lines in France, together with 70 hostels, and that you have furnished 46 ambulances, manned and officered by Salvationists. I am particularly interested to learn that 6000 women are knitting under the direction of the Salvation Army, and with materials furnished by this organization here in America, in order to turn out garments and useful articles for the soldiers at the Front.

> Faithfully yours,
> (Signed) Theodore Roosevelt.

April 21st, 1919.
Commander Evangeline Booth,
120 West 14th Street, New York, N.Y.
Dear Commander Booth:

I have known the Salvation Army from its beginning.

The mother of the Salvation Army was Mrs. Catherine Booth, and her common sense and Christian spirit laid the foundations; while her husband, General William booth, in his impressive frame, fertility of ideas, and invincible spirit of evangelism always seemed to me as if he were closely related to St. Peter, the fisherman—the man of ideas and many questions, of the Lord's family.

General William Booth was of a discipleship that kept him always on the "long, long trail" with a self-sacrificing spirit, but with a cheerfulness that heard the nightingales in the early mornings that awakened him to duty and service. He was never tired. The Salvation Army under the present leadership of your brother, Bramwell Booth, has "carried on" along the same roads, and with the same methods, as the great General who has passed into the Beyond.

The Salvation Army has been itself true to the spirit of its mighty originator during the present war. No work was too hard; no day was long enough; no duty too simple, no self-denial was too great.

From my personal knowledge, the Salvation Army workers were consecrated to their work. Just as the brave boys who carried the Flag, they were soldiers fighting a battle, to find comforts, and a song to put music into the hearts of the noble fellows that now lie sleeping on the ridges of the Marne, with their graves unmarked save with a cross.

The sleepless vigilance of the Salvation Army extended from their kitchens where they cooked for the boys, to the hospitals where they prayed with them to the last hour when life ended in a silence, the stillest of all slumbers.

The Armies of every country in which they labored have a record of their faithfulness and devotion which will be sealed in the hearts of the many thousands they helped in the days of the struggle for peace.

The question is, what can we do now to perpetuate the Salvation Army and its work, and my reply is, that there is nothing they ask or want that should be refused to them. They are worthy; they are competent; they can be trusted with responsibility; and their splendid leader seems to have almost a miraculous power for management in the work which her father committed to her so far as America is concerned.

> Very sincerely yours,
> (Signed) John Wanamaker.

Cardinal's Residence, 408 Charles Street, Baltimore.
April 16, 1919.
Hon. Charles S. Whitman, New York City.
Honorable and Dear Sir:

I have been asked by the local Commander of the Salvation Army to address a word to you as the National Chairman of the Campaign about to be launched in behalf of the above named organization. This I am happy to do, and for the reason that, along with my fellow American citizens, I rejoice in the splendid service which the Salvation Army rendered our Soldier and Sailor Boys during the war. Every returning trooper is a willing witness to the efficient and generous work of the Salvation Army both at the Front, and in the camps at home. I am also the more happy to commend this organization because it is free from sectarian bias. The man in need of help is the object of their effort, with never a question of his creed or color.

I trust, therefore, your efforts to raise $13,000,000 for the Salvation Army will meet with a hearty response from our generous American public.

> Faithfully yours,
> James, Cardinal, Gibbons.

Commissioner Plenipotentiary of the United States of America.
Paris, April 7th, 1919.
My Dear Commander Booth:

Those of us who have been fortunate enough to see something of the work of the Salvation Army with the American troops have been made proud by the devotion and self-sacrifice of the workers connected with your organization.

I congratulate you and, through you, your associates, and I wish you the best fortune in the continuance of your splendid work.

> Very sincerely yours,
> L. M. House.

Commander Evangeline Booth, Salvation Army.
Evangeline Booth,
Salvation Army Headquarters, New York.

I have seen the work of the Salvation Army in France and consider it very helpful and valuable. I trust you will be able to secure the means not only for its maintenance but for the enlargement of its scope. It is a good work and should be encouraged.

Leonard Wood.
Camp Funston, Kansas.

Brigadier-General Duncan wrote to Colonel Barker the following letter:

December 7, 1917.

The Salvation Army in this its first experience with our troops has stepped very closely into the hearts of the men. Your huts have been open to them at all times. They have been cordially received in a homelike atmosphere and many needs provided in religious teachings. Your efforts have the honest support of our chaplains. I have talked with many of our soldiers who are warm in their praise and satisfaction in what is being done for them. For myself I feel that the Salvation Army has a real place for its activities with our Army in France and I offer you and your workers, men and women, good wishes and thanks for what you have done and are doing for our men.

G. B. Duncan, Brigadier-General.

The Salvation Army is doing a great work in France and every soldier bears testimony to the fact.

Omar Bundy, Major-General.

Headquarters First Division,
American Expeditionary Forces.
France, September 15, 1918.
From: Chief of Staff.
To: Major L. Allison Coe, Salvation Army.
Subject: Service in Operation against St. Mihiel Salient.

1. The Division Commander desires me to express to you his appreciation of the particularly valuable service that the Salvation Army, through you and your assistants, has rendered the Division during the recent operation against the St. Mihiel salient.

2. You have furnished aid and comfort to the American soldier throughout the trying experiences of the last few days, and in accomplishing this worthy mission have spared yourself in nothing.

3. The Division Commander wishes me to thank you for the Division and for himself.

CK/T.
Campbell King, Chief of Staff.

Cablegram.
Paris, December 17, 1917.
Commander Miss E. Booth,
120 W. 14th St., New York.

I am glad to be able to express my appreciation of the work done by the Salvation Army in the way of providing for the comfort and welfare of the Command. I think the efforts of the Salvation Army are admirable and deserving of appreciation and commendation, and I consider the effort is made without advertisement and that it reaches and is appreciated by those for whom it is most needed.

L. P. Murphy, Lieut.-Colonel of Cavalry.

Cablegram.
Paris, December 17, 1917.
Commander Miss E. Booth,
120 W. 14th Street, New York City.

I wish to express my most sincere appreciation of the work of your organization with my regiment. Your Officer has done everything that could be expected of any organization in carrying on his work with the soldiers of this command, and has surpassed any such expectations. He has assisted the soldiers in every way possible and has gained their hearty good will. He has also shown himself willing and anxious to carry out regulations and orders affecting his organization. As a matter of fact, all the officers and soldiers of this command are most enthusiastic about the help of the Salvation Army, and you can hear nothing but praise for its work. The work of your organization, both religious and material, has been wholesome and dignified, and I desire you to know that it is appreciated.

> J. L. Hines,
> Colonel, Sixteenth Infantry.

In sending a contribution toward the expenses of the War Work, Colonel George B. McClellan wrote:

Treasurer, Salvation Army,
July 24, 1918.
120 West 14th Street, New York City.
Dear Sir:
All the Officers I have talked with who have been in the trenches have enthusiastically praised the work the Salvation Army is doing at the front. They are agreed that for coolness under fire, cheerfulness under the most adverse conditions, kindness, helpfulness and real efficiency, your workers are unsurpassed.

Will you accept the enclosed check as my modest contribution to your War Fund, and believe me to be

> Yours very truly,
> Geo. B. McClellan, Lt.-Col. Ord. Dept., N.A.

Cablegram.
Paris, December 17, 1917.

Commander Miss E. Booth,
120 West 14th Street, New York City, N.Y.

I have carefully observed the work of the Salvation Army from their first arrival in Training Area First Division American Expeditionary Force to date. The work they have done for the enlisted men of the Division and the places of amusement and recreation that they have provided for them, are of the highest order. I unhesitatingly state that, in my opinion, the Salvation Army has done more for the enlisted men of the First Division than any other organization or society operating in France.

> F. G. Lawton,
> Colonel, Infantry, National Army.

To Whom It May Concern:

The work of the Salvation Army as illustrated by the work of Major S. H. Atkins is duplicated by no one. He has been Chaplain and more besides. He has the confidence of officers and men. Major Atkins, as typifying the Salvation Army, has been forward at the very front with what is even more important than the rear area work.

> Theodore Roosevelt.

The following letter was sent to Major Atkins of the Salvation Army:

Headquarters, 1st Battalion, 26th Infantry,
France, December 26, 1917.

I wish to thank you for the great work you have been doing here among the men of this battalion. You have added greatly to the happiness and contentment of us all; giving, as you have, an opportunity for good, clean entertainment and pleasure.

In religious work you have done much. As you know, this regiment has no chaplain, and you have to a large extent taken the place of one here.

For myself, and on behalf of the officers stationed here, I wish to express my appreciation of the work that you have been doing here, and the hope that you can accompany the battalion wherever the fortune of war may lead us.

Wishing you a very happy and successful New Year, I am

> Yours sincerely,
> (Signed) Theodore Roosevelt, Jr.,
> Major (U.S.R.), 26th Infantry.

When Captain Archibald Roosevelt was lying wounded in Red Cross Hospital No. 1 he wrote the following letter to the same officer:

Red Cross Hospital No. 1.
July 10, 1918.

You have, by your example, helped the men morally and physically. By your continued presence in the most dangerous and uncomfortable periods, you have made yourself the comrade and friend of every officer and man in our battalion. It is in this way that you have filled a position which the other charitable organizations had left vacant.

Let me also mention that, perfect Democrat that you are, you have realized the necessity of discipline, and have helped make the discipline understood by these men and officers.

If all the Salvation Army workers are like you, I sincerely hope to see the time when there is a Salvation Army officer with each battalion in the camp.

Before leaving France for the United States, two Salvation Army lassies received the following letter:

I was very sorry to hear that you had been taken from this division, and desire to express my appreciation of the excellent assistance you have been to us.

In all of our "shows" you have been with us, and I wish that I knew of the many sufferers you have cheered and made more comfortable. They are many and, I am positive, will always have grateful thoughts of you.

I have seen you enduring hardships—going without food and sleep, working day and night, sometimes under fire, both shell and avion—and never have you been anything but cheerful and willing.

I thank you and your organization for all of this, and assure you of the respect and gratitude of the entire division.

> J. I. Mabee, Colonel, Medical Corps,
> Division Surgeon.

Cable.
January 17, 1918.
The Salvation Army, New York:

As Inspector General of the First Division I have inspected all the Salvation Army huts in this Division area and I am glad to inform you that your work here is a well-earned success. Your huts are warm, dry, light, and, I believe, much appreciated by all the men in this Division. To make these huts at all homelike under present conditions requires energy and ability. I know that the Salvation Army men in this Division have it and am very willing to so testify.

> Conrad S. Babcock, Lieut.-Colonel,
> Inspector General, First Division.

The Salvation Army keeps open house, and any time that a body of men come back from the front lines, in from a convoy, there is hot coffee and sometimes home-made doughnuts (all free to the men) I was in command of a town where the hut never closed till 3 or 4 in the morning, and their girls baked pies and made doughnuts up to the front, under shell fire, for our infantrymen. A Salvation Army lassie is safe without an escort anywhere in France where there is an American soldier. That speaks for itself. I am for any organization that is out to do something for my men, and I think that it is the idea of the American people when they give their money. What we want is someone who is willing to come over here and do something for the boys, regardless of the fact that it may not net any gain—in fact, may not help them to gather enough facts for a lecture tour when they return home.

Headquarters, Third Division,
September 5, 1918.
My Dear Mr. Leffingwell:

Your letter of July 22d just received. It has, perhaps, been somewhat delayed in reaching me, owing to the fact that I have recently been transferred to another division.

I only wish things had been so that I might have granted you or a representative of the Salvation Army an interview when I was in the States recently, but, being under orders, I could wait for nothing. Whatever I may have said, in a casual way, of the work of the Salvation Army in France, I assure you was all deserved. Your organization has been doing a splendid work for the men of my former division and other troops who have come in contact with it. I have often remarked, as have many of the officers, that after the war the Salvation Army is going to receive such a boom from the boys who have come in touch with it over here that it will seem like a veritable propaganda! Why shouldn't it? For your work has been conducted in such a quiet, unostentatious, unselfish way that only a man whose sensibilities are dead can fail to appreciate it. I have found several of your workers, whose names at this moment I am unable to recall, putting up with all sorts of hardships and inconveniences, working from daylight until well into the night that the boys might be cheered in one way or another. Your shacks have always been at the disposal of the chaplains for their regimental services. Whether Mass for the Catholic chaplains or Holy Communion for an Episcopalian chaplain, they always found a place to set up their altars in the Salvation Army huts; and the Protestant chaplains, also the Jewish, always, to my knowledge, were given its use for their services. I have found your own services have been very acceptable to the boys, in general, but perhaps your doughnut program, with hot coffee or chocolate, means as much as anything. Not that, like those of old, we follow the Salvation Army because we can get filled up, but we all like their spirit. More than on one occasion do I know of troops moving at night—and pretty wet and hungry—that have been warmed and fed and sent on their way with new courage because of what some Salvation Army worker and hut furnished. And as they went their way many fine things were said about the Salvation Army. I am sure, as a result of this work, you have won the favor and confidence of hundreds of these soldier lads, and, if I am not terribly mistaken, when we get home the Salvation tambourine will receive greater consideration than heretofore.

I am glad to express my feelings for your work. God bless you in it, and always!

Sincerely yours,

Lyman Rollins, Division Chaplain,

Headquarters, Third Division, A.E.F., via New York.

At the Front in France, June 12, 1918.

Commissioner Thomas Estill,

Salvation Army, Chicago.

My Dear Commissioner:

We are engaged in a great battle. My time is all taken with our wounded and dead. Still I cannot resist the temptation to take a few moments in which to express our appreciation of the splendid aid given our soldiers by the Salvation Army.

The work of the Salvation Army is not in duplication of that of any other organization. It is entirely original and unique. It fills a long-felt want. Some day the world will know the aid that you have rendered our soldiers. Then you will receive every dollar you need.

Your work is also greatly appreciated by the French people. I have never heard a single unfavorable comment on the Salvation Army. They are respected everywhere. Their unselfish devotion to our well, sick, wounded and dead is above any praise that I can bestow. God will surely greatly reward them.

I heartily congratulate you on the class of workers you have sent over here. I pray that your invaluable aid may be extended to our troops everywhere. God bless you and yours,

> In His name,
> (Signed) Thomas J. Dickson,
> Chaplain with rank of Major,
> Sixth Field Artillery, First Division, U.S. Army.

An appreciation written concerning the first Salvation Army chaplain that was appointed after the war started:

Camp Cody, New Mexico,
January 16, 1918.
Major E. C. Clemans,
136th Infantry, Camp Cody, N.M.
Commissioner Thomas Estill, Chicago, Ill.

I have been associated with the chaplain now for nearly four months. I have found him a Christian soldier and gentleman. He is "on the job" all the time and no Chaplain in this Division is doing more faithful and effective work. He is thoroughly evangelistic, is burdened for the souls of his men and is working for their salvation not in but from their sins. He is a "man's man," knows how to approach men and knows how and does get hold of their affections in such a way that he is a help and a comfort to them. He brings things to pass.

The Salvation Army may be well pleased that it is so well represented in the Army as it is by Chaplain Kline.

Sincerely yours,
(Signed) Ezra C. Clemans,
Senior Chaplain, 34th Division.

July 11, 1918.

I have been familiar with the work of the Salvation Army for years, and the organization from the beginning of the war has been doing a wonderful work with the Allied forces and since the entering of the United States into the struggle has given splendid aid and cooperation not only in connection with the war activities at home but also with our forces abroad.

Their work is entitled to the sincere admiration of every American citizen.

Major Edwin F. Glenn.

To Whom It May Concern:

It gives me the greatest pleasure to testify to the very excellent work of the Salvation Army as I have seen it in this division. I have seen the work done by this organization for ten months, under all sorts of conditions, and it has always been of the highest character. At the start, the Salvation Army was handicapped by lack of funds, but even under adverse conditions, it did most valuable work in maintaining cheerful recreation centres for the men, often in places exposed to hostile shell-fire. The doughnut and pie supply has been maintained. This seems a little thing, but it has gone a long way to keep the men cheerful. All the Salvation Army force has been untiring in its work under very trying conditions, and as a result, I believe it has gained the respect and affection of officers and men more than any similar organization.

Albert J. Myers, Jr., Major, National Army.
1st Div., A.E.F. (Captain, Cavalry, U.S.A.)

Extract from letter from Captain Charles W. Albright:

Q. M., R. C., France.

As to the Salvation Army, well, if they wanted our boys to lie down for them to walk on, to keep their feet from getting muddy, the boys would gladly do so.

From everyone, officers and men alike, nothing but the highest praise is given the Salvation Army. They are right in the thick of danger, comforting and helping the men in the front line, heedless of shot, shell or gas, the

U.S. Army in France, as a unit, swears by the Salvation Army.

I am proud to have a sister in their ranks.

An old regular army officer who returned to Paris last week said:

"I wish every American who has stood on street corners in America and sneered at the work of the Salvation Army could see what they are doing for the boys in France.

"They do not proclaim that they are here for investigation or for getting atmosphere for War romances. They have not come to furnish material for Broadway press agents. They do not wear, 'Oh, such becoming uniforms,' white shoes, dainty blue capes and bonnets, nor do they frequent Paris tea rooms where the swanky British and American officers put up.

"Take it from me, these women are doing almighty fine work. There are twenty-two of them here in France. We army men have given them shell-shattered and cast-off field kitchens to work with, and oh, man, the doughnuts, the pancakes and the pies they turn out!

"I'm an old army officer, but what I like about the Salvation Army is that it doesn't cater to officers. It is for the doughboys first, last and all the time. The Salvation Army men do not wear Sam Browne belts; they do as little handshaking with officers as possible.

"They cash the boys' checks without question, and during the month of April in a certain division the Salvation Army sent home $20,000 for the soldiers. The Rockefeller Foundation hasn't as yet given the Salvation Army a million-dollar donation to carry on its work. Fact is, I don't know just how the Salvation Army chaplains and lassies do get along. But get along they do.

"Perhaps some of the boys and officers give them a lift

now and then when the sledding is rough. They don't aim to make a slight profit as do some other organizations.

"Ever since Cornelius Hickey put up 'Hickey's Hut,' the first Salvation Army hut in France, they have been working at a loss. I saw an American officer give a Salvation Army chaplain 500 francs out of his pay at a certain small town in France recently.

"The work done in 'Hickey's Hut' did much to endear the Salvation folks to the doughboys. When a letter arrived in France some months ago addressed only to 'Hickey's Hut, France,' it reached its destination *toute de suite,* forty-eight hours after it arrived.

"The French climate has hit our boys hard. It is wet and penetratingly cold. Goes right to the marrow, and three suits of underwear are no protection against it. When the lads returned from training camp or the trenches, wet, cold, hungry and despondent, they found a welcome in 'Hickey's Hut.'

"Not a patronizing, holier-than-thou, we-know-we-are-doing-a-good-work-and-hope-you-doughboys-appreciate-it sort of welcome, but a good old Salvation Army, Bowery Mission welcome, such as Tim Sullivan knew how to hand out in the old days.

"Around a warm fire with men who spoke their own language and who did not pretend to be above them in the social scale the doughboys forgot that they were four thousand miles from home and that they couldn't 'sling the lingo.'

"I saw a group of lads on the Montdidier front who had not been paid in three months, standing cursing their luck. They had no money, therefore, they could not buy anything.

"The Salvation Army had been apprised by telegraph that the doughboys were playing in hard luck. Presto!

Out from Paris came a truck loaded with everything to eat. The truck was unloaded and the boys paid for whatever they wanted with slips of paper signed with their John Hancocks. The Salvation Army lassies asked no questions, but accepted the slips of paper as if they were Uncle Sam's gold.

"And one of the most useful institutions in Europe where war rages is one that has no publicity bureau and has no horns to toot. This is the Salvation Army. In the estimation of many, the Salvation Army goes way ahead of the work of many of the other war organizations working here. I see brave women and young women of the Salvation Army every day in places that are really hazardous."

First Lieutenant Marion M. Marcus, Jr., Field Artillery, wrote to one of our leading officers:

October 9, 1918.

If the people at home could see the untiring and absolute devotion of the workers of the Salvation Army, in serving and caring for our men, they would more than give you the support you ask. The way the men and women expose themselves to the dangers of the front lines and hardships has more than endeared them to every member of the American Expeditionary Forces, and they are always in the right spot with cheer of hot food and drink when it is most appreciated.

Extracts from letters.

Away up front where things break hard and rough for us, and we are hungry and want something hot, we can usually find it in some old partly destroyed building, which has been organized into a shack by—well, guess—the Salvation Army.

They are the soldier's friend. They make no display or show of any kind, but they are fast winning a warm corner in the heart of everyone.

I feel it is my duty to drop you a few lines to let you know how the boys over here appreciate what the Salvation Army is doing for them. It is a second home to us. There is always a cheerful welcome awaiting us there and *I have yet to meet a sour-faced clerk behind the counter.* One Salvation Army worker has his home in a cellar, located close to the front-line trenches. He cheerfully carries on his wonderful work amid the flying of shells and in danger of gas. He is one fine fellow, always greeting you with a smile. He serves the boys with hot coffee every day, free of charge, and many times he has divided his own bread with the tired and hungry boys returning from the trenches. In the evening he serves coffee and doughnuts at a small price. Say, who wouldn't be willing to fight after feasting on that?

In the many rest camps you will find the Salvation Army girls. They are located so close to the front-line trenches that they have to wear their gas masks in the slung position, and they also have their tin hats ready to put on. The girls certainly are a fine, jolly bunch, and when it comes to baking pies and doughnuts they are hard to beat. The boys line up a half hour before time so as to be sure they get their share. I had the pleasure of talking to a mother and her daughter and they told me they had sold out everything they had to the boys with the exception of some salmon and sardines on which they were living—salmon for dinner and sardines for supper. They stood it all with big smiles and those smiles made me smile when I thought of my troubles.

In the trenches the boys become affected with body lice, known as cooties. A good hot bath is the only real cure for them. While on the way to a bath-house a Salvation Army worker overtook us. He was riding in a Ford which had seen better days. The springs on it were about all in and it made a noise like someone calling for mercy. The Salvation Army worker pulled up in front of us and with a broad smile on his face said: "Room for half a ton!" We did not need a second invitation and we soon had poor Henry loaded down. I thought sure it would give out, but the worker only laughed about it and kept on feeding the machine more gas as we cheered until it started away with us.

I want to tell you what the Salvation Army does for the moral side of the soldier. The American soldier needs the guidance of God over here more than he ever did in his whole life. Away from home and in a foreign land in every corner, one must have Divine guidance to keep him on the narrow path of life. If it was not for the *workers of God over here the boys would gradually break away and then I'm afraid we would not have the right kind of fighters to hold up our end*. Of course, prayers alone won't satisfy the appetite of the American soldier, and the Salvation Army girls get around that by baking for the boys. They believe in satisfying the cravings of the stomach as well as the craving of the soul and mind. I always enjoy the sermons at the Salvation Army. A good, every-day sermon is always appreciated. The Salvation Army helps you along in their good old way, and they don't believe in preaching all day on what you should do and what you shouldn't do. The girls are a fine bunch of singers and their singing is enjoyed very much by all of the boys. It is a treat to see an American girl so close to the front and a still better treat to listen to one sing.

The Salvation Army does much good work in keeping the boys in the right spirit so that they are glad to go back to the trenches when their turn comes. There is no

Salvation Army hut on this front. I often wish there was one on every front. I believe the Salvation Army does not get its full credit over in the States. Perhaps the people over there do not understand the full meaning of the work it is doing over here. I want the Salvation Army to know that it has all of the boys over here back of it and we want to keep up the good work. We will go through hell, if necessary, because we know the folks back home are back of us. We want the Salvation Army to feel the same way. The *boys over here are really back of it and we want you to continue your good work.*

There is just one thing more I wish to speak of, and that is the little old Salvation Army. You will never see me, nor any of the other boys over here, laugh at their street services in the future, and if I see anyone else doing that little thing that person is due for a busted head! I haven't seen where they are raising a tenth the money some of the other societies are, but they are the topnotchers of them all as the soldiers' friend, and their handouts always come at the right time. Some of those girls work as hard as we do.

The Salvation Army over here is doing wonderful work. *They haven't any shows or music, but they certainly know what pleases the boys most,* and feed us with homemade apple pie or crullers, with lemonade—a great big piece of pie or three crullers, with a large cup of lemonade, for a franc (18 1/2 cents).

These people are working like beavers, and the people in the States ought to give them plenty of credit and appreciate their wonderful help to the men over here.

We were in a bomb-proof semi-dugout, in the heart of a dense forest, within range of enemy guns, my Hebrew comrade and I. We were talking of the fate that brought us here—of the conditions as we left them at home. There was the thought of what "might" happen if we were to return to America minus a limb or an eye; we were discussing the great economic and moral reform which is a certainty after the war, when through the air came the harmonious strumming of a guitar accompanying a sweet, feminine voice, and we heard:

> Lead, Kindly Light, amid the encircling gloom;
> Lead Thou me on;
> The night is dark and I am far from home,
> Lead Thou me on.
> Keep Thou my feet; I do not ask to see
> The distant scene—
> One step enough for me.

It was the Salvation Army! In a desert of human hearts, many of them wounded with heartache, these brave, brave servants of the Son of David came to cheer us up and make life more bearable.

In our outfit are Greeks, Italians, Bohemians, Irish, Jews—all of them loyal Americans—and the Salvation Army serves each with an impartial self-sacrifice which should forever still the voices of critics who condemn sending Army lassies over here.

Those in the ranks are men. The Salvation Army women are admired—almost worshipped—but respected and safe. Men by the thousands would lay down their lives for the Salvationists, and not till after the war will the full results of this sacrifice by Salvation Army workers bear fruit. But now, with so many strong temptations to go the wrong way, here are noble girls roughing it, smiling at the hardships, singing songs, making doughnuts for the doughboys, and always reminding us, even in danger, that it is not all of "life to live," bringing to us recollections of our mothers, sisters, and sweethearts, and if anyone questions, "Is it worth while?" the answer is: "A thousand times yes!" and I cannot refrain from sending my hearty thanks for all this service means to us.

A few miles in back of us now, a half dozen Connecticut girls representing the Salvation Army are doing their bit to make things brighter for us, and say, maybe those girls cannot bake. Every day they furnish us with real homemade crullers and pies at a small cost, and their coffee, holy smoke! it makes me homesick to even write about it. The girls have their headquarters in an old tumble-down building and they must have some nerve, for the Boche keeps dropping shells all around them day and night, and it would only take one of those shells to blow the whole outfit into kingdom come.

In a letter from a private to his mother while he was lying wounded in the hospital, he says of the Salvation Army and Red Cross:

Most emphatically let me say that they both are giving real service to the men here and both are worthy of any praise or help that can be given them. This is especially so of the Salvation Army, because it is not fully understood just what they are doing over here. They are the only ones that, regardless of shells or gas, feed the boys in the trenches and bear home to them the realization of what God really is at the very moment when our brave lads are facing death. Their timely phrases about the Christ, handed out with their doughnuts and coffee, have turned many faltering souls back to the path and they will never forget it. "Man's extremity is God's opportunity" surely holds good here. You may not realize or think it possible, but a large majority of the boys carry Bibles and there are often heated arguments over the different phrases.

I have just turned my pockets inside out and the tambourine could hold no more, but it was all I had and I am still in debt to the Salvation Army.

For hot coffee and cookies when I was shivering like an aspen, for buttons and patches on my tattered uniform, for steering me clear of the camp followers; but more than all for the cheery words of solace for those "gone West," for the blessed face of a woman from the homeland in the midst of withering blight and desolation—for these I am indebted to the Salvation Army.

Cablegram.
Paris, December 17, 1917.
Commander Miss E. Booth,
120 W. 14th Street, New York, N.Y.

Being a Private, I am one of the many thousands who enjoy the kindnesses and thoughtful recreation in the Salvation hut. The huts are always crowded when the boys are off duty, for 'tis there we find warmth of body and comradeship, pleasures in games and music, delight in the palatable refreshments, knowledge in reading periodicals, convenience in the writing material at our disposal, and other home-like touches for enjoyment. The courtesy and good-will of the hut workers, combined with these good things, makes the huts a resort of real comfort with the big thought of salvation in Christ predominating over all. Appreciation of these huts, and all they mean to the soldier in this terrible war, rises full in all our hearts.

Clinton Spencer,
Private, Motor Action.

I just used to love to listen to the Salvation Army at 6th and Penn Streets, but I never dreamed of seeing them over here. And when I first saw four girls cooking and baking all day I wondered what it was all about.

But I didn't have long to find out, for that night I saw these same girls put on their gas masks at the alert and start for the trenches. Then I started to ask about them. I never spoke to the girls, but fellows who had been in the trenches told me that they came up under shell fire to give the boys pies or doughnuts or little cakes or cocoa or whatever they had made that day. I thought that great of the Salvation Army. And many a boy who got help through them has a warm spot in his heart for them.

You can see by the paper I write on who gave it to us. It is Salvation Army paper. Altogether I say give three hearty cheers for the Salvation Army and the girls who risk their own lives to give our boys a little treat.

I am going to crow about our real friends here—and it is the verdict of all the boys—it is the Salvation Army, Joe. *That is the boys' mother and father here. It is our home.* They have a treat for us boys every night—that is, cookies, doughnuts or pie—about 9 o'clock. But that is only a little of them. The big thing is the spirit—the feeling a boy gets of being home when he enters the hut and meets the lassies and lads who call themselves the soldiers of Christ, and we are proud to call them brother soldiers. We think the world of them! So, Joe, whenever you get a chance to do the Salvation Army a good turn, by word or deed, do so, as thereby you will help us. When we get back we are going to be the Salvation Army's big friend, and you will see it become one of the United States' great organizations.

My life as a soldier is not quite as easy as it was in Rochester, but still I am not going to give up my religion, and I am not ashamed to let the other fellows know that I belong to the Salvation Army. Sometimes they try to get me to smoke or go and have a glass of beer with them, but I tell them that I am a Salvationist. There are twenty fellows in a hut, so they used to make fun at me when I used to say my prayers. Once in awhile I used to have a *pair of shoes* or a coat or something thrown at me. I used to think what I could do to stop them throwing things at me, so I thought of a plan and waited. It was two or three nights before they threw anything again. One night, as I was saying my prayers, someone threw his shoes at me. After I got through I picked up the shoes and took out my shoe brushes and polished and cleaned the shoes thrown at me, and from that night to now I have never had a thing thrown at me. The fellow came to me in a little while and said he was sorry he had thrown them. There are four or five Salvationists in our company—one was a Captain in the States. The Salvation Army has three big huts here among the soldier boys. We have some nice meetings here, and they have reading-rooms and writing and lunch-rooms, so I spend most of my time there.

Letter of Commendation re Salvation Army.

U.S.S. Point Bonita, 15 October, 1918.
Miss Evangeline Booth, Commander,
Care of Salvation Army Headquarters,
14th Street, New York City.
Dear Miss Booth:—

We want to thank you for presenting our crew with an elegant phonograph and 25 records. We are all going to take up a collection and buy a lot of records and I guess we will be able to pass the time away when we are not on watch.

We have a few men in the crew who have made trips across on transports and they say that every soldier and sailor has praised the Salvation Army way-up-to-the-sky for all the many kindnesses shown them.

We also want to thank you for the kindness shown to one of our crew. The Major who gave us the present was the best yet and so was the gentleman who drove the auto about ten miles to our ship. That is the Salvation Army all over. During the war or in times of peace, your organization reaches the hearts of all.

We all would like to thank Mr. Leffingwell for his great kindness in helping us.

The undersigned all have the warmest sort of feeling for you and the Salvation Army.

Many, many thanks, from the ship's crew.

I was down to the Salvation Army the other day helping them cook doughnuts and they sure did taste good, and the fellows fairly go crazy to get them, too. Anything that is homemade don't last long around here, and when they get candy or anything sweet there is a line about a block long.

Notice the paper this is written on? Well, I can't say enough about them. They sure are a treat to us boys, and almost every night they have good eats for us. One night it is lemonade, pies and coffee, and the next it is doughnuts and coffee, and they are just like mother makes. There are two girls here that run the place, and they are real American girls, too. The first I have seen since I have been in France, and I'll say they are a treat!

Hogan and I have been helping them, and now I cook pies and doughnuts as well as anyone. We sure do have a picnic with them and enjoy helping out once in awhile.

One thing I want you to do is to help the Salvation Army all you can and whenever you get a chance to lend a helping hand to them do it, for they sure have done a whole lot for your boy, and if you can get them a write-up in the papers, why do it and I will be happy.

From Lord Derby.

The splendid work which the Salvation Army has done among the soldiers during the war is one for which I, as Secretary of State for War, should like to thank them most sincerely; it is a work which is deserving of all support.

State of New Jersey
Executive Department
Trenton.
December 27, 1917.
My Dear Mr. Battle:
    I have learned of the campaign of the Salvation Army to raise money for its war activities. The work of the Salvation Army is at all times commendable and deserving, but particularly so in its relation to the war.
    I sincerely hope that the campaign will be very successful.
        Cordially yours,
        (Signed) Walter E. Edge,
        Governor.
        Mr. George Gordon Battle,
        General Chairman, 37 Wall Street, New York City.

Governor Charles S. Whitman's address at luncheon at Hotel Ten Eyck, Albany, New York, December 8, 1917.

I take especial pleasure in offering my tribute of respect and appreciation to the Salvation Army. I have known of its work as intimately as any man who is not directly connected with the organization. In my position as a judge and a district attorney of New York City for many years, I always found the Salvation Army a great help in solving the various problems of the poor, the criminal and distressed.

"Frequently while other agencies, though good, hesitated, there was never a case where there was a possibility that relief might be brought—never was a case of misery or violence so low, that the Salvation Army would not undertake it.

"The Salvation Army lends its manhood and womanhood to go 'Over There' from our States, and our State, to labor with those who fight and die. There is very little we can do, but we can help with our funds."

The Salvation Army is worthy of the support of all right-thinking people. Its main purpose is to reclaim men and women to decency and good citizenship. This purpose is being prosecuted not only with energy and enthusiasm but with rare tact and judgment.

The sphere of the Army's operations has now been extended to the battlefields of Europe, where its consecrated workers will cooperate with the Y.M.C.A., K. of C., and kindred organizations.

It gives me pleasure to commend the work of this beneficent organization, and to urge our people to remember its splendid service to humanity.

> Very truly yours,
> Albert E. Sleeper,
> Governor.

January 25, 1918.
Endorsement of
Governor Hugh M. Dorsey, of Georgia.

The Salvation Army has been a potent force for good everywhere, so far as I know. They are rendering to our soldiers "somewhere in France" the most invaluable aid, ministering not only to their spiritual needs, but caring for them in a material way. This they have done without the blare of trumpets.

Many commanding officers certify to the fact that the Salvation Army is not only rendering most effective work, but that this work is of a distinctive character and of a nature not covered by the activities of other organizations ministering to the needs of the soldier boys. In other words, they are filling that gap in the army life which they have always so well filled in the civil life of our people.

State of Utah
Executive Office
Salt Lake City, January 21, 1918.

I have learned with a great deal of interest of the splendid work being done by the Salvation Army for the moral uplift of the soldiers, both in the training camps and in the field. I am very glad to endorse this work and to express the hope that the Salvation Army may find a way to continue and extend its work among the soldiers.

(Signed) Simon Bamberg,
Governor.

From a Proclamation by Governor Brumbaugh.

To the People of Pennsylvania:

I have long since learned to believe in the great, good work of the Salvation Army and have given it my approval and support through the years. This mighty body of consecrated workers are like gleaners in the fields of humanity. They seek and succor and save those that most need and least receive aid.

Now, THEREFORE, I, Martin G. Brumbaugh, Governor of the Commonwealth of Pennsylvania, do cordially commend the work of the Salvation Army and call upon our people to give earnest heed to their call for assistance, making liberal donations to their praiseworthy work and manifesting thus our continued and resolute purpose to give our men in arms unstinted aid and to support gladly all these noble and sacrificing agencies that under God give hope and help to our soldiers.

[SEAL]

Given under my hand and the great seal of the State, at the City of Harrisburg, this seventh day of February, in the year of our Lord one thousand nine hundred and eighteen, and of the Commonwealth the one hundred and forty-second.

By the Governor:
Secretary of the Commonwealth.
copy/h

The Commonwealth of Massachusetts,
Executive Department,
State House, Boston, February 15, 1918.

It gives me pleasure to add my word of approval to the very noble work that is being done by the Salvation Army for the men now serving the country. The Salvation Army has for many years been doing very valuable work, and the extension of its labors into the ranks of the soldiers has not lessened in any degree its power of accomplishment. The Salvation Army can render most efficient service. It should be the aim of every one of us in Massachusetts to assist in every way the work that is being done for the soldiers. We cannot do too much of this kind of work for them—they deserve and need it all. I urge everybody in Massachusetts to assist the Salvation Army in every way possible, to the end that Massachusetts may maintain her place in the forefront of the States of the Union who are assisting the work of the Army.

(Signed) Samuel W. McCall,
Governor.

Proclamation.
To the People of the State of Maryland:

I have been very much impressed with the good work which is being done in this country by the Salvation Army, and I am not at all surprised at the great work which it is doing at the front, upon or near the battlefields of Europe. It is doing not only the same kind of work being done by the Y.M.C.A. and the Knights of Columbus, but work in fields decidedly their own.

It is now undertaking to raise $1,000,000 for the National War Service and it is preparing a hutment equipped with libraries, daily newspapers, games, light refreshments, etc., in every camp in France.

Now, THEREFORE, I, Emerson C. Harrington, Governor of Maryland, believing that the effect and purposes for which the Salvation Army is asking this money, are deserving of our warmest support, do hereby call upon the people of Maryland to respond as liberally as they can in this war drive being made by the Salvation Army to enable them more efficiently to render service which is so much needed.

IN TESTIMONY WHEREOF, I have hereunto set my hand and caused to be hereto affixed the Great Seal of Maryland at Annapolis, Maryland, this fourteenth day of February, in the year one thousand nine hundred and eighteen.

(The Great Seal of the State of Maryland)
Emerson C. Harrington.
By the Governor,
Thos. W. Simmons, Secretary of State.

The Salvation Army is peculiarly equipped for this kind of service. I have watched the career of this organization for many years, and I know its leaders to be devoted and capable men and women.

Of course, any agency which can in any way ameliorate the condition of the boys at the front should receive encouragement.

(Signed) Frank C. Lowden,
Governor of Illinois.

I join with thousands of my fellow citizens in having a great admiration for the splendid work which has already been accomplished by the Salvation Army in the alleviation of suffering, the spiritual uplift of the masses, and its substantial and prayerful ministrations.

The Salvation Army does its work quietly, carefully, persistently and effectively. Our patriotic citizenry will quickly place the stamp of approval upon the great work being done by the Salvation Army among the private soldiers at home and abroad.

(Signed) Governor Brough of Arkansas.

Lansing, Michigan, June 13, 1918.
To Whom It May Concern:

Among the various organizations doing war work in connection with the American Army, none are found more worthy of support than the Salvation Army.

Entering into its work with the whole-hearted zeal which has characterized its movement in times of peace, it has won the highest praise of both officers and soldiers alike.

It is an essential pleasure to commend the work of the Salvation Army to the people of Michigan with the urgent request that its war activities be given your generous support.

Albert E. Sleeper,
Governor of the State of Michigan.
Mark E. McKee,
Secretary, Counties Division, Michigan War Board.

State of Kansas
Arthur Capper, Governor,
Topeka
August 8, 1917.

I have been greatly pleased with the war activities of the Salvation Army and want to express my appreciation of the splendid service rendered by that organization on the battlefield of Europe ever since the war began. It is a most commendable and a most patriotic thing to do and I hope the people of Kansas will give the enterprise their generous support.

Very respectfully,
(Signed) Arthur Capper, Governor.

Best wishes for the success of your work. As the Salvation Army has done so much good in time of peace, it has multiplied opportunities to do good in the horrors of war, if given the necessary means."

(Signed) Miles Poindexter,
Senator from Washington.

House of Representatives
Washington, D.C.
January 8, 1918.

Colonel Adam Gifford, Salvation Army,
8 East Brookline Street, Boston, Mass.
My Dear Colonel Gifford:

I desire to write you in highest commendation of the work the Salvation Army is doing in France. During last November I was behind the French and English fronts, and unless one has been there they cannot realize the assistance to spirit and courage given to the soldiers by the "hut" service of the Salvation Army.

The only particular in which the Salvation Army fell short was that there were not sufficient huts for the demands of the troops. The huts I saw were crowded and not commodious.

Behind the British front I heard several officers state that the service of the Salvation Army was somewhat different from other services of the same kind, but most effective.

With kindest regards, I remain,

Very sincerely yours,
(Signed) George Holden Tinkham,
Congressman.

This Condolence Card conveyed the sympathy of the Commander to the friends of the fallen. Forethought had prepared this some time before the first American had made the supreme sacrifice.

Greater love hath no man than this,
that a man lay down his life for his friends.

122 W. 14th Street
New York

My dear Friend:

I must on behalf of the Salvation Army take this opportunity to say how deeply and truly we share your grief at this time of your bereavement. It will be hard for you to understand how anything can soothe the pain made by your great loss, but let me point you to the one Jesus Christ, who acquainted Himself with all our griefs so that He might heal the heart's wounds made by our sorrows and whose love for us was so vast that He bled and died to save us.

It may be some solace to think that your loved one poured out his life in a War in which high and holy principles are involved, and also that he was quick to answer the call for men.

Believe me when I say that we are praying and will pray for you.

Yours in sympathy,
Evangeline Booth

Commander Evangeline Booth:

The comfort and solace contained in the beautiful card of sympathy I recently received from you is more than you can ever know. With all my heart I am very grateful to you and can only assure you feebly of my deep appreciation.

It has made me realize more than ever before the fundamental principles of Christianity upon which your Army is built and organized, for how truly does it comfort the widow and fatherless in their affliction.

Tucked away as my two babies and I are in a tiny Wisconsin town, we felt that our grief, while shared in by our good friends, was just a passing emotion to the rest of the world. But when a card such as yours comes, extending a heart of sympathy and prayer and ferrets us out in our sorrow in our little town, you must know how much less lonely we are because of it. It surely shows us that a sacrifice such as my dear husband made is acknowledged and lauded by the entire world.

I am, oh! so proud of him, so comforted to know I was wife to a man so imbued with the principles of right and justice that he counted no sacrifice, not even his life, too great to offer in the cause. Not for anything would I ask him back or rob him of the glory of such a death. Yet our little home is sad indeed, with its light and life taken away.

The good you have done before and during the war must be a very great source of gratification for you, and I trust you may be spared for many years to stretch out your helping hand to the sorrowing and make us better for having known you.

With deepest gratitude.

Commander Evangeline Booth:

I have just seen your picture in the November *Pictorial Review* and I do so greatly admire your splendid character and the great work you are doing.

I want to thank you for the message of Christian love and sympathy you sent to me upon the death of my son in July, aeroplane accident in England.

Without the Christian's faith and the blessed hope of the Gospel we would despair indeed. A long time ago I learned to pray Thy will be done for my son—and I have tested the promises and I have found them true.

May the Lord bless you abundantly in your own heart and in your world wide influence and the splendid Salvation Army.

Dear Friends:

Words fall far short in expressing our deep appreciation of your comforting words of condolence and sympathy. Will you accept as a small token of love the enclosed appreciation written by Professor ——— of the Oberlin College, and a quotation from a letter written August 25th by our soldier boy, and found among his effects to be opened only in case of his death, and forwarded to his mother?

> I am
> Yours truly.

Enclosure:
"November 16, 1918.

"If by any chance this letter should be given to you, as something coming directly from my heart; you, who are my mother, need have no fear or regret for the personality destined not to come back to you.

"A mother and father whose noble ideals they firmly fixed in two sons should rather experience a deep sense of pride that the young chap of nearly twenty-one years does not come back to them; for, though he was fond of living, he was also prepared to die with a faith as sound and steadfast as that of the little children whom the Master took in His arms.

"And more than that, the body you gave to me so sweet and pure and strong, though misused at times, has been returned to God as pure and undefiled as when you gave it to me. I think there is nothing that should please you more than that.

> "In My Father's House are many mansions,
> I go to prepare a place for you;
> If it were not so, I would have told you.

> "Your Baby boy,"
> (Signed) Paul.
> Chatereaux, France.
> August, 1918.

N.B.—Written on back of the envelope:
"To be opened only in case of accident."

Commander Evangeline Booth:

Permit me to express through you my deep appreciation of the consoling message from the Salvation Army on the loss of my brother, Clement, in France. I am indeed grateful for this last thought from an organization which did so much to meet his living needs and to lessen the hardships of his service in France. I shall always feel a personal debt to those of you who seemed so near to him at the end.

Miss Evangeline Booth:

I was greatly touched by the card of sympathy sent me in your name on the occasion of my great sorrow—and my equally great glory. The death of a husband for the great cause of humanity is a martyrdom that any soldier's wife, even in her deep grief, is proud to share.

Thanking you for your helpful message.

Miss Evangeline Booth:

Of the many cards of condolence received by our family upon the death of my dear brother, none touched us more deeply than the one sent by you.

We do indeed appreciate your thoughtfulness in sending words of comfort to people who are utter strangers to you.

Accept again, the gratitude of my parents as well as the other members of our family, including myself.

May our Heavenly Father bless you all and glorify your good works.

Miss Evangeline Booth,
Commander of the Salvation Army,
New York City, N.Y.
Dear Miss Booth:

I beg of you to pardon me for writing you this letter,

but I feel that I must. On the 17th day of March I received a letter from my boy in France, and it reads as follows:

"Somewhere in France, Jan. 15, 1918.
"My Dear Mother:

"I must write you a few lines to tell you that you must not worry about me even though it is some time since I wrote you. We don't have much time to ourselves out here. I have just come out of the trenches, and now it is mud, mud, mud, up to one's knees. I often think of the fireplace at home these cold nights, but, mother, I must tell you that I don't know what we boys would do if it was not for the Salvation Army. The women, they are just like mothers to the boys. God help the ones that say anything but good about the Army! Those women certainly have courage, to come right out in the trenches with coffee and cocoa, etc., and they are so kind and good. Mother, I want you to write to Miss Booth and thank her for me for her splendid work out here. When I come home I shall exchange the U.S. uniform for the S.A. uniform, and I know, ma, that you will not object. Well, the Germans have been raining shells to-day, but we were unharmed. I passed by an old shack of a building—a poor woman sat there with a baby, lulling it to sleep, when a shell came down and the poor souls had passed from this earthly hell to their heavenly reward. Only God knows the conditions out here; it is horrible. Well, I must close now, and don't worry, mother, I will be home some day.

"Your loving son,"

Well, Miss Booth, I got word three weeks ago that Joseph had been killed in action. I am heart-broken, but

I suppose it was God's will. Poor boy! He has his uniform exchanged for a white robe. I am all alone now, as he was my only boy and only child. Again I beg of you to pardon me for sending you this letter.

December 10, 1917.
Commander Evangeline C. Booth, New York City.
My Dear Commander:

I have just read in the New York papers of your purpose and plan to raise a million dollars for your Salvation Army work carried on in the interests of the soldiers at home and abroad, and I cannot refrain from writing to you to express my deep interest, and also the hope that you may be successful in raising this fund, because I know that it will be so well administered.

From all that I have heard of the Salvation Army work in connection with the soldiers carried on under your direction, I think it is simply wonderful, and if there is any service that I can render you or the Army, I should be exceedingly pleased.

I have read "Souls in Khaki," and I wish that everyone might read it, for could they do so, your million-dollar fund would be easily raised.

With ever-increasing interest in the Salvation Army, I am,

> Cordially yours,
> (Signed) J. Wilbur Chapman.
> Moderator of the General Assembly of the Presbyterian Church in the U.S.A.

Raymond B. Fosdick, chairman of the War Recreation Commission, on his return from a tour of investigation into activities of the relief organizations in France, gave out the following:

Somewhat to my surprise I found the Salvation Army

probably the most popular organization in France with the troops. It has not undertaken the comprehensive program which the Y.M.C.A. has laid out for itself; that is, it is operating in three or four divisions, while the Y.M.C.A. is aiming to cover every unit of troops.

But its simple, homely, unadorned service seems to have touched the hearts of our men. The aim of the organization is, if possible, to put a worker and his wife in a canteen or a centre. The women spend their time making doughnuts and pies, and sew on buttons. The men make themselves generally useful in any way which their service can be applied.

I saw such placed in dugouts way up at the front, where the German shells screamed over our heads with a sound not unlike a freight train crossing a bridge. Down in their dugouts the Salvation Army folks imperturbably handed out doughnuts and dished out the "drink."

War Department
Commission on Training Camp Activities, Washington
45, Avenue Montaigne, Paris.
Apr. 8, 1919.
Commander Evangeline Booth,
Salvation Army, New York City.
My Dear Commander Booth:
The work of the Salvation Army with the armed forces of the United States does not need any word of commendation from me. Perhaps I may be permitted to say, however, that as a representative of the War and Navy Departments I have been closely in touch with it from its inception, both in Europe and in the United States. I do not believe there is a doughboy anywhere who does not speak of it with enthusiasm and affection. Its remarkable success has been due solely to the unselfish spirit of service which has underlain it. Nothing has been

too humble or too lowly for the Salvation Army representative to do for the soldier. Without ostentation, without advertising, without any emphasis upon auspices or organization, your people have met the men of the Army as friends and companions-in-arms, and the soldiers, particularly those of the American Expeditionary Force, will never forget what you have done.

> Faithfully yours,
> (Signed) Raymond B. Fosdick.

From Honorable Arthur Stanley,
Chairman British Red Cross Society.
British Red Cross Society
Joint War Committee
83 Pall Mall, London, S.W.,
December 22, 1917.
General Bramwell Booth.
Dear General Booth:

I enclose formal receipt for the cheque, value £2000, which was handed to me by your representative. I note that it is a contribution from the Salvation Army to the Joint Funds to provide a new Salvation Army Motor Ambulance Unit on the same conditions as before.

I cannot sufficiently thank you and the Salvation Army for this very generous donation.

I am indeed glad to know that you are providing another twenty drivers for service with our Ambulance Fleet in France. This is most welcome news, as whenever Salvation Army men are helping we hear nothing but good reports of their work. Sir Ernest Clarke tells me that your Ambulance Sections are quite the best of any in our service, and the more Salvation Army men you can send him, the better he will be pleased. I would again take this opportunity of congratulating you, which I do with all my heart, upon the splendid record of your Army.

> Yours sincerely,
> (Signed) Arthur Stanley.

Extract from Judge Ben Lindsey's picture of the Salvation Army at the Front:

A good expression for American enthusiasm is: "I am crazy about"—this, or that, or the other thing that excites our admiration. Well, "I am crazy about the Salvation Army"—the Salvation Army as I saw it and mingled with it and the doughboys in the trenches. And when I happened to be passing through Chicago to-day and saw an appeal in the *Tribune* for the Salvation Army, I remembered what our boys so often shouted out to me as I passed them in the trenches and back of the lines: "Judge, when you get back home tell the folks not to forget the Salvation Army. They're the real thing."

And I know they are the real thing. I have shared with the boys the doughnuts and chocolate and coffee that seemed to be so much better than any other doughnuts or coffee or chocolate I have ever tasted before. And when it seemed so wonderful to me after just a mild sort of experience down a shell-swept road, through the damp and cold of a French winter day, what must it be to those boys after trench raids or red-hot scraps down rain-soaked trenches under the wet mists of No Man's Land? . . . Listen to some of the stories the boys told me; "You see, Judge, the good old Salvation Army is the real thing. They don't put on no airs. There ain't no flub-dub about them and you don't see their mugs in the fancy magazines much. Why, you never would see one of them in Paris around the hotels.

You'd never know they existed, Judge, unless you came right up here to the front lines as near as the Colonel will let you!"

And one enthusiastic urchin said: "Why, Judge, after the battle yesterday, we couldn't get those women out of the village till they'd seen every fellow had at least a dozen fried cakes and all the coffee or chocolate he could pile in. We just had to drag 'em out—for the boys love 'em too much to lose 'em—we weren't going to take no chances—not much—for our Salvation ladies!"

In speaking of the Salvation Army's work before the Rotary Club of San Francisco, Harry Lauder said:

"There is no organization in Europe doing more for the troops than the Salvation Army, and the devotion of its officers has caused the Salvation Army to be revered by the soldiers."

Mr. Otto Kahn, one of America's most prominent bankers, upon his return to this country after a tour through the American lines in France, writes, among other things:

I should particularly consider myself remiss if I did not refer with sincere admiration to the devoted, sympathetic, and most efficient work of the Salvation Army, which, though limited in its activities to a few sectors only, has won the warm and affectionate regard of those of our troops with whom it has been in contact.

Mr. David Lawrence, special Washington correspondent of the New York Evening Post and other influential papers, in an article in which he comments on the work of all the relief agencies, says of the Salvation Army in France:

Curiously enough the Salvation Army is spoken of in all official reports as the organization most popular with the troops. Its organization is the smallest of all four. Its service is simple and unadorned. It specializes on doughnuts and pie, which it gives away free whenever the ingredients of the manufacture of those articles are at hand.

The policy of the organization is to place a worker and his wife, if possible, with a unit of troops. The woman makes doughnuts and sews on buttons, while the man helps the soldiers in any way he can.

The success of the Salvation Army is attributed by commanding officers to the fact that the workers know how to mix naturally. *In other cases there had been sometimes an air of condescension not unlike that of the professional settlement house worker.*

In a recent issue of the Saturday Evening Post, Mr. Irvin Cobb, who has just returned from France, has this to say of the Salvation Army:

Right here seems a good-enough place for me to slip in a few words of approbation for the work which another organization has accomplished in France since we put our men into the field. Nobody asked me to speak in its favor because, so far as I can find out, it has no publicity department. I am referring to the Salvation Army. May it live forever for the service which, without price and without any boasting on the part of its personnel, it is rendering to our boys in France!

A good many of us who hadn't enough religion, and a good many more of us who, mayhap, had too much religion, looked rather contemptuously upon the methods of the Salvationists. Some have gone so far as to intimate that the Salvation Army was vulgar in its methods and lacking in dignity and even in reverence. Some have intimated that converting a sinner to the tap of a bass drum or the tinkle of a tambourine was an improper process altogether. Never again, though, shall I hear the blare of the cornet as it cuts into the chorus of hallelujah whoops, where a ring of blue-bonneted women and blue-capped men stand exhorting on a city street-corner under the gaslights, without recalling what some of their enrolled brethren—and sisters—have done, and are doing, in Europe!

The American Salvation Army in France is small, but, believe me, it is powerfully busy! Its war delegation came over without any fanfare of the trumpets of publicity. It has no paid press agents here and no impressive headquarters. There are no well-known names, other than the names of its executive heads, on its rosters or on its advisory boards. None of its members are housed at an expensive hotel and none of them have handsome automobiles in which to travel about from place to place. No campaigns to raise nation-wide millions of dollars for the cost of its ministrations overseas were ever held at home. I imagine it is the pennies of the poor that mainly fill its war chest. I imagine, too, that sometimes its finances are an uncertain quantity. Incidentally, I am assured that not one of its male workers here is of draft age unless he holds exemption papers to prove his physical unfitness for military service. The Salvationists are taking care to purge themselves of any suspicion that potential slackers have joined their ranks in order to avoid the possibility of having to perform duties in khaki.

Among officers, as well as among enlisted men, one occasionally hears criticism—which may or may not be based on a fair judgment—for certain branches of certain activities of certain organizations. But I have yet to meet any soldier, whether a brigadier or a private, who, if he spoke at all of the Salvation Army, did not speak in terms of fervent gratitude for the aid that the Salvationists are rendering so unostentatiously and yet so very effectively. Let a sizable body of troops move from one station to another, and hard on its heels there came a squad of men and women of the Salvation Army. An army truck may bring them, or it may be they have a battered jitney to move them and their scanty outfits. Usually they do not ask for help from anyone in reaching their destinations. They find lodgment in a wrecked shell of a house or in the corner of a barn. By main force and awkwardness they set up their equipment, and very soon the word has spread among the troops that at such and such a place the Salvation Army is serving free hot drinks and free doughnuts and free pies. It specializes in doughnuts—the Salvation Army in the field does—the real old-fashioned home-made ones that taste of home to a homesick soldier boy!

I did not see this, but one of my associates did. He saw it last winter in a dismal place on the Toul sector. A file of our troops were finishing a long hike through rain and snow over roads knee-deep in half-thawed icy slush. Cold and wet and miserable they came tramping into a cheerless, half-empty town within sound and range of the German guns. They found a reception committee awaiting them there—in the person of two Salvation Army lassies and a Salvation Army Captain. The women had a fire going in the dilapidated oven of a vanished villager's kitchen. One of them was rolling out the batter on a plank, with an old wine-bottle for a rolling pin, and using the top of a tin can to cut the dough into circular strips; the other woman was cooking the doughnuts, and as fast as they were cooked the man served them out, spitting hot, to hungry, wet boys clamoring about the door, and nobody was asked to pay a cent!

At the risk of giving mortal affront to ultradoctrinal

practitioners of applied theology, I am firmly committed to the belief that by the grace and the grease of those doughnuts those three humble benefactors that day strengthened their right to a place in the Heavenly Kingdom.

My Dear Colonel Jenkins:

I take pleasure in sending you a copy of my report as Commissioner to France, in which I made reference to the work of the Salvation Army with our American Expeditionary Forces.

I cannot recall ever hearing the slightest criticism of the work of the Salvation Army, but I heard many words of enthusiastic appreciation on the part not only of the Generals and officers but of the soldiers.

I saw many evidences showing that the unselfish, sometimes reckless, abandon of your workers had a great effect upon our men.

I am sure that the Salvation Army also stands in high respect for its religious influence upon the men.

It was pleasant still further to hear such words of appreciation as I did from General Duncan regarding the work of Chaplain Allan, the divisional chaplain of General Duncan's unit. He has evidently risen to his work in a splendid way. It is a pleasure to have this opportunity of rendering this testimony to you.

> Faithfully yours,
> Charles S. MacFarland,
> General Secretary.

The New York Globe *printed the following:*

Huns don't stop Salvation Army. Meeting held in deep dugout under ruined village—mandolin supplants the organ, By Herbert Corey.

Just behind the Somme Front, May 31.—Somewhere in the tangle of smashed walls there was a steely jingle. At first the sound was hard to identify, so odd are acoustics in this which was once a little town. There were stub ends of walls here and there—bare, raw snags of walls sticking up—and now and then a rooftree tilted pathetically against a ruin, or a pile of dusty masonry that had been a house. A little path ran through this tangle, and under an arched gateway that by a miracle remained standing and down the steps of a dugout. The jingling sound became recognizable. Some one was trying to play on a mandolin:

"Jesus, Lover of My Soul."

It was grotesque and laughable. The grand old hymn refused its cadences to this instrument of a tune-loving bourgeoise. It seemed to stand aloof and unconquered. This is a hymn for the swelling notes of an organ or for the great harmonies of a choir. It was not made to be debased by association with this caterwauling wood and wire, this sounding board for barbershop chords, this accomplice of sick lovers leaning on village fences. Then there came a voice:

"By gollies, brother, you're getting it! I actually believe you're getting it, brother. We'll have a swell meeting to-night."

I went down the steps into the Salvation Army man's dugout. A large soldier, cigarette depending from his lower lip, unshaven, tin hat tipped on the back of his head, was picking away at the wires of the mandolin with fingers that seemed as thick and yellow as ears of corn. As I came in he stated profanely, that these dam' things were not made to pick out condemn' hymn tunes on. The Salvation Army man encouraged him:

"You keep on, brother," said he, "and we'll have a

fine meeting for the Brigadier when he comes in to-night."

Taking His Chances.

Another boy was sitting there, his head rather low. The mandolin player indicated him with a jerk. "He got all roughed up last night," said he. "We found a bottle of some sweet stuff these Frogs left in the house where we're billeted. Tasted a good deal like syrup. But it sure put Bull out."

Bull turned a pair of inflamed eyes on the musician.

"You keep on a-talkin', and I'll hang somep'n on your eye," said Bull, hoarsely.

Then he replaced his head in his hands. The Salvation Army man laughed at the interlude and then returned to the player.

"See," said he, "it goes like this———" He hummed the wonderful old hymn.

The floor of the dugout was covered with straw. The stairs which led to it were wide, so that at certain hours the sun shone in and dried out the walls. There were few slugs crawling slimily on the walls of the Salvation Army's place. Rats were there, of course, and bugs of sorts, but few slugs. On the whole it was considered a good dugout, because of these things. The roof was not a strong one, it seemed to me. A 77-shell would go through it like a knife through cheese. I said so to the Salvation Army man.

"Aw, brother," said he. "We've got to take our chances along with the rest."

At the foot of the stairs was a table on which were the few things the Salvation Army man had to sell, up here under the guns. There were some figs and a handful of black licorice drops and a few nuts. Boys kept coming in and demanding cookies. Cookies there were none, but there was hope ahead. If the Brigadier managed to get in to-night with the fliv, there might be cookies.

No Money, But Good Cheer.

"Just our luck," said some morose doughboy, "if a shell hit the fliv. It's a hell of a road—

"No shell has hit it yet, brother," said the Salvation Army man, cheerily.

Fifteen dollars would have bought everything he had in stock. One could have carried away the whole stock in the pockets of an army overcoat. The Salvation Army has no money, you know. It is hard to buy supplies for canteens over here, unless a pocket filled with money is doing the buying. The Salvation Army must pick up its stuff where it can get it. Yesterday there had been sardines and shaving soap and tin watches. To-day there were only figs and licorice drops and nuts.

"But if the Brigadier gets in," said the Salvation Army man, "there will be something sweet to eat. And we'll have a little meeting of song and praise, brother—just to thank God for the chance he has given us to help."

Here there is no one else to serve the boys. Other organizations have more money and more men, but for some reason they have not seen fit to come to this which was once a town. Shells fall into it from six directions all day and all night long. Now and then it is gassed. A few kilometres away is the German line. One reaches town over a road which is nightly torn to pieces by high explosives. No one comes here voluntarily, and no one stays willingly—except the Salvation Army man. He's here for keeps.

Men come down into his little dugout to play checkers and dominoes and buy sweet things to eat. He is here to help them spiritually as well as physically and they know it, and yet they do not hear him. He talks to them just as they talk to each other, except that he does not swear and he does not tell stories that have too much of a tang. He never obtrudes his religion on them. Just once in a while—on the nights the Brigadier gets in—there is a little song and praise meeting. They thank God for the chance they have to help.

That night the Brigadier got in with his cookies and chocolates and his message that salvation is free. Perhaps a dozen men sat around uncomfortably in the little dugout and listened to him. The man of the mandolin had refused at the last moment. He said he would be dam' if he could play a hymn tune on that thing. But the old hymn quavered cheerily out of the little dugout into the shell-torn night. The husky voices of the Brigadier and the Ensign and Holy Joe carried it on, while the little audience sat mute.

> *While the nearer waters roll,*
> *While the tempest still is high.*

Then there was a little prayer and a few straight, cordial words from the Brigadier and then, somewhere in that perilous night outside, "taps" sounded and the men were off to bed. They had no word of thanks as they shook hands on parting. They did not speak to each other as they picked their way along the path through the ruins. But when they reached the street some one said very profanely and very earnestly:

"I can lick any man's son who says THEY ain't all right."

I have just received your letter of the 30th of July, and it has cheered my heart to know you take an interest in a poor Belgian prisoner of war.

Since I wrote to you last we have been changed to another camp; the one we are now in is quite a nice camp, with lots of flowers, and we are allowed more freedom, but it is very bad regarding food. We have so very little to eat, it is a pity we can't eat flowers! We rise up hungry and go to bed hungry, and all day long we are trying to still the craving for food. So you will understand the longing there is in our hearts to once again be free—to be able to go to work and earn our daily bread! But the one great comfort that I find is since I learned to know Jesus as my Saviour and Friend I can better endure the trials and even rejoice that I am called to suffer for His sake, and while around me I see many who are in despair—some even cursing God for all the misery in which we are surrounded, some trying to be brave, some giving up altogether—yet to a number of us has come the Gospel message, brought by the Salvation Army, and I am so glad that I, for one, listened and surrendered my life to this Jesus! Now I have real peace, and He walks with me and gives me grace to conquer the evil.

When I lived in Belgium I was very worldly and sinful—I lived for pleasure and drink and sin. I did not then know of One who said, "Come unto Me, all ye that labor and are heavy-laden, and I will give you rest." I did not know anything about living a Christian life, but now it is all changed and I am so thankful! Salvation Army officers visit us and bring words of cheer and blessing and comfort. You will be glad to know that I have applied to our Commissioner to become a Salvation Army officer when the war is over. I want to go to my poor little stricken country and tell my people of this wonderful Saviour that can save from all sin!

On behalf of my comrades and myself, I want to thank the American nation for all they have done, and are still doing, for my people. May God bless you all for it, and may He grant that before long there will be peace on earth!

I remain, faithfully yours,
Remy Meersman.

A copy of the "Stars and Stripes," the official publication of the American Expeditionary Forces published in France by the American soldiers themselves, just received in Chicago, contains the following:

Perhaps in the old days when war and your home town seemed as far apart as Paris, France, and Paris, Ill., you were a superior person who used to snicker when you passed a street corner where a small Salvation Army band was holding forth. Perhaps—Heaven forgive you—you even sneered a little when you heard the bespectacled sister in the poke-bonnet bang her tambourine and raise a shrill voice to the strains of 'Oh death, where is thy sting-a-ling.' Probably—unless you yourselves had known the bitterness of one who finds himself alone, hungry and homeless in a big city—you did not know much about the Salvation Army.

Well, we are all homeless over here and every American soldier will take back with him a new affection and a new respect for the Salvation Army. Many will carry with them the memories of a cheering word and a friendly cruller received in one of the huts nearest of all to the trenches. There the old slogan of "Soup and Salvation" has given way to "Pies and Piety." It might be "Doughnuts and Doughboys." These huts pitched within the shock of the German guns, are ramshackle and bare and few, for no organization can grow rich on the pennies and nickels that are tossed into the tambourines at the street-corners of the world. But they are doing a work that the soldiers themselves will never forget, and it is an especial pleasure to say so here, because the Salvation Army, being much too simple and old-fashioned to know the uses of advertisement, have never asked us to. You, however, can testify for them. Perhaps you do in your letters home. And surely when you are back there and you pass once more a "meeting" at the curb, you will not snicker. You will tarry awhile—and take off your hat.

We have received a letter from Mr. Lewis Strauss, Secretary to Mr. Herbert Hoover, who has just returned from France, and he says that Mr. Hoover's time while in Europe was spent almost wholly in London and Paris, and that he had no opportunity for observing our War Relief Work at the front. The concluding paragraph of the letter, however, is as follows:

Mr. Hoover has frequently heard the most complimentary reports of the invaluable work which your organization is performing in invariably the most perilous localities, and he is filled with admiration for those who are conducting it at the front.

The Chicago Tribune *(May 17, 1918), quoting from the above, also speaks editorially.*

The acid test of any service done for our soldiers in France is the value the men themselves place upon it. No matter how excellent our intentions, we cannot be satisfied with the result if the soldiers are not satisfied. Without suggesting any invidious distinctions among organizations that are working at the front, it is nevertheless a pleasure to record that the Salvation Army stands very high in the regard of American soldiers.

The evidence of the Salvation Army's excellent work comes from many sources.

Appendix: A Few Facts About The Salvation Army

It has been truly said that within four days after the German Army entered Belgium, another Army entered also—the Salvation Army! One came to destroy, the other to relieve distress and minister to the wounded and dying.

The British Salvation Army furnished a number of Red Cross Ambulances, manned by Salvationists when the Red Cross was in great need of such. When these arrived in France and people first saw the big cars with the "Salvation Army" label it attracted a good deal of attention. The drivers wore the Red Cross uniform, and were under its military rules, but wore on their caps the red band with the words, "Salvation Army."

There is a story of a young officer in sportive mood who left a group of his companions and stepped out into the street to stop one of these ambulances:

"Hello! Salvation Army!" he cried. "Are you taking those men to heaven?"

Amid the derisive laughter of the officers on the sidewalk the Salvationists replied pleasantly:

"I cannot say I am taking them to heaven, but I certainly am taking them away from the other place."

One of the good British Salvationists wrote of meeting our American boys in England. He said:

"Oh, these American soldiers! One meets them in

twos and threes, all over the city, everlastingly asking questions, by word of mouth and by wide-open trustful eyes, and they make a bee-line for the Salvation Army uniform on sight. I passed a company of them on the march across London, from one railroad station to another, the other day. They were obviously interested in the sights of the city streets as they passed through at noon, but as they drew nearer one of the boys caught sight of the red band around my cap among the hats crowning the sidewalk crowd. My! but that one man's interest swept over the hundred odd men! Like the flame of a prairie fire, it went with a zip! They all knew at once! They had no eyes for the crowd any more; they did not stare at the façade of the railway terminus which they were passing; they saw nothing of the famous 'London Stone' set in the wall behind its grid on their right hand. What they saw was a Salvation Army man in all his familiar war-paint, and it was a sight for sore eyes! Here was something they could understand! This was an American institution, a tried, proved and necessary part of the life of any community. All this and much more those wide-open eyes told me. It was as good to them as if I was stuck all over with stars and stripes. I belonged—that's it—belonged to them, and so they took off the veil and showed their hearts and smiled their good glad greeting.

"So I smiled and that first file of four beamed seraphic. Two at least were of Scandinavian stock, but how should that make any difference? Again and again I noticed their counterpart in the column which followed. . . . It was all the same; file upon file those faces spread out in eager particular greeting; those eyes, one and all, sought mine expecting the smile I so gladly gave. And then when the last was past and I gazed upon their swaying forms from the rear I wondered why my eyes were moist and something had gone wrong with my swallowing apparatus. Great boys! Bonny boys!"

The Salvation Army was founded July 5, 1865, as a Christian Mission in East London by the Reverend William Booth, and its first Headquarters opened in Whitechapel Road, London. Three years later work was begun in Scotland.

In 1877 the name of the Christian Mission was altered to the Salvation Army, and the Reverend William Booth assumed the title of General.

December 29, 1879, the first number of the official organ, "The War Cry," was issued and the first brass band formed at Consett.

In 1880 the first Training School was opened at Hackney, London, and the first contingent of the Salvation Army officers landed in the United States. The next year the Salvation Army entered Australia, and was extended to France. 1882 saw Switzerland, Sweden, India and Canada receiving their first contingent of Salvation Army officers. A London Orphan Asylum was acquired and converted into Congress Hall, which, with its large Auditorium, with a seating capacity of five thousand, still remains the Mammoth International Training School for Salvation Army officers, for missionary and home fields all over the world. The first Prison-Gate Home was opened in London in this same year.

The Army commenced in South Africa, New Zealand and Iceland in 1883.

In 1886 work was begun in Germany and the late General visited France, the United States and Canada. The First International Congress was held in London in that year.

The British Slum work was inaugurated in 1887, and Officers sent to Italy, Holland, Denmark, Zululand, and among the Kaffirs and Hottentots. The next year the Army extended to Norway, Argentine Republic, Finland and Belgium, and the next ten years saw work extended in succession to Uruguay, West Indies, Java, Japan, British Guiana, Panama and Korea, and work commenced among the Lepers.

The growing confidence of the great of the earth was manifested by the honors that were conferred upon General Booth from time to time. In 1898 he opened the American Senate with prayer. In 1904 King Edward received him at Buckingham Palace, the freedom of the City of London and the City of Kirkcaldy were conferred upon him, as well as the degree of D.C.L. by Oxford, during 1905. The Kings of Denmark, Norway, the Queen of Sweden, and the Emperor of Japan were among those who received him in private audience.

On August 20, 1912, General William Booth laid down his sword.

He lay in state in Congress Hall, London, where the number of visitors who looked upon his remains ran into the hundreds of thousands.

His son, William Bramwell Booth, the Chief of the Staff, by the appointment of the late General, succeeded to the office and came to the position with a wealth of affection and confidence on the part of the people of the nations such as few men know.

(Editor's Note: The following information was current when *The War Romance of the Salvation Army* was originally published in 1919. We include it in our 1991 edition as a source of interest and awareness regarding the extensive activities and services provided by the Salvation Army during World War I.)

SALVATION ARMY WAR ACTIVITIES

    77 Motor ambulances manned by Salvationists.

    87 Hotels for use of Soldiers and Sailors.

   107 Buildings in United States placed at disposal of Government for war relief purposes.

   199 Huts at Soldiers' Camps used for religious and social gatherings and for dispensing comfort to Soldiers and Sailors.

   300 Rest-rooms equipped with papers, magazines, books, etc., in charge of Salvation Army Officers.

  1507 Salvation Army officers devote their entire time to religious and social work among Soldiers and Sailors.

 15,000 Beds in hotels close to railway stations and landing points at seaport cities for protection of Soldiers and Sailors going to and from the Front.

 80,000 Salvation Army officers fighting with Allied Armies.

100,000 Parcels of food and clothing distributed among Soldiers and Sailors.

100,000 Wounded Soldiers taken from battlefields in Salvation Army ambulances.

300,000 Soldiers and Sailors daily attend Salvation Army buildings.

$2,000,000 Already spent in war activities.

    45 Chaplains serving under Government appointment.

    40 Camps, Forts and Navy Yards at which Salvation Army services are conducted or

which are visited by Salvation Army officers.

2184 War Widows assisted (legal and other aid, and visited).

2404 Soldiers' wives cared for (including medical help).

442 War children under our care.

3378 Soldiers' remittances forwarded (without charge).

$196,081.05 Amount remitted.

600 Parcels supplied Prisoners of War.

1300 Cables sent for Soldiers.

275 Officers detailed to assist Soldiers' wives and relatives; number assisted, 275.

40 Military hospitals visited.

360 Persons visiting hospitals.

147 Boats met.

324,052 Men on board.

35,845 Telegrams sent.

24 Salvationists detailed for this work.

20 Salvationists detailed for this work outside of New York City.

SALVATION ARMY WORK IN UNITED STATES OF AMERICA

1218 Buildings in use at present.

2953 Missing friends found.

6125 Tons of ice distributed.

12,000 Officers and non-commissioned officers actively employed.

11,650 Accommodations in institutions.

68,000 Children cared for in Rescue Homes and Slum Settlements.

22,161	Women and girls cared for in Rescue Homes.
30,401	Tons of coal distributed.
175,764	Men cared for in Industrial Homes.
342,639	Poor families visited.
399,418	Outings given poor people.
668,250	Converted to Christian life.
984,426	Jobs found for unemployed poor.
1,535,840	Hours spent in active service in slum districts.
6,900,995	Poor people given temporary relief.
40,522,990	Nights' shelter and beds given to needy poor.
52,674,308	Meals supplied to needy poor.
	Constituency reached with appeal for Christian citizenship.
132,608,087	Out-door meeting attendance.
134,412,564	In-door meeting attendance.

NATIONAL WAR BOARD

Commander Evangeline C. Booth, President.

East.
Peart, Col. William, Chairman.
Reinhardsen, Col. Gustave S., Sec'y. and Treas.
Damon, Col. Alexander M.,
Parker, Col. Edward J.,
Jenkins, Lt.-Col. Walter F.,
Stanyon, Lt.-Col. Thomas,
Welte, Brigadier Charles

West.
Estill, Commissioner Thos., Chairman.
Gauntlett, Col. Sidney,

Brewer, Lt.-Col. Arthur T.,
Eynn, Lt.-Col. John T.,
Dart, Brigadier Wm. J., Sec'y.

FRANCE

Barker, Lt.-Col. William S., Director of War Work.

As indicated in the above list, the National War Board functions in two distinct territories—East and West—the duty of each being to administer all War Work in the respective territories. The closest supervision is given by each War Board over all expenditure of money and no scheme is sanctioned until the judgment of the Board is carried concerning the usefulness of the project and the sound financial proposals associated therewith. After any plan is initiated, the Board is still responsible for the supervision of the work, and for the Eastern department Colonel Edward J. Parker is the Board's representative in all such matters and Lieut-Colonel Arthur T. Brewer fills a similar office in the Western department. Each section of the National Board takes responsibility in connection with the overseas work, under the presidency of COMMANDER EVANGELINE C. BOOTH for the raising, equipping and sending of thoroughly suitable people in proper proportion. Joint councils are occasionally necessary, when it is customary for proper representatives of each section of the Board to meet together.

The National Board is greatly strengthened through the adding to its special councils all of the Provincial Officers of the country.

About the Author

Grace Livingston Hill is well-known as one of the most prolific writers of romantic fiction. Her personal life was fraught with joys and sorrows not unlike those experienced by many of her fictional heroines.

Born in Wellsville, New York, Grace nearly died during the first hours of life. But her loving parents and friends turned to God in prayer. She survived miraculously, thus her thankful father named her Grace.

Grace was always close to her father, a Presbyterian minister, and her mother, a published writer. It was from them that she learned the art of storytelling. When Grace was twelve, a close aunt surprised her with a hardbound, illustrated copy of one of Grace's stories. This was the beginning of Grace's journey into being a published author.

In 1892 Grace married Fred Hill, a young minister, and they soon had two lovely young daughters. Then came 1901, a difficult year for Grace—the year when, within months of each other, both her father and husband died. Suddenly Grace had to find a new place to live (her home was owned by the church where her husband had been pastor). It was a struggle for Grace to raise her young daughters alone, but through everything she kept writing. In 1902 she produced *The Angel of His Presence, The Story of a Whim,* and *An Unwilling Guest.* In 1903 her two books *According to the Pattern* and *Because of Stephen* were published.

It wasn't long before Grace was a well-known author, but she wanted to go beyond just entertaining her readers. She soon included the message of God's salvation through Jesus Christ in each of her books. For Grace, the most important thing she did was not write books but share the message of salvation, a message she felt God wanted her to share through the abilities he had given her.

In all, Grace Livingston Hill wrote more than one hundred books, all of which have sold thousands of copies and have touched the lives of readers around the world with their message of "enduring love" and the true way to lasting happiness: a relationship with God through his Son, Jesus Christ.

In an interview shortly before her death, Grace's devotion to her Lord still shone clear. She commented that whatever she had accomplished had been God's doing. She was only his servant, one who had tried to follow his teaching in all her thoughts and writing.

Don't miss these Grace Livingston Hill romance novels!

If you are unable to find any of these titles at your local bookstore, you may call Tyndale's toll-free number **1-800-323-9400, X-214** for ordering information. Or you may write for pricing to **Tyndale Family Products, P.O. Box 448, Wheaton, IL 60189-0448.**